Acclaim for

THE NORDIC WARS

"*Winter's Chill* is a captivating adventure into secrets, discoveries, and a bond that will grip your heart as surely it has the characters'! I'd been waiting breathlessly for this installment of the Nordic Wars series and now will be waiting just as breathlessly for the next one. Busse's stories always take hold of my heart and mind and linger with me long after the last page, and *Winter's Chill* is no exception!"

— **ROSEANNA M. WHITE**, best-selling, Christy Award–winning author

"*Winter's Chill* is just what I wanted for a sequel! Epic, stunning, Viking-esque, with a fantastical lore that I can only describe as addictive. I was a fan of Morgan Busse before the The Nordic Wars, but now I'm a full-on groupie!"

— **JAIME JO WRIGHT**, Christy Award–winning author of *The House on Foster Hill* and *The Vanishing at Castle Moreau*

"I am loving Busse's newest series—a heroine to admire, a budding romance, an against-the-odds task, a troop of loyal friends working through hard things, and a uniquely drawn cold world—made warmer by the love these characters share."

— **LISA T. BERGREN**, award-winning author of *Estuary*

"*Winter's Chill* has everything you want in a second book and more. With powerful prose and characters who make you want to stand up and fight, Morgan Busse has created a story world that will transport readers into the depths of winter from the first page. The rich fantasy and beautiful allegory will leave you wishing you could experience the story for the first time all over again. A must-read for fans of Morgan's Follower of the Word series."

— **SARA ELLA**, award-winning author of *The Wonderland Trials* and the *Unblemished* trilogy

Books by Morgan L. Busse

Follower of the Word
Daughter of Light
Son of Truth
Heir of Hope

The Soul Chronicles
Tainted
Awakened

The Ravenwood Saga
Mark of the Raven
Flight of the Raven
Cry of the Raven

Skyworld
Secrets in the Mist
Blood Secrets

The Nordic Wars
Winter's Maiden
Winter's Chill

THE NORDIC WARS | BOOK 2

WINTER'S CHILL

MORGAN L. BUSSE

Winter's Chill
Copyright © 2025 Morgan L. Busse

Published by Enclave Publishing, an imprint of Oasis Family Media, LLC

Carol Stream, Illinois, USA.
www.enclavepublishing.com

All rights reserved. No part of this publication may be reproduced, digitally stored, or transmitted in any form without written permission from Oasis Family Media, LLC.

This is a work of fiction. Names, characters, places, and incidents are products of the author's imagination or are used fictitiously. Any similarity to actual people, organizations, and/or events is purely coincidental.

ISBN: 979-8-88605-214-5 (printed hardcover)
ISBN: 979-8-88605-215-2 (printed softcover)
ISBN: 979-8-88605-217-6 (ebook)

Cover design by Emilie Haney, www.EAHCreative.com
Interior design by Jamie Foley, www.JamieFoley.com
Typesetting by Collin Smith, www.CollinSmithCreative.com

Printed in the United States of America.

To Jaden, a woman of extraordinary strength and character.
We are so glad you are part of our family.

1

A chill as cold as winter hung in the air as the sun began to rise. Kaeden blew on his hands and rubbed them furiously against the wind as he stood by the wagon, where an empty manacle thumped against the wooden side. He glanced at the hills and mountains beyond. Where was Brighid now? What choice would she make? Would they meet again on the battlefield, or would she find a way to free her people? In the end . . . it was her choice alone. He had set her free. And now he had his own path to walk, one that would eventually lead to the Shadonae.

He let out his breath, a cold wisp in the air, and headed for the campsite where the healers slept. A couple blanket-covered mounds lay around a fire that had burned down to glowing embers. Kaeden grabbed a log from the small pile nearby and placed it on the coals, then blew softly. The sky steadily changed as dawn broke across the land. A few minutes later and a robust fire roared.

As he held his hands to the flame, he looked one more time to the Ari Mountains. *Stay safe, Brighid. Stay warm.*

Minutes later, a group of Avonain soldiers marched his way. He remained hunched near the fire as they approached. He'd wondered how long it would take before they discovered Brighid was gone and that he freed her. She had almost half a night's head start. He flexed his fingers against the heat. He would try to give her more time.

Captain Bertin's shadow fell next to his knee. "By order of the Southern Alliance, Kaeden, you are under arrest."

At his words, some of the healers stirred and looked around.

"*Master* Kaeden," he replied without turning. He didn't care about his new title, but he found a dark pleasure in reminding Captain Bertin whom he was dealing with.

Captain Bertin paused behind him. "*Master* Kaeden," he finally said with a hint of sarcasm.

Kaeden pushed off the ground. More healers awoke and watched the exchange with frowns. He brushed off his robes and turned around. "What am I being arrested for?" He crossed his arms and stood to his full height.

"Freeing a prisoner of the Alliance."

He raised one eyebrow. He could deny it. He was sure they had no proof unless someone other than Treyvar had seen him free Brighid. But he was a Truthsayer—lies did not become him. "I see," he said instead. "Lead the way, Captain."

He felt the stares of the healers behind him and heard their fading murmurs as he followed Captain Bertin through the camp and toward the tents ahead—the same tents where, the night before, he had convinced Commander Warin and the others to let him use his power on Brighid.

Brighid. She filled his thoughts again as he remembered fragments of her memories and soul. Her strength, her perseverance, her fighting spirit. If all the Nordics were like her, they were indeed fighting a powerful foe.

Most of the camp still slept, despite the commotion Captain Bertin and his men made as they escorted Kaeden to the commander's tent. Normally the soldiers would have been awake and preparing for another day of marching. No doubt his actions had delayed everyone. He didn't feel guilty about it.

Upon entering the middle tent, he found the same group of men from the previous night. Commander Warin watched him from across the table with dark circles under his eyes, while it appeared a few of the others had risen hastily from sleep.

Captain Bertin shoved him from behind. Kaeden caught himself and looked back. "I wouldn't touch me if I were you. After all, I'm not like Master Mathias." He raised his gloved hand as a reminder.

Captain Bertin opened his mouth, then closed it.

"The Nordic prisoner was discovered missing early this morning," Commander Warin said, "and there are those who say they saw you with her again after you used your power on her."

"Where are those who say these things?" Kaeden went to stand on the other side of the table. He glanced around. None of these men were present when he revisited her.

"Call in the soldier," Commander Warin said.

One of the guards exited then returned a minute later with a scrawny young man. The soldier glanced at Kaeden then looked away. Kaeden vaguely recognized him as one of the men who had thrown stones at Brighid.

"Is this who you saw free the Nordic woman?" Commander Warin asked.

The young man nodded.

Captain Reginar, the head of the White City forces, tapped his finger on the table. "But wasn't there someone else? Surely the woman wasn't left alone without a guard. Or was that your job?"

The soldier looked up.

"What do you mean by that, Captain Reginar?" Captain Bertin asked.

Captain Reginar faced Captain Bertin. "You have brought Master Kaeden before us but not her guard. We should also be interrogating the man who oversaw her."

"You mean the healer Treyvar?" Commander Warin asked. Was that a sheen of sweat collecting along the commander's forehead?

"Yes."

Kaeden pinched his lips together. He had hoped by coming alone with Captain Bertin he could keep Treyvar out of this. But apparently Captain Reginar wanted all the details. If worse came to worst, he would take whatever punishment they chose and find a way to save Treyvar. The young man did not deserve to carry the weight of Kaeden's decision.

"Well, this will complicate things." Commander Warin ran a hand along the back of his neck.

"How?" Both captains looked questioningly at Commander Warin.

The commander let out a sigh. "Please call the healer Treyvar to our tent," he told one of his aides. The young man nodded and left. They waited in an uncomfortable silence as the other aides continued to pack the few items still left in the tent.

Minutes later, Treyvar arrived. "Commander. Captains," he greeted them as he stopped just inside the tent and glanced around. "And Master Kaeden is here as well. What is this about?"

"Were you there when Master Kaeden released the prisoner?" Commander Warin asked.

"Yes, I was. I had been assigned to guard the Nordic woman."

"What happened when Master Kaeden arrived for a second visit with the prisoner?"

"He freed her."

"And you didn't try to stop him?" one of the other officers asked in disbelief.

Treyvar turned his attention to the man and clasped his hands behind his back. For the first time, Kaeden saw something in his appearance, an air of authority he had not witnessed before. "No, I did not."

Commander Warin continued. "May I ask why?"

Treyvar glanced over at Kaeden. "The Truthsayer told me he was under orders from the Word to free the Nordic woman. Despite our rocky relationship with the Eldaran people, both Avonai and the White City highly respect and listen to the Truthsayer as the voice of the Word. Who was I to stand in the way of Master Kaeden?"

Captain Reginar tilted his head. "Is that the only reason?"

"Before I answer that, may I ask those gathered a question of my own?"

A few of the captains glanced at each other while Commander Warin nodded. "You may."

"What were your plans for the young woman?"

"We hadn't made a decision yet," Captain Reginar said. "We were going to hold her until we reached Mostyn."

"And then what?"

Captain Bertin glared at Treyvar. "Why are we answering this healer? He has no say in the decisions made in this tent." He pointed a finger at the young man. "You should have reported Master Kaeden's actions immediately and let us decide whether the Truthsayer had any right to free the woman."

Treyvar's demeanor changed as if a mask had been pulled away. The earnest scholar and healer disappeared, replaced with hardened intensity. "I made the decision as a representative of Avonai."

Captain Bertin laughed darkly. "Since when did a healer hold such authority?" He turned toward Commander Warin. "Sir, Master Kaeden may not be an Avonain, but Treyvar is. Freeing a prisoner of war is treasonous, is it not? And wouldn't Master Kaeden's conduct be considered aiding and abetting? These are acts of aggression toward our alliance. Truthsayer or not, he has harmed our forces by his deeds. I say he should be stripped of his authority at the very least. Perhaps even imprisoned at the next outpost."

Others murmured their agreement.

"Enough!" Commander Warin slapped the table. He stared hard at Bertin, taking each breath through his nose while a vein throbbed along his temple. "You have no idea who you are speaking about."

Captain Bertin worked his jaw. "I know Master Kaeden is the Truthsayer, but what he did is not permissible, no matter what authority Treyvar thinks he has as a healer—"

"This man is not just a healer!" Commander Warin's eyes blazed as he stared at Captain Bertin. "He is *Prince* Treyvar, second son of King Erhard of Avonai and the coastal lands. He is your *lord*."

An invisible shockwave burst across the tent, leaving a wake of silence. Even Kaeden struggled to maintain his composure. *Did Mathias know?* Yes, he had to. Kaeden had suspected there was more to this quiet scholar, but this?

Every eye turned toward Treyvar. No, *Prince* Treyvar. Bertin's eyes grew wide as his face lost all color. "I . . . I . . ." he stuttered. "I had no idea."

Treyvar dipped his head. "I have been working under the pretense of healer, although I truly did want to learn the healing arts under Master Mathias. And I am a scholar. I feel it is my duty to my people and land to gather information, whether that is by book, scroll, or searching beyond the borders of Avonai."

"My lord," Captain Bertin found his voice. The other Avonains also bowed. Kaeden remained standing. The Truthsayer bowed to no one but the Word. Still, he couldn't believe the man he had been working with over the last few months was Avonain royalty.

"As a prince of our nation, Prince Treyvar was within his power to allow Master Kaeden to free the prisoner," Commander Warin said, breaking the silence for the rest of them.

Treyvar spoke. "That is true. But I should also share that there are more things at work here than this war between the south and Nordica. I know there are beings assisting the Nordics in their war effort, powerful beings whom we cannot hope to overcome by ourselves."

"You mean those shadow things that have been wiping out our villages up north?" one officer asked, glancing from Commander Warin to Treyvar as if to check if he could speak of such things.

"More than that," Treyvar said. "There are Eldarans working on their side."

Kaeden narrowed his eyes. How did Treyvar know about that? Did Mathias tell him at some point?

"Yes," Commander Warin said. "We know."

"They are not true Eldarans but Shadonae," Treyvar continued. "Eldarans who have twisted their power and walked away from the Word."

"Did the Nordic woman tell you this?" one of the other captains asked.

"No," Treyvar replied. "I'm not sure how much she understood of the powers at play among her people. Master Mathias is the one who informed me. We know one of the Shadonae is a former Oathmaker and has bound the Nordic army. That is why the Nordic prisoners of war died. Their binding unraveled."

"Why did Master Mathias not inform us?" Commander Warin asked.

"He never got a chance. He was still investigating when he was called to use his power on the soldier Captain Bertin was interrogating." Treyvar glared at Captain Bertin. "Instead, he gave his life."

Captain Bertin had enough sense to look away.

Commander Warin frowned. "What does the Nordic woman have to do with this and why did you free her?"

"Master Kaeden?" Treyvar said.

Kaeden looked over the group present and felt a familiar, bitter taste fill his mouth. *Old man, I wish you were here right now. I'm struggling. I want nothing to do with these men or this place.* He took a deep breath. "I serve the Word, Speaker of the World and Savior of the Great Battle. I do not know what her future holds, but He has called the Nordic woman. And He told me to free her."

"That sounds like gibberish to me," one of the younger men muttered.

Kaeden raised an eyebrow at him. Many gave only verbal credence to the Word and didn't actually believe in Him. In many ways, that was how Kaeden had lived the last few years.

"Quiet," his companion whispered and jabbed him in the side with his elbow.

"If you think about it from another perspective, she may be the only one who can stop the Nordics," Kaeden said.

"What do you mean?" Commander Warin asked.

"She is a highly admired warrior if you consider the moniker her people have given her. I believe they—at least a few—will listen to her. She saw what happened here in the camp and how the oath the Nordics took killed them."

"That doesn't mean she wouldn't go back and fight us again," Commander Warin said. "The Nordics are a proud people. And she is a capable fighter."

"More than capable," Captain Reginar chimed in. "She is one of the fiercest fighters I've ever seen. I was acquainted with the Bear Clan many years ago and have seen what the Nordic people could offer as warriors."

Kaeden shrugged. "She might return and choose to fight us once again. But who of us will the Nordics listen to?" He looked around. A few shook their heads while Commander Warin watched thoughtfully with tight lips. "I believe she realizes the real enemy is not us, but the Shadonae. They are our enemy as well. I even dare say they helped fan these flames of war."

Treyvar crossed his arms. "They might have had a part in that, but I think some of the responsibility lies with us as well."

"We did nothing," Captain Bertin protested. "They invaded our countries and killed our people."

"True, but we invaded their land as well." Those gathered looked at one another, puzzled. Treyvar bowed. "I cannot say more, but I believe there is much at work here, and more than one group is complicit in starting this war." Silence fell throughout the tent. "Anyway"—Treyvar waved his hands as if to clear the air—"the deed is done. She is gone. And we will hope that we might have an ally on the other side. If not, we haven't lost much. We will still fight and protect our lands."

"So what happens to those who freed the Nordic?" Captain Bertin asked, casting a side glance at Kaeden.

"Nothing," Commander Warin said. "The Eldarans still hold authority here in the Ryland Plains and the White City, and Prince Treyvar gave his consent on behalf of Avonai to release her. But it will not do for the morale of the soldiers to hear the Stryth'Veizla was released, so the official word will be that she escaped. And a scouting party should be sent to look for her."

"I agree," Captain Reginar said. "Or else there will be questions about why we didn't pursue her." The others nodded around him.

Captain Bertin glanced up at his suggestion. Kaeden didn't like his look. Perhaps the man was still hoping to capture and interrogate Brighid. But she'd been running all night. And he'd restored her strength and stamina before she left. The chances of a scouting party finding her were slim. Still, he whispered a prayer for her inside his mind.

"In the end, the Nordics are still our enemy," Commander Warin said. "And we are at war. We need to keep the enemy at the forefront of our soldiers' minds. There will be no revelation of her release to anyone. Understand?"

Everyone nodded.

Kaeden folded his arms. Commander Warin was right, as much as he wished otherwise. If it was this difficult explaining to these commanders and captains why he freed Brighid, he couldn't imagine telling the soldiers outside. This was a better choice and outcome.

"We march in one hour." Commander Warin waved toward the tent opening. "You are all dismissed."

Kaeden turned and headed outside with Treyvar right behind him.

2

Kaeden frowned as he headed back to the wagons and healers. Selma—the other Eldaran—packed her belongings a few fires away. Did she know who Treyvar was?

"So, surprised?"

Kaeden turned as Treyvar caught up to him. "Yes. I suspected you were hiding something all these months, but not that."

Treyvar passed him and headed to where their bedrolls and possessions had been left the night before. "I admit I enjoyed the look of shock on your face," he said without glancing back.

Kaeden snorted as he caught up to the other man. "And the look of shock on everyone else's faces?"

"Especially Captain Bertin's." This time, a small smile spread across his lips. "I had hoped to go longer without revealing my identity. But seeing his face was worth it."

Kaeden silently agreed and joined in his smile. "What are you going to do now? No matter if Commander Warin silences everyone, word might get out who you are."

Treyvar shrugged. "The same thing I'm doing. I'll continue as a healer and scholar. I've learned a lot more firsthand than I ever could sitting in Avonai."

"But people will treat you differently."

"Maybe. In the end, the time had come for me to reveal myself. I wasn't going to let the Truthsayer be imprisoned for following the Word. It wouldn't be right. And I consider you a friend."

Friend. Kaeden mulled the word over in his mind. When was the last time he had considered anyone a friend? As he thought on it, it seemed right to call Treyvar a friend. "Just curious," he said, breaking the silence. "Why were you hiding the fact that you're the Prince of Avonai?"

Treyvar huffed. "Not *the* prince. That title belongs to my older brother. I'm the second son. And probably not even missed. I came because I want to know what's going on. We had envoys from Nordica a year ago, and my father turned them away at the city gates. Why did they come? Why did my father not see them? And why is it a year later we are fighting for our lives?"

"Those are good questions," Kaeden said.

"Yes. And I'm hoping to find answers."

Kaeden felt kinship with the young man beside him. They were both more than they appeared and carried a great deal of responsibility.

"Since you woke yesterday, I don't know if you were told that most of the Avonain forces will be parting today for the Tieve Hills in preparation for winter."

Kaeden stopped. "Are you going back with them?"

"No. I am going to seek an audience with Lord Rayner of the White City. And you should come with me and introduce yourself as the new Truthsayer. I'm assuming you had already planned to go all the way to the White City to inter Mathias, correct?"

"Yes. My first priority is to see Mathias put to rest."

"And then what?"

Kaeden stared off into the distance. "I'm not sure. I know what I must do, but how to do it . . ."

"You mean confront the Shadonae."

Kaeden turned back. "Yes."

"You'll have time to plan your strategy this winter."

"Winter?"

"Yes, there will be no more battles until at least early next spring."

Kaeden frowned. "What do you mean?"

Treyvar shook his head. "You've never experienced a winter in the Ryland Plains. Snow as high as your knees on a good day. And when the wind blows, the plains become such a flurry of white that you can't see your hand in front of you. There will be no battles, no confrontations with the Nordics. One bad snowstorm would take care of them."

Kaeden blinked. Having lived in calmer climates, he had never experienced such a thing. "Is it the same way in Nordica?"

"I don't think so. They get more snow, but they don't have the winds like they do on the plains."

"I wondered what you meant when you said some of the Avonain troops were preparing for winter."

"In some ways, winter brings rest. Wounds can be healed and more supplies acquired. Perhaps you might find some information on the Shadonae in the White City. After all, it is the birthplace of your people."

Kaeden slowly nodded. Treyvar might be right. It wasn't as if he could walk through an entire army of Nordics, reach the Shadonae, and then . . . and then what? He wasn't even sure what he would do. What did Mathias mean when he said he would have to judge his people? What would he say? How would he stop them?

The two started again toward the fire. He had never visited the White City, nor the Sanctuary where his people first stepped foot in the Lands. He suddenly found himself curious what he would find and was thankful he could ensure Mathias was honored in death. Having never been able to retrieve the bodies of his parents, he could at least see that his mentor made it home.

Selma approached them minutes later, her dark cloak fluttering in the chilly wind and her pack on her back. "Where were you two?"

Treyvar and Kaeden glanced at each other. "Commander Warin wanted to see me," Kaeden replied as he looked over his shoulder.

"What for?"

"As the new Truthsayer."

"Oh." A dark look passed over her face for but a moment. Kaeden frowned. Was she . . . jealous? Had she been hoping she would become the next Truthsayer? The thought disturbed him. They hadn't really talked since he woke up from the change. But in a way, it would make sense. The position of Truthsayer brought respect and power. He had a feeling many would covet the power and status. Including her.

He let out a sigh and glanced up at the ever-brightening sky. *Why me?* But the air was silent.

He bid farewell to the healers from Avonai, including Darry and Leon, then joined Treyvar and the wagon carrying Mathias's body. Selma accompanied them. "I thought you would return to Avonai," Kaeden said as she kept pace at his side, despite his long gait.

"I thought about it, but I wish to see Mathias put to rest in the Sanctuary. Besides, there is a need for healers with the Ryland side of the alliance, and I volunteered."

"I see." But was there something more? Only once did he glance back at the Avonains heading southeast toward the Tieve Hills. A tiny part of him wished he was going that direction. But his path had been laid out for him the moment Mathias died and the mantle of Truthsayer fell on him. A path that would eventually lead north.

A couple days later, they arrived at the Garring Stronghold on the edge of Anwin Forest. Mostyn was a three-day journey from there, then the White City almost a full day after that. At least, that was what the men were saying. Most of the forces would be stationed here, to winter and prepare for Nordica's next move.

The stronghold was an unadorned structure of stone surrounded by fields of dry grass. From the looks of it, Kaeden was sure the structure could hold a couple thousand soldiers. The rest—including Kaeden—would continue to Mostyn and the White City.

Captain Reginar found them as they made camp outside the massive gates, while those stationed there moved in. "I will be escorting Master Mathias to the White City. Will the three of you be attending his body?"

"Yes," Treyvar said. "And we hope to seek an audience with Lord Rayner."

"I don't think that will be an issue given your statuses as prince and the new Truthsayer." His eyes flitted to Selma. "And I believe I can have the Eldaran healer invited as well."

"That will not be necessary." Selma pulled her woolen blanket from her pack. "I am only here for Master Mathias."

He bowed. "As you wish."

Kaeden didn't say anything. A storm seemed to be brewing inside Selma and he wanted no part of it. Instead, he arranged his own bedding near the fire and then lay down with his hands behind his head. The night was chilly, but the fire kept him warm. He stared up at the dark sky and for the second time wondered where Brighid was. Was she gazing up at the same night sky? Was she warm?

Why am I thinking about her? He turned on his side, his back to the fire, and closed his eyes. But Brighid remained firmly in his mind, almost as if he could see her running through hills of gold and evergreen trees with towering mountains ahead of her. The images were so vivid that they seemed real, and he continued to dream about her through the night.

The next day they entered Anwin Forest. Rumors claimed this forest had stood since the beginning of time. Some said that when the Word formed the Lands with His words, Anwin Forest sprang up from the ground fully formed as if it had stood there for centuries.

As they entered, darkness replaced the bright sunlight. Only slips of light appeared through the thick foliage above. Trunks as wide as three men filled the forest, and years of pine needles and leaves covered the ground. A single road wove through the trees, wide enough for wagons. The path was well maintained, and greenery grew where the sun reached the forest floor.

Birds chirped in the trees above, and occasionally a rustling sounded in thick bushes, evidence of life in this ancient place.

Kaeden looked around in wonder and felt a connection inside his soul. He still preferred the Tieve Hills and the abundance of deciduous trees, hills, and meadows, but there was something hauntingly beautiful about this forest.

The first night they made camp in a small clearing. The smell of smoke and roasting meat filled the area, attracting a few peering eyes in the darkness. The next two days were the same until almost night on the third when they approached the fortress of Mostyn.

Stone walls surrounded the garrison with a thick wooden gate in the middle. A lantern hung above, lighting the entrance. A small gatehouse stood nearby and an older man exited as the massive party approached. Captain Reginar spoke to him and, minutes later, the gates opened as a cold rain began to fall. Treyvar and Kaeden quickly worked to cover the wagon carrying Mathias's body. As Kaeden pulled the waterproof covering over the box, he felt grateful to those who had prepared the body so it would last the journey to the White City. He couldn't imagine what it would look or smell like now if it hadn't been prepped.

Most of the soldiers headed to the main fortress, a massive structure of wood and stone. Mostyn was considered the first line of defense for the White City should an army ever march on it. Admiring it in person, Kaeden could understand why it would take an army to defeat it. Like Garring, the stone was wide and solid with multiple defenses.

However, rumor suggested Dallam was the same, and it took the Nordic forces nigh a day to overtake the northern citadel. Looking back on the Battle of the Plains, the only reason the Nordics lost was because of the surprise arrival of the Avonains. If Commander Warin hadn't hurried the troops from the bridge south to Tieve, then across the Onyx River and north, it might be the Nordics here in Mostyn this evening instead of them.

Lights from lamps twinkled along the rainy street as they entered the barracks. The cart that held Mathias's body rumbled across the uneven cobblestones inside and toward the stables. Rivulets of water ran between the stones like tiny rivers. Once under the extended roof, the horses were taken care of, and Kaeden checked on the burial box again. No rain had gotten inside.

"Shall we find a place to spend the night?" Treyvar said beside him.

"I wish to stay with Mathias." He doubted anyone would want to watch over the burial box anyway.

Treyvar nodded. "I understand. I'll find us some food and be back."

Kaeden looked up. "What do you mean?"

"I'm staying here with you."

"Here? In the stable?"

"If it's good enough for the Truthsayer, it's good enough for a prince."

Before Kaeden could protest, Treyvar disappeared into the rainy night with the others. Captain Reginar approached him. "I can have my men stay with Master Mathias."

Kaeden shook his head. "I will watch over him tonight."

His eyes widened. "Are you sure?"

"Yes." He placed his hand on the box. "This is something I want to do."

Captain Reginar paused, his eyes on Kaeden. "All right. Let me at least get you some food."

"Someone already is." He didn't mention Treyvar's name. He had a feeling there would be a lot more protesting if the captain knew a prince of Avonai planned to sleep in the stable. But did it really matter? They had all been sleeping on the ground the last few days.

"Then I'll let you be. We will start for the White City at dawn."

"I'll see you tomorrow, Captain."

Kaeden watched him go, then let out his breath and listened to the gentle tapping of the rain on the roof above. "You're almost home, old man." He started to pull out his bedding and lay it on the hay nearby.

The sooner they arrived in the White City and put Mathias to rest, the better. And yet once Mathias was interred, the last thread that tied him to his former mentor and father would be severed, leaving him drifting without an anchor.

3

Brighid lay poised on the thick branch of an evergreen tree twenty feet above the ground a day later, a knife in hand. Midmorning sunlight streamed through the forest below as the scouting party wove through the trees, stopping every few minutes to check out a broken twig or a print in the soil. She had purposefully left a cluttered mess of tracks that led to the river nearby in hopes that whoever followed her would be deceived. But just in case they were cleverer than the average scout, she was ready.

"Here," one of the nearby southern scouts said, pointing to a bush. "It looks like she was heading toward the river."

"Perhaps." The leader's voice barely carried across the forest as he looked around. Even if he glanced up, the needles and branches hid her from view. But she wouldn't take any chances.

I really don't want to kill you, she thought as she tightened her grip on the knife's handle. *But I will not be taken again.* She let each breath blend in with the wind, never moving on the branch.

After twenty minutes of sweeping the entire area, the group headed for the river. Brighid released a relieved sigh, but remained still despite developing cramps in her back, arms, and legs. She breathed in the scent of pine, listening to the birds singing again now that the humans were gone, and waited.

The sun moved through the sky, and thick white clouds formed as the afternoon passed. Sweat gathered on her chest where she clung to the branch, and a bit of sap pooled beneath her left hand, leaving a sticky residue that coated her palm. Her throat was parched from the need to drink, but she would not go down until evening.

As the light began to vanish and dusk settled over the forest, Brighid checked her surroundings one more time, then quietly pulled herself into a sitting position and removed the pack Kaeden had given her. She leaned against the trunk, placed the knife back in the pack, and pulled out the waterskin. The water was tepid and tasted like leather, but it was something and she drained the waterskin dry.

Revived, she shouldered the pack once more and started down the tree in the dark. Once she slipped and caught herself, gouging her palm on a broken branch. "Bolva," she whispered. She scrambled the rest of the way down, then headed for the river. Only a haze of light remained.

She dipped her hand in the water and hissed. She washed it the best she could, then searched for something to wrap it in. As she drew out the contents of the pack, her heart swelled in gratitude and wonder despite the stinging pain. She had only drawn out the knife that morning before scurrying up the tree. There wasn't much, but it was clear Kaeden had thought about what she would need for her journey. Aside from the knife, there was also a flint stone, travel biscuits, and the waterskin. She tore into a biscuit and counted the rest. If she rationed the food, it would last her five days in addition to what she could find and catch along the way.

After she finished the biscuit, she pulled out the last item. A dark wool cloak. It was thick and in good shape. She hesitated, then held it to her face and breathed in. It smelled like mint, leather, and an undefined masculine aroma. It must be his cloak. Even as she thought this, she saw Kaeden in her mind, kneeling before her, his healer's robes tight across his shoulders, his dark hair disheveled from the wind as he held his hand between them, the light spilling from his palm.

Will I see you again? she had asked him.

I don't know, he replied.

She knew the chances of another encounter were slim. And if they ever did meet again, it would most likely be as enemies. She was Nordic. He was an Eldaran and healer for the Southern Alliance. But for one moment she hoped they would, and they could be as they were for those few days when neither were foe. Just two beings surviving in this cold, dark world. Perhaps they could even be friends.

She took the knife and cut a small strip from the bottom of the cloak and wrapped it around her hand. She glanced longingly at the biscuits, then shook her head. No. She would need them later.

She quietly placed everything back into the pack, then followed the river south for about a mile, the opposite direction the scouts went. She doubted they would head this way, which hopefully would give her a couple hours to rest. Around the corner of the river grew a patch of thick berry bushes. She found a small spot where deer had bedded. Perfect. She crawled into the space, pulled out the cloak, and wrapped it around her body.

The scent conjured dreams of Kaeden. She watched him walk with the southern forces toward an ancient forest where light barely shone through the branches. She'd never seen a forest like that before, not even in the Northern Wastelands. An ancient forest with trees as thick as three men and as dark as night.

The buzz of insects and bright morning sunlight woke her. Brighid broke her fast on a few shriveled berries that hadn't been taken by birds or beasts. After she ate enough to ward off hunger, she went down to the river, entered the chilly water, and headed north. The brush and overhanging trees hid her from the surrounding hills. Within minutes, her toes and lower legs grew numb. The rocks were slippery beneath the frigid water, and twice she almost plunged in. As she neared the area where she had first spotted the scouts, she left the river and headed for the peaks on the other side.

Evergreens covered the foothills with the occasional deciduous changing into its autumn foliage. A tiny stream gurgled at the bottom of the next valley, just deep enough to wade. Brighid entered the water. The more she could throw off any evidence of her trail, the better.

One day turned into two. And two turned into three. And she never saw the scouts again.

Evenings were spent in trees or under brush. By the morning of the fourth day, she was sure the scouts wouldn't find her. The thought brought a chill of realization: She was alone, with nothing but woods and wildlife for hundreds of miles.

She stared at the sky that night with those thoughts swirling inside her mind and Kaeden's cloak tucked beneath her chin. The wind blew, bringing a soft song her heart knew, in the same place where she could feel death. But this was not death, it was something more. And she closed her eyes, not feeling quite so alone.

Her journey northward grew slower as she was forced to forage for berries and roots and catch fish in the stream she followed. Fish was much better than rat or squirrel. She caught herself wishing she and Elphsaba had never moved to Ragnbork years ago as the skewered fish cooked over the fire. She could have provided for them off the bounty of the mountains. Then she sighed. But where would she be now? Could she really have survived in the wilderness? Would she have ever discovered the red haze? Learned to fight? Met people like Johan and Marta? Even Mathias and Kaeden?

Maybe Elphsaba knew what she was doing, and Brighid's past—no matter what it was—made her who she was today.

The nights grew increasingly chilly, as if winter was ready to lay claim to the land early. It rarely snowed before the end of harvest, but once in a while, snow-laden clouds would descend from the northern mountains and cover the world in unexpected white. Brighid peered at the mountains ahead with unease in her heart. Even the most seasoned Nordic knew that one did not gamble with a surprise snowstorm.

I just need to get to those mountains, she thought before descending into the valley where the forest swallowed the view from her sight. The northern Ari Mountains marked the border of Nordica. Once she reached them, she would search for Rokr Valley, which served as the passage between the north and the south, travel through, and find her people. A fortnight at most, if the weather held and she could find food relatively easy.

I can do that. Brighid readjusted her pack and started into the forest. *Twelve more days. Maybe fourteen. Then I'm home.*

4

"We searched as long as we could. There was no sign of her."

Captain Bertin slammed his fist against the table and let out a curse. Then he turned his eyes on Kaeden as the messenger left the main hall inside the Mostyn fortress. Others glanced up at the captain's reaction from the surrounding tables, but Captain Bertin ignored them, and they returned to breaking their fasts. Spoons scraped wooden bowls while dim light filtered in from the long narrow windows. No one wanted to engage the storm brewing inside the captain.

Kaeden ignored him as well as he finished his early morning meal. But inside, he smiled. Brighid had escaped. Or at least she had avoided capture. Then his heart constricted. This was only the beginning. He had dreamed about her again last night, the second time since he released her. The dream had been so vivid he could almost feel the vastness of the mountain range around her and the brightness of the stars overhead. Could the young Nordic woman really make it across the wilds of the north alone?

He hesitated, then sent up a prayer for her journey.

Captain Bertin glared at him as he left the room. Kaeden shook his head once he was out in the narrow stone hallway. Men like Bertin seemed to have a particular hatred for the Nordics. And it was hatred like his that would continue to fuel this war.

He reached the main doors and stepped outside. Grey hazy clouds covered the sky, blotting out the rising sun and creating a gloomy atmosphere over the fortress and surrounding town. Most of the southern forces had remained at Garring, but a small company would be stationed here for the winter, including Captain Bertin. Why the Avonain captain had been chosen to stay here instead of sent to the Tieve Hills, Kaeden didn't know. All he knew was he would be happy to leave the captain behind.

Kaeden made his way to the stables. As he walked along the dirt street, he noticed crowds of people with packs across their backs or satchels clutched to their chests standing in the gaps between the buildings. There were children among the adults, their eyes wide and no smile on their faces. He slowed his pace and eased into the shadows.

"Momma," a child said and tugged on his mother's skirts. "When do we get to go home?"

"Shh, child." The woman patted his head. "Soon, after the soldiers defeat those filthy Nordics."

At the word "filthy," Kaeden's chest tightened.

"Why did they take our home from us?" the child continued.

"Because they are selfish. But soon we will have our land back. See those men?" She pointed across the street. Kaeden covertly looked the same direction. A handful of White City soldiers milled around the center of town, jostling one another and laughing. "They fight for us."

The boy dropped his head. "I miss my dog. I hope she's all right."

The other people around the woman and child spoke in hushed whispers. Kaeden sighed and continued along the street. These people were refugees, displaced from the villages taken by the Nordics. Of course they would detest the Nordic people. But did they know some of their own countrymen had done the same thing to the Nordic people? It seemed hatred begot hatred, and the innocent paid for it. He hoped the boy would see his dog again.

He met Selma near the stables, where the wagon that carried Mathias waited, ready to make the trek to the White City.

Captain Reginar and Treyvar arrived minutes later, along with a handful of soldiers who would see them the rest of the way. Treyvar looked as tired as he felt. Sleeping on the floor of the stable might have lent some protection against anyone wishing to tamper with the box that held Mathias's body, but it did not leave one feeling refreshed the next day.

"Ready to go?" Captain Reginar asked.

"Yes," both Kaeden and Selma responded. Reginar gave the command to the gatekeepers, and moments later, the gates slowly opened with a loud creak. A dirt road led through the town toward a second set of gates. Kaeden placed his gloved hand on the side of the wagon as it started rolling toward the exit. He let out a sigh. Shades of grief still held his heart, sometimes intense, sometimes a dull ache. Today it felt much like the clouds overhead: bleak and dreary. The air was cool with a wind that blew a chill through his clothes.

A few people looked out from narrow doorways to watch the small procession, while more refugees huddled in the alleys. Kaeden spotted looks of surprise and reverence as he walked by in his white robes and golden cord. His hand tightened along the edge of the wagon, and the leather gave way beneath his grip. Going from an Eldaran with no power to the most powerful of their people still didn't feel real. How could he fill Mathias's position? Yes, he was ready to forge his own path as the Truthsayer, but deep inside he felt inadequate, with no one to speak to. Selma remained distant and Treyvar was not an Eldaran.

He glanced at the wooden box that carried his former mentor and a new wave of grief washed over him. "I wish I'd had more time with you," he whispered. He turned his face forward and held on to the rumbling wagon.

Minutes later they reentered Anwin Forest. The rain from the night before left the air humid with the scent of soil and pine. Kaeden breathed the smell in deeply, letting it fill his lungs and clear his mind and heart. They journeyed along the dirt road steadily upward, stopping only once for rest. As the sun began to set, they crested a hill and the forest opened to reveal the mountain capital of the Ryland Plains, the White City.

The last of the sun's rays hit the white stone from which the city was hewn, casting the capital in a rosy hue. Towering walls as thick as three wagons surrounded the city. Peaks loomed high above the city, which was carved from the face of the cliffs beyond. Before the entrance lay a meadow, green and lush, with a handful of wildflowers still clinging to their summer petals.

The wagon rumbled along the dirt path that led through the meadow to the massive gates ahead. Kaeden stared in wonder. Such a feat to carve a city from a mountain. And the beauty of such architecture stood to this day. Almost as if it had sprung into being the same moment Anwin Forest was formed by the Word.

"The Sanctuary is that direction." Selma came alongside him and pointed to the left. "You can't see it yet, but there is a waterfall that springs from the cliffs above and forms a pool in the forest. That is where our people first came from."

In his mind, Kaeden saw Eldarans emerging from a crystal-clear pool, donning flesh and choosing to live with humans for the Word's sake. His ancestors loved the Word so much they accompanied Him to rescue mankind. He glanced at Selma from the corner of his eye as they approached the city gates. Did they still love the Word? Did they still love mankind?

Did he?

Apart from Brighid, he still hadn't touched another human and wasn't sure if he could. Even the thought caused a small wave of revulsion inside his middle. How could he be the Truthsayer if he could never touch another person? He glanced at the covered burial box within the cart and, once again, wished his mentor was still there.

The sun disappeared just as they reached the gates. Captain Reginar spoke to the gatekeepers, then a minute later they were ushered in. The city inside was as beautiful as the outside. Cobblestone streets wove throughout, with quaint stone stores and shops lining each side. Lamps on every corner lit the capital from within. Soaring above it all, Celestis Castle emerged from the face of the mountain as if the two were one. Lights twinkled inside the windows like stationary fireflies.

"We will seek lodging within Celestis Castle tonight," Captain Reginar said, addressing the group as they rolled their way upward. "Then we will meet with Lord Rayner, hopefully, tomorrow."

"Sounds good," Treyvar said, replying for all of them.

It took almost twenty minutes to arrive at a second set of gates that led into the courtyard of the castle. These gates required Captain Reginar speaking to the guards before they were admitted.

The courtyard was busy despite the lateness of the day. Guards patrolled the walls above and switched shifts with those who would cover the night. Stable hands crossed the wide area, ready to take care of the wagon and horses. A fountain made from the same white stone stood in the middle with water tumbling into the pool below, the soft splashing echoing across the area. Past the fountain were wide stairs that led to the entrance into Celestis Castle.

Captain Reginar talked to one of the guards and pointed to the wagon. The guard nodded, hurried up the staircase, and disappeared inside the castle. Reginar turned and walked toward Kaeden and the rest. "I told the guard we have the body of Master Mathias. He is checking with his captain to learn where the body can be stored until the burial ceremony and to make sure it is watched."

Kaeden bowed. "Thank you, Captain Reginar."

The man nodded. "It is the least we can do for the former Truthsayer." He placed a hand on the box, and the scar near his left eye wrinkled as his face furrowed. "I made a mistake many years ago and Master Mathias helped me. I wish . . ." He took in a deep breath. "Anyway, it is my honor to escort Master Mathias and help put him to rest."

A warmth expanded inside Kaeden's chest. How many people had Mathias helped over the course of his life? Every time he turned around, another person spoke of Mathias with praise and admiration. The Eldaran truly lived the way of the Word.

After the guards came and took the burial box, and the horses and wagon were taken care of, the group was led into Celestis Castle. "Lord Rayner will meet with us tomorrow, and the day of the burial ceremony will be planned," Captain Reginar said as they entered. He continued into the details, but his voice faded as Kaeden took in the castle's massive entryway. Long, dark tapestries hung from the high ceiling above with an iron candelabra in the middle lighting the area. Ornate blue rugs covered the pale floor. Silver ornamentals decorated matching tables on each side of the room, their polished surfaces twinkling in the candlelight. Simple but awe-inspiring, and what he would expect from the pinnacle of the mountain city.

A man dressed in light armor with a dark blue tabard approached them. A sprinkling of grey aged his brown hair and lines creased his eyes. He was of medium stature, but an aura of power rested around him. He bowed when he stopped. "Captain Reginar, guests of Celestis Castle. I am Wilmar, Captain of the Guard for the White City. Welcome."

"Captain Wilmar." Reginar returned the bow.

"My lord instructed me to show you to your quarters and assure you of a safe visit while you are here in the White City."

"Thank you, Captain," Reginar replied.

"This way." The captain turned and headed down the hallway. Everyone fell in line behind him.

"Does Captain Wilmar know who you are?" Kaeden asked Treyvar quietly as they walked the darkened hall. "I noticed he didn't address you."

"Perhaps. Or perhaps not." He gave Kaeden a wry smile. "I'm not as well-known as my elder brother."

Interesting. Commander Warin knew Treyvar's status, but perhaps he was one of a few. Then again, he was Avonain.

Kaeden glanced at the walls as they passed portraits of previous White City rulers. Men dressed in regal clothing with neatly trimmed black beards and full heads of hair. There were also beautiful ladies clothed in white with long flowing hair, equal rulers who had led the White City and Ryland Plains during their own time.

At the end of the hall, the guard turned right and led them up a staircase. Another hall, and another corner, then Captain Wilmar opened the first door on the right. He held it open and bowed. "Servants will be sent to attend to your needs. Please rest in ease tonight, gentlemen."

"Thank you, Captain Wilmar," Captain Reginar said, speaking for all of them.

As the captain turned and left, Reginar held the door. "My apologies, I'm not sure why Captain Wilmar didn't address either of you. I made sure to share who you both are."

Kaeden shrugged. "It does not matter to me."

"Nor me," Treyvar replied. "I prefer being known as a scholar from Avonai."

Reginar frowned. "Still . . ." He glanced down the dark hall, then let out his breath. "Feel free to take whichever rooms you desire."

They entered a suite with a main room fit with a stone fireplace, a set of chairs, and tall narrow windows. Two doors—one to the right and one to the left—led to individual bedchambers.

Kaeden took the one on the right. The room was simple with a single bed, chest, and small table with a bowl and pitcher. No candles were lit, only the chandelier from the main room provided light. He let his pack hit the floor, then rolled his shoulders. He walked toward the window to his right. A full night sky filled the view with twinkling lights of the city below. Where was Brighid tonight? Had he provided enough for her? Certainly not enough food. But she had his cloak, a knife, and a flintstone to make a fire. Hopefully she could make do with those.

He sighed and turned. A servant entered minutes later with water for the pitcher and bowl.

"Thank you," Kaeden said.

The servant bowed and left.

He washed, shut the door, and settled on the bed. After sleeping on the ground for months, the bed felt strange to his body. Too soft. Too warm. He tossed and turned until he lay on his back and stared at the ceiling. Then, as had started to become custom, he prayed for the Nordic woman making her way north.

5

The inside of Celestis Castle was grander than Kaeden had imagined. He admired the beautiful alabaster stone from which the castle was hewn, the ornate rugs that covered the floors, the simple but beautiful wooden furniture and carvings, and tapestries woven with an eye for detail and color. Not for the first time he was thankful that a clean set of healer's robes had been procured for his audience with Lord Rayner. They were a little tight in the shoulders, but unless clothing had been made specifically for him, it rarely fit right.

Treyvar walked quietly beside him as Captains Reginar and Wilmar led the way to the main audience chamber. Captain Wilmar still had not addressed them, despite his quick glance at the golden cord Kaeden wore around his midsection, one of the few symbols of his status as Truthsayer. If the captain was like this, it made Kaeden wonder what King Erhard or the crown prince were like.

A guard stood on each side of a set of double doors near the end of the hallway. At Captain Wilmar's silent command, they opened the doors and stepped aside. He went in first, followed by the other three.

If the castle itself was stunning, the main audience chamber put it to shame. Pillars of white stone held the loft ceiling with tapestries of deep blue between them. Long, narrow windows lined each side of the chamber, letting in pale light. An exquisite blue runner followed the length of the room to a platform supporting three silver thrones: one each for the lord and lady, and one for the heir.

A man sat on the center throne with a simple circlet upon his hair as black as raven feathers. An equally dark beard and mustache graced his chin. He wore a white tunic with silver embroidery along the neckline, the rest of his middle hidden behind a surcoat of blue. Silver jewelry twinkled along his fingers and neck, and his boots were fine black leather.

He watched them approach with a stony look in his dark eyes. Captain Wilmar stopped at the edge of the platform and bowed while placing a fist across his chest. "My lord, your guests have arrived."

Lord Rayner glanced over each person, his gaze lingering longest on Kaeden. Kaeden didn't waver. Instead, he returned Lord Rayner's intense look. Mathias probably would have chastised him for not bowing, but the lord of the White City was not his master, and he already didn't like the treatment they'd received.

"Prince Treyvar. It has been a long time since a royal from Avonai has graced my court."

Treyvar bowed. "Thank you for welcoming me to the White City."

Kaeden listened to their exchange in frigid silence. Only now was Prince Treyvar being acknowledged?

"And Captain Reginar. Thank you for your hard work on the battlefield."

Reginar also bowed. "For the glory of the White City and the Ryland Plains."

Lord Rayner's gaze landed on Kaeden once again. "I am told you are the new Truthsayer. I was sorry to hear that Master Mathias died on the battlefield. The news was shocking."

"It was shocking to all of us and he will be greatly missed," Kaeden replied.

"What is your name, Truthsayer? I do not believe I have met you before."

"Master Kaeden."

"And your surname?"

"I do not carry one."

Lord Rayner pulled on the tip of his beard. "Interesting. Where do you hail from, Master Kaeden?"

"Many places. I have lived in the Tieve Hills, Khodath, Mistsylver Island, and Avonai."

Lord Rayner straightened. "Are you pledged to Avonai?"

Ah, there it was. Lord Rayner wanted to know whom he called master. "I am pledged to no one but the Word."

He sat back. "I see. Is that why you freed the Nordic prisoner?"

So Lord Rayner had heard what had happened. "Yes."

"You hear the Word?"

"He speaks to me at times," Kaeden answered carefully, watching Lord Rayner's face.

"And what did He tell you to do with the prisoner?"

"Save her." Kaeden left out the part about her being the Word's special instrument. He had a feeling Lord Rayner—or anyone of the south—would not like to hear that. Nor that the Word would give her a choice.

"Just that? 'Save her'? How do you know that meant freeing her?" Lord Rayner leaned forward. "Could you have been mistaken? Did the Word mean then or later? Did you ever think that bringing her to our side might have been the salvation the Word spoke of?"

Kaeden fought the urge to snort. The thought that Brighid could only be saved by aligning with the south was hubris. He never considered joining the Nordics in this war, but he wasn't blind to the bias and hatred the south held for them, a feeling that continued to fuel this fight.

"I did what I did under the authority of *my* Lord."

A dark look came over Lord Rayner's face. Kaeden stood firm, holding eye contact. Mathias probably would have handled Lord Rayner and his questions in a more diplomatic way, but that was not who Kaeden was. He was stubborn, resolute, and blunt.

Lord Rayner finally straightened. "Let us hope you were correct in your thinking. Now we should discuss how to honor Master Mathias and put him to rest."

A handful of men and women were called to the audience chamber, leaders of the city and part of the council. A viewing was scheduled to be held the next day. Afterward, Mathias's body would be carried to the Sanctuary and placed in the crypt beneath.

Noon came and went by the time Kaeden and Treyvar were dismissed. Additional details and preparations were left up to the

White City. Once they arrived back in their rooms, Treyvar spoke. "Lord Rayner doesn't like you."

"He doesn't seem to care for you either," Kaeden responded. "He hardly spoke to you."

Treyvar shrugged. "I've never claimed my royal roots. All I want to be is a scholar and healer and help my people."

"Perhaps that is what people need the most."

"They also need someone who will not be swayed. Like an oak tree with roots deep in the earth that will stand against wind and rain. Master Mathias was that way. And I think you will be too. A Truthsayer for these times."

Kaeden blinked at Treyvar's words, surprised by the sincerity. "Thank you, my friend."

Treyvar smiled and nodded.

Kaeden stretched out his back and shoulders. "I think I'm going to find a place to exercise. All I've done is walk for the last few months." And physical exercise had a way of cleansing the mind. He didn't want to think anymore. Just push his body to the limit so he could sleep tonight.

"I believe there is a training area on the eastern side of the castle." Treyvar paused and glanced at him. "You know, I never asked. What did you do before you joined the war?"

Kaeden looked up in surprise. Neither of them had really spoken about their private lives. "I worked in a quarry for a couple years. I've always done manual work until I came to serve under Mathias."

Treyvar's eyebrows shot up. "A quarry?" His gaze slid to Kaeden's arms. "That explains your physique."

Kaeden snorted. "Strength is the only thing that has ever come naturally to me."

"Why did you become a healer, then?"

Kaeden paused and glanced out the nearby window. The White City spread beyond the windowsill. "I'm not a fighter. I never will be, not if I can help it. My parents were healers. I had also hoped to become one. But the Word had different plans for me." He held his palm up, covered by his glove. Although he wasn't sure if he could become a true healer. He still felt an aversion to touch. The only one he had ever truly healed was Brighid.

Kaeden looked back and found Treyvar watching him thoughtfully. "You know, there is more to strength than fighting. I am familiar with some of the teachings on the Eldarans. I know that to heal requires taking on the wound and then healing yourself through your inborn power. I would wager a body like yours could handle more than the usual person."

Kaeden glanced at his hand again. He had never thought of that before. "You might be right." He had healed Brighid from near death. Something not many Eldarans he knew of could do. And his physical stature allowed him to break through the crowd to reach her and carry her back. Perhaps the Word had created him this way for a reason. His heart squeezed and he dropped his hand. Mathias would have told him the same thing. Lands, he missed that old man.

After changing into a simple tunic and trousers, he located the training room Treyvar had spoken of. He stood in the doorway for a moment, taking in the massive space. It was two stories tall with a roof made of glass, allowing natural light to filter inside. Thick wooden beams held the walls and roof up. Racks lined the walls with both practice and real weapons. Two combat circles were painted on the ground, one currently in use. The rest of the room was used to stretch and warm up.

His heart squeezed again. There was a dam inside him and he could feel the pressure of grief pressing against his chest. But there was no release. He couldn't seem to let slip a tear or a groan for his former master and friend, not since the day he held Mathias's body, then underwent the change. The pressure grew as the ceremony and interment drew near.

Kaeden turned right and headed to an area devoid of people. He closed his eyes and took in a couple deep breaths. He started stretching his arms, then legs. When he first started working the quarry, an older man showed him the wisdom of preparing his muscles for the laborious work so he didn't injure himself. He found the movements freeing. With each pull and tug, the pressure in his chest lessened. Then he began to pray with each movement. Part of him felt strange engaging with the Word, but another part felt a connectedness he hadn't known before.

Soon, his body was warm and limber. He turned to face the room, wondering what to do next when he saw that a handful of guards had stopped their exercise to watch him. One of them stepped away from the group and approached.

"Are you a new recruit?" the young man asked. He was taller than the others but with an average build.

"No, just a visitor to the White City," Kaeden replied. "I was given permission to exercise here."

"We were wondering if you would like to spar," the young man said.

Kaeden glanced past him to the other men. "I don't use weapons."

"Then what do you do?"

He raised one eyebrow. "I sometimes participate in grappling."

A heavyset man in back began to grin. Kaeden could read the look on his face. He wanted to test his strength against Kaeden's. The man stepped forward. "I would like to challenge you." The others murmured and laughed.

The first young man glanced at the heavyset guard, then at Kaeden. "What say you? Will you accept Branok's challenge?"

Kaeden tilted his head. "I would be honored."

"Clear the nearest circle," the young man shouted. The murmurs grew louder and more smiles broke out.

Kaeden mentally checked the status of his body. Everything was limber and warm. He was ready.

He and Branok entered the circle. Branok looked to be about his age, a couple inches shorter, with thick brown hair and a clean-shaven face. While both were heavy built, Kaeden possessed a speed not normally seen in a man his size. This usually gave him an advantage.

The others gathered around and a few bets were exchanged. A bittersweet joy filled his heart. Mathias loved grappling matches and would sometimes wager a little bit for fun. *This is for you, old man,* Kaeden thought as he faced off with his opponent.

The moment the first man shouted "Go!" Kaeden burst across the circle, head forward, and caught Branok by the back of the thighs. He lifted the other man, and together they fell to the floor. Before

Branok could react, Kaeden gripped him in a hold and held him to the ground. Using his weight, Kaeden pressed Branok down. After a moment of intense struggling, Branok shouted, "I yield!"

Shouts and groans filled the training room as those who had bet on Kaeden looked gleefully on those who had wagered on Branok.

Kaeden helped Branok to his feet.

"You're fast," Branok said with a touch of awe in his voice. "Care to try once more?"

"I would be honored."

The crowd settled as Branok and Kaeden lined up again. This time, Branok was prepared, but after a takedown and a minute of grappling, Kaeden won again. He was smiling now. His body pulsed with energy and exaltation. He wiped the sweat from his brow as those around the ring debated who would take him next. The last time he had grappled was back at the quarry when the foremen gave them a night off. Mathias had wagered on him during that first year they were there, and he always won.

After a couple more rounds, they stopped for water. A few of the men gathered around him, asking about his techniques and where he had learned to fight.

As he spoke, Kaeden realized he had felt no revulsion during the matches. How was it he couldn't stand human touch, but he had no problem fighting?

Was it the competition? He didn't have to think while grappling, but when ministering to patients, he was constantly reminded of their humanness and of his parents. Was that it?

He didn't know. And deep down, he wasn't sure how much he wanted that to change.

The next day, Mathias's burial box was placed on a platform in the main audience chamber, and black flags replaced the blue ones across the White City. Although Eldarans had not dwelt in the White City for over a hundred years, the city still saw itself as the birthplace of the race and keepers of their lore. Storm clouds gathered at noon, dark and menacing, and a sudden chill hung in the air.

Kaeden kept his vigil over Mathias from a nearby alcove, watching the various dignitaries, councilors, and people of worth parade in and out to view the burial box and pay their respects. A cloth of blue with an intricate design of a moon and stars was placed over the box. Candles were lit, leaving the room feeling somber. Only a few glanced his way, and of those, a handful recognized the golden cord around his waist. One came and spoke to him.

The man bowed. "You are the new voice for the Word, I presume."

"I am," Kaeden replied.

"Rem Palancar, at your service." He was tall and lanky, with greying hair pulled back at the nape of his neck and hazel eyes. His fine clothing suggested he was important. "May I ask why you do not stand beside the burial box?"

"I prefer to serve the Word from the shadows." He had no desire to stand in a spot where he might have to touch people. Given how heavy his heart was today, his reaction to a simple hand clasp might send him over the edge.

"May I ask who your parents were?" When Kaeden blinked,

Rem amended his words. "I was once acquainted with a handful of Eldarans a long time ago."

Kaeden rarely spoke of his parents, and a piece of him didn't want to part with their names. But he was also curious now about this man in front of him, and if he had indeed known his parents. "Telent and Rosenwyn."

The man smiled. "Yes, I knew them. They visited here once and stayed in my home."

"When?" Kaeden asked, his heart beating faster.

"Many years ago. If you are their son, it was before your birth. But you look like them. You have Telent's face."

It had been ages since he had been compared to his father. By the time he became an adult, he was over a head taller than both of them and much broader than his father. But they had the same face, a face his mother loved and constantly mentioned with a smile on hers.

"They were wonderful, kind people," Rem said. Then his expression grew serious. "I assume their missing presence means they are no longer with us."

Kaeden swallowed the lump in his throat. "You are correct."

Rem glanced at the cord around his middle again. "It appears the mantle of Truthsayer fell to you."

"Yes." He barely squeezed the word out.

"Thank you for carrying such a heavy burden. Word knows we need a Truthsayer now more than ever with this war. Perhaps you will be the one to broker peace."

"Only the Word knows," Kaeden replied. But he doubted that. His real path lay with the Shadonae and stopping them. However, that could pave the way to peace. He thought again of Brighid. *She is my special instrument.* Was the Word hinting she would be the one to bring peace?

"If you need a place to stay, or anything else, please ask for me."

Kaeden bowed. "I will. Thank you."

Rem walked away. Palancar. The name sounded familiar. Maybe he had heard it from his parents a long time ago. He watched the man approach another group of people and begin to talk. There was a regal air to the older man, and Kaeden wondered what position he held here in the White City.

As afternoon descended, the crowd finally thinned. Selma spoke with the few people still present. A servant came and offered Kaeden a drink. He declined. In remembrance of his parents, he chose never to imbibe alcohol. A minute later, Treyvar approached him from the side with a goblet of water. "You must be thirsty. You've been standing here all morning. And I saw you dismiss the servant, so I figured you don't drink wine." He offered the glass to Kaeden.

Kaeden drained the goblet in one gulp. "Thank you."

"I spoke to Captain Reginar. He and a handful of soldiers will be ready to carry Mathias's box to the Sanctuary in the next hour."

"It will be a small party, correct?" Kaeden said as he returned the goblet to Treyvar.

"Yes. Very few are allowed to approach the Sanctuary of the Eldarans. I feel honored to be one of the escorts."

"Have you informed Selma?"

"Yes, before she came to the audience chamber."

"I will be ready when it is time."

Treyvar looked as if he would say more, then nodded and walked away. Perhaps he sensed a heavy presence descending on Kaeden. As the hour approached to take these last steps with Mathias, his heart grew heavier. He knew Mathias was dead, and what lay in the box was just the shell left behind. But in those crazed, grief-filled moments, he wanted nothing more than for Mathias to sit up and tell everyone he had simply been asleep.

Twenty minutes later, Captain Reginar entered the audience chamber with six guards. Lord Rayner walked in a minute later with Captain Wilmar in tow. The small group headed for the burial box.

Kaeden left his place in the shadows and stepped into the dim light pooling on the stone ground. It was time.

Selma headed across the hall, and they both stopped a couple feet from the box. Kaeden kept his eyes on the embroidered moon and stars as Lord Rayner said something about the service of the Eldarans and Mathias in particular. He had no patience to the listen to this man, not with grief hanging so heavily over him.

Lord Rayner finished and the guards assigned to carry the box took their places. With a single swift movement, they raised the box and started forward. Kaeden and the others followed, save for Lord Rayner. He stood at the pedestal with the light from outside falling across his shoulders and cloak.

The group moved as one through the castle and the double-set doors to the outside. A few raindrops fell as they left the protective awning over the castle entrance. Through the courtyard, out the gates, and then they turned right down a narrow street.

"There is a small city gate to the west that leads to the Sanctuary," Treyvar explained.

"How do you know this?" Kaeden asked.

"I might not have visited the Sanctuary, but I know where it is, and how to get to it."

"What keeps others from the Sanctuary if it is so close to the city?" Or vandalizing it, or worse?

"A seal on the door. Only an Eldaran can open it. The place is held in awe, almost a fearful reverence by many. Very few venture to the Sanctuary, or so I've heard."

"I see." That made sense. And it gave him a small measure of comfort that at least some aspects of his people were still respected.

They reached a smaller gate set within the walls. One of the guards opened it and the procession continued outside. Not far from the walls, the Forest of Anwin rose with only a slim path leading through the trees. The forest was even darker today with the barest hint of light filtering through the thick foliage above. Only a handful of raindrops made it through the canopy, keeping the group dry as they made their way through the forest.

After twenty minutes, the evergreens opened to reveal a breathtaking view. Waterfalls spilled from the cliffs high above into a pool of water so clear it was like glass. Around the pool spread a meadow of emerald green with courageous wildflowers bracing for the first frost.

Kaeden slowly let out his breath as his gaze settled on the white structure next to the lake. It stood two stories tall with wide stairs that led to a set of doors covered by a portico. The simple and elegant design blended in with the natural splendor of the place. Moss and ivy rose across the walls as nature gradually took hold of the ancient setting.

This was the Sanctuary of his people. And the pool of water was where the Eldaran race first came forth into the Lands to fight and serve alongside the Word.

"This place is more splendid than the scrolls described," Treyvar said in a hushed voice.

"I haven't been here in ages," Selma murmured.

A lump rose inside Kaeden's throat. As much as he was grateful that Mathias would be interred here in the place of their ancestors, he couldn't help but remember his parents and their charred remains. They deserved to be here with the rest of the Eldarans. Why had the Word allowed them to die in a foreign country in such a horrid manner? And not even let them return to their home for their final rest?

That grief followed him as the small party made its way across the field to the Sanctuary. They paused at the bottom of the stairs. Kaeden spotted runes across the thick wooden doors and wondered if this was one of the protective measures Treyvar had spoken of.

He had his answer when Selma asked him to follow her. "Place your hand on the wood," she said once they reached the top. Kaeden removed his glove. The mark on his hand shone like a small candle in the shadows. He still wasn't used to this sight. Selma pressed her palm along the wood and he did the same. At the touch, his mark flared to life.

There was a loud creak and the doors began to open. Kaeden poured his thoughts and feelings into the doors until they stood fully expanded. Selma glanced at him and nodded. They turned and motioned for those below to follow with the body of Mathias.

The inside of the Sanctuary was just as beautiful and wild as the outside. White alabaster stone walls, a high arching ceiling, ivy weaving its way up the sides, and smooth stone floor. As he made his way through the first room and into the main, for the second time, his breath escaped his lungs. Ahead stood a wall made entirely of colored glass.

Others gasped as they entered. At the same moment, the sun came out from behind the clouds and hit the colored glass, sending a rainbow of colors across the cavernous hall. The grief he had been holding inside blossomed in his chest and rose into his throat. Tears came unbidden, and only with sheer determination did he hold them back.

He walked across the stone slabs, his boots barely making a sound, and went to stand before the wall of glass. Each square held the memories of the Eldarans. The first glass portrayed two Eldarans kneeling before the sick and healing them. Another was a Guardian holding his sword of light aloft as he banished the shadow-wraiths to the unseen world. Another was an Oathmaker strengthening soldiers for the battle ahead.

Kaeden stood there, taking in the history of his people. At last, his eyes rested on the top image where a woman dressed in white stood with her right hand held high and beams of light spreading toward the top corners of the glass. Above that, in the ancient language, the letters for the Word were molded from lead and woven into the rest of the panels, completing the wall of glass.

Before he could think, Kaeden stepped forward and placed his marked hand on the glass. He crushed his other hand into a fist and held it against his chest. So many emotions swirled inside. It was as if a hurricane had erupted within the deepest parts of his soul, sweeping his entire being into its harrowing tempest.

"Kaeden?" Selma asked from the other side of the room.

"I need a moment," he said without turning.

Treyvar came up alongside him and placed his hand on Kaeden's shoulder. "Spend all the time you need here," he said quietly. "We will take Mathias's body below. Join us when you are ready."

Kaeden nodded. Selma hesitated beside Treyvar, but he didn't look at her. He needed time and he hoped she would understand.

Eventually, she followed the others to the left side of the room, where stairs led down to the crypt.

After the last person disappeared, Kaeden fell to his knees and pounded his chest with his clenched hand. He wanted to raise a fist to the wall of glass and hit it as well, but he wouldn't let his emotions destroy this piece of history.

The sun disappeared and the colors faded. One tear rolled down his cheek before he wiped it away with the back of his hand.

Questions rose and swirled inside his mind. Why were the ones who gave everything to help mankind treated with such contempt by the very ones they served? These glass pictures showed the power and beauty of the Eldarans, but they didn't show the end to some of them. Lives that ended in betrayal, in pain, and in sorrow.

Kaeden glanced up at the wall of glass again. These Eldarans were his ancestors. Each walked the hard path of serving the Word and giving their all for mankind, just like the Word had. And now they were witnesses of the next generation, encouraging them to keep going.

"I don't know if I can do this," he whispered. "I don't know if I can walk this path You've laid out for me. I'm tired. I'm weak. And it hurts."

The main room was silent, but he heard the others speaking below. Then a song began, so quiet at first he didn't notice. It rose inside his mind and heart, a thunderous, beautiful voice. He didn't know the words, but they touched him deep inside. Light grew within the cavernous hall and he felt a soothing warmth, as if a thousand hands were lightly brushing his back. Maybe they were real. It was as if his ancestors were there with him, placing their own wounded hands upon him and leaving behind encouragement and blessing. A beautiful host of beings who had walked this path and were now here to give him the strength to walk the same road.

He slowly rose and held up his marked hand as the song reverberated in his heart. The light flared across his palm, dancing along the wall of glass, and shot toward the ceiling.

You are mine, Son of Light. And I will be with you, as I have always been with all who follow Me.

"Word?" Kaeden looked up. The light faded from his palm until only a soft glow remained.

"Kaeden?"

He twisted around to find Selma had come back upstairs.

"Are you all right?"

"Yes." He lowered his hand. "Just grieving." For some reason, he didn't want to share the intimate moment he had experienced.

"Do you still need time?"

"No, I'm fine now. But what about you?"

Her gaze moved to the glass wall behind him. "I've been here before. It's a beautiful tribute to our people."

Tribute? Didn't she feel something more? What about the song? Did she hear it? Or feel this intimate connection with their people?

Selma had already turned around. "I'll show you where the rest of our group is waiting." Kaeden blinked. Perhaps it was only a monument in Selma's eyes and nothing more. The thought left a sliver of sorrow in his heart.

He followed her to the opening in the stone slabs and the stairs that descended into the crypt. The light from her hand reflected off the white stone, adding a gentle ambiance to the area. At the bottom, fre stones were imbedded in the walls, trading the white light of her hand for a soft blue. Down a narrow hallway they walked. After a minute, it opened into a space with a low ceiling and a dozen walls and columns, like a dark maze deep within the earth. There the rest of their group waited with the box that held Mathias's body.

Treyvar came to Kaeden's side as the group started forward again, with Selma leading the way with confidence. Their boots echoed across the vast place with a solemn sound. Kaeden glanced at the areas that opened to the right and to the left that disappeared into darkness. Long, narrow ledges were built into the alabaster walls. Most held boxes similar to Mathias's, but a few were empty, waiting for the next Eldaran who had achieved their eternal rest.

Near what seemed to be the center of the crypts, Selma came to a stop. "Here." Four walls made a square opening with curved archways that led in the directions of the compass. "This is where the Truthsayers are put to rest."

Kaeden jolted at the word "Truthsayer." He glanced at the walls. Each held nine long and narrow gaps carved into the stone: three from top to bottom, and three across. Most of the hollows were occupied with burial boxes. Only four spots remained.

Truthsayers. The voice for the Word in the Lands. A chill went down his spine. For a moment, he felt like he didn't belong. Not long ago, he had been Eldaran in name only, with no power. How could he now be this world's Truthsayer?

The vibration of a faint song thrummed again in his soul and Kaeden took a deep breath. No. He belonged here because the Word had chosen him. Selma directed the men to place Mathias's burial box in the narrow gap in the wall to the right. The box slid into the empty space with a hushed whisper.

The men stepped back. "Do you have any words for us?" Selma asked Kaeden.

He shook his head. "No, you may speak first."

She nodded and raised her hand, sending the light of her palm across the room. She spoke in the ancient tongue, quoting the passages from the texts that spoke of the Eldarans who followed the Word to the Lands to fight in the Great Battle. A few of the men glanced at each other, puzzled. They didn't know the ancient tongue. But Treyvar seemed to understand as he listened to Selma.

When she finished, she glanced at Kaeden. "Your turn."

He took in a long breath and looked at the burial box that held Mathias. Then he knelt and placed his hand on the box. Instead of speaking, he began to sing. There were a few stifled gasps and he himself was surprised. He rarely sang. But something took over his mouth, and he couldn't help but begin the song that had first entered his heart upstairs when he stood before the wall of colored glass.

His baritone echoed across the room and through the archways, reverberating through the crypts. The words were a mixture of joy and sorrow, and the longing for something more. As he ended the song, his voice faded into silence. *I'll miss you, old man*, he thought as he brushed his hand one last time across the box and stood.

Treyvar gave instructions for the others, and together they started for the exit.

"Why did you sing that song?" Selma whispered as she came to Kaeden's side.

He glanced over to find a look of fear and horror on her face, enhanced by the blue fre light. "It captured what I am feeling. Why?"

"That song is sacred to our people and not to be sung in front of others."

Kaeden frowned. "I don't understand. It's the words of the Word. Why would He not want the people He loves to hear it?"

"It is *our* song. Not theirs."

Kaeden wasn't so sure. If it was really that important, wouldn't his parents or Mathias have taught him as much? The Word loved mankind enough to battle for their souls. Why would He withhold His song from them?

An unease spread in his chest. He glanced at Selma again as they made their way out of the crypt and up into the main part of the Sanctuary. What was happening to the Eldaran race?

7

Brighid slowly opened her eyes. The song that had filled her dream faded from her mind. She lay beneath a brightening sky trying to recall the words or why they touched her heart so much, but the longer she lingered on it, the more it slipped away like water through her fingers, until the only thing she remembered was the beautiful baritone voice.

Finally, she sat up. The smell of the fire from the night before mingled with the pine needles strewn about her. She looked around, still feeling a longing in her soul for the song. But it was gone. And so was the night. Already the sun started to peek above the treetops.

She sighed and placed Kaeden's cloak to the side. It no longer smelled like him, only like dirt and her sweat. She brought her knees up and held the cloak beneath her chin. More than fifteen days had passed, but she hadn't seen a village or any sign of human life. Maybe her estimate was wrong. She thought she would be near Nordica's border by now, but that was only based on a fleeting understanding of maps and the world. Perhaps—her gut clenched—she was lost.

She stood and shook out the cloak. No. She would not linger on such thoughts. They would gut her and wipe out the strength she needed to get back. At the moment she was healthy, and she had been through hardship many times before. *I can do this. I must do this.*

And then what? Kaeden told her to return to her people and tell them the truth about the Shadonae and the war. But how? Who would listen to a clanless woman who been captured by the enemy?

She held her hand up, then closed it into a fist. She had never cared about the name others had given her on the battlefield. But at that moment, it felt like a cord she could cling to. *I am the Stryth'Veizla. And I will fight for an opportunity to be heard. No matter how long it takes or if I must traverse all of Nordica. Because if I don't . . .*

Images of Johan and Marta flashed across her mind. And others she had fought with. On the battlefield, it didn't matter the clan one belonged to or if one was clanless. They all fought for Nordica. They were her people. The people of the North. And these Shadonae had enslaved them.

She gathered the cattail roots she had roasted over the fire the night before. Combined with the stems and the last of the berries, she had enough food for a day or two. She could also take a day off to hunt or fish, but there was no guarantee she would get anything. But meat would give her more stamina than these tubers and berries. And she had no idea how far she still needed to travel or how much strength she would need to get home.

Soon, something would give.

Brighid shook her head and finished packing. No, none of those thoughts today. She ate a few of the stems and berries, then started north again. As she settled into a quick walk along the ridge of a hill, she glanced around. When had the trees started changing color? Had she not noticed because mainly evergreens grew in this part of the country? Or did it happen overnight? As beautiful as fall appeared, a premature change in the trees meant winter would come early.

"Bolva," she said under her breath and gripped the straps of her pack. She wasn't a stranger to winter. The Nordic people counted years by winter. But it could slow her down if she didn't reach the border soon.

Just as the sky changed from day to night, she spotted a handful of lights between the trees. Finally. A village.

I guess I didn't need to worry about food. She hurried through the trees until the forest gave way to small wooden houses, crudely fashioned fences, and haystacks. She came to a stop.

These buildings weren't Nordic.

"Where am I?" she whispered as she ducked, blending in with the shadows. Twilight had settled over the mountains, and the only thing she could see was light from candles escaping through the oiled skins that covered the windows. Were there really Ryland villages this close to the Nordic border? Or had she somehow wandered off course?

No, she was close the northern edge of the Ari Mountains. She couldn't miss those massive snow-topped peaks. But she hadn't found the valley yet that bridged the two countries. Either this was a village along the foothills, or it was one of the villages near Rokr Valley.

Hopefully the valley, she thought as she watched the occupants. Shadows passed by the windows as families gathered for the evening inside their homes. Her legs began to cramp from hunching down. Nearby, the branches of a pine tree hung like a skirt around its trunk. She crawled inside, then sat and parted the branches so she could continue to watch.

Muffled voices blended with the sounds of the night. Crickets chirped, and somewhere in the woods behind her an owl began its night song. Brighid brought her knees to her chest and wrapped her arms around them. It felt peaceful here. With families, and animals, and life. It reminded her a little of her early days with Elphsaba, when they lived in the Northern Wastelands, traveling from one small village to another. They always shared a small cabin with a goat or two. And evenings were spent watching the sun set together.

Tears no longer came when she thought about Elphsaba. Just a sigh and a feeling of emptiness. As night settled in, she began to doze. Crickets. The soft hoot of an owl. The song from last evening . . .

Brighid jerked awake. Everything was dark except for slips of moonlight. How long had she slept? She blinked, then scanned the village. Everyone was asleep, as far as she could tell. She had thought about circumventing the village, but this was a rare opportunity to find more supplies. Especially if winter did, indeed, come early.

Cautiously, she left the cover of the pine tree. The house closest to her was small with a thatched roof and an animal pen on the side. She slipped past while looking for a storage shed or smokehouse. Nothing. She moved on to the next, following the outer edge of the village.

The third house held promise. A lean-to was built on the side facing the forest. Brighid found the latch, then carefully lifted the wooden handle. It was well oiled and didn't make a sound. Same with the door as she pushed it inward. The aroma of smoked meat hung around the barest shadow of barrels against the wall. After lifting the lid from the first barrel, she reached inside and felt barley. She pulled back the flap on her pack and grabbed handfuls and shoved them inside. Next, she found another crate filled with potatoes. She grabbed a half dozen and stuffed them in.

She encountered cheese wheels on the shelf above, but they were much too big to take. Navigating the rest of the room by feel, she found the meat. Most were large hunks, but she did find a string of sausage. Perfect. Quickly pulling out her knife, her fingers counted four links, and she began to saw the casing. A dog barked outside. She jumped and lost the knife.

"Bolva!" She dropped to her knees and searched the straw that covered the floor. She couldn't afford to lose her knife. The barking continued, followed by a man's voice. Her heart beat faster. "Come on, come on. Where are you?" she muttered. As the voice drew close, she found the knife and stood. For one heartbeat, she contemplated the sausage. Meat meant no need to hunt. It was worth it.

She grabbed the sausage and sliced at one of the links, then stuffed everything into the pack.

She slipped through the door. More voices spoke. Brighid ran for the forest. Shouts and barking followed. She reached the forest edge within seconds and plunged into the underbrush. Twigs cracked and snapped, branches grabbed her exposed skin, and her leg twisted as she came down on a root. But like a wild animal on the run, she broke through and rushed between the trees.

The barking drew closer.

Brighid found a narrow game trail and sprinted for all she was worth. The dog hit her from behind. She fell, her hands landing on rocks that sliced through her palms. Teeth clamped down on the fleshy part of her calf just above her boot.

She clenched her own teeth against a scream. Twisting around, she tore loose from the dog's jaws, then kicked out with her good leg. A wild yelp split the air. She scrambled up and then kicked the dog again. There were no thoughts, only actions and the need to survive.

The dog didn't jump again. In the moonlight, it looked to be crouching down.

She twisted around and ran again. Pain tore along her leg, and a sticky wetness coated her calf. But it didn't seem like the bite was deep, and her leg moved fine, so she shunted the pain and focused only on the trail ahead, aiming to get as far away as she could.

After a few minutes, she slowed. The dog was no longer following her, either because it had been injured or called off. She really hoped it was the latter. Though it had attacked, she had no desire to hurt an animal.

Brighid resumed running until she felt like she would collapse. Sweat dripped down her hot face and stung her eyes as she slipped to the ground next to a giant pine tree. Her leg throbbed, but she couldn't see enough to assess the wound. She leaned her head back and slowed her breathing. She would check it tomorrow.

After a few minutes, her heart no longer thrashed, and the sweat cooled across her body. She took a few more deep breaths, then pulled out the sausage. With her teeth, she tore a chunk off the half link she had sliced. She chewed quietly, savoring the meaty taste and texture. Despite the pulsing pain of her calf, this was, indeed, worth it. So much better than squirrel or fish. She tore off another chunk and chewed in the darkness.

Once she had finished the half link, she pulled out her cloak and stored the rest in her pack. Now full and tired, she lay down on her side, her back against the trunk of the tree. The air was cold, but the cloak was thick and comforting. She snuggled inside the warm cloth and closed her eyes. Even the aching of her leg couldn't stop sleep from taking over.

Morning came in a hazy grey. Brighid slowly blinked her eyes open. She didn't want to move. The cloak was tugged tight around her head and shoulders, leaving only her face exposed. The tip of her nose was numb from the chilly air. The scent of pine needles and soil filled her nostrils, and sleep hovered in her mind like a morning mist.

She took stock of her body as she lay beneath the cloak. Though sore, everything felt fine—except her calf. Now it was warm and swollen. Brighid sat up and pulled back the cloak. She gasped at the chill in the air. It was colder than she had expected. And her leg . . .

She stared at the mess of torn cloth, caked blood, and inflammation. It was almost twice the size of her other calf. "Bolva," she whispered. This was going to make things slower. She took the waterskin, wiped as much blood away as she could, then tore the rest of her pants. The bite marks weren't large, but given how her leg felt, an infection must be setting in.

She looked around. If only she could find honey. It would help with the wound. However, the chances of finding a nest were slim. Usually, bees' nests were hidden deep within the forest or in rocks between crevices. Her second option was to continue northward, find a Nordic village, and receive help there.

Brighid cut more of the cloth around her leg, this strip free of blood. After pouring water over it and wringing it out, she wrapped it around her calf. The damp cloth felt good against her heated skin. She tied off the end, then stood. Even though her leg hurt, she could walk and use it.

She quickly ate a breakfast of roasted cattails, then lifted the pack to her shoulder and started north again. One or two days. *Please let it be just a couple more days,* she silently prayed. A shadowed passed over her heart as she made her way through the brush and trees. The last thing she wanted was for death to visit her out here in the middle of nowhere. She closed her eyes for a brief moment, but she didn't feel the chill of death. It wasn't here. Not yet. But she knew more than most how fast it could steal across a person and carry off their soul.

The next day brought both heat and ice. Brighid sucked in a breath as she rewashed her wound, her fingers stiff from cold. After tightening the bandage, she looked up at the grey sky and held her hand out. Maybe she had imagined that bit of white from a moment ago. Seconds later, another snowflake drifted down and landed on her palm, melting on contact.

No, she hadn't. It was snowing.

She closed her hand into a fist. It rarely snowed this early in the season. She had never experienced early snowstorms herself, just heard about them from Elphsaba. Strange winters when the harvest was still ripe in the fields and snow had wiped out the crops.

Standing, she pulled her cloak tight around her neck. Last night, she had finally reached what appeared to be the Rokr Valley. The Ari Mountains towered on each side of the wide vale. But she wasn't sure how long the valley was or how many days it would take to reach the other side and Nordica. And now, with snow . . .

She hefted her pack and started north along the eastern side of the mountains. As more snow fell, she increased her pace. Narrow trees spread out ahead of her. Nothing that would provide shelter if this turned into a snowstorm.

As the day passed, the sky grew darker, and more snowflakes fell. The temperature dropped until she rolled her fingers inside her cloak to protect them. It was afternoon, but it felt—and looked—like evening. A half hour passed, and the snow fell in earnest. At the same time, what had been a constant, dull pain in her leg turned into heated throbbing, slowing her gait and causing a wince every few steps.

Her thoughts darkened like the sky above, and desperation took hold of her heart. She knew what could happen to people caught in a snowstorm. Lost and frozen to death, only to be found later.

Was that her fate? Had she survived hunger and war and being a prisoner just to die after she finally escaped? She limped on, pushing her way through the brush, taking each game trail she could find. Did the Word exist? Had He really rescued her from captivity, or was it all a coincidence and she would die out here?

A wind blew gently through the trees, sending flakes dancing in the sky.

Brighid looked up. *Is that You?*

Only the wind answered.

She turned her attention back to the trail. She wanted to believe, but belief was hard when her reality was full of bleakness and pain.

No, she had also seen glimpses of beauty. Mathias's kindness. The light from Kaeden's hand. Was it possible these were hints of an invisible being Who held the world by His words?

How did she know what was true and what were just stories?

Or did everything end in darkness, and Morrud and the Abyss took the dead?

She clutched the front of her cloak. *Please don't let that be my end.* She closed her eyes. *Let there be a reason for this life. It's already full of so much pain and suffering.*

Her leg gave another hard throb, causing her to gasp. She stopped and took a few deep breaths, letting the pain wash away. The ground was white with snow, but she could still make out a narrow trail through the forest and the mountains on her right.

She paused for a moment and reached out with her senses. Cold air blew past and snowflakes melted on her face. But this chill was normal. It wasn't death. She let out her breath in a long, wispy trail. If death was coming for her, she would feel it now that she was no longer under Armand's oath.

She would live—for now.

After a short search, she found a long stick suitable for walking.

Leaning on the makeshift staff, she continued. *I can do this.* She huffed a breath. *I can do this.*

One hour turned into two. Her pace was half of what it was yesterday, and her leg burned as if a fire had been lit inside it. Sweat combined with the melting snow across her face. The sun was nowhere to be seen, but she knew it was setting by how dark the sky continued to grow. She stumbled twice, and her fingers and toes had lost feeling. She might not die, but if she didn't find shelter soon, she could lose a limb.

The snow reached the top edge of her boots when she arrived at a denser part of the forest. There, the conifers provided some shelter from the falling flakes.

Just a little deeper into the forest, she thought and trudged ahead. Minutes later, she found what she had been looking for: an old pine tree as thick as her body. The branches hung low, creating a natural shelter where she would be protected from the elements. Pushing aside one branch, she discovered dirt and pine needles along the base, but no snow. Perfect.

She ducked inside and fell against the trunk with a sigh of relief. The pine needles were soft but also poked her here and there. At the moment, she didn't care. Brighid closed her eyes and laid her head against the scratchy trunk. The heat from her leg spread across her body, a constant, aching throb.

No, can't sleep yet. She struggled to open her eyes. *Need to eat and drink and take care of my leg.* She brought her pack around and reached inside. After downing a sausage and potato, she drank deeply from her waterskin. She could barely see enough to look at her leg. She carefully unrolled the material, panting. Her calf was hot and swollen, and the chill of her fingers felt good against her skin. With a grunt, she reached for a bit of snow to wash her wound, then rewrapped it. Without honey or a proper poultice, her only hopes were that her body would heal on its own or she would find her people. Soon.

Carefully, she lay on her side, her wounded leg on top of her good one. She pulled the cloak up to her neck, making sure her entire body was covered, and tucked her fingers in her armpits to keep them warm. The cloak was thick, and although she wasn't comfortably warm, she would be safe from frostbite.

The air was silent as snow gently fell across the land. Nothing stirred around her. She closed her eyes, and the darkness of slumber came. When she woke later, everything was black. She readjusted and let sleep take her again.

The next time she woke up, the world outside was grey and white. Snow had collected beyond the pine branches, forming a wall around the conifer. It took her a moment to realize just how much snow had fallen in the night. How long had she slept?

Brighid blinked, then sat up. "This can't be," she whispered as she crawled toward the nearest branch, letting out a gasp of pain. She tapped the outermost branch and let the snow fall in a pile, then looked between the cleared branches. Knee-deep snow covered everything. She let out a shaky breath. This would make traveling difficult.

She sat back and stared at the world of white. Why did it have to snow? No, why did she have to run into that dog? She pressed the knuckles of her fist to her mouth. Maybe she should have avoided that village entirely and taken a different route. Or returned to the Nordic army instead of trying to get to Nordica.

All these thoughts swirled inside her mind as her throat constricted and her heart raced. *What am I going to do? I can barely walk . . .*

Word, why?

There was no wind, song, or soft words. All was silent.

She dropped her head and held it between her fingers. *Why am I even asking Him?*

The Word is always here, even if we don't hear Him. Mathias's voice drifted through her mind, and she recalled their brief conversations those few days she was in captivity.

She pressed her head into her knees and squeezed her eyes shut. *I wish he was here now, or Kaeden. Or Johan or Marta. I miss them.* She swallowed and lifted her head. *But right now, I need to survive.*

Survive. She excelled at that.

Without a second thought, she stood and slung the cloak around her shoulders. Best to start now and get as far as she could today. And pray it didn't snow more.

She hefted her pack and emerged from the conifer's protection. The snow reached above her boots. But if she followed the areas beneath the trees, it would be less deep.

"All right, let's go." She grabbed her walking stick and continued toward northward. One day. Just one day and she would hopefully reach civilization.

9

Kaeden woke from a dream full of snow and heat, and his leg throbbed as if on fire. He sat up and threw the covers off. His leg looked fine. He stretched it out and moved it back and forth. There was no more heat, just the feel of cool air against his skin. He shook his head, puzzled. Never had he experienced dreams so real that they blurred illusion and reality. Was this an unknown side effect of being the Truthsayer? But why were these his dreams? Why did he dream of Brighid and mountains and snow?

He swung his legs around and stood. The stone floor felt as real as the pain in his calf from minutes before. Did Mathias experience this? He sighed. *I wish I could talk to you. I have so many questions.*

But Mathias was no longer here. He was with their ancestors now in the Celestial Halls.

And I am alone.

Well, that wasn't fully true. Selma was here. Maybe she had answers. But something inside him hesitated at the thought of sharing with her. She was a fellow Eldaran, but he felt no kinship with her.

Someone knocked on his door.

"Give me a moment." Kaeden grabbed his tunic from the top of the dresser and pulled the shirt over his head. As he tucked the tunic into his pants, he caught sight of the window on the other side of the guest room and stopped. White fluttered beyond the glass. "What the—?" He finished tucking his shirt in and walked toward the window. It was snowing. In the middle of autumn. It was also snowing in his dream.

Did he have a premonition of snow? Was that what his dream was telling him?

There was another knock.

Kaeden answered the door, and Treyvar stood on the other side. "Did you see?" A new fire had been lit in the fireplace in the common room they shared.

"Yes, it's snowing."

A concerned look shadowed Treyvar's face. "Do you think it's snowing up north as well?"

"Are you worried about the Nordic woman?"

Treyvar hesitated. "She did cross my mind."

Kaeden shook his head. "There's nothing we can do."

Treyvar let out his breath. "True."

"But you're wondering if we did the right thing?"

"I know freeing her was better than the alternative."

"You mean what Captain Bertin would have done to her."

"Or others. I'm familiar with the methods used to retrieve information from the enemy." Treyvar looked away. "It's not pleasant. But was it still right to send a woman alone into the wild? And with the truth about her people? The fact that those beings were able to deceive the clan hjars gives weight to how influential they are."

Kaeden glanced at the main window, where snow left wet patches along the glass. On closer examination, it wasn't sticking to the rooftops or collecting along the sill. That was a good sign. Still, Treyvar had a point. *Did I make the right choice?*

The Word said she would be His tool to the Nordic people. He wanted to believe that meant the Word would take care of Brighid. But his parents went to Khodath to serve the Word, and they ended up dead. Following the Word didn't always mean everything turned out well.

His stomach clenched at the thought. How did one serve and follow the Word with no guarantee?

"Kaeden?"

He turned back. "Sorry, Treyvar, just thinking."

"Care to share?"

"No. Not really." He looked at the glass again, and a silent prayer went up from his soul for Brighid.

The two men spoke of other things as they left the guest rooms and headed for the dining hall. "Do you plan to return to Avonai?" Kaeden asked.

Treyvar shook his head. "No. If Lord Rayner allows it, I hope to winter in the White City. The library is vaster than the one in Avonai. I hope to learn more and perhaps work with the healers here so I can be ready when Nordica makes a move again. What about you?"

"I'm not sure. I spoke to Captain Reginar, and they are restricting travel."

"If you want to go back to Avonai, I can make it happen."

"Thank you for the offer, but there's nothing to return to." *And there's nothing here either,* Kaeden thought. *I have no home. All I have is a mission.* The thought left a hollow feeling inside his chest.

"Then let's find a reason for you here," Treyvar said. "There are books on the Eldarans in the library. Old scrolls written by your people."

Kaeden glanced up, surprised. "There are?"

"Yes. You might find some information that can help you in your new role as Truthsayer."

Maybe they would explain his strange dreams. And he could find out more about the various gifts the Eldarans possessed, including the Oathmaker and what the Shadonae did to the Nordic people. Perhaps even find a way to free the Nordics without the unraveling of the oath killing them. "I think I would like that."

"Then let us both meet with Lord Rayner."

He nodded to himself. A part of him feared he would be wasting his time here in the White City all winter. But understanding who he was and why his people were here in the Lands might help him when the time came to confront the Shadaone. Then he frowned. Should he invite Selma to join them? He should be working with her. After all, she was also an Eldaran and an Oathmaker. But he had never seen her use that particular gift. In fact, apart from the mark on her hand, she seemed like every other healer. Why didn't she use her gifts more? Maybe he should ask her. But something held him back.

They entered the dining hall where the staff and guests of Celestis Castle ate. A fire crackled in the large stone fireplace, warming the area, while snow continued to fall outside the tall, narrow windows along the other wall. A long table made of dark wood that contrasted with the white stone took up most of the room. Blue banners hung from the lofty ceiling with the crest of the White City.

A single table near the back held baskets of bread and rounds of cheese. Watered-down ale waited in pitchers. Breakfast was a simple affair, with little time spent dining. Selma joined them a couple minutes later, wearing her healer robes. Her dark, wavy hair was pulled back, and her pale blue eyes matched the belt around her waist. Her beauty had started attracting attention around the castle, but Kaeden felt no pull.

"Good morning," she said to Kaeden and Treyvar before helping herself to a slice of bread and cheese. A handful of other guests moved in and out of the dining hall, their eyes lingering on the three foreign visitors.

Selma ignored them as she sat down opposite of Treyvar and started a conversation revolving around her current work in the Healers Quarters.

"Would you like to join us?" she asked, glancing at Kaeden.

"Join you?" He hadn't been keeping up with the conversation.

"I am working with the Chief Healer here in Celestis Castle. I know you were learning from Mathias before he passed away. Perhaps you could continue your studies with Healer Weylin. We could use the help. With more people arriving in the White City, there is a need for healers."

"More people arriving?" Kaeden asked.

"Refugees." Selma took a bite of bread. The way she said the word so nonchalantly, it was as if she were commenting on the weather.

Refugees were coming to the White City as well. It made sense. If the Nordics attacked the White City, they would be met with an impenetrable wall and the high cliffs of the Ari Mountains that served as the rearguard. It was one of the safest places for the fleeing people of the Ryland Plains. But . . .

Kaeden glanced down at the wooden plate and the half-eaten slice of bread. No one knew of his revulsion to physical touch except Mathias. How would he explain he couldn't touch a human? Mathias had been working with him, and he had made some progress. He healed Brighid. And he was able to assist Mathias in the healer's tents. His mentor would want him to continue to heal, but could he?

"Let me think about it."

Selma picked up a wedge of cheese. "At least let me introduce you to Healer Weylin and show you where the Healers Quarters are here in the castle." She popped the bite of cheese into her mouth.

"All right." He could do that. "Tomorrow morning."

"I will see you then." Selma finished chewing, then cleaned the area around her and deposited her plate at the end of the table.

"It would appear there are two reasons for you to stay here in the White City," Treyvar said as Selma left the dining room. "Knowledge about your heritage and helping others."

"Yes. I was also thinking about exercising with the guards I met in the training room."

"Oh?" Treyvar asked.

"I've been sharing some of my grappling techniques. And I want to maintain my strength. I was a runner during the last battle. It would be best to keep my body conditioned for whatever role I play when the war starts again."

"That is wise."

"You are welcome to join."

Treyvar laughed. "I'm more a man of intellect than brawn."

Kaeden grinned. "You can be both."

"I think I will stick to my books. But thank you."

That evening, Kaeden accompanied Treyvar to meet with Lord Rayner. He waited for them in the grand audience chamber, sitting on his throne with a cold, casual air. Kaeden balked at his look. He really didn't like the lord of the White City and wondered what secrets the man held.

They stopped at the bottom of the wide stairs that led to up to the platform where Lord Rayner sat. Treyvar explained his desire to stay in the White City, and Lord Rayner listened, then leaned forward and tugged on his chin, his eyes set on Treyvar.

"Does your father not desire to have you back in Avonai?" he asked. Kaeden did not like the glint in his eyes.

"King Erhard has given me freedom to do as I wish," Treyvar answered. "I am a seeker of truth and wisdom, and as such, I travel the Lands. Currently, I hope to learn as much as I can to help when the war recommences."

Kaeden peered at Treyvar from the corner of his eye. Interesting. He referred to his father as the king instead of using a more familial title.

Lord Rayner pursed his lips and nodded. "A worthy endeavor for a prince. Feel free to use all resources the White City has to offer."

Treyvar bowed. "Thank you, Lord Rayner."

Lord Rayner turned his attention to Kaeden. "And you, Truthsayer. What are your plans?"

"I also wish to stay here in the White City over the winter." He was glad he had spoken to Treyvar earlier and had a firm idea of how he would spend his time waiting out the winter.

"What will you do while you are here?"

"I will continue my studies in the healing arts and would like to learn more about my people. As the birthplace of the Eldaran race, the White City holds much information."

"I see. What will you do with what you learn about your heritage?"

"Find a way to end this war."

Silence fell across the audience chamber. Kaeden could feel Treyvar's side glance. He ignored his friend and pressed on. "After all, that is the purpose of my people. To be messengers of peace and hope. You desire that, don't you, Lord Rayner?"

Lord Rayner stared at him for a moment with a look so cold it could freeze a lake. Kaeden sensed the discomfort around him. Probably no one had ever spoken to their lord in such a manner. But he was tired of these quibbles. Better to be frank and open.

After a moment, Lord Rayner laughed. "Of course, I want peace. War is a nasty business."

"I'm glad you agree. I'm sure we can find a way to bring harmony to these lands." Kaeden was sure if he could see Treyvar right now, the young man's face would be either pale or flushed. As for himself, it felt refreshing to speak his mind. *Blunt as always,* as Mathias would have said. Yes, he was.

"I, too, would like to know more about your race." Lord Rayner sat back. "I spent most of my youth studying how to govern, trade, and negotiate. But not as much on history. Please share with me what you discover. And maybe together we can find a way toward this peace you speak of."

There was that glint again in his eyes. Kaeden fought the urge to clench his jaw. Instead, he bowed. "I would be happy to enlighten you, Lord Rayner."

Lord Rayner stared at him, then slowly smiled. "Lastly, there is one thing I ask while you both stay in this castle. Dine with me once a week. I would like to hear what each of you learn."

It sounded like a simple request, but Kaeden had a feeling there was a shadow side to the invitation. However, the best way to find out what Lord Rayner really wanted was to accept his invitation. He returned Lord Rayner's smile. He would play this game, for a little while. "As you wish."

※○※

The moment the door closed to their shared suite, Treyvar rounded on him. "Why did you answer Lord Rayner like that?"

"Why not? It's true. My goal is to reach the Shadonae and stop them. But what good is stopping them if this conflict continues?" Kaeden crossed the room until he reached the fireplace. "I wanted to plant a seed: an end to this war." He placed his hand on the mantel and stared down at the flames. "You said envoys visited Avonai a year ago and were turned away at the gates. Were envoys sent here as well?"

He heard Treyvar cross the common room and take a seat behind him in one of the chairs. "Yes. It was the fourth bitter winter for the northern country. Food was scarce. And there were rumors that Rylanders were crossing the ancient boundary and stealing from those along the border."

Kaeden glanced back. "Hunger and desperation will drive people to fight."

"Yes. It's not surprising Nordica retaliated."

"And with the power of the Shadonae backing them up, they've proven to be almost unstoppable."

"I don't think my father or Lord Rayner thought Nordica would fight back."

Kaeden frowned. "That doesn't make sense. It's an entire nation of warriors—"

"Who were starving and poor," Treyvar pointed out. "For a long time, there has been fear that the North would march down and take our lands. So perhaps my father and Lord Rayner hoped that by ignoring their plight, their numbers would dwindle and shrivel up, leaving Nordica a weak nation."

"That is a gruesome thought."

"That is one of my darker conclusions, but it makes sense. You've seen the bias between the north and south."

"Yes." Kaeden remembered how Captain Bertin and others had treated the Nordics. And how Brighid was almost beaten to death on the battlefield. "Instead, they awakened the fighting spirit of the North."

"Yes."

Kaeden turned back toward the fire. Once again, he was reminded of the darkness and cruelty of mankind. He crushed his hand into a fist. Why did the Word love a people such as this? Take on their wounds and forgive them? "I do not understand," he said quietly. And yet Mathias served. And so did his parents.

He let out a sigh. "And I will too."

10

Snow.

Gurmund held his hand up and watched as a white flake landed across his palm, melting on contact. He looked over the battlement at the rest of the Dallam Fortress and the Onyx River beyond, which ran as dark as its namesake.

Snow.

Bad things happened when winter came early.

He crushed his hand into a fist and entered the fortress. The bodies and blood from the battle that summer had been washed away, leaving behind cold stone and flickering torches. The halls were filled with the voices of those who had been stationed there after the Battle of the Plains. They lost a lot of warriors to that battle and were forced to retreat to the northern border and regroup.

Including the clanless blond woman.

Gurmund entered the main hall, where long tables had been set up and a fire burned in the hearth across the room. The heat from the fire barely reached him by the entrance. He rubbed his arms and crossed the hall. Nordic soldiers filled every table. The rooms beyond were also filled with those recovering from the battle. He let out a sigh as he approached the fireplace. Almost a fourth of their forces died in that battle. He rested a hand on the mantel and stared into the fire.

Was it worth it?

His heart clenched at the thought. On his right, a handful of people from his own clan broke their fast. He lost the least number of warriors. The Stag and Eagle Clans took the brunt of the battle. Along with the clanless who had been sent to the forefront.

He let out his breath. He had seen glimpses of the blond woman. The one the others called the Stryth'Veizla. The term didn't fit her, not really. Yes, she fought like a berserker from his own clan with overwhelming strength, like those carrion bird women from myth. But there was a grace to her fight, not brutality, that had set her apart.

In some ways, she was the epitome of their people. A physical representation of what they stood for. But all warriors eventually fell, and apparently she had been captured according to Volka. Even the Wolf Clan hjar had seemed troubled by her capture.

Gurmund sighed again and turned. Stein looked up and nodded in his direction. Gurmund joined his second in command at the table. The man looked like an oversized bear between his thick black hair and beard. "Saw snow this morning," Stein said in a gruff voice before taking one last bite of gruel.

"Aye. Bodes bad tidings," Gurmund replied.

Stein placed his spoon in the wooden bowl. "I hear Hjar Bodin and a few of the mystics from the Owl Clan will be performing rituals today to see what the future holds."

Gurmund grunted. As a fighter, he held little stock in mystical beliefs. But he had witnessed enough of the Owl Clan to know they could see more than the average human. "Ready to run our warriors through their drills?"

"Yes." Stein stood from the table. "Did you eat?"

"No. I have no appetite."

Stein's face darkened. "My Hjar—"

Gurmund raised his hand. "I will eat at noon, after our morning drills."

Stein looked as if he wanted to say more but shut his mouth. Once they were out in the hallway, he couldn't stay silent. "Have you spoken to a deathkeeper?"

Gurmund wrinkled his nose. "No. I wouldn't trust them to patch a scratch on my little toe. I sent word to Ana the moment we arrived, so she knows where I am. I also asked for more herbs." The only one he trusted with his health was his wife.

"Will Bard be joining us at some point?"

"No. I still need him at the border. And . . ." He subtly glanced around and lowered his voice. "I need him away from Armand and his power. If only I'd known at the beginning, I could have saved the others."

Stein gave him a slight nod, his face tight. A handful of their warriors had fought against the binding early in the war. Later, they disappeared. But Gurmund knew what happened. The words had poisoned their minds, sending them into convulsions and death. It had been a warning to him to keep his other warriors in line and obey. He had been suspicious of Armand and his power. After that event, he started covertly searching for a way to rid the Nordics of these strangers. But he needed to be very careful, or he would find himself on the other side of the veil, just like his men.

They turned the corner and exited the building. Snow coated the ground in a thin blanket of white. Stein's face fell. "Bolva. I hate doing drills in the snow." He pulled up the collar of his outer coat.

"It'll feel like home once you start."

Stein scowled. "This place feels nothing like home. I hate it here."

Gurmund had to admit Stein was right. It wasn't so much the cold stone of Dallam Fortress or even the militaristic feel of the place. Most everything was made of thick lumber and stone in Nordica. It was the unfamiliar mountains that towered nearby and the furnishings that weren't quite Nordic. A scent in the air reminded him of the south, and more deciduous trees surrounded them than pines and had recently turned into brilliant colors of yellow and orange and red. Pretty, but not like the everlasting green of his homeland.

That, and he missed Ana.

"Will you be calling Bein in to work with him?" Stein asked.

"No," Gurmund replied as they crossed the bailey. "I'll let him hibernate for the winter." He sighed. "We're both getting old and both could use a good nap."

Stein laughed. "Don't let the others hear you saying such things."

Gurmund smiled for the first time in days. "I'm sure the others can hear my joints creak every time we warm up."

"Probably, but you're still one of the best warriors among us."

"That's because I've lived longer than all of you, and I have the blood of my ancestors."

"For which we are thankful."

They reached an area near the outer wall where over a hundred men and a handful of women from the Bear Clan waited for Gurmund's arrival. Some grumbled about the snow, but soon those words disappeared as Stein led the clan in their morning drills. Snow continued to fall, but this was nothing to the people of the North. Gurmund warmed up alongside the others, then worked with the younger warriors. He noticed the gaps in their ranks, gaps that were the result of injury or death.

Near noon, when the snow became a thick flurry, the Bear Clan dispersed. As he reentered the main fortress, he heard the far-off thumps in one of the training rooms where some of the Eagle Clan, who had been left to protect the fortress, practiced with their bows. In another area, a skal from the Stag Clan worked with the clanless. The Owl Clan was somewhere above.

With that thought in mind, he spotted Aisling, Hjar Bodin's owl, swoop past the window and up toward the tower. He watched it disappear and wondered why the nocturnal creature was out during the day. Perhaps collecting information for her master. Or returning from her hunt.

The four groups had come to an uneasy truce with regard to the living quarters in Dallam. The Eagle and Wolf, along with half of the Stag Clan, were stationed east, across the Onyx River, in Mistcairn. Smaller groups from all five clans rotated with clanless along the border of the Lands, which the Nordics now held due to the war.

After stomping the snow off his boots and shaking out his cloak, he walked through the fortress and headed upstairs, where a hint of mint hung in the air. A handful of deathkeepers moved between the two main rooms where the injured convalesced. Unlike the healers of the south, the deathkeepers would provide basic treatments for the sick and wounded, but their main purpose was to assist with one's journey toward life or death.

Gurmund wrinkled his nose as he passed. This was one area he believed the south had correct. He was thankful Ana was skilled in the healing arts for the sake of their clan. But she wasn't here, and he wasn't as knowledgeable, so his warriors were left to heal themselves or be at the mercy of the deathkeepers. But he wouldn't let them face the beyond by themselves.

He stepped into the last room, where hay and blankets had been laid out for the wounded from the Bear Clan. Long, narrow windows lined one wall, revealing dark grey skies and snow beyond. He started his walk between the beds and then noticed a figure standing in the back at a table and crushing something in a stone bowl. The man was as large as one of the berserkers, but he wasn't of the Bear Clan.

"Who are you?" Gurmund crossed the room in five long strides.

The man placed the bowl on the table and turned. Gurmund slightly recognized him. His hair was brown and cropped short. A rune for wisdom was tatted on his forearm. He was one of the clanless. The man bowed when he saw Gurmund. "I am Johan, from Udenhalla."

"Stag territory," Gurmund said.

"Yes. I know a little about healing, so I was asked to assist up here."

"You're not a deathkeeper, are you?" Gurmund said with a frown.

"No, Hjar Gurmund. Just a humble warrior who knows about herbs and bandages."

"Show me."

Johan nodded and reached for the small pouch around his waist. "I found some witch's leaves near Ragnbork before we left Nordica and dried them out." He took a pinch of what looked like tiny green leaves and held them out to Gurmund. The leaves emitted an earthy, minty scent. "I crush the dried leaves and place them in hot water. They help relieve fever and pain. I also carry a small jar of honey for wounds and bandages."

"Where did you learn this?"

"My mother and grandmother. They were very knowledgeable about plants."

"And you've been treating the warriors in this room?"

"Yes, since last night."

Gurmund glanced around. There were almost twenty here with wounds that couldn't be handled alone. Most were sleeping, without faces pinched in pain and with fresh bandages on limbs. "I'm impressed, Johan."

"Thank you, Hjar."

"Please stay here and continue to watch over these warriors."

"I can come every few hours. However, I am also caring for the clanless since there is no one else."

Gurmund nodded. "I understand. I would be grateful for whatever you provide. Please let me know if you need more supplies, both for these men and the clanless. I will do whatever I can to procure them for you."

Johan's eyebrows rose. "Thank you."

"No, thank you for the work you are doing. We will need all the healthy warriors we can get for the next battle, whether clan members or clanless."

"I will do what I can."

Gurmund smiled. He liked this strong man before him. He could use more warriors like this one. "That's all I ask."

11

The sky remained grey and the forest empty as Brighid trudged through the trees. The only sound was the soft crunch of her boots and walking stick sinking through the snow. Sweat trickled down her face from pain and labor. With each step, her leg throbbed, but she pushed on.

An hour later, the first snowflake fell for that day. She didn't bother to stop. Instead, she furrowed her brow, gritted her teeth, and kept going. More sweat collected beneath her clothing, and her legs felt the strain of shoving against the snow and the now constant throbbing pain in her calf. With each minute that passed, more snow fell, and the afternoon became a reflection of yesterday.

I'm close to the border. I must be. She imagined a warm fire and food, soft furs, and four walls and a roof to protect her from the snow. Just over the next rise. And when she reached that hill, she told herself it was the next one. It worked the first few times, but disappointment and fear began to chip at her determination, until finally the air was filled with so much snow it was almost white. She stumbled to a stop, panting as she leaned against the walking stick.

Tears filled her eyes and her chest tightened. The feverish heat from her leg seemed to have spread throughout her body, leaving her weak and nauseated. "Maybe I made a mistake," she whispered into the silent snowfall. "Maybe I shouldn't have left the south at all." She dropped her head. "What do I do now?"

One tear fell, leaving a cold trail across her cheek. *What do I do?*

Well, she knew one thing. Standing here would be the death of her. She had to find shelter again under a tree, in a cave, or in a house.

She shifted her pack and adjusted the grip on her stick. She lifted her head, a stubbornness taking hold of her body, almost as strong as the red haze. "I can't give up. I can still walk, and it's not night yet." She wiped her face. "I'll go until I can't."

So she started again. Her steps were slower as the cold finally seeped through her cloak. Her head and cheeks grew even hotter, melting the flakes as they fell on her skin. She could see just far enough ahead to take her next step.

And another step.

And another.

It grew dark as twilight descended. Still nothing. The trees were thin and spindly, and there were no cliffs or overhangs. No cheery lights in the distance.

I can't give up. I can't give up. I can't—

Brighid stumbled over a buried log and fell into the snow. Her bad leg twisted, sending a sharp cry from her mouth as her hands and knees sank deep into the chilly wetness. She closed her eyes as a strangled sob lodged itself inside her throat. Deep inside her bones, her body burned with an unusual fire, and her head pulsated with pain.

As if to confirm her fears, she finally felt it. The deeper, biting chill of death. Her heart clamored at the feeling. She had felt death in the past, passing from soul to soul, claiming lives for the Abyss, but never moving toward her. To feel it now, washing over her with a frigidness and loneliness, stole her breath.

"So . . . you're here for me." She curled her fingers beneath the snow to keep them from shaking. "And I can't even fight you."

It's not fair. She closed her eyes as her lower lip began to quiver. *This isn't fair.* Somewhere in the back of her mind, she could feel her fingers growing numb beneath the snow, but what did that matter if she was going to die?

No. She clenched her jaw to stop her chattering teeth. *Not yet. I won't go down that easily.*

Brighid felt around for her walking stick, found it, and heaved herself up. The chill increased like an invisible fog as death moved around her. She glared into the darkness and put one foot in front of the other. "I dare you to come get me," she said, her voice even despite the frantic thumping of her heart.

Night seemed to follow death, leaving the world in darkness and ice. Within minutes, what little light had guided her disappeared. No moon, no stars. Just invisible snow that kept falling. She stumbled again, and this time the stick was nowhere to be found. "Fine. I'll crawl, then," she growled. In her delirium and fever, she could almost see death in the darkness, a figure draped in black robes with nothing but a wicked grin showing from beneath his hood. He stood a few feet away, watching her, the hem of his clothes hovering above the snow.

At the sight of him, the stubbornness inside her took hold, taking away the edge of fear, moving her, giving her that last gasp of strength.

Something brushed along her side. Adrenaline shot through her body. What was that? She reached out blindly with her hand and felt fur. She breathed faster, her hand still. It felt like an animal. It moved and she flinched. She couldn't see it, but every awful thought flew through her mind. A bear? A wolf? Something else?

The creature let out a warm huff just above her head, sending her hair flying back across her forehead. Another huff.

Brighid remained frozen. Did the creature know she was there? What should she do? She tested her wounded leg. No way she could stand without the help of her walking stick.

She lowered her head, her heart clenching. Death had brought an animal? Was that how it was going to harvest her soul?

This was it, then. This was the end. She might have been able to keep hobbling through the snow, but she couldn't escape a predator. "Are you death's companion?" she finally asked and laughed darkly.

The creature grunted. Brighid almost laughed again. It sounded like it said no. The fever began to burn through her adrenaline, bringing back a degree of delirium. "Well, if you're going to eat me, best do it soon."

The animal sniffed her. A nose and then fur brushed against her face.

Brighid blinked at the touch. Something shifted deep inside her, spreading from her, connecting with the animal. "Who are you?"

she whispered, slowly raising her head. She couldn't see, but she felt warm breath against her forehead.

The furry face nuzzled her again. The chill from minutes ago vanished in that warm breath. Even . . . the chill of death. Her eyes widened. She turned her head, feeling, waiting for death to make itself known, but its presence was gone. Had this creature banished it?

The animal nudged her and let out a quiet whine.

Before she could think, Brighid rose from her knees and felt the mound next to her. The creature was quite large and covered in thick, coarse fur. She could feel her consciousness slipping away from the fever and snow.

The mound huffed. Brighid paused for a moment, then placed her face against the warm fur. It smelled musky and like the dry leaves of autumn. Had the Word sent this animal to save her? Could she trust it?

What's the worst that could happen? her fevered mind thought. Her fingers were frozen and devoid of feeling. She buried her hands into the fur and sighed. So warm.

After a second, she felt along the body until she found what seemed to be a shoulder. Then she gripped the fur and pulled herself up. Her legs could barely straddle the broad back of this creature. But it didn't buck or startle at her mounting. Instead, it began to move forward with a steady lope.

Brighid leaned down and pressed her cheek into the fur and let out a sigh. Darkness beckoned her forward. And as she slipped away, she figured that even if this was all a dream, she felt safe for the first time.

12

Bard dismounted from Amro just inside the Bear Clan compound. Snow fell in white flakes, covering the evergreens beyond the walls in a thick, cold blanket. He pulled the hood of his cloak back, sending a flurry of white to the ground, and stomped his boots. He couldn't remember a time when snow had come so early to the Northern Wastelands, especially this far south, near the Ryland Plains border. As he pulled off his fur gloves, Amro huffed beside him.

"I'm almost done, my friend." Bard tucked the gloves into his belt. The other men who had patrolled the border with him the last few days were already attending to their mounts or finding shelter in the great hall. Bard ran a hand over Amro's thick, brown fur, checking for any tightness before undoing the clasp of the saddle. With a short command in the ancient tongue, Amro raised one massive paw, and Bard slid the chest harness off. He went around to the other side, then gave the same command and pulled the saddle over the bear's head.

From the corner of his eye, he spotted Konal waiting for the saddle. The stable boy always seemed to anticipate what he needed. "Here." He handed the saddle to Konal. "Please oil it, then hang it."

The boy bowed. "Yes, Hjaren."

Bard watched Konal head into the longhouse, where most of the mounts and livestock were kept. Konal had arrived at their compound two years ago, just skin and bones after losing his family to Ryland raiders. He wasn't the only person the Bear Clan had taken in over the years, and he wouldn't be the last. Bears might be solitary creatures, but the clan itself believed in family. At least he thought they did until he visited Ragnbork and witnessed how many Nordics had been displaced due to their clanless status. They could do more. They *needed* to do more.

"Wait here, Amro."

The bear lightly huffed but remained still as Bard crossed the open area and entered the storage house. Within, bags of hide hung from the rafters on one side of the room. The rest of the area was filled with barrels of grains, potatoes, and herbs drying from the ceiling. Inside the bags was pamon, a food made of powdered meat and fat. It was the perfect sustenance for both warrior and bear. And Bard didn't want to send Amro into the forest without eating first.

He reached into the bag and pulled out a large chunk. After closing the door to the storage building, he returned to Amro and held out the meaty fat piece. Amro sniffed the dark brown square, then opened his mouth. Bard placed the pamon inside his waiting jaws. As the bear chewed, Bard ran his hand along the beast's shoulder. "Rest well, my friend. I will need you again soon."

When Amro was done, Bard walked alongside him toward the stronghold gates, his hand resting against Amro's side. Another layer of snow coated them as Bard bid farewell to his companion and watched the massive bear lumber into the forest. He would be back in a few days, when both had rested and were ready to patrol the border again.

Bard let out a tired sigh as Amro disappeared. There was very little activity along the border since the war began. He suspected the fight was keeping the Rylanders occupied elsewhere. Not that he was complaining. It seemed peace had finally come to the valley, peace they hadn't seen in almost twenty years. But at what cost?

He turned and headed for the great hall. Smoke swirled above the roof line, a welcome sight on this cold morning. As he entered the hall, loud conversation and the smell of food greeted him. Most of the patrol sat at the long tables on each side of the hall. A large fire burned in the firepit, where an iron pot hung over the low flames. An older woman laughed as she spoke with the men at one table, then headed toward the pot and stirred the contents. Bard smiled as he crossed the hall. "Mother."

The older woman turned. "Bard! I was wondering when you would arrive."

They embraced in a lingering hug. There was a strength in his mother's arms and a warmth that filled his heart and body. Her grey hair, bound in a braid and wrapped around her head, appeared like a crown more beautiful than one of gold.

"How was your patrol?" she asked, taking a step back, her hands still grasping his forearms.

"Quiet."

She nodded, a concerned look on her face. "That is to be expected with the war and all." Her hands dropped.

"Have you heard from Father?"

"Yes," she said quietly. "They lost the latest battle and retreated north, back to Dallam. I think they plan on wintering there. They might also secure the rest of the northern border, so we might see some of our fellow countrymen in the coming months, unless winter is brutal this year."

"I think it will be. It's been snowing for over a day now."

"Yes, such a strange storm. What does it bode . . ." She glanced at the pot and sighed. "Best to eat before the food gets cold. We can talk more later in our rooms."

Bard nodded. His mother returned to the cooking fire, while he retrieved a wooden bowl and spoon from a nearby table. Thick porridge bubbled in the pot. He ladled some into his bowl and found an empty seat near the firepit. He shed his fur cloak, added honey and milk to his porridge, and dug in. The simple food was filling and warmed his insides.

Just as he finished his breakfast, one of the guards from the compound burst through the double doors. Finn took a moment to look around, spotted Bard, and rushed over.

"Hjaren Bard, there is a stranger at our gate. And the person is riding a bear."

"What do you mean?" Bard asked as he rose from the table.

"It's just as I said. I didn't see them until they were almost to the gate. The person seems to be clinging to the bear, a massive one I do not recognize."

"Take me to them."

The two hurried from the great hall, across the open space, toward the gates. Among the fluttering flakes beneath the gate frame, Bard spotted the lumbering bear with a small figure on top. Thoughts rammed through his mind as he quickly approached the pair. Who was this person? Who was the bear? And how were they together?

The bear stopped just before the gates and lifted his massive head. His fur was brown with a silver sheen, and his small black eyes held intelligence. Bard blinked. He was by far the largest bear he had ever seen, and at the prime of his life.

Bard lifted his hands in an unthreatening manner. "Who do you have, my friend?"

The bear grunted and lowered his head. Bard brought his hands down and eased closer. The bear didn't seem hostile or threatened by his approach. Strange. Unless a bear had bonded with a member of the clan, they never came near humans. Even stranger, an unbonded bear would never let a person ride on his back. But as Bard made his way around the bear's side, there was clearly a person, covered in a cloak, clinging to the bear's fur.

"Thank you for bringing this stranger to us," Bard said. Then he paused. Was it possible this alpha knew the ancient tongue? He gave a short command and the bear knelt. What in the Lands was going on?

Bard pulled the stranger from the bear's back. The cloak slipped down, revealing a young Nordic woman. The symbol of the sun curved around her left eye. Her hair was matted and dirty but still fashioned in common braids.

"Who are you?" Bard asked, but her eyes remained tightly shut. "Finn, take this woman to my mother's room, but not through the great hall." Finn's eyes went wide as he held out his arms. Bard felt the same disbelief, but there would be time enough to find out what was going on later. He still wasn't sure what this bear would do.

Finn took the woman and headed toward the great hall.

"Well, my friend," Bard said to the bear, who rose up on all fours and let out a massive shake, sending snow flying across the ground. "Thank you for bringing this daughter of the North here."

The bear grunted and turned, lumbering away into the forest, the silver tips of his fur glistening with moisture. "I wonder if we will meet again," Bard murmured. The bear was a true alpha.

Minutes later, he bypassed the great hall and entered through the back, where his family had their own private rooms. A small stone fireplace blazed against the left wall, and stairs to the loft stood to the right. Bard headed upstairs, where Finn placed the woman on a stack of furs and blankets. He lit the lamp on the nearby table and came to stand beside the bed. "Thank you, Finn."

The man turned and bowed. "Who do you think she is?" he asked quietly.

Bard shook his head as he gazed at the woman. "I have no idea."

"How did she come to be riding a bear?"

"I don't know. Perhaps the bear took pity on her and brought her to us." It was rare, but it was known to happen. There was a sacred bond among all life in the north.

"Her leg is badly wounded."

Bard looked down. Dark blood crusted what looked like haphazard bandaging around her right calf. "Can you get my mother for me? This woman needs a healer."

"Yes, Hjaren." Finn hurried away, leaving the room silent. Bard bent down and placed his hand on the woman's forehead. Hot. She was burning with fever. He heard the door open downstairs and went to meet his mother at the top of the stairs.

"Bard, what's going on?" Ana said as she ascended to the loft.

"Finn found an injured woman at our gates. Riding a bear."

"Riding a *what*?"

"A bear. I wouldn't believe it myself if I hadn't seen it. I think he took pity on her and brough her to us. I didn't recognize the alpha, but he's the biggest bear I've ever seen, with silver-tipped fur."

"Strange," his mother murmured as she approached the bed. "She's Nordic," she said a moment later. "With an interesting Mark of Remembrance around her eye."

"Do you recognize it?"

"It's not common. And it's not a clan symbol."

Bard shook his head. The mystery around this young woman deepened.

Ana assessed her, clicking her tongue as she did so. She first checked the leg, then touched the woman's forehead. "Bard, please retrieve a fresh linen dress from my chest. I need to get her out of these wet clothes first and see her leg."

Bard retrieved the dress, handed it to his mother, then went downstairs and stood by the fire while his mother tended to the young woman. He couldn't help but think there was something familiar about the young woman's face. Almost like—

"Bard, I need a small bucket with cold water and a handful of rags," Ana said over the railing. "And also ground Ammelica and Black Milfoil."

Bard retrieved the supplies and returned minutes later. He went up the stairs and found a pile of clothing to one side and a pack and cloak on the other. The woman lay in the bed with his mother kneeling beside her. One of her legs was exposed, revealing a red and swollen calf. Bard let out a low whistle at the sight.

"It's bad," his mother said. "I've seen worse. Place the bucket, rags, and Black Milfoil here." She patted the floor beside her. Bard did as she asked and set the bowl of Ammelica nearby.

Ana poured a small amount of water in the bowl, stirred the Ammelica with her finger, then gently raised the woman's head and dribbled the green liquid into her mouth. "There you go," she murmured. "This will make you feel better."

Once again, Bard felt there was something familiar about the woman's face as his mother lowered her head back down on the pillow.

His mother turned the woman's leg over and hissed. Puncture wounds were deep in the calf. "She must have been bit. By what, I wonder." She shook her head and began to wash the leg. The only sound in the room was the crackling of the fire below. Just as Bard thought it was best to leave his mother to care for the stranger, she spoke quietly as she began to wrap Black Milfoil leaves around the calf. "She looks a bit like your sister did when she was young."

A jolt shook him to his core. Yes. His chest tightened as he gazed at the young woman. She looked a lot like Kalla, right before . . . He swallowed the lump in his throat and looked away. Kalla disappeared twenty winters ago, at the end of summer, never to be seen again.

The disappearance of his older sister had devastated their family. No one knew what happened to her, or why she vanished. Only guilt and questions had been left behind.

"Bard, please bring me a stool. I'll sit with her until she wakes." Ana reached for the wool blanket and pulled it over the woman, carefully tucking it around her.

"I'll bring two." Bard returned minutes later with the stools and placed them both beside the bed. His mother hadn't stopped staring at the woman, and it made his heart hurt more. He knew she was still thinking about his sister. But this stranger wasn't Kalla.

Kalla was never coming back.

13

Slowly, Brighid rose from the darkness. She still felt hot, but that chilling edge of death no longer hung on to her. The warm fur was gone, replaced with wool. She could also feel bandages wrapped around her bad leg.

"I wonder where she came from," an older woman murmured nearby. "And to arrive during a snowstorm. What strange tidings . . ."

"Yes," a man replied.

"What happened to the bear that brought her here?"

Bear?

"He left. He knew the ancient tongue. I was able to speak to him and retrieve the young woman. It's almost like—"

"Like he was protecting her," the older woman finished.

"Yes. I wonder if there is some distant Bear Clan blood in her."

"It must be potent enough for a bear to be willing to carry her. And bring her here to our clan."

Brighid tried to open her eyes. Where was she? Who were these people? Were they speaking about her? Her fingers twitched. Where was the fur she had clung to? And that sweet scent, like grass in the autumn when it turns golden.

"Bard, her fingers just moved."

Bard. That name sounded familiar.

A hand touched her forehead. "Are you awake?" a feminine voice asked.

Brighid blinked, then finally opened her eyes. She slowly took in the room. A solid wooden roof hung over her with thick beams. A hint of smoke and meat hung in the air. Two figures sat nearby: a man with a thick, honey-colored beard and an older woman with silver hair wrapped in a braid around her head.

"How are you feeling?" the woman said, while the man looked on.

"Who are you?" Brighid's voice croaked. "And where am I?"

The woman glanced at the man. "My son, Bard, found you outside our gates. He brought you to our home. You have an injured leg and a fever."

Brighid blinked. She could still feel pain in her leg, but it no longer throbbed like it had the last few days. And the fever, although it burned, no longer carried the chill of death. Yes, death had vanished, for now. "Is this Nordica?" she asked, glancing at the two.

"Yes," the mother replied. "I knew you were one of us by the Mark of Remembrance on your face."

She let out her breath. "Then I made it home."

The woman patted her shoulder. "Yes, you are safe."

Brighid closed her eyes. Darkness and warmth began to sweep her away, but not before she heard Bard and the woman resume their hushed tones.

"The Ammelica seems to be setting in," the woman said. "It will help her rest and bring the fever down. I'll stay and watch over her."

A stool scraped along the floor. "I'll let Tola know to tend to the fires and cooking," Bard said.

"Thank you, my son."

Brighid opened one eye and saw Bard bend down to kiss his mother on the head, then leave.

Bear Clan? Brighid shut her eye. Bard. Hjar Gurmund's son. That's why she recognized the name. A sense of safety and warmth enveloped her as she drifted back to sleep.

The next time she awoke, the older woman was sitting beside her stitching a piece of cloth. The woman looked up. "Awake again, are you? Want to try eating?"

Brighid nodded. The woman put her sewing in a nearby basket, headed across the loft, and disappeared. Brighid struggled up to a sitting position. As her vision came into focus, she studied the room a bit more. A railing stood to her right, overlooking a large room with a steep roof. A lamp was lit on the table next to the bed where she lay. The bed was big enough for two, and she wondered who it belonged to. The older woman she recalled was Bard's mother. Which meant she was also Hjar Gurmund's wife, and this was his home.

Strange. She looked around again. The Bear Clan lived near the border and protected the ancient boundary, but she didn't think she would end up there. And what did they mean she arrived on a bear? She scrunched her face. She scarcely remembered the last few days. Only the aching of her leg, the bitter cold of snow and death, and some animal with thick, musky fur.

The stairs creaked, and moments later, the older woman arrived with a steaming wooden bowl. "Here." She held it out to Brighid. "Tola made it this morning. I added milk to cool it."

Brighid's stomach gurgled at the smell, and she took the bowl and spoon with willing hands. "Thank you."

She dug in and sighed at the first taste. Food. Real food. Not whatever she could scavenge. Halfway through her bowl, the older woman laughed. "You eat like my husband and son after a long day out in the woods."

Brighid slowly wiped her mouth. "It's delicious." She couldn't remember the last time she had eaten porridge with milk. Maybe when she was young and she and Elphsaba owned a goat.

"My name is Ana. What is yours?"

Brighid hesitated. What information should she give?

Ana placed her hand on top of Brighid's. "Remember, you are safe here."

Brighid lifted her chin. She had nothing to be ashamed of. She had fought with honor. And had returned with honor. "My name is Brighid."

"Brighid." Ana rolled the name off her tongue. "Strength. A good, strong Nordic name. Your mother named you well."

"Yes, she did."

"Do you remember anything before you arrived here? Where you are from? Or who your clan is?"

Her lips tightened.

Ana nodded. "I understand. Know that you are welcome here, and we will help you."

"Thank you." She might not have anything to be ashamed of, but she hardly knew these people. And words could be twisted. Better to remain silent and wait than to be tossed aside. Time would tell if she could trust the Bear Clan.

Ana gave her more of the green medicine called Ammelica, then rewrapped her leg with black leaves. "Your leg is looking better."

"It is feeling better as well."

"May I inquire how you came to be bitten?"

"A dog," Brighid replied.

The older woman nodded and finished bandaging her calf. The heat was gone, and only the pain of healing remained. "It'll scar, but the infection has passed, which is good. Do you need anything else?"

Brighid shook her head. The medicine was already making her drowsy.

"Then I will leave you be. The best healing is done in sleep."

The next few days were filled with rest, food, and Ana's help to the privy outside. The snow melted somewhat, leaving slush and mud inside the walled confines of the bear compound, which resembled a village, complete with stables, over a dozen thatched long homes, the main hall, a smokehouse, and training grounds. The first day she emerged from the loft and ventured outside with Ana's assistance, a few heads turned her way, but their glances didn't linger long, and she wondered what Ana and Bard had said about her.

By the third day, she felt almost whole.

"Would you like to join us for our evening meal?" Ana asked as she handed Brighid her old clothes, freshly washed. Brighid could smell the faint scent of soap from the clothing and balked inwardly. How long did it take the older woman to wash these foul things that had been covered in mud, sweat, and blood? Threading caught her eye and she lifted the trousers. The tear from the dog had been mended along with added material to replace where she had cut away the fabric to bandage her leg.

"Thank you for repairing my clothes," Brighid said and held the rough clothing to her chest.

"I thought you would want your own clothes returned. And my wool dress was a bit large on you. However, I couldn't help but notice your clothing is for a Nordic fighter. As the wife of a hjar who oversees the warriors of our clan in my husband's stead, and once a fighter myself, I recognize your outfit."

Brighid froze, the clothes still clutched to her chest. Did she dare tell Ana she was from the Nordic forces? That she was a clanless warrior who had been fighting down south? Would she be labeled a deserter?

Something Mathias did back when she was a prisoner suddenly filled her mind. He spoke to her. And by talking, they shared truth and built trust.

The memory faded, but she could still hear his words as she looked at Ana. She had made it to Nordica, but now the next part of her journey began. And whether by design or luck—or perhaps even the Word Himself—she had been found by the Bear Clan. She would be honest, but she would need to be prudent in how she shared the truth. Bit by bit.

"Yes, I am a fighter. It is my trade."

"Which clan do you fight for?"

Brighid swallowed. Time for the first hint of truth. "None." She squeezed the clothes tight. "I am clanless."

Ana gave her a soft smile. "Clanless are welcome at our fire. Were you on your way to a post?"

"Yes." In a way. Brighid licked her lips. Would Ana ask if she had fought in the war? Was she ready to answer? She would need to unpack her truth carefully.

"I see." Ana studied her face, and for one moment, Brighid thought she saw a look of grief pass over the woman's features before her expression smoothed. "I want to hear more, but the evening meal is ready. I'll head down and let you dress. Meet me at the threshold."

Brighid ducked her head as relief filled her chest. It was not yet time to share her journey. "I will."

After Ana disappeared down the steps, Brighid pulled off the oversized wool dress and donned her old clothes. Scars ran along her calf beneath the colorful thread Ana had used to patch her pants. They weren't her only scars. There were knicks and wounds across her body from the war. "It's a good thing I told her I'm a fighter," Brighid murmured. It would explain her scars.

But then what? How could she say anything that wouldn't make her out to be a deserter? In many ways, she was. She didn't return to the Nordic forces. Even worse, she could be branded a coward.

Find a way to free your people. Share the truth with them.

Kaeden's words filled her mind. Then memories of Johan and Marta and her comrades. Still bound by their oath and Armand's words. And, if ever captured, they could succumb to the same fate as those who died after the Battle of the Plains. A cruel and excruciating death.

Brighid lifted her head. She would find a way to share the reality of what was happening in this war. This time, her battle was with words and the truth. She would need to navigate carefully so she would be understood. And if the Bear Clan didn't believe her, she would move on. Travel all the way to Ragnbork if she had to. Until she found someone who would.

14

Brighid entered the main hall that evening a step behind Ana. This was her first time meeting the others who lived with and served the Bear Clan. Multiple long tables were set up on each side of the room with a pathway between and a large firepit in the middle. The roof towered above with thick wooden beams and pillars. Shields bearing the image of a bear hung on the walls, along with spears, swords, and axes. Runes for strength and family were engraved in the wooden pillars. The faint scent of dried herbs and fur filled the air.

There were at least two dozen people in the room, along with a handful of children. The men sported long beards, some braided and a few with beads. The women wore their hair long. Marks of Remembrance ranged from full-on tattoos across faces and necks, to covert ones barely peeking out from beneath collars and sleeves.

As she stepped into the hall, heads turned in her direction, eyes glancing between her and Ana.

"Good evening," Ana said and made her way to the firepit, where a black pot sat over burning coals.

A few answered, while others raised their hands in greeting. Then they returned to their food. No doubt they already knew of the recent arrival. Brighid followed Ana, bowing her head to those who spoke to her. After dishing up two bowls of venison stew, Ana led them to the closest empty table and sat. "I usually help with the evening meal, but Tola filled in for me so I could be with you."

"Tola?" Brighid asked.

"One of the women who helps me manage the affairs of our home. She is also my cousin. Most of us who live here are related, but there are a few who are part of the Bear Clan by bonding." She pointed to a man at the next table with a wide girth and light brown hair. "Asher is from the Stag Clan. He married Hylli, another cousin of mine. And Geisl is of the Eagle Clan. Torsten was born clanless but proved himself hardworking and loyal, so my husband brought him into our clan."

"You allow clanless to join?"

"Yes. I know other clans strictly observe rituals and lineages, but here along the border and in the wastelands, everyone is trying to survive. This unites us. Not everyone wants to be a part of the Bear Clan, for various reasons. And part of our duty to the people of Nordica is to protect the border, maintain peace when we can, and we are warriors, which means we are the first to fight. Some people do not want to carry those burdens. But for those who do, we have a place in our hall for such warriors." Ana gazed at Brighid. "Warriors such as yourself."

Brighid nodded. "Thank you." The offer was tempting. To stay and forget about the war. To be accepted and be part of something better than an eljun. To not be alone.

She sighed inwardly and spooned up a chunk of meat. This peace was an illusion. Eventually, Armand's words would reach Nordica. She doubted even a war could take him out. So who could? Her thoughts turned to Kaeden.

Bard sat down next to Brighid with a bowl of stew. She started at his sudden presence. He didn't seem to notice as he took a bite. "I can tell Tola made this," he said after a spoonful. "It's good, but it's not yours, Mother."

"Be thankful you have food." Ana waved her spoon in Bard's direction.

He smiled as he took another bite, then glanced at Brighid. "Good to see you out and about."

His hands were calloused and scarred. She furtively glanced at the rest of him as he ate. He appeared to be past thirty winters, with wheat-colored hair and beard, both kept trimmed and short, a contrast to most of the men in the hall. Then a tattoo of two interwoven circles on the inner part of his arm caught her eye. Interwoven circles were Marks of Remembrance worn when a beloved husband or wife died. Which meant Bard had lost his wife. One he had loved enough to wear this particular mark for.

She turned her attention back to her stew and finished the food, while questions and thoughts filled her mind about the people around her. Elphsaba had once known these people. She recalled the first time she met Bard years ago when they were traveling to Ragnbork, and Elphsaba mentioned his name. Why didn't Elphsaba join their clan? Was the death of her intended, one of their warriors, so devastating that she couldn't bear the thought of living with his people? Or did she enjoy her independence as clanless, despite the stigma? Life was hard but good when they lived in the Wastelands. It wasn't until they moved to Ragnbork that the prejudice against clanless affected their lives.

Brighid moved the chunks of meat around in the broth, while Ana and Bard talked nearby. What would life have looked like if she'd grown up here? If she wasn't a warrior? What if she found a man worth bonding with? A man worth wearing the eternal circles for? Would she want to be a wife and mother? She pushed the last bits of food around again. She wasn't sure. Life was hard and she was clanless.

After dinner, Brighid helped Ana and the others clean up. People asked her many questions as they cleaned. Brighid shared the barest details. Ana was nice, despite her suspicions. And Bard was like an older brother—a *much* older brother. But what would the others think if they discovered she had been fighting in the south and had escaped back to Nordica? That she was clanless? Would they be as embracing? She had seen too much of humanity to trust them with her secrets. But soon she would need to decide what to do next.

Brighid stared at the ceiling later that night. A bed had been made for her near the firepit, and Ana had returned to bedding in the loft. Bard slept with the warriors in another building. The light from the low-burning fire flickered against the wooden walls, and she could hear Ana shift on the bed, followed shortly by the heavy breathing of sleep.

Find a way to free your people.

Kaeden's declaration came roaring back into her mind. Those were some of his last words to her before he sent her fleeing into the night. As she recalled his voice, her heart suddenly ached in loneliness. Though they had known each other for only a few days, a connection had been made between them. A connection that made her miss him now.

She let out a deep breath, rolled onto her side, and watched the flames dance above the rim of the firepit. She had held on to those words, and they gave her the strength to cross mountains and valleys. And she had finally returned to her people. But . . .

What allegiance did she owe to the people of Nordica? To some she willingly gave her loyalty, like her comrades Johan, Marta, and the other clanless still oathbound and fighting in the south. And to the warriors who had stood by her side during the battles. But what about those who had looked down on her? Those who saw her as less than a pebble to be kicked down the street? Or the ones who used those like her?

For the first time, she felt a hesitation in her soul. Tonight, Ana had offered her a place in the Bear Clan. She could stay here, have a home, and never return to war. And she could forget about Armand and his companions and their strange gifts. But the hesitation faded as fast as it came. That was not who she was.

Her hands were not meant for healing or tending a hearth, even one as nice as Ana's. Even though she was far from the battleground, she was still a warrior. Her hands were created to hold a shield and sword. The red haze called to her in the deepest parts of the night. She was still afraid of death and had no pleasure in delivering it to others. But she couldn't escape who she was. She was the Stryth'Viezla. And because of that, she couldn't stay. She was made to fight for others.

This isn't where I belong.

15

Kaeden woke up with hazy images of firelight flickering off log walls and a sense of restlessness. He didn't recognize the place in his dreams. But he did relate to the restlessness. And somewhere in his consciousness, the presence of Brighid faded from his mind.

Had he dreamed of her again? Was it possible the dream was a vision and an assurance that she made it north? He closed his eyes. *Word, let it be so.*

After dressing, he met Treyvar in the sitting room they shared. Winter had a hold on Celestis Castle, leaving the air chilly and the stone cold. He crossed the room and warmed himself by the fire, while Treyvar finished reading a book he had started the night before. The man was always reading, and the few times he wasn't, he was learning in the Healers Quarters with the chief healer.

Treyvar looked up as he closed the book and placed it on the small table between the chairs. He stood. "Do you still want to accompany me to the Healers Quarters?"

Kaeden stared into the fire with his hands toward the flames, his right one covered with the fingerless glove he always wore. *No,* he wanted to say. It would be easier to never touch a person again. But that would require leaving civilization and leading a hermit life. Deep down, he knew that wasn't what he was made to do. For reasons he still didn't understand, the Word had chosen him to be the Truthsayer, both to his people and humanity.

Kaeden dropped his hands and turned. "Yes. I still have much to learn." Something inside him refused to let go of the journey he and Mathias had started toward his healing.

Treyvar led the way. Kaeden pulled his new cloak closer to his body to ward off the chill in the corridors. Unlike his old grey one, this one was white and embroidered in gold thread, matching his healers robes and the gold cord he wore around his waist signifying his status.

His status.

He fingered the gold thread along the edge of the cloak and let out his breath. It took almost a week to convince the guards in the training room to let him work out with them and teach them to grapple. A few still held back, in awe of his position. He understood their hesitation. He remembered the same awe he held for Mathias. But Mathias led an unpretentious life where anyone could approach him. Kaeden wanted the same thing. Which meant taking this step to overcoming his revulsion at touch.

A couple minutes later, after a flight of stairs and two more hallways, they arrived at the Healers Quarters.

The room was cavernous with bookshelves lining the right side around a stone fireplace, three long tables set up in middle, and doors to separate rooms on the left. Long, narrow windows were set against the far wall, letting in dim light from this cold and dreary day. As they walked in, he caught a dozen different herbal scents from lavender to mint to ones he couldn't quite name.

The bookshelves held more than just books. There were scrolls in metal tubes, jars of herbs, mortar and pestles, and even a handful of skulls from various animals.

"Welcome, welcome," a deep voice boomed as a rotund man stepped out of one of the side rooms. Thick grey hair stood on end, and a full beard covered his jaw. He wore white healer robes that barely reached around his girth. He smiled and one word came to Kaeden's mind. Cheery.

Treyvar nodded toward the man. "Healer Weylin."

"Treyvar. It is good to see you this morning." His warm brown eyes turned toward Kaeden. "And it seems you brought the Truthsayer with you." Healer Weylin bowed. "It is an honor to meet you, Master Kaeden."

Kaeden returned his bow. "And you likewise, Healer Weylin."

The man's head came up with that cheery smile on his face again. "I had the pleasure of working with Master Mathias when he first came north from Hont. He was quite the rascal when he was young." Weylin laughed, and his booming chortle filled the room.

A smile crept across Kaeden's face. He wanted to know what kind of mischief a young Mathias had gotten into. Maybe he would find out as he trained here.

"So, how can I help you, Master Kaeden?"

"I wish to continue my training in the healing arts. I am a healer for the Avonain forces, but I'm afraid my knowledge is still lacking."

"I see. Treyvar said you might be visiting. I am happy to share all I know."

"Thank you."

Healer Weylin started by showing him around the room, pointing to the different objects on the shelves, naming the books, and describing the various herbs. "This is witch's leaves," he said, pointing to a jar filled with dark leaves. "Also known as Ammelica. It is found in the Keshmin Mountains, deep in the heart of Nordica. It works as a fever and pain reducer. It can also help prevent infection. One of the best herbs I've ever used."

"If it's from the North, how did you obtain it?" Kaeden asked.

"I received the dried leaves two years ago. I wish I could get more, but with the war, obtaining anything from the North is impossible now. I use these sparingly."

Kaeden stared at the dark leaves for a moment longer, then continued the tour with Healer Weylin. How many things would be lost to the south if this war continued? And what would the north lose?

As they finished touring the Healers Quarters—including the additional room where more supplies were kept and an area where patients could rest—two more healers walked in. They greeted Healer Weylin and Treyvar, then were introduced to Kaeden. One held out his hand to shake and Kaeden hesitated. With his glove on, his revulsion seemed to be less, but it still made him nervous. The young man began to withdraw his hand when Kaeden grabbed it. "Forgive me, I'm not used to a hand being offered to me."

The young man smiled and nodded shyly. "It is an honor to meet you, Master Kaeden."

Kaeden smiled inwardly, thankful he had taken the young man's hand and hadn't winced at the touch. *Mathias, I did it. I'm still touching humans.* After all, that was why he was there.

Kaeden spent the rest of the day familiarizing himself with more of the herbs, speaking to the other healers, and discussing what he learned with Treyvar. There were moments he was amazed at how well Treyvar interacted with everyone. Did they know his status as prince of Avonai? Treyvar put on no airs about who he was, which was probably why Kaeden never knew he was a prince until the end of the Battle of the Plains. It reminded him a little of Mathias. And it made him wonder what Treyvar's family was like. Based on what he knew and what he had heard from Treyvar himself, it seemed the prince was different. More like a commoner than royalty.

As the afternoon waned, Selma walked in. A few of the healers paused and glanced at her. She ignored them as she caught sight of Kaeden and made her way toward him. Treyvar looked up from the table where he was crushing herbs, while Kaeden bunched lavender together for drying.

"Have you decided to join us?" she asked.

"Yes." Kaeden finished tying twine around the bundle. "I wish to continue what Mathias and I started. I want to be ready for when the war begins again."

She looked at the table and frowned. "But you're preparing herbs."

"I'm helping Healer Weylin replenish his stores. These herbs will aid us when we go to battle."

"That is usually a job assigned to an acolyte. Certainly not to the Truthsayer."

Treyvar's head snapped up as Kaeden answered. "He did not assign me this task. I volunteered. Mathias taught me that any job is worthy of an Eldaran."

"Perhaps when you have established your position. But what will people think if they see you doing menial tasks as the new Truthsayer?"

He raised one eyebrow. "That I'm not above it?"

She shook her head. "It is not respectable."

Kaeden placed the bundle of lavender down. "Selma, I once worked in the quarries on Mistsylver Island."

"Yes, but that was before you were the Truthsayer. Now you hold one of the highest places of honor among our people." She lowered her voice. "I know you spent a lot of time away from these lands and may not understand the place Eldarans hold in society, but it is important that you carry yourself with respect so others do the same."

A pang of annoyance rose inside Kaeden's chest. "And what part of helping another healer is not respectable?"

Treyvar tapped the top of Kaeden's hand. "You should take this conversation elsewhere."

Kaeden sighed as Selma glanced around. Heads bowed as fingers went back to work. "You are right. This conversation is not for the ears of others."

"I also apologize. I should have been more aware." Selma bowed toward Kaeden before taking a place on the other side of the room. Kaeden watched her go, the same unease as before settling across his heart. Were all Eldarans like her? It wasn't that she was unkind, and she certainly did her part to serve humanity, but there was something in her attitude that rubbed him the wrong way. A distance she placed between herself and others.

Once again he found himself wishing he'd had more time with Mathias and his parents.

16

Autumn teased the land, sending snow one day, then allowing the sun to shine the next. This particular day was a sunny one, and Kaeden decided to take advantage of it by walking along the outer wall of the White City. The wall was wide, almost like a narrow street with a stone ledge on each side. But unlike a street boxed in by buildings, the view was open and wide, allowing breathtaking views of the White City, the Ari Mountains, and the ancient forest of Anwin to the south.

Inside the city, buildings shone with the famous alabaster stone of the Ari Mountains. Kaeden stopped, leaned across the ledge, and studied the dark forest past the open field that lay beyond the front gates. Towering trees as old as the Lands acted as canopy over the forest, letting in very little light and moisture. To the right, beyond a set of younger trees, he glimpsed shimmering water and the lake where the Sanctuary of the Eldarans stood. Where Mathias was buried.

He wanted to visit again. One more time. Hopefully before war resumed.

He continued his walk around the walls, coming to the other side as the noon came. The rest of the afternoon was spent with Treyvar and Healer Weylin in the Healers Quarters. Selma concentrated her time and efforts in the other rooms, attending to patients and working with the younger healers. She really did help people. Kaeden couldn't deny that. Perhaps he was wrong about the underlying, superior attitude he sensed from her.

The next day, Treyvar invited him to the library. He wasn't much of a reader, but ever since Treyvar told him there were old books and scrolls about the Eldaran race kept safe in the library, Kaeden was curious to look. They walked the cold corridors, passing by windows filled with a dreary sky and trees bereaved of their leaves. A young man met them on the first floor. As they approached, Kaeden noticed he was dressed far finer than the servants of the castle, but he didn't seem to be a visiting dignitary or councilman. His black hair hung along his shoulders, and his face was young and handsome.

"Lord Teduin," Treyvar said, his voice echoing along the corridor.

The man stopped and a sly smile rose across his face. "Prince Treyvar. I heard you were wintering here in Celestis Castle. Why didn't you return home?"

Treyvar's face darkened. "I am here serving on behalf of Avonai."

"As a captain? Or commander? Wait, no. I heard you are a healer." He smirked.

Kaeden narrowed his eyes. Who was this arrogant cur? He looked vaguely familiar. Maybe from Mathias's viewing?

Lord Teduin's gaze moved to Kaeden. "Ah, the Truthsayer."

Kaeden straightened to his full height and crossed his arms. He felt a certain satisfaction when the man was forced to look up. This was one of the moments he didn't mind his large stature. "Yes, I am the Truthsayer. I am Master Kaeden. And I'm afraid I have no idea who you are." Although he had an inkling now.

The man's face reddened. "I am Lord Teduin, son of Lord Rayner and future High Lord of Celestis Castle."

Kaeden saw the resemblance to Lord Rayner. And the same attitude. "I am also a healer for the Southern Alliance. It is a worthy endeavor for anyone who desires to help with the war."

"Well, that may be . . ." A sheen of sweat rose across Lord Teduin's face. "But, eh, perhaps Prince Treyvar would serve better as someone in command."

"Why?" Kaeden held firm his looming posture.

"That is, as a future leader of his country . . ."

Treyvar balked.

"He should be leading on the battlefield."

Kaeden almost laughed. Only people who craved power saw the

world that way and couldn't imagine that sometimes leading was best done by serving. Something both his parents and Mathias had taught him.

"Occasionally what a country needs most is healing." *And people too*, Kaeden thought as he reflected on his own journey.

Lord Teduin regained his composure. "I suppose. You are, after all, the Truthsayer and voice for the Word. You speak wisdom." He bowed. "Good day, Master Kaeden. Prince Treyvar."

"Good day, Lord Teduin," Treyvar replied.

Kaeden watched Teduin continue down the hall from the corner of his eye. "I take it you're not close." They started toward the library again.

"It depends on what you mean by close. We grew up together, Lord Teduin, my brother, Elion, and I. Our families met at least twice a year. Elion and Teduin are close. And similar. I was different. I had different thoughts, different dreams, different aspirations. Therefore, many times I found myself alone."

"I see. Is that why you don't share who you are?"

Treyvar let out a snort. "Contrary to what Teduin said, I am not the future leader of Avonai. Elion is. My father made that clear a long time ago. I'm not even sure if my father wants me to carry the title prince. Everything belongs to Elion. But I still love my people and my country, despite that I will never lead them. I will serve in another way: by healing and knowledge. I will support from the shadows."

Kaeden smiled. The more he grew to know the man beside him, the more he admired him.

"But I did find it satisfying to see you put Lord Teduin in his place."

"Oh?"

"Usually, people flatter him, hoping to gain his approval and therefore advance their own agendas through his name. I quite enjoyed how steady and unmoving you were with him. It was refreshing."

Kaeden laughed. "I have certainly never been afraid to stand for justice. To do what is right and speak for what is right. Besides, it annoyed me to hear him speak of leading on the battlefield when neither he nor your brother nor the lords have marched with us. Only you."

"It is easier to command from the safety of one's castle."

"A true leader doesn't stand behind others. That's not leading."

"You were mentored by Master Mathias, a man who led others by his own example. Those kinds of leaders are few and far between. You're also not afraid to stand up to those in authority. You saved the Nordic woman on the battlefield from Captain Bertin and his men, then freed her despite what the commanders wanted. Even now, you continue to speak truth. Perhaps that is why the Word chose you to be the next Truthsayer." Treyvar glanced at him.

Kaeden sobered. "Maybe."

They reached the library and entered. Kaeden took in the space with admiration. Despite holding a wavering interest in books, he could appreciate a place that held history and learning in esteem.

Two stories of wooden shelves lined wall after wall with a ladder leading up to a narrow ledge along the second story. The curved ceiling matched the curved windows, intentionally carved into the white stone to allow enough sunlight in for reading, but not enough to touch the books, only the stone floor below.

To see the actual titles along the shelves, one could light a lamp from a table set near the door and carry it throughout the library. Between the shelves were more tables, where one could bring a book and read by lamplight. The room held a leather, woody scent that seemed comforting and old. There was not a trace of dust to be found, indicating meticulous care of the tomes and books here.

Treyvar lit one of the lamps and held it up. Although plenty of light came through the windows during that time of day, it would be easier to see the titles with the added illumination. "This way." Treyvar crossed the room and Kaeden followed, passing multiple shelves until they reached the back. There they found scrolls in metal tubes set in cubbies, a rack of books chained to a wheel, allowing only enough space to take the book to the one table nearby, and handfuls of parchments tied together with leather strips.

"This is where you will find the history of your people," Treyvar said.

Kaeden glanced around the area again. "Where should I begin?"

"Hmm." Treyvar held the lamp close to the etchings on the end of the metal tubes. "What kind of information are you looking for?"

Kaeden paused. He knew of their origins, of following the Word to the Lands. And fighting in the Great Battle. That knowledge was passed down by his parents. "Is there anything specifically about the Truthsayers? Or the Shadonae?" He had never even heard the term until Mathias shared it months ago. Had there been other Shadonae in ages past?

"Let's see." Treyvar moved the light along the cubbies, then walked over to the strange wheel where books were chained. "Here, hold this." He handed Kaeden the lamp, then gripped the side of the wheel and began to turn. With each pull, a new shelf appeared with four to five books lined across it.

"No, not this one," he muttered. "No, no." He turned the wheel again, then one more time. "Hmm," he said again, gazing at a dark leather-bound book.

One word graced the front, embossed in the leather and inlaid in silver. *Sonja*. Kaeden stared at the name. He knew that name. The first Truthsayer who stepped from the waters and entered the Lands with the Word.

Treyvar glanced at Kaeden. "These are the collected writings of Sonja."

"Sonja herself?"

"Yes. They are kept here, and only here, under lock and key."

Kaeden stared at the book. What would it be like to read the words of the very first Truthsayer? His ancestor?

"Want to read it?"

"Yes."

Treyvar made sure the wheel was locked in place, then carefully lifted the tome. The chain attached to the book clanked softly as he started toward the table nearby. The chain followed him, one end attached to the wheel.

Treyvar placed the book down, then pulled a cloth from the inside of his surcoat. "It's important to keep your fingers clean before touching the pages of a book." He carefully wiped his hands, then held the cloth out to Kaeden. While Kaeden cleaned his hands, Treyvar opened the book. Words and images adorned the first page in beautiful calligraphy. "This is written in the old tongue. Do you know how to read it?"

"Yes." Kaeden placed the cleaning rag on the table and took a seat in front of the tome.

"Then enjoy. I'll be near the front of the library if you need me. I've been studying the historical relationships between the White City, Avonai, and Nordica to see if I can find anything that might help bring this war to an end."

Kaeden looked up. "I'm not sure any kind of discussions can happen if the Nordic clans are being influenced by the Shadonae. Their hold on the people of the North is powerful." He knew that only too well after watching the Shadonae's very words annihilate the minds and bodies of the Nordics.

"Well, my friend, that is your area of expertise. And I believe you will find a way to free them. When that happens, I want to be ready to negotiate peace."

"Will your father let you? Or Lord Rayner?"

Treyvar shrugged. "I will exert what power I can. And that power will come from any knowledge I can obtain. I am arming myself now with ideas and understanding."

"That is wise."

Treyvar placed a hand on his shoulder. "Word willing, together we can bring peace and stability back to these lands."

Treyvar's hand felt heavy on his shoulder, as if the weight of the Lands were in that touch. Only he could judge the Shadonae. Only he could ultimately stop their destruction. But he couldn't do it alone. He would need help from others. Comrades who would stand by him and bring the world into a better future afterward. People like Prince Treyvar. And maybe the Nordic woman, Brighid, working on behalf of the Nordic people. And others he hadn't met yet.

Treyvar lifted his hand. "Now I must be off to read and see what I can discover." He turned, and Kaeden listened to his footsteps grow faint.

Kaeden took in a deep breath and let it out slowly. Then he looked down again at the beautiful script. It curved and flowed with a feminine feel. Sonja's own handwriting. The first Truthsayer of the Lands. He started reading where swirls formed the first words at the top of the page.

In the Beginning was the Word . . .

17

Winter sealed the north. Snow reached midway up the outer walls, and it would take an hour of shoveling to free the gates. But the woodpile was high, there was meat in the smokehouse, along with barrels of tubers and vegetables, dried herbs hung from the rafters, and plenty of pelts and wool for creating all that was needed to stay warm and comfortable in the dark months ahead.

Bard folded his arms and nodded to himself as he stood in the middle of the compound, surveying the buildings around him. Yes, they were ready. Only the warriors and his father were missing, but they remained stationed south beyond the Ari Mountains.

A hand slapped his back. "Missing Gurmund?"

Bard turned to find Thorald leaning on his walking stick, a grin on his face. His thick brown beard hung to the middle of his chest and his hair was captured with a leather tie. They were the same age, almost born on the same day, but something happened during Thorald's birth that caused a complication, leaving his left leg crippled. However, he possessed a sensible mind, and Father had made him steward of their holdings when he was away. And now that Father was away, Bard counted on his help. And his friendship.

"I worry only about his return," Bard said.

"Have you heard anything lately?"

"No. But that's not surprising. It takes weeks for letters to come and go from the south. The last we read, he is stationed at the Dallam Fortress for the winter."

"The fortress our forces took at the beginning of the war? Near the mouth of the Onyx River?"

"Yes."

"Have you told him about the young woman who arrived?"

"Mother sent a letter a few days after she woke up."

"I wonder what Hjar Gurmund will say." Thorald tugged on his beard with his free hand. He paused and glanced at Bard. "What do *you* think?"

"She doesn't say much. But I know she is a warrior."

"A warrior? Have you thought about sparring with her? Testing her abilities and strength? We could always use another fighter while your father and the others are away."

"That's not a bad idea. I'm curious to see what she is capable of. There are certainly Nordic women who fight, but not many." Bard turned to look at Thorald. "I think I'll invite her to do just that. And have the others participate. Besides, it will hold off the boredom of winter."

The two continued around the compound, following the paths dug through the snow. Thorald pointed out a few things that needed to be replaced or repaired. They entered the main hall later that morning. The building was alive with activity. A handful of children chased each other with screams and squeals, while the women sat near the firepit sewing and talking, including his mother and Brighid.

Bard watched their guest for a moment. If he didn't know about Brighid's recent past, he would almost think she belonged. She was working on a small wool dress and quietly listening to the others. Her hair was pulled back in a long braid that hung over one shoulder. Again, he was struck at how similar she looked to his sister. Then he shook his head and walked over to the fire. Those gathered glanced up as he approached, including Brighid.

"May I speak to you for a moment?" he asked her.

She blinked in surprise, then nodded.

"Here, I'll hold on to that." His mother reached for the dress. As Brighid passed the clothing over, he noticed beautiful curves and circles in bright blue thread that she had been sewing along the edge of the collar. He wasn't knowledgeable in the area of art, but even he could see there was a quality and unique beauty to her work.

"Hjaren Bard?" Brighid said.

"Come over here." He headed toward a long table and stood beside the edge. She came to a stop nearby and folded her hands. The sun mark around her eye stood out against her face. Strange, it wasn't a common symbol. Who did she wish to remember with her mark? With it in such a prominent spot, it was clearly someone she had loved. Maybe a cherished parent.

"My mother told me you are a fighter," Bard began. "And, as such, I wanted to invite you to spar with me and the other warriors here. It would be a way to keep your skills honed during the winter months."

Brighid's eyes widened. "I would like that."

"What weapon do you use?"

"Sword and shield."

"I'll make sure to provide you with what you need. We start this afternoon." He glanced over her attire. She wore the clothes she had arrived in: pants, tunic, boots, and a leather jerkin. That would be sufficient. "I'll meet you here and show you where we practice."

She nodded. "Thank you." She returned to the fire. His mother had been watching them. She handed Brighid the dress, then Brighid sat down and started working again. Just as he went to leave, she paused for a moment and held up one hand, studying her fingers. A smile crept across her face before she gripped the dress again and began sewing.

Brighid was waiting for him after the noon meal in the main hall, her braid secured and any loose clothing tucked away.

"Ready?" Bard asked as he approached.

"Ready." And she looked it. There was a determination on her face, almost like a fire had been lit inside her.

They left the main hall, crossed the snow-covered ground to the training hall, and entered the double doors. The room was bare with a packed dirt floor and a firepit in the middle for warmth. Lamps were lit, and a handful of warriors waited near the weapons racks. At their entrance, the men and one woman hailed them loudly.

"Hjaren Bard! It's about time you showed up!"

"Looks like he brought a guest with him."

"Can you fight?" Nora asked as she approached Brighid. Nora was around Brighid's age, with nutbrown hair and matching eyes. She was a couple inches taller and leaner as well, her body straight rather than curved. She wasn't quite ready to go to battle a year ago, so Bard kept her here to patrol the border with his other handpicked warriors.

"Yes." Brighid replied. Neither Bard nor his mother had shared Brighid's story, only that she had arrived and was a guest of the Bear Clan. "I've been fighting since I was seventeen winters."

A few eyebrows raised at her comment, while Nora grinned. "I've been wanting a sparring partner who wasn't a brute."

Arngrim shoved his shoulder into Nora's side. "You're the only brute here, Nora."

She shoved him playfully back. "No, I think that title belongs to you."

Arngrim's facial hair shone like copper in the lamplight, and his dark eyes twinkled as he laughed with Nora. He was built like a small bear, arms as thick as tree trunks. Bard wondered when the two would realize there was a bond between them.

The others introduced themselves to Brighid. Galt, a gangly young man and youngest in his family and the only one not at the frontlines. Heming, as blond as the sun and Bard's right-hand man. Vigi and Lodin, twins and distant cousins of Bard's, with dark hair they had inherited from their Wolf Clan mother. Small braids wove through Lodin's shoulder-length hair, while Vigi kept his long and free.

The five continued to ask Brighid questions and laugh with each other. Brighid answered each with a short sentence.

"So how did you come to be at the bear compound?" Arngrim asked after letting Vigi go from a head grip.

"It was snowing and I needed a place to stay," Brighid replied.

"I heard you arrived on a bear," Galt said.

The others stilled and glanced at Brighid. "That is what I also heard. But I was sick and don't remember," she replied.

"A bear?" Lodin asked Bard.

Bard ignored his look, wondering how Galt had heard about that. Had Finn shared, even though Bard asked him to stay quiet? Or had

Galt seen it? "I think it's time for us to start. Vigi, Lodin, get your weapons. You will go first."

The two young men groaned and went to the weapons rack. "The rest of you might as well prepare." Bard watched as Brighid approached the rack, studied the weapons available, and chose a small sword and round shield. She tested the weight of the weapon, gave it a couple swings, then stepped back.

Lodin chose a longsword, while his brother favored a bearded axe and dagger. The others grabbed their own weapons of choice, then stood around the room. For a few minutes, everyone warmed up, swinging their arms, testing their practice weapons, and stretching their legs. Then Bard called Vigi and Lodin to one side of the room beyond the firepit.

He folded his arms. "All right, let's see what you have today," he said to the twins.

Lodin dropped into a stance with his sword, his hair hanging over one shoulder. Vigi grinned, his axe and dagger ready.

"Shall we wager, brother?" Lodin asked. "I'm on patrol this week. But if I win, I get to stay here and guard the compound in your place."

"And if I win, you will be the last to bathe." Vigi twirled his axe. "Enjoy that cold water."

Bard raised his hand. The two men stilled. Then Bard dropped his hand. In the blink of an eye, the brothers clashed, their weapons ringing throughout the room. Lodin held his ground, using his sword to pummel his brother. But then Vigi caught the blade with the curved edge of his axe, hooked and shoved it away, and went in with his dagger. Lodin jumped back, barely escaping the slash. He freed his sword, then charged his brother again. They circled each other like wolves, Lodin going in with his sword, Vigi returning his attack.

After a few minutes, both men were panting, and sweat dripped down their faces. Bard was about to call it a draw when Vigi hooked Lodin's blade again, held it away from his body, and was finally able to get his dagger past Lodin's defenses.

"Bolva," Lodin shouted as Vigi whooped and hollered in victory.

"All right, who's next?" Bard asked. The others glanced at each other, then Brighid stepped forward. "I'll go."

Bard arched his eyebrows. He hadn't expected her to volunteer so quickly. "Who wishes to go against our guest?"

Vigi raised a hand while bringing his breathing down. "Give me a moment and I'd be happy go against her."

Heming stepped forward. "I'll do it." He looked at her. "I'll be your partner."

Brighid nodded and headed to the empty space beyond the firepit.

Bard lifted his head and folded his arms. This would be interesting. Heming also used the sword and shield. Watching them fight would allow him to see what Brighid was capable of and how skilled she was as a warrior.

Heming was average size and height. While Bard kept his hair short, Heming wore his light blond hair long and currently held back in a handful of braids. The man swung his sword in anticipation as he approached Brighid.

She watched him coolly, her sword and shield ready. As they came to stand in front of each other, Bard could almost sense the tension coiling in their bodies as they prepared to spar.

He lifted his hand, then dropped it.

Both rushed each other.

Brighid reached Heming first with her sword, causing him to go on the defense. Heming caught her blade just in time with his shield, a brief look of surprise flashing across his features. Brighid continued to bring her sword down on his shield in a flurry of hits. Heming took a few steps back, then was finally able to return a blow of his own.

Their fight became a dance. Back and forth they moved across the packed earth. The sound of constant thumps of blades against wooden shields filled the air. Heming's braids swung around his face and sweat collected along his temple. There was a cool fierceness to Brighid's countenance. Bard glanced at the others, watching their reaction. They were captivated. Not many could hold their own against Heming. The only reason the man was here and not down south with Hjar Gurmund was because Bard had asked him to stay.

Then something changed in Brighid. She moved faster, her sword darting in and out from behind her shield. Her blade appeared to hit harder, causing Heming to buckle slightly under her blows. Bard tightened his grip on his folded arms as he watched the fight. How was she doing that? He had no doubts now that she was an excellent warrior. The evidence was before him. He even wondered why she was here and not fighting down south. Even so . . . this was on a different level. The look on her face now was savage, with a fire in her eyes that would not be extinguished.

Heming could not keep up, and a moment later, Brighid made it past his defenses when she caught his sword with her shield and thrust past the edge of his own shield with her blade. He let out a grunt when her dull blade contacted his side.

"I concede," he said and lowered his weapons.

The only sound in the room was Brighid and Heming panting. Then Brighid bowed her head toward Heming. "It was an honor to fight with you."

"And you as well," Heming answered. "If our warriors are as good as you, we will win the south."

A shadow passed over her face, then she answered, "Our people are strong and courageous."

Bard narrowed his eyes. Wait, was it possible she *had* been a fighter down south? But then, how did she end up this far north?

A hand slapped his shoulder, bringing him out of his reverie. Vigi stood next to him, a look of excitement on his face. "That woman fights just like you. Is it possible the blood of the bear runs in her veins?"

Bard glanced at Brighid again as Nora and Angrim spoke with her. He replayed the fight again in his mind as a cold sweat swept across his body. Was it possible?

One way to find out.

Bard stepped forward. "Brighid, would you be willing to spar with me?"

All eyes turned toward Bard in surprise. Brighid bowed her head. "Yes, it would be an honor to fight with the hjaren."

Bard walked over to the weapons rack and chose two small axes. He swung both around a couple times to warm his arms up, then he turned to Brighid. The contours of her face and nose were familiar, like those of his sister. Same with her wheat-colored hair. But there was a lean, muscular strength to her body, unlike the litheness his sister had possessed. And a fire filled her bright blue eyes, whereas Kalla always had mischief and merriment in hers. Maybe Vigi and the others were right. There may be a distant trace of the Bear Clan in Brighid's blood.

The two stood before each other. "Heming, let us know when to start," Bard said without looking at the man.

"Yes, Hjaren," Heming replied.

Brighid waited, as still as a cat poised to pounce. The moment Heming dropped his hand, she sprang into action. Bard barely had time to deflect her sword with the side of his axe. The strength of her blow surprised him. He cleared his mind and swung around with his other axe.

Brighid kept up with his speed, answering each hit with one of her own. He tried to hook her shield with the curved edge of his axe, but she slipped out of his reach, only to return with her sword. Her fighting was impressive, but there wasn't that spirit of the bear he thought he would encounter. He had hoped that by fighting her, he would ignite the ember inside her so he could experience it himself. Instead, she was simply a gifted fighter.

Oh well, best to end this fight—

Then the air shifted. Before he could ready himself, Brighid slammed into his body with her shield. He staggered back. Her sword jutted out from behind and almost caught him at his side. He hooked the blade with his axe and swung out with his other, but she deflected with her shield and slammed him again.

Hoots and hollers came from those watching. He fought to keep his balance. What was with this change? Had she finally ignited the spirit inside her? If so . . .

Bard dug his feet into the ground and took in a deep breath, allowing his own Vilrik to flood his body. Then he answered her fight.

The Vilrik guided his movements, anticipating her moves, answering her blows and returning ones of his own. He could barely see beyond the red fog that enveloped his vision, but he never lost control of the Vilrik. He had trained for years to channel the gift of his clan.

After a minute, he finally hooked both her shield and sword, held her arms and weapons away, then kicked her in the middle, sending her flying back. She hit the wall with a soft thump.

There were a few gasps and one "bolva." Bard hooked one axe into the loop along his belt, then walked over and held out his hand. "Good fight," he said as he helped her up. The heat of the battle still lingered on her face, along with an expression of awe.

"Yes," she answered as she came to her feet. "I have not had the privilege of fighting such a worthy opponent, Hjaren Bard."

"That was amazing!" Vigi slapped Bard across the shoulders. Bard turned and glared at the younger man, but he didn't seem to notice. "Not many of us can keep up with Hjaren Bard."

The others chimed in their praise.

As they began to settle, Bard looked over the group. "Nora, Angrim, let's see what you can do."

Nora laughed and taunted Arngrim as she went toward the center of the room. Arngrim just smiled back. Bard continued the sparring matches for the next hour, then let the warriors break. As he followed the others out, he glanced at Brighid a few feet ahead of him. Yes, he was sure of it now. The way her fighting style changed halfway through their sparring confirmed it. There was Bear Clan blood in her, and somehow she had inherited the fighting power of his family: the Vilrik.

18

Brighid rested against the back wall while the others sparred. At the end of an hour, Bard raised his hand and signaled the end of their session. As she followed them out, she felt their eyes again on her. The same glances she received every time the red haze came upon her.

Especially Hjaren Bard's gaze.

She hadn't meant to unleash it. It usually came upon her only in the heat of battle. But the feeling of the sword and shield back in her hands after weeks of emptiness, along with the thrill of fighting again, had ignited the fire inside her soul. And like a fire, it couldn't be hidden. Once ablaze, it burned brightly. The way she fought. The way of the Stryth' Viezla.

The one named Vigi paused and waited for her to pass. "That was amazing," he said with a full grin as he walked beside her. "I've only seen Heming and Hjar Gurmund go toe-to-toe with Hjaren Bard. I heard you were clanless. Do other clanless fight like that?"

"The ones I know are exceptional warriors," she said, remembering Johan and Marta. Her heart tightened at the memory of her comrades. Where were they now? Had they survived the Battle of the Plains?

"Really?" He held his hand out and clenched it. "I would love to test my strength against theirs." He continued to grin.

"Why didn't you join your clan and fight down south?" Brighid asked, curious to know why capable warriors were here and not fighting with their hjar.

"Hjaren Bard asked my brother and me to stay and continue the patrol along the border. There might be a war down south, but that doesn't stop bandits and trespassers from looting those left behind. However"—he glanced ahead at Bard, then the others, and lowered his voice—"I would rather be fighting for our country."

Brighid gave him a small smile. Inside, she couldn't help but be relieved there were still warriors in Nordica who had not been deceived by Armand's oath. Nor would they die because of the oath's unraveling if they were ever captured.

But what about those still under the bondage of Armand's words? Brighid let out a sigh as they walked along the path through patches of deep snow toward the main hall. Clan or clanless, none of them deserved such slavery.

Find a way to free your people.

But how? She still hadn't spoken about her past to Ana or Bard. But the time was coming when they would probably question her.

She entered the hall and stomped her boots. At the moment, the north was sealed in by snow and winter. That gave her time to think. To figure out her words.

That moment came sooner than Brighid anticipated. After dinner, Ana invited her to sit by the firepit in her private room off the main hall. Brighid followed, her insides twisting like snakes. This was it. Ana was going to ask her questions. She was sure of it.

The two women settled around the fire. "I found some extra wool yarn from this past spring's shearing and made a wool-strap dress for you. Something you can wear when your other clothes need cleaning. I appreciate you helping this morning, but I think you would welcome working on your own dress."

Brighid took the material. She hadn't worn a dress in over a year, not since before she joined the eljun. "Thank you." The woven yarn was soft and warm and had been dyed a light brown. Already her mind envisioned what design she would embroider around the edges. Scarlet and gold circles would look striking if the thread was available.

Ana handed over a basket woven from thin willow branches.

Inside were sewing items. "I guessed your size and used one of our young women to measure."

Brighid turned the material over. The stitching along the seams was small and precise. While she looked inside the basket for thread and bone needles, Ana brought over a larger basket of items that needed mending. The two women sat quietly around the fire, working on their projects. Brighid found some scarlet thread and started decorating the neckline. Yes, interconnecting circles would look nice.

The fire crackled and spat. Brighid waited for the questions to come. It didn't take long. And she was ready with answers.

"Where are you from?" Ana asked a few minutes into their work.

"Folkvar," Brighid answered. "But my mother and I traveled the Wastelands for her work."

"And that was?"

"She was a midwife."

Ana paused and looked up. "Do you mind if I ask her name?"

"Elphsaba."

Ana's eyes grew wide. "I know that name. From a long time ago."

"We met Hjaren Bard a few years ago when traveling to Ragnbork. Elphsaba recognized him."

Ana smiled. "She probably hadn't seen Bard since he was little. It was Elphsaba who helped me deliver him." Then she sighed and began working again. "Shortly afterward, Eirik passed and Elphsaba moved away from here. That was over thirty years ago. I didn't realize she had bonded since then."

Time for a crumb of truth. "She didn't. I was adopted."

Ana stopped and glanced at her.

Heat climbed Brighid's neck. "My mother died at my birth. And my father didn't want me. So Elphsaba took me in."

"I see." No doubt Ana understood what she meant. That she had been an illegitimate birth. "I'm not surprised. I didn't know her well, but what I did know was that Elphsaba was a gruff but kind woman."

"Aye, that she was." Tears prickled Brighid's eyes and she blinked them away.

"Do you know who your mother or father was?" Ana returned to her work again.

Despite her fingers moving the needle in and out of the fabric, Brighid knew Ana was trying to figure out who she might be. "No. I was never told their names." She wasn't about to reveal her father was a Rylander. Not yet.

"So you grew up in the Wastelands. What was that like for you?"

Brighid poked her own bone needle into the fabric. "Simple. We traveled from village to village, staying anywhere for a season to a year. We went where there was a need for a midwife."

"How did you become a fighter? Usually, one learns the family trade."

Brighid swallowed. "I did not have the hands of a healer."

Ana glanced over. "So how did you learn to fight?"

Brighid started working on the dress again. "We eventually moved to Ragnbork. It was... difficult. Things were not easy for the clanless. Elphsaba was many winters by then, so I did what I could to help. But there wasn't much work to be found." Brighid shoved the needle hard through the fabric and pricked herself. "Bolva," she whispered, then quickly glanced up to see if Ana had heard her curse.

Ana seemed to focus on her work. "So you learned to fight instead." She continued to patch the tunic.

"I had to. I was attacked on the streets." She didn't share that she had stolen bread. Already, her entire body felt warm from her past shame. She doubted the wife of a hjar had ever experienced such want. "I was able to hold my own. Then, when Elphsaba died—" She drove the needle through the dress. "I had to find my own way to survive."

Ana looked up. "By fighting?" There was no condemnation in her face, just curiosity, so Brighid took a chance.

"I joined an eljun. For a clanless like me, it meant a place to live in the bitter winter, food to eat, and a purpose. Almost like a clan."

"I have heard of these eljuns. My husband wrote to me about them. He wrote to me about many things and the situation in Ragnbork. It was an inescapable solution for those who had nothing else."

So Ana understood. Brighid finished the first circle and started the next. "I fought for the eljun. I discovered that, instead of the hands of a healer like Elphsaba, I had the hands of a fighter. That gave me worth."

"What happened to your eljun? And how did you come to be out this far from Ragnbork?"

Brighid glanced down at the dress. Her mouth grew dry. She could lie, but what logical reason would she have to travel this way? It would have been better to stay in Ragnbork. She also had a feeling the Bear Clan—the leading warriors of Nordica—would not take kindly to someone who left the war.

"It is . . . a long story," Brighid said slowly.

"I can see it on your face."

Brighid glanced up. What if Ana deemed her a deserter? Asked her why she didn't return? Should she share about the Shadonae who controlled the Nordic army, or about her capture during the Battle of the Plains? What about her real fighting ability, the red haze?

"What if I told you I'm willing to hear your story with no judgment?"

Brighid looked down, her insides tense. Should she trust this woman? What if traveling all this way was for nothing? Her mind flashed back to that first night after she escaped the southern camp, and all the stars in the night sky. *I'm just one in a thousand. Apart from the red haze, I am nobody. Who would believe me?*

A log broke and fell into the coals of the fire, sending up a spray of sparks. At the same time, a wind hit the longhouse and sent the home creaking. Ana glanced at the ceiling. "Appears we have another storm coming in."

Brighid blinked. There were words in those fiery sparks and the sudden gust of wind. The same barely audible voice from that first night. And Mathias's words came back again. Talk. Share truth. Build trust.

An earnest desperation rose from her heart to the Word. A prayer without words. Only that she would be believed.

Then Brighid started her story.

19

Bard stood just beyond the doorway, listening to his mother and Brighid converse. At first, he waited for a pause in their conversation so he could enter and interrupt, but then he found himself drawn in. He didn't remember a midwife named Elphsaba. Another woman had assisted his wife during the delivery of their son. Shortly after, both his wife and child died, and those memories were shrouded in pain and darkness.

His curiosity grew when his mother asked what brought Brighid away from Ragnbork. He had wondered the same thing. After their sparring, he knew what kind of warrior she was. Not only was she exceptional as a clanless fighter, but somehow she carried the Vilrik of the Bear Clan. Had she gained her skills through the eljun? He wouldn't have thought that. But perhaps the leader had taught her.

But what about the Vilrik? A suspicion had been growing inside his mind ever since Brighid arrived at their door. One that he had a feeling would dredge up deep and hurtful memories for his mother. He would listen now to Brighid's tale to see if it was worth the hurt.

"I competed in the trial and was chosen to be part of the Nordic forces," Brighid said.

"Are you talking about the war?" Ana replied.

"Yes."

"My husband wrote about this competition. So you were one of the clanless chosen?"

"I was."

Bard froze. His father had written much about the trials. He even named a few clanless warriors he had been impressed with. Including a woman with blond hair who fought with a sword and shield. It couldn't be her, could it?

"How did you come to be here?"

Bard leaned against the wall. Was Brighid a deserter? He didn't want her to be. There was a solid honesty to her character that seemed to point to the young woman his father had written about.

"I was captured during the Battle of the Plains. Many of our warriors died during our imprisonment."

"The southern forces put to death prisoners of war? I thought they handled their hostages differently," his mother said.

"No, it wasn't our captors. Something else caused their deaths."

"Disease? Wounds?"

Another pause. "Did Hjar Gurmund ever share about our allies?"

Bard's throat tightened. Yes, his father had written about them. In their ancient tongue that very few knew so what he wrote could be read only by his wife and son. His first letter was the main reason Bard was there and not fighting in the south.

Bard stared at the log wall that separated him from the women in the next room. Should he walk in? Ask questions? Find out more about these beings that scared his father more than Morrud himself?

"Yes," his mother answered.

Bard held his breath.

"And you know of the oath given to our warriors before the war?"

"Yes, my husband wrote about it."

"Did he tell you what happens to those who do not renew their oath?"

"No."

"The oath gave us power. Whatever hindered us from fighting, Armand's words took that away and replaced it with strength. After each battle, we had to renew our oath or we started losing that power. But we didn't realize what would happen if we didn't return after a battle. In one night, almost every Nordic warrior captured after the Battle of the Plains died."

"They just dropped dead?" his mother asked.

Bard felt the same incredulity he heard in his mother's voice. He decided to risk looking past the doorway. His mother sat on one side of the firepit, and Brighid sat opposite of her. The look on Brighid's face made his insides freeze.

"No." Brighid gripped her fingers, and whatever she had been working on slipped to the floor. "It was the most excruciating pain ever. Like someone was taking an axe to my skull, while my body thrashed. There was no escape. I couldn't stop it, and I couldn't pass out. The only way was to endure." Brighid looked down at her fingers. "I almost didn't survive."

"What about the others?"

"They all died. Later, I saw them hanging from posts, every one of them gone."

"What happened to you?" his mother whispered. He could see the same horror on her face that he was feeling.

"I lived. The only one who did."

"How? Were you not also under the oath?"

"I was. I don't know why I survived. What I do know is every time our warriors are not bound again by their oath, there is the possibility of death by that same oath."

Mother took in a deep breath. "Gurmund told us he was wary of Armand and the other two, and that a handful of our warriors passed away shortly after taking the oath. But he didn't go into detail about the torture they went through. At the time, he believed they died as a warning to keep his clansmen in line. I don't think he knows that every Nordic who has taken the oath carries a death sentence."

"And maybe he won't know. If it is discovered that those taken during the battle died, it could be said the southerners killed them. After all, that is what the Wolf Clan does with their prisoners. That is why I am here. I came to warn you."

Bard could remain silent no longer. "Forgive me," he said as he entered the room. Both women startled. "I came to speak to my mother and overheard your conversation."

Brighid drew back.

"Please, I want to hear more. My father might not have known the extent of malice these 'allies' possessed, but now I know. And we must warn him."

Brighid held still and watched as Bard approached the firepit. He lowered himself into the remaining chair. "First, I heard you lived. But how did you escape?"

Brighid narrowed her eyes, then seemed to reach a conclusion within herself because she spoke again. "The southern forces have allies like Armand, Peder, and Viessa. But also not like them. Different. Better. With marks of light across their palms."

Bard blinked. "There are more of these powerful beings?"

"Yes."

He shook his head. When his father first wrote about Armand and the other two, Bard struggled to believe such power existed. But with each letter, his belief grew, and he held the same wariness as his father, despite how powerful their warriors had become. Now he knew their promises came with a terrible price. "So you're saying those allies are opposite of Armand. And fight for the south."

Brighid paused. "They don't fight. At least I didn't see them fight. One of them rescued me from the battlefield. I was on the verge of death and he . . ." Brighid scrunched her face as if trying to find words. Then she shrugged. "He healed me. I don't know how. But with the power Armand has. And his palm was different. The skin along Armand's hand and the others' is black, like it's rotting flesh. But Kaeden's was full of light and healing."

"Kaeden?"

"That is the name of the one who saved me. And he wasn't the only one. There was another named Mathias. When I was brought to the southern camp, they made sure I wasn't chained up with the other prisoners. They treated me like a human."

"But why didn't they help the other Nordic prisoners?" Bard asked.

"They did. When our people started dying, both Kaeden and Mathias did everything they could to save them. Somehow, Mathias died helping them. And afterward, Kaeden became the Truthsayer."

"Truthsayer?" Bard rubbed his forehead. This was all very confusing.

"Truthsayer," his mother whispered, a look of awe and fear on her face. Bard glanced at her. "That is a word I haven't heard since I was young."

"Mother?" he said.

"Stories from far away. I only remember the Truthsayer. A being with the ability to see inside a person's soul. Stories from the Great Battle. But that's all I thought they were: stories." She turned her attention back to Brighid. "This Truthsayer saved you?"

"Yes," Brighid said. "Not only did he save me, but he also released me and told me to return north, back to my people, and warn them of Armand and the others."

Bard let out his breath. What a tale. But he had no reason *not* to believe her. He already knew his father did not trust their allies. And Brighid had brought a tangible reason. He needed to tell Father. "What a tangled mess. What were the hjars thinking, aligning themselves with these beings?"

Brighid spoke up. "If they are anything like the Truthsayer, perhaps the hjars were swayed by their power."

Bard glanced at her. "Did this Kaeden say how we could free ourselves?"

Brighid shook her head. "No. However, I do remember he said these Shadonae were his jurisdiction."

"Shadonae?" Bard said.

"That is what Kaeden called Armand and the others."

"Even the name hints at their nature," his mother said softly.

"Probably why they didn't say what they were," Bard replied darkly. "We should have asked more questions. Probed more deeply. Instead, Volka and the others were so hungry for power and conquest, they joined hands with these Shadonae. Bolva! What do we do now?"

The three of them sat quietly around the fire. "Well, we have all winter to think," Bard said, breaking the silence after a few moments. "And to write to my father. Perhaps between us, we can find allies, both here and within the Nordic camp, and find a way to break away from the Shadonae."

"Kaeden will be searching for a way to confront the Shadonae himself," Brighid said.

Bard eyed her. "I know he freed you, but do you think we can really trust this being?"

"He told me to find a way to free our people, and he would find a way to stop the Shadonae."

"As a Truthsayer, he might have the power to do just that," Ana said. Then she looked at Brighid. "I want to know how you were able to travel all the way here."

Brighid looked down at her fingers. "It wasn't easy. There were times I wondered if I should return to our forces. But I know Armand's secret. That the oath our people took would someday be their death. So either I would be bound again or put to death as a deserter."

Bard huffed. "Hjar Volka has strong feelings about deserters."

"So you traveled north instead. All by yourself," Ana said.

"Yes."

"Through an autumn snowstorm. With an injured leg."

"And with the help of a bear," Bard pointed out.

"Yes," Brighid said. "Although, I was well for most of the journey. The dog bite happened a few days before the bear found me and brought me here."

"That is a tale for the fires," Ana said, sitting back. "I would like to hear it."

Brighid seemed to be more relaxed, her hands no longer clenched in her lap, though her voice was low. As she spoke about how she traveled north, Bard stared into the fire, his heart heavy. Bolva! How in the Lands could they separate themselves from these Shadonae? The threads between the Nordic forces and Armand seemed to be woven too tightly. All this Armand would need to do is step back and do nothing, and almost the entire Nordic army would perish from his words.

What have we done? Bard ran a hand across his mouth, then down his beard. *How do we fix this?*

20

Kaeden sat on the left side of Lord Rayner at dinner that night. Almost two months had passed since he first arrived in the White City. True to his word, the great lord invited both he and Treyvar to dine with him once a week. Tonight, Lord Rayner's son, Teduin, joined them, along with many of the other nobles, counselors, and people of note in the White City.

A long dark wood table took up most of the room. Narrow windows lined the east side and were currently filled with darkness and condensation as the snowflakes outside melted on contact with the glass. A fire burned cheerily in the ornate stone fireplace behind Lord Rayner. The rest of the room glowed beneath a chandelier that hung above the table, the candles set between boughs of pine and winterberries.

The room hummed with low conversation as various parties spoke with one another. A servant offered Kaeden wine, but he declined. So did Treyvar, who sat next to him. Minutes ticked by. Treyvar spoke with a couple on his left: a merchant family with ties to Avonai. Kaeden suspected they had no idea who Treyvar was. Most Avonains did not, which he found interesting. Treyvar said he was the second son, and from what Kaeden had gathered, not important, but he wondered if Treyvar also purported that image of himself. Kaeden had a feeling the Avonain prince liked being incognito.

As Kaeden reached for the glass of water that had been brought after the wine, he felt a pair of eyes on him. He looked up and Teduin watched him from across the table. He appeared as a younger version of his father, only without the facial hair. His dark hair glistened in the candlelight and fell in waves along his shoulders.

"So, Master Kaeden, I heard you've been practicing with our guards."

"Yes, that is true." Kaeden took a sip from his goblet.

"What exactly do you do? Fight with swords? I thought you were a pacifist."

Kaeden raised one eyebrow. "I wouldn't necessarily call myself a pacifist. I simply choose not to fight when it comes to battles."

Teduin scoffed. "Why not? You've been gifted with a body for it."

Kaeden placed his cup down. Others turned their way. "A strong body can be used in many ways, not just for fighting."

"Such as?"

"Moving injured people, packing wagons, setting up healing tents. Even when there isn't a war, able bodies are always needed. As far as practicing with your guards, daily exercise is needed to keep my body in shape for when spring comes, and the war starts again. Besides, they asked me to teach them."

"What could a healer possibly teach our guards?" Even Lord Rayner was listening now.

"I am proficient in grappling. It is something I learned when I was young and have improved upon over the years. Swords can be lost during a fight, so it is important to have other skills. It is also something I enjoy."

"Interesting." Teduin took a sip of wine from his goblet. "What would you say to a little competition?"

"Are you suggesting you're interested in grappling?"

"I am. I also have some experience."

Murmurs stirred around the table. Lord Rayner frowned but didn't say anything.

"You want to challenge me?"

"Yes. I'm curious what a Truthsayer can do."

Kaeden smirked inwardly. Mathias would have loved this. Not just the potential of a grappling competition, but the surprise on Teduin's face when he realized a Truthsayer and healer could go toe-to-toe physically with a lord of the White City. A moment later, he realized this was the first time he was remembering Mathias without the sharp pang of grief in his chest.

Before Kaeden could answer, the servants entered with steaming plates of meat and root vegetables, baskets of bread, and platters with cheese. The smells of roasted venison and fresh bread filled the room, causing his stomach to rumble. He didn't really like these formal weekly meals, but the food from the main kitchen always made up for it.

The conversation from moments ago was forgotten as people helped themselves to the dishes.

Kaeden took a serving of meat and vegetables. But unlike the fickle onlookers, he had not forgotten Teduin's challenge. "I would be open to a challenge, my lord. I'm available most days."

Treyvar spoke up. "What if we had a little wager?"

Kaeden almost choked on his first bite of meat. He glanced at Treyvar from the corner of his eye as he tried to hide his struggle to swallow. He wouldn't have thought Treyvar would be the one to suggest such a thing.

"I would be interested," a man sitting near Teduin said.

"And I," declared a younger man farther down the table.

Teduin smiled. "Yes, let's do that. Treyvar, what do you say to overseeing this little competition?"

Treyvar wiped his lips with a linen cloth. "I could do that. And record the wagers."

"I'll send word with my aide to let you know which day is best for me," Teduin said. "I am a bit busier than someone who merely spends time with Healer Weylin and studies in the library."

Kaeden narrowed his eyes. Was Teduin watching him? That would explain why he knew about his grappling sessions with the guards. But why?

Teduin turned to the young man beside him and started a new conversation. Kaeden continued to eat, watching those around him. Lord Rayner had been silent during the exchange, and Kaeden was curious what he thought of this. In fact, Lord Rayner had been silent during most of their dinners, which surprised Kaeden. He thought the

High Lord wanted to get more information out of him since their first meeting. Perhaps Lord Rayner was content to watch and listen and, like his son, had been observing Kaeden's daily activities from afar.

After dinner, Kaeden and Treyvar walked alone toward the guest rooms that had become their more permanent accommodations for the winter. The dark halls were chilly and bore down on Kaeden with an uncomfortable weight. It wasn't the first time since winter had finally taken hold of the White City that he decided he did not like these cold months here in the mountains. Both Khodath and Mistsylver Island had been warm and sunny all year. And the Tieve Hills were mild with more light. Because of that, he wasn't sure if the White City would ever become his permanent home, despite it being the birthplace of his people. He definitely didn't like winter.

"What do you think?" Treyvar asked, breaking the silence.

"About Lord Teduin and his challenge?"

"Yes."

Kaeden glanced around before answering. "I think the young man is bored, despite his claim of busyness. And he's competitive. I suspect we are near the same age. But I'm different. I've seen more. Carry more weight and responsibility. I believe he's challenged by that."

The two men entered the sitting room of the guest suite. A fire burned in the stone fireplace. Kaeden went immediately to it, pulled the glove off his right hand, and held both palms out. The heat and light felt good, like life was washing over him.

"Celestis Castle definitely gets cold in the winter." Treyvar joined him. "I don't know which is worse, the snow and cold here, or the cold and rain in Avonai."

"Both," Kaeden replied. The men laughed. After a moment, Kaeden spoke up again. "Lord Rayner scarcely speaks at these meals he's asked us to attend, and he didn't react to his son's suggestion for a competition."

"Yes, I observed the same. Perhaps it's simply to keep us in check while we winter here. And probably a gesture of hospitality toward me."

"Because of your status as a prince of Avonai?"

Treyvar hesitated. "Yes."

Kaeden wanted to ask more, but Treyvar's response made him think the young man wasn't ready to share his background. Made sense—for years Kaeden hid who he was.

"I don't know much about grappling, but I've seen you practice a couple times," Treyvar said, breaking the silence. "And I remember how fondly Master Mathias spoke about you and your ability."

"Is that why you brought up the idea of a wager?"

Treyvar grinned. "Yes. Not a large amount. But enough to make Teduin feel the weight of competition. Master Mathias once spoke of how he liked to wager. I was shocked at first, but then I could see it. He was not what I thought he would be when I first met him. I thought he'd be solemn and upright. And he was, at times. But he could laugh and loved life and people. Something I hadn't seen before."

Kaeden decided to press. "When did you meet Master Mathias?

"Almost three years ago when he arrived in Avonai. My father invited him to stay in the castle. I usually kept to myself. Studied, walked the city, observed everything and everyone from afar. I lived just as my father wanted me to: in the background. Then Master Mathias . . ." Treyvar smiled and shook his head. "He would have none of that. He would join me in the library, on my walks around the city, and talk to me at dinner. He saw something in me that neither my family nor I saw in myself: a man who had much to offer this world."

"That definitely sounds like Mathias." Kaeden's heart swelled with affection tinged in sadness. Mathias was always helping others. Always.

"Master Mathias helped me find my own path. And grew in me a desire to help my people in whatever capacity I could. I found a reason to study more so I could assist in diplomacy. I watched how my people lived every day in order to know what policies would help them most. And when the war broke out, I knew I wasn't a fighter. I decided I would help the healers and be with my people in the fight. Something my father and brother chose not to do." A hint of bitterness seasoned his tone. Treyvar turned away.

Kaeden waited, but Treyvar remained quiet. He reached over and gripped his friend's shoulder. Treyvar was probably a year or two younger than him. And from his story, it sounded like after Mathias left Kaeden on Mistsylver Island, he came to Avonai and helped another young man.

For a moment, Kaeden wondered what would have happened if they had both returned to Avonai? Would he and Treyvar have met earlier? Become friends and comrades?

"Mathias did exactly what the Word asked of him: He helped others. And we can honor his legacy by doing the same." Kaeden dropped his hand.

"Yes," Treyvar said in a firm tone. He turned around, and Kaeden wasn't sure if it was anger or grief in his eyes. Maybe both. "Let us do that together. You as the Truthsayer, and me as a prince of Avonai."

Kaeden smiled. "Yes. And maybe together we can help end this war."

21

Three days later, Kaeden stood in the training room in the early afternoon. Word of the grappling match must have spread around Celestis Castle because the space was full of spectators, and not just guards. Snow fell across the glass roof high above, creating a ceiling of warm grey. The torches burned along the stone walls for light, and the weapons racks had been moved to make way for more people.

The room was warm with all the compressed bodies and smelled of sweat and stone. Kaeden stood almost a head taller than those gathered and spotted both Teduin and Treyvar on the far side of the room, where a circle was painted on the wood floor.

Teduin glanced up and a smirk crossed his lips. "Ah, here he is, the Truthsayer himself," he shouted. The crowd murmured around them, and Kaeden caught bits of conversation as people parted to let him through.

"He's a big man."

"Does the Truthsayer really fight?"

"Maybe I should have bet on him."

Kaeden walked toward the two men. At the edge of the white-painted circle, he stopped and inclined his head toward Teduin. "Lord Teduin."

"Master Kaeden." There was no return bow.

More murmurs and Kaeden barely heard, "Why doesn't our lord show respect for the Truthsayer?" Teduin apparently didn't hear their questions or ignored them. Treyvar gave the lord a sideways glance, a cold look on his face.

Teduin raised his hands. "I didn't realize so many of you would want to watch a friendly competition between myself and Master Kaeden. I'm merely here because I want to see what the Truthsayer is capable of. Maybe there is more to him that just a healer on the battlefield."

A few people snickered, but most leaned in, curious as well.

Teduin turned toward Kaeden. "Are you ready?"

"Let me warm up first." Kaeden undid the cord around his waist. "Will you hold this for me?" he asked Treyvar.

"Of course."

He removed his robes, then his tunic, leaving only his trousers. Then he took his boots and socks off.

"I told you he was a big man," one of the guards said. A man named Lance. "He's been teaching me his techniques."

That warmed Kaeden's heart. At first he had joined the guards to keep his body in shape for when the war resumed, but he soon found himself laughing and making friends with the men. He took a few minutes to stretch and ensure his muscles and limbs were warm and ready. Teduin did the same.

"Look at that scar on his side," someone whispered. "Where do you think he got that?"

Kaeden turned away from the crowd and finished his last stretch. He knew what scar they were talking about. The one he received when he healed Brighid. It would always be there, a reminder of his first healing and the awakening of his power. And of her.

"All right." Teduin headed toward the center of the circle. "I'm ready."

Kaeden entered the ring. "I am also ready."

Without his jerkin or tunic on, Kaeden could see Teduin was a tall, lean man. There was form to his body, which meant the man didn't spend his days idling but actually did some training. Just how much, he would soon know.

"First, some rules," Treyvar said, stepping between them.

The crowd groaned. "We just wanna see them fight!" someone shouted.

"Yes, that's true," Treyvar said. "But fairly."

"He's right," Kaeden said, raising his hands. The crowd quieted.

"The fight must stay in the circle." Treyvar laid out other rules, including no use of violent actions. Teduin stood beside him with his arms crossed and a bored look on his face. Kaeden glanced at those gathered, the majority of whom were guards and soldiers. Most already knew the guidelines, but it was good that Treyvar was going over them one more time, because he had a feeling Teduin would not hesitate to do anything he could to win in front of the others.

Over the last three days, Kaeden wondered if he should let Teduin win—after a couple of holds—so the man could save face in front of his people. Kaeden was already highly regarded, not only because of his rank as Truthsayer but also because of his time spent with these men and the training he had given them. However, Teduin was their lord and the future ruler of the White City. Winning would earn him some respect.

"And that's it," Treyvar said.

"Finally," Teduin said under his breath.

Irritation bloomed inside Kaeden's chest, and his lips tightened into a thin line. From the expressions of those in front of them, the crowd hadn't heard Teduin's words, but there were a few frowns, indicating a couple knew what he had said. Such disrespect. His eyes narrowed. No, he had no intention of letting the man win. He would take Teduin down.

"Now." Treyvar turned toward Kaeden and Teduin. "Enter the ring."

Both men walked across the floor. The wood was cold, but it was better than the unrelenting stone of the rest of the castle. Once they reached the middle, they turned and faced each other. Teduin cracked his neck and grinned. Kaeden met his gaze with a cool look.

"On the count of three, you may begin," Treyvar said. "One." Kaeden sank into his stance, his fingers slightly curled, his body bent. "Two." He drew in a breath. "Three."

Kaeden exploded across the ring, knees bent, and cleared Teduin's arms. He brought his head and shoulder beneath Teduin and shoved up, causing him to lean on his other leg, then grabbed the leg closest to him. Teduin slammed onto the ground. There was a moment of shock on his face before he countered Kaeden.

After that, the match became a blur of limbs, grabs, and balance. There was no delayed thinking, no hesitation, just instinct and muscle memory. Kaeden's body moved with the flow of the fight. At one point, he found himself on the ground, but he was able to twist out of Teduin's grip. Then he saw his opportunity.

He grabbed Teduin's arm and rolled with his back on the ground, twisting until the man's arm was caught between Kaeden's legs. He continued to roll, forcing Teduin to follow his movement. Teduin's face thumped against the floor. He squirmed, but he couldn't get out of Kaeden's hold.

"Relent!" Kaeden yelled.

"No!" Teduin struggled against his hold. But Kaeden held on, locking Teduin in place.

"Relent, now!"

"Never!" Teduin yelled with a hard yank. His fingers scrambled for a grip and found the edge of Kaeden's glove, forcing the leather to dig between Kaeden's fingers. Teduin pulled harder, bending Kaeden's hand, then shoved his thumb inside the glove.

"Wait!" Kaeden shouted. "Don't do that—"

It was too late. His mark reacted the moment Teduin's thumb grazed his palm. Light flared from the glove as Kaeden sank inside Teduin's mind.

Memories, images, and feelings flashed across Kaeden's thoughts: Teduin storming out of the throne room when Lord Rayner once again pointed out how far he fell short as his son. Dark glee in taking out his frustration on one of the old servants. Finding camaraderie in Prince Elion and harassing the prince's younger brother, Treyvar. Jealousy over how much Elion's father doted on him when his own was never pleased.

More and more feelings and memories rushed by until he reached the deepest part of Teduin's soul: longing and hatred. The two were entangled in each other, creating a dark, twisting monster in Teduin's heart.

The connection broke and Kaeden found himself staring up at the ceiling, cold sweat coating his forehead. So that was the real Teduin.

"How *dare* you use your power on me!"

Kaeden turned his head and found Teduin on his knees, his face deathly pale, his eyes dark and dilated. A vein throbbed along his temple.

"I tried to stop you," Kaeden replied as he struggled to sit up. Nausea swept up his throat. Diving into Teduin's soul was very different from entering Brighid's.

Teduin pointed a finger at him. "You cheated! And therefore this match is forfeited to me."

A dark burn bloomed in Kaeden's midsection. "You gripped my glove, and I told you to stop!"

Teduin stood. "Grappling is all about winning."

"There are *rules*," Kaeden snarled, also standing.

"Nothing about gloves."

"I wear this glove to protect people from my power."

"Well, you didn't do a good job. You used your power on me without my consent."

"My mark reacts to touch!"

The guards murmured around them. Kaeden looked away. He was stooping to Teduin's level. He needed to stop, despite still feeling the swirls of darkness inside his body, leftover from his encounter with Teduin.

Treyvar stepped forward, his hands raised. "Let us consider this match a draw."

"No." Teduin's nostrils flared as he glared first at Treyvar, then at Kaeden. "I would have thought a Truthsayer would have more integrity."

Kaeden clenched his hand at the verbal attack. He barely restrained his anger. "Let him have the victory," he said to Treyvar.

"We could do a rematch," Treyvar replied.

"No, Lord Teduin was right. There were no *spoken* rules against gloves. And I inadvertently used my power." Although holding clothing was usually frowned upon in grappling matches.

Treyvar studied him one more time, then addressed the crowd. "Lord Teduin is the winner of this grappling match by default."

A few men voiced their discontent, but a scathing look from Teduin silenced them.

Kaeden turned toward Teduin, and it took everything inside of him to bow his head. "Thank you for the match, Lord Teduin," he said.

"It was my pleasure." His voice held a hint of gloating.

Kaeden swallowed and held his composure. Teduin had no idea how his words and actions came across to the people around them—the very people from whom he desired respect. Instead, his determination to win at any cost and bend the rules to his will made him lose face with those in this room.

"Please excuse me." Kaeden crossed the fight circle, where his clothes waited on a nearby table.

"The Truthsayer has spoken." Teduin raised his hands in triumph.

Kaeden ignored him as he donned his robes and cord, then tugged his boots on. A few voices rose around him as he made his way through the crowd toward the door in back. The crowd was not pleased.

"I was hoping for more of a fight," someone whispered.

"Grabbing the Truthsayer's glove was a bit of a cheat if you ask me," another person said.

"Did the Truthsayer really use his power on Lord Teduin?"

Kaeden paused at the last whisper. He didn't want these guards to fear him. Not after spending time building camaraderie with them. But if that happened, there wasn't much he could do about it. This was who he was. Funny how months ago he held no power. And now he hid his power beneath a glove.

At the door, he turned back. Most of the crowd was ignoring Teduin and his crowing. In that brief moment, Kaeden felt bad for the young lord. Having seen Teduin's life, he knew the man's greatest desire was to be recognized. But he wasn't ready to do the hard work of earning his people's respect. Instead, it seemed he would remain petty, willing to do anything to win.

Kaeden sighed and left the training room. Word help the White City with their future High Lord.

Kaeden stood by the fireplace in the guest quarters, his glove tossed on the chair, his hand in a fist as he pressed it against the mantel. He stared at the flames as the door opened behind him.

"I'm sorry," Treyvar said, then the door closed. Boots stepped softly against the stone floor. "I shouldn't have mentioned a wager. It brought out Teduin's competitive spirit." Treyvar came to stand beside him. He shook his head. "I should have known he would do something like that."

"Even without a wager, Teduin would have found a way to win." Kaeden scoffed darkly. "Too bad he used my mark to do it. I know him now."

"Oh?" Treyvar glanced at him.

Kaeden turned away from the fire. "I also saw your past through his eyes."

"Oh."

"It is I who is sorry. Sorry for how you have been treated. And I am sorry this beautiful city and land will inherit such a man for its ruler."

"I can imagine what you saw to cause you to say such a thing." Treyvar let out a long sigh. "It is the same for my own country."

Kaeden lifted his hand and stared at his mark, which now glowed with a soft light. "What good is it being the Truthsayer when it feels like I can do nothing to bring about change? Did Mathias feel this way?"

"You can't force change, not the good kind anyway. You are doing what a Truthsayer is supposed to do: Show the truth. You did something back in the training room. I've never seen Teduin react so viciously before. And that's saying something. Whatever he saw—whatever he experienced—it affected him. And maybe good might come of that someday."

Kaeden dropped his hand and reached for his glove. "I've barely had this power, and already I can tell there is a temptation to touch those I dislike, to force my thoughts and will on them through my mark." He tugged on the glove and looked over at Treyvar. "Does that statement scare you?"

Treyvar paused. "I think it would if you were any other man or woman. Your gift is powerful. In the wrong hands, it could control entire nations." His face sobered. "And that is a terrifying thought."

But would it be a bad thing? Kaeden glanced at his hand again, now covered. He could use his mark to shape Teduin, turn him into the man this city needed. And the man Teduin wanted to become.

He turned away. He didn't even have to think twice. Yes, it would be bad. As much as he desired to bring change to this world, Treyvar was right. Change brought by force—and not by the willingness of the heart—was no change at all. Even men like Teduin deserved the chance to change themselves.

"I think that's why Mathias's gift passed on to you."

Kaeden looked up. "What do you mean?"

Treyvar let out his breath. "I've only known you since the start of the war, but what I've seen is a person who doesn't set himself above others, whether that be humans or the enemy. I've met other Eldarans. They weren't the same."

"You mean Selma."

"Yes. She is a good healer, and we are very thankful she is serving the Southern Alliance. But sometimes . . ."

Kaeden folded his arms. "Sometimes she's arrogant."

"Yes, bluntly speaking. I thought serving with Mathias would have changed her, but there are moments when I see or hear something."

"She may still change."

Treyvar nodded. "Yes. I hope so."

Kaeden remembered Selma's interest in the group of Eldarans who lived in the far northwest, beyond the Ari Mountains. What were they like? Mathias had said they kept to themselves and had little to do with humanity, hence why his father left them years ago. Was Selma's interest based on her desire to be with her own kind?

He could understand that. For a long time, he felt different, even when others didn't know about his Eldaran heritage or his lack of power. And now, as the Truthsayer, he felt even more alone. The accident during the grappling match didn't help. It reminded everyone that there was a powerful mark beneath his glove. And with one touch, they could trigger his power.

"You're thinking dark thoughts. I can see it on your face," Treyvar said.

Kaeden grunted in reply.

"I may not be an Eldaran, but I am your friend."

Treyvar was right. He was allowing grim feelings to invade his mind, sending him into a black vortex. And like a friend, Treyvar was calling him back.

Kaeden huffed. "Thank you."

"Of course. I may not be Mathias, but I will be here for you. As one Follower of the Word to another." Treyvar held out his hand.

Kaeden clasped it. "Thank you, friend."

"Always."

22

Brighid sat up in bed, her face red and hot. She had dreamed of Kaeden again—a dream so real she almost felt like *she* was the one in the strange training room with the glass roof, surrounded by a crowd, breathing in the smell of sweat, and feeling the heat of compressed bodies. Why had she dreamed of Kaeden? And why . . .

She pressed a hand against her heated cheek. Why had she dreamed of Kaeden without a tunic on? She could still see the contours of his muscles. Strong, broad, and powerful. She had seen many men without their shirts on during the war. But this was different. Her reaction was different.

Bolva! Brighid swung her feet around the plank bed and pressed her toes against the cold, hard-packed soil. The firepit nearby had burned down to glowing embers during the night, and the air held an icy chill.

Her dream ended when another man stepped in front of Kaeden, also shirtless, and they charged each other. The last emotion was the thrill of the fight.

She shook her head and stood. What a strange and disturbing dream. "Why do I keep seeing him?" she whispered as she quickly pulled on her own clothes. The wool-strap dress she had been embroidering was not quite finished, so her old clothes would have to do. Then she grabbed Kaeden's dark cloak. She held the thick, warm cloth to her face. It now smelled of smoke and fire. Nothing lingered that reminded her of him.

"Why do I keep dreaming of you?" she murmured into the cloth. They had spent only a handful of days together, yet there seemed to be a connection between them, forged from that brief time.

She drew the cloak around her shoulders and fastened it, then placed a few logs on the firepit to get the flames going again. In the loft above, she could hear Ana's deep breathing of sleep. Brighid glanced up at the railing. The members of the Bear Clan were not who she had thought they would be. Not that she had a lot of interaction with the clan the last few months on the battlefield.

They weren't like the Wolf Clan, who stayed to themselves and acted superior toward the clanless unless a person showed potential. And the Owl Clan didn't mingle with anyone. None of the clans really had anything to do with the clanless, despite fighting together. But here, the Bear Clan not only welcomed her, they seemed to welcome others, both from other clans and clanless.

And the other night, when she finally shared her past and what brought her here, Ana and Hjaren Bard had listened to her. They reminded her a little of Johan and Marta and the other clanless fighters who shared the evening fires during the war.

Brighid remained hunched by the firepit, blowing softly on the embers, coaxing a new fire into the stone circle. Once the flame took hold of the small wood pieces, it greedily started devouring the larger logs.

Where were Johan and Marta now? Were they still alive? Was there a way Hjaren Bard could find out through his father? She shook her head. No. Why would a Hjar care about two clanless warriors? But maybe she would still ask. Just in case.

And what was going on with the war now? Where was everyone stationed? What happened after the Battle of the Plains?

Ana rustled upstairs. Brighid glanced up, then stood and brushed off the bits of bark and wood from her cloak. Already the area was warming from the fire.

A minute later, Ana made her way down the stairs. Her silver hair hung in a long braid over one shoulder. An aura of warmth and strength seemed to emanate from the Bear Clan matron. She spotted Brighid by the firepit. "Thank you for tending the fire," she said as she reached the bottom. She rubbed her hands together. "Winter feels colder with every year that passes."

Brighid weighed her thoughts, then decided to risk her question. "Have you heard from our forces? From . . . Hjar Gurmund?"

Ana held her hands to the fire. "Yes, briefly. My husband sent me a letter when he arrived in one of the fortresses taken. Dallam, I believe."

Dallam. Brighid remembered that place. The Stag Clan spent a night and a day building a floating bridge to cross the Onyx River. And it took only one day to take the fortress. "Are all of the Nordic forces stationed there?"

"I'm not sure. His message was brief, to let me know he was alive and where to send letters."

"Oh." She looked down at the cheery fire that was now consuming all the logs.

"You are wondering about your comrades."

Brighid swallowed. "Yes."

"If you give me their names, I can ask the next time I send a letter."

Brighid looked up. "They're clanless. I doubt Hjar Gurmund would have heard of them."

Ana smiled softly. "I can still ask."

It was a fleeting hope, but it was still hope. "Johan and Marta."

"Johan . . . and . . . Marta." Ana said the names as if etching them into her mind. "Clanless. I sent a letter not too long ago and haven't heard back. But I'll be happy to send another one with your inquiry."

Brighid's chest swelled with gratitude. "Thank you."

Ana nodded with a smile. "I understand your worry. When I was young, and Gurmund and I were preparing for our bonding, we spent a summer on the border during a time of unrest. Many fights broke out, and we were separated for most of it. Each night I worried for him, and he for me. Every letter I received brought a sliver of hope for the day we would be reunited."

For some reason, Ana's words made Brighid think back on the dream she had woken from that morning. And the other dreams. Many dreams. Of Kaeden. Was there a hidden hope in her heart of seeing him someday? Was that why she kept seeing him during her sleep? But they were such strange dreams and felt so real.

They can't be, Brighid thought. *They're just dreams. And we will probably never meet again.* However, she couldn't deny the sliver of hope deep inside that she *would* see him again.

Maybe when this war was over.

A couple of mornings later, Brighid sat near the firepit in the main hall, breaking her fast with the day's first meal. Bard had finished and left minutes before, leaving only the twins, Vigi and Lodin, beside her.

"Going out on patrol today?" Instead of braids, Vigi wore his dark hair down, letting it fall past his shoulders.

"Not this time." Brighid replied.

"We are!" Vigi punched Lodin's arm.

His brother rolled his eyes and shook his head. "Must you be so excited?" he muttered.

Brighid hid her grin by placing a spoonful of porridge in her mouth. They might be twins, but they were as different as day and night. Even their hairstyles reflected their differences. Lodin had shaved most of his hair close to his scalp yesterday, keeping just the top long and gathered at his crown by a leather strap.

"It's snowing, or haven't you noticed?" Lodin glared at the nearby window. "I hate patrolling in the snow."

Before Vigi could answer, the far door opened with a slam, sending in a blast of cold air and white flakes. In the entryway stood a grizzled man, his face and body hidden deep within a fur-lined hood and cloak with a grey-speckled beard emerging from the collar line. The rest of him was covered in snow. He remained in the doorway as he shook off the white flakes like a dog, then stomped his boots.

"Wait, is that Orest?" Vigi said.

"Orest?" Brighid asked.

"Is that you, Orest?" someone else shouted.

"Aye! It is!" a deep voice hollered as the figure pulled back his cloak, letting lose thick peppered hair that hung below his shoulders.

"Shut the door, you mountain hound, you're letting in the cold," Thorald yelled from two tables over. He slowly stood, using a staff to help him to his feet, and started toward the front door. "You'd think he was born in a cave," Thorald grumbled.

There were a few chuckles when Orest grunted and shut the door. Thorald shook his head and sat back down. Those in the hall welcomed Orest as he crossed the room, stopping every few feet to let out an exuberant greeting or answer a question.

"I wonder where he traveled this time," Vigi said with a grin.

"We could have used him a few months ago," Lodin answered.

Orest made his way to their table. "Vigi, Lodin! Til Val!" he yelled with a raised fist.

The twins stood. "Til Val!" they answered. The rest of the room joined in, yelling the Nordic chant until it felt like the hall was shaking. Then everyone broke out in laughter and good cheer.

Brighid stared up at the strange man from the bench where she sat. She wasn't sure what to make of him. Then his gaze landed on her and he froze. Pale blue eyes stared down at her from his grizzled face.

"By the Lands," he said as he stared at her. "Kalla, is that you?"

The cheerful atmosphere from moments before melted away, leaving behind a cold, silent wake.

Brighid blinked. Kalla? Who was that?

Before she could answer, Orest leaned across the table, his forearms resting on the wooden surface. His gaze moved along her face until Brighid inched back, uncomfortable. "No, you're not Kalla."

"No," Brighid answered, finally finding her voice. From the corner of her eye, she could see discomfort on both Vigi's and Lodin's faces. Farther away, a few people shifted uncomfortably and one person coughed. Their unease seeped into her body.

"Who are you, young lady?"

Brighid raised her chin. "Brighid. I'm a guest here."

"Brighid." He rolled her name across his tongue. "Brighid," he said again.

"She arrived a few weeks ago," Vigi finally answered.

He straightened and looked over his shoulder. "What's wrong with the lot of you? You all are acting like someone died." He turned around and huffed. "That's right. I said her name. Kalla would be laughing at you all, with your jaws hanging and eyes bulging."

Vigi and a few others let out uneasy chuckles.

"Humph." Orest crossed his arms. "The best thing we can do is remember her spirit. *I* will remember her spirit."

The door to the back opened, and Brighid heard Bard's voice. "Orest?"

The old man turned around and broke out in a big smile. "Bard, my boy!" His voice boomed across the room. He bypassed Brighid's table as he strode toward rear and clasped Bard by the shoulders. "You're looking good."

"And you as well, Uncle. We haven't seen you in almost a year. Where did you travel this time?"

The hall returned to a gentle hum of conversation, tinged with only a hint of the unease from minutes earlier. Vigi stood. "I'm going to get ready for patrol."

Brighid went to grab his hand, but he moved quickly away. Lodin followed his brother out of the hall. She had half a mind to follow them and demand an answer. But something held her back. Was it the disquiet that name brought to those here? She didn't want to open old wounds, if that was the case.

She sighed and returned to her half-eaten porridge, dipping her spoon in the bowl while she caught snippets of Orest and Bard's conversation.

"—then I finally made it to the far north," Orest said. "To the edge of the Wastelands." Brighid watched him drop his hands. "What is this I hear of a war?" he asked in a hushed tone.

"You knew there was the possibility before you left."

"Yes. But I never thought the south would actually move on us."

"They didn't. The council decided. We took the war to them."

Orest let out a low whistle. "Well, well. Can't say I'm surprised. The bear will attack when threatened. How do we fare so far?"

Brighid leaned in a little more, hopefully without catching their attention. She wanted to hear as well, while in the back of her mind the name Kalla echoed.

"We won most of our battles and took the entire northern border along the Ari Mountains, along with the Onyx River. But the last battle before autumn was won by the White City and Avonai. Father is now stationed at Dallam Fortress."

"We hold Dallam? Good. Good. What about Stelriden Fortress?"

"No."

"It's not far from here, on the other side of the valley, south of our border. Maybe we should take a group of our own warriors—"

"No, Uncle."

"Why not? It wouldn't be that hard. Who is still here? I saw Heming on my way in, and the twins. I've visited the fortress once or twice and remember the layout. What victory it would bring to our clan, what glory! I can still fight, even if I don't have the Vilrik—"

"Right now we are holding the border, as we have always done."

Orest's face darkened. "Guard duty? Is that what you're doing? Is that why Gurmund left you? That fortress is on our doorstep. We should be bringing the fight to them."

Bard sighed. "Not here. We can discuss it around our own fire. And I will tell you more."

Orest's gaze landed on Brighid, and she pretended to be lost in thought while staring at the fire. "Who's the young woman? By the gods, she looks like Kalla. Spittin' image. Is she Kalla's daughter perhaps?"

"Uncle! Not here." Bard placed a hand on Orest's shoulder. "Come. I'm sure Mother would love to see you. And I need to go on patrol."

"Ana!" Orest's face brightened. "My dear sister. Yes, yes. Take me to her."

Bard gently guided his uncle toward the door. "You still haven't told me who the young woman is," Orest said as they walked through the doorway. The door shut before Brighid could hear Bard's answer.

Brighid finished her food and stood. She wished she was on patrol today and could ask who Kalla was. Instead, she would be here. And Ana would be visiting with Orest. Which didn't leave anyone else close enough she could ask.

But there was something there—between the reactions of everyone and Orest's claim that she looked like this Kalla—that prickled the edges of her mind. Like the first few flakes of snow before the winter storm. A forewarning of things to come.

23

"I heard Orest arrived this morning."

Bard grunted in reply to Heming as he stored his weapons on the designated rack inside the training hall. He had sent the twins on patrol that morning and chose to remain behind. With Orest there, it was better to stay back and watch his uncle.

"Everyone's talking about what he said in the main hall. About Kalla."

Bard hung the last sword. "I told him not to bring up Kalla's name with Mother. At least not unless I'm present."

"And what are you going to say? Many of us have wondered the same thing."

Bard twisted around. "Then why didn't you say anything?"

Heming walked over to the firepit burning in the middle of the room and sat on his haunches. "I know the trauma your family went through when Kalla disappeared. I was there. How could I bring up such hurt again?"

"You're right." Bard turned back and started straightening the shields that hung on the wall, his gut clenching at Heming's words. "And thank you."

"Of course. But now you seem open to talking about it."

Bard let out his breath. "I am."

"She looks like Kalla. She fights like one of ours and was brought to us by a bear." Heming stared into the fire. "Is there any possibility that Brighid is your sister's daughter?"

Bard's hand paused on the edge of the shield. He said he was ready to talk, but how did he give voice to the suspicions that had been swirling inside his head ever since Brighid arrived?

And how did he speak of Kalla? Just the mention of her name stirred up a hornet's nest of feelings and memories, leaving a physical ache in his chest. She had been a wild thing. Laughing, dancing, singing, without a care in the world. That careless, passionate life had led to many conflicts between her and their parents. Despite her lack of the Vilrik, as firstborn, Kalla was destined to be leader of the Bear Clan someday. But she desired neither the position nor the responsibility, and she constantly bucked against their father.

Then came the first of many bitter winters, bringing a terrible blizzard and a contingent of Rylander soldiers.

"Bard?"

He let out a sigh and turned. He walked toward the fire and hunched down across from Heming, then held his hands toward the flames. The fire felt hot, but his skin was cold. "I won't deny the thought has passed through my mind many times." He shook his head. "But how would that have happened? And where is Kalla now?"

"Did Brighid say who her mother is?"

"Her adoptive mother was clanless. A midwife named Elphsaba who lived with our clan a long time ago."

"I see."

Both men sat silently around the firepit. Unease stirred inside Bard. Yes, he had wondered about Brighid when she first arrived, and he couldn't shake how much she looked like his lost sister. But her personality and behavior were so completely opposite of Kalla's that he had suppressed his suspicions. Now they stirred again. He ran a thumb along his bottom lip. Could Heming be right? "Bolva."

"What?" Heming glanced over at him.

"You're making me think now." He brought his hand away. "Not only does Brighid fight like our warriors but she possesses the Vilrik. I tested her the first day we sparred."

"I wondered if you did," Heming said.

"Not just that," Bard continued. "It might even be stronger than my own."

Heming's head snapped up. "What?"

"I will need to work with her more to see if that is true. But the power I felt that day reminded me of Father's."

"Hjar Gurmund's?"

"Yes."

Heming muttered some exclamation.

"And the bear that brought Brighid to us responded to the ancient language. Not every bear does that. Only those with a connection to our people."

Heming shook his head. "How is that possible for a young clanless woman? Unless she is not clanless . . ."

The fire snapped and crackled, the only sound in the silence.

"Bard, I know your faith is in the Word and not the gods of our ancestors, but either way, I think someone—or something—brought her to us. And given what we know of Brighid, I think she is of your blood—and Hjar Gurmund's and Ana's."

For a moment, Bard froze at Heming's words. All this time, these thoughts had swirled deep inside his soul, but to hear them spoken aloud by a friend released something inside him. A moment of dizziness took him and his chest tightened. Then the dam broke loose.

Wetness coated his eyes, and he clenched his hand as waves of emotions rolled over him. "My sister," he whispered. Could she have been restored to them through her child? The possibility was there. No, more than that. He felt the truth like an anchor in his soul. Yes, he believed it was possible that Brighid was his sister's daughter.

His . . . niece.

Another wave rolled over him at that thought and he hunched over. His family had lost so much over the years: the disappearance of Kalla, the death of his wife and newborn son, the bitter winters, and now a war that took their warriors.

Could this really be?

"I miss her, Heming," Bard said after regaining control over his emotions. "I miss so many who have passed over the veil. I always wondered what kind of person Kalla would have become. Would life have tempered the fire inside her? Shaped that unbridled flame into a strong, burning influence for our people?" He shook his head. "We will never know." He bowed as his heart lingered on the others. "So many things we will never know."

"So you believe it to be true?"

Bard swallowed. "I do. Perhaps in His vast mercy, the Word has brought Kalla back to us."

"Will you speak to your mother?"

"Yes. I'm sure she believes this as well. And as painful as it will be for her to speak of Kalla, this might be the very thing to help her heal. To see that Kalla left something beautiful behind. A legacy for us. A hope for our future."

Heming stood and walked around the fire. He placed a hand on Bard's shoulder. "Your mother is a strong woman. Although revisiting the past will hurt, I believe this knowledge will ultimately bring healing. Go to her, my friend. You've all suffered long enough."

Bard pushed off the ground and stood. Yes, it was time to share his thoughts with his mother. Then they could both share the news with his father. Orest could be blunt sometimes, like a bear in a tiny cabin, but this time his unchecked words might have presented a hidden gift to their family.

Maybe someday he would be able to thank his uncle.

24

It wasn't until evening that Bard was able to find his mother alone. Well, not quite alone. Orest was there, too, sitting by the firepit within their family's rooms off the main hall. The two conversed quietly as his mother rested for once. Given her peaceful voice and relaxed posture, Orest hadn't said anything about Kalla. Good, at least his uncle had followed that part of his advice.

At his entrance, Orest looked up. "Ah, Bard, my boy. Joining us by the fire?"

His mother glanced over her shoulder and smiled at him. "Yes, come join us."

Bard walked toward the stairs that led into the loft and retrieved a chair. He pulled it toward the fire, then sat down. His pulse quickened. All day he was certain about this conversation, but now that he was ready to share, he hesitated.

He looked around the room. Signs of generations of the Bear Clan hung from the walls and rafters in the firelight. Painted shields depicting battles, tapestries of bears, mountains, and snow. A single shelf with a thick rolled parchment containing the birth and death of Gurmund's lineage. His gaze lingered on the last. A lineage that most likely held a new member. It was time to share.

Bard took in a deep breath and began. "Do you remember when Brighid first arrived?"

Ana spoke. "You mean amid that blizzard during harvest?"

"Yes. What were your thoughts at that time?"

His mother settled in her chair, but there was a rigidness to her posture. He could already tell she suspected his purpose in asking. He swallowed and clenched his hands together.

Ana let out her breath. "That she looked like Kalla."

"Yes."

"Are you saying there is more?"

Bard turned his attention to the fire. "I had her spar with a few of our warriors a while ago. Then I sparred with her. I believe she possesses our Vilrik."

Ana blinked. "Some of our berserkers have the same fighting spirit. Are you saying there is Bear Clan blood flowing through her?"

"Yes . . . and more. It is powerful in her. It not only gives her strength, but it also possesses her." He looked at her. "Like it does me. And Father."

Orest perked up. "You mean she falls into that—how did Gurmund describe it? Red fog?"

"Yes."

His mother's face tightened. "What are you saying, Bard?"

Now came the hard part. He leaned forward. "What if Kalla was with child when she disappeared?"

Ana slammed her hand down on the arm of her chair. "That's not possible! She was promised, but the bonding never took place."

"Mother, you know she was fascinated by those Rylanders who stayed with us that winter."

His mother's nostrils flared. "She wouldn't do that."

"We both know Kalla was wild and stubborn."

"She was many things!" Ana shouted.

Orest sat back and folded his hands on his lap, a concerned look on his face. "Ana, you could no more restrain Kalla than you could a winter storm. You know that is what I loved about my niece."

"I know. But still . . ."

Bard pressed forward. "It's possible, if Kalla got it in her mind and she loved one of those Rylander men, she would follow him."

"No!" Ana shook her head vigorously. "No, it can't be. She wouldn't leave our family. I know we had our fights, but she wouldn't leave us . . ." Tears sparkled in her eyes as she looked up. "Would she?"

Bard swallowed the lump in his throat. "I'm so sorry," he whispered, his heart breaking at her agitation. "I didn't want to bring up bad memories. But I needed to say something."

Ana shook her head again. "No, I'm sorry. I shouldn't have reacted like that. I just . . . I just . . ." She ran a hand down her face. "We loved her. Perhaps we indulged her too much. Should have said no . . ."

Bard reached over and placed his fingers over the top of his mother's. "Kalla was like the wind, coming and going. Soft as a breeze and wild like a tempest. You loved her, you did your best. I saw."

"You were six years younger than her. Still a child. How can you say we did our best?"

Bard gave her a soft smile. "Mother, I was just becoming a man. Don't underestimate what a child can see and feel. You and father always loved us. You guided her the best you knew how."

"Bard's right," Orest said softly. Bard glanced over. This was one of those rare moments his rough and gruff uncle was showing his softer side. A side that only came out for his sister.

A tear trickled down her weathered cheek, twinkling in the firelight. "Sometimes I wonder how Kalla didn't possess the bear spirit. She was so strong and independent."

"She didn't need the Vilrik to be strong. But perhaps it was passed on to her daughter." There. Bard was able to bring the conversation back around.

His mother grew silent. The fire popped and cracked. Outside, the wind howled as a winter storm blew in. "I'll admit, I had my suspicions. You know that. I said it the first day Brighid arrived. But I couldn't accept it. So I buried it. Believed that she was really a clanless young woman who perhaps had inherited the Bear Clan blood from a distant relative. But now . . ."

Bard waited, letting his mother sift through her thoughts. When it had been quiet long enough, he spoke up. "We may never truly know, not if Brighid doesn't know who her own mother was. But I know her Vilrik is strong. And I'm going to test her another way. I'm going to call for the bear that brought her to our village. He seemed to have a connection to her."

"It might just be her connection to the Bear Clan that caused the bear to bring her to us."

"I want to know for certain. I want to see if there is something more. And if there is—if there is an unseen connection between them—I think we need to consider the possibility that Brighid might be part of our family. There would be too many coincidences to say otherwise."

Ana stared into the fire. Bard watched her face, but she betrayed none of her thoughts or feelings. He went to remove his hand, but she snatched his fingers. "You're right," she whispered. Her face softened. "There would be too many coincidences. Her Vilrik, her bonding with a bear, and her appearance." More tears shone in her eyes. "She looks like Kalla, doesn't she?"

"Yes, she does," Bard said softly.

"I like Brighid. If she really is part our family, it would be almost like receiving Kalla back. I wonder why Elphsaba never told us."

"It was a long time ago," Bard said. "Kalla was a young woman then. And you know she chose not to have a Mark of Remembrance for our clan. How would this Elphsaba have known she was our family?"

Ana sighed. "That is true. And I'm not ignorant of how many young women find themselves with child outside of bonding. I just never thought . . ." her voice trailed off.

Bard nodded. He knew how much Kalla's disappearance ripped the hearts out of his parents and left questions behind. But he also knew they would be strong enough to accept Brighid and not compare her to Kalla. To let Brighid be herself. Because as much as she looked like Kalla, she was different. If Kalla was summer, Brighid was winter. Opposites. And yet an undertone of similarity.

"When are you going to call the bear?" Ana asked, finally withdrawing her hand.

He glanced at the rafters as another wind shook the longhouse. "After this storm. If she really does have a bond, I want to start training her in the ways of the bear, not just her Vilrik, but with her companion as well."

"I will await your conclusion."

Bard stood. "I'll let you rest now." He leaned down and kissed her forehead. "Sleep well, Mother."

"Sleep well, my son."

"Good night, Uncle."

"Good night, Bard. I will keep watch over your mother."

Bard nodded. He had been the one to open old wounds. It was good his uncle would be there to comfort his mother. Then he turned and headed for his own room, leaving his mother to ponder beside the firepit.

25

"Hjar Gurmund, a letter arrived for you early this morning."

Gurmund looked up from the table, his bowl of gruel still cooling, and held out his hand. The messenger gave him a small folded piece of parchment stamped with the crest of the bear in wax. "Thank you, Alfar."

"The falcon also had this attached to his leg." Alfar handed over a small pouch.

Gurmund let out a sigh. Ana's herbs. His body had been aching ever since the Battle of the Plains. *Thank you, my love.* He tucked the pouch into his inner tunic. "You are dismissed."

The young man bowed and left the hall.

Gurmund turned the tightly folded parchment over in his hand. He had sent a letter home the moment they arrived in Dallam Fortress. There were still traces of Ryland influence around the place: the deep blue banners that currently hung from the rafters above the common room, the food supplies of southern wheat and something called sourdough, and tapestries depicting the victories of the White City. Past victories. Now this fortress belonged to Nordica.

Gurmund retrieved the small knife from the sheath at his side and broke the seal. He unfolded the parchment and found the familiar, strong, and firm handwriting of his wife. Emotions swelled in his chest. Lands, he missed her.

As he read, a frown crept across his face.

A young woman arrived at our gates near the beginning of winter. She was injured and sick, so Bard brought her in. As I attended her, I discovered she was one of the warriors who fought down south but was captured, then escaped during what she called the Battle of the Plains. I don't know how she made it all the way to our border, especially with the strange snowstorm that swept the wastelands shortly before her arrival.

I don't believe she is a deserter. When I questioned her, she spoke of those strange beings who bestowed power on the Nordic forces by their words. However, she also told me of what happened to those who were captured during the Battle of the Plains, and how they died.

Gurmund, the south didn't put to death the Nordic prisoners of war. Their own oaths killed them. She barely lived through the experience. And because of that, she chose to travel here to tell us the truth of what is going on.

Also, another anomaly occurred at her arrival. She appeared at our gates riding a bear . . .

Riding a *what*?

Gurmund stared at his wife's writing, rereading the words again. A young warrior woman. Captured during the Battle of the Great Plains. Escaped to the north after surviving the oath.

And arrived on a bear?

He looked up to see if anyone was watching him. The hall was mostly empty with only a handful of warriors breaking their fasts in the large stone room. A chill hung in the corners, while the fire ahead provided some warmth against the deep winter cold.

He quickly read the letter a second and third time, then sat back and stared at the fire that burned nearby. "Curse Armand," he whispered. "Curse him and his oath from the Abyss." A small part of him had hoped those captured during the Battle of the Plains were still alive and that there would be an opportunity to get their comrades back. The south usually didn't execute their prisoners. But if what Ana wrote was true, then their own allies had killed them.

A sickening feeling filled his middle. He lost a handful of warriors last spring before they marched to war. Good fighters who no longer wanted to be bound by Armand's oath. Instead of being freed, their oath sent them into convulsions. At the time, he thought their deaths had been a warning to keep his warriors in line. Only now to realize every single Nordic who had taken the oath was infected by the same deathly words.

What do we do? He leaned forward and held his face in his hands. *Ana, I wish you were here right now. I could use your wisdom.* After a moment, he lifted his head and stood, his gruel now cold in his bowl. Stein would chastise him again for not eating, but he had no appetite.

The evening before had brought more snow, covering Dallam in another layer of white. Gurmund usually didn't mind winter. It was part of the cycle of the north. But winter usually meant time around the firepit, exchanging stories, warm food made by his wife, and much-needed rest from the months before.

Here, winter was cold and barren. The fortress had little to offer for warmth of the soul. He could see it in the eyes of the warriors stationed with him: the Bear Clan, Stag Clan, and even the Owl Clan who hailed from the Keshmin Mountains. The only ones who didn't seem fazed were the clanless. Something told him they were used to bleak winters.

"We need to do better," he muttered as he walked out into the dark stone hallway. "When this war is over, we need to find a way to take better care of all our people."

As he headed toward the training room, he passed others who were wintering in Dallam.

"Hjar Gurmund," an Eagle Clan warrior said with a dip of his head.

"Morning," Gurmund replied.

He approached the training room when a commotion filled the hallway. He turned around and stared down the long corridor. The noise grew louder.

"What in the Lands?" He started back. The sound seemed to come from the front doors. He heard a woman's voice and his stomach dropped. Viessa, Armand's comrade. What was she doing here?

He approached the massive front doors as they closed, but not before a flurry of snow made its way into the wide entrance hall. Flames flickered in the sconces before settling into a steady burn.

Viessa stood in the middle of the stone corridor, her hood pulled over her head, surrounded by a handful of Wolf Clan warriors and a few clanless. Her voice rose over the din. "Where is he? Where is Hjar Gurmund? I thought he would have greeted me on my arrival."

"I'm here," Gurmund answered, standing in the doorway of the corridor, his arms folded over his chest. "But I never received word that you were coming to Dallam."

She turned and pulled back her hood. Dark, straight hair pooled over her shoulder, with that one white stripe following the side of her face. Her eyes and lips were edged in black, giving her a grim appearance. He wondered for a moment if that was her intention.

"What do you mean you never received word?" The warriors parted to let her through. "I had a falcon sent weeks ago."

Gurmund shook his head. "Never arrived."

Her face grew hard. "I will have to see who was in charge of that message." Then her face relaxed and she smiled. It reminded Gurmund of a cat. "I've been with Hjar Volka, Hjar Adrian, and Armand. Plans for spring are already being discussed. I am here because we will be overseeing the northwest. Specifically, we are looking at Stelriden Fortress."

Gurmund dug his fingers into the fleshy part of his arms. "You discussed spring battle plans without all the hjars present?"

"How else? You are all scattered."

"That is not how we do things." His gaze fell on the warriors around them, and he let out his breath. "Come, such discussions do not belong on the doorstep. Follow me."

Stelriden Fortress. The Ryland Plains bastion that stood at the entrance to Rokr Valley and Nordica. His own clan stronghold stood at the northern end of the valley. Despite Rylanders crossing the ancient boundary over the last few years, neither his warriors nor their soldiers had clashed. There was an unspoken agreement between them, one of peace. Well, that peace was broken now with the war.

His boots clapped against the cold stone floor, and he heard Viessa and her entourage from the Wolf Clan following him. He bypassed the main hall and headed toward a smaller room that had been used by the Ryland officers before the Nordics took over.

Gurmund entered the room first and headed for the fireplace. The fire had burned down so he tended it, placing a few logs on the embers and coaxing the flame back. A table was set in the middle with a handful of wood chairs. A map of the Lands hung on the wall to the right, and a collection of papers left by the previous occupants were rolled and stored in the cubicle shelving. Two windows let in cool grey light, causing the room to feel cold and gloomy.

Behind him, Viessa instructed those with her to wait out in the corridor. The flames took to the logs and Gurmund stood. Viessa's presence felt as cool as the stone walls around him. He had a feeling they regarded each other the same: with stony indifference.

"Come, sit by the fire." Gurmund pulled one of the chairs near the fireplace. "I'm sure your journey was long and cold."

Viessa made her way around the main table as he brought another chair to the fire and sat down. He folded his arms over his chest. "Now, tell me about this plan that was made in my absence."

He was sure he saw Viessa bristle before she swept down into the other chair. "As you know, Stelriden Fortress is the only stronghold we don't control along the northern Ari Mountains. Once we have that, we will control everything along the border between Nordica and the south. We would have taken it sooner, but time did not allow us to secure everything we desired before winter."

Gurmund nodded slowly. Since they chose to attack Mistcairn and Dallam first, then secure the Onyx River, the fortress had been left alone. Not that the hjars had been worried. Gurmund was able to use the fortress as an excuse to hold his son and a contingent of his warriors back. To keep the fortress and boundary in check. And secretly keep them away from Armand and his oath.

Viessa kept her fingers curled within the sleeves of her robe. "I will winter here and take care of the few small villages between Dallam and Stelriden as the snow permits. When spring comes and the threat of winter is gone, I will lead the warriors to Stelriden."

"You? You will lead the group?" Gurmund flared his nostrils. "It is the *hjars* of the clans who lead our warriors, not an outsider."

"You and your Bear Clan will be needed south. Volka has already sent a few of his warriors under my command. And his skal, Hauss, will bring more when spring comes."

"Hjar Volka decided this, did he?" Gurmund gritted his teeth. "Did Hjar Adrian say anything?"

"He agreed."

Bolva! What was Adrian thinking? Or was he? Gurmund clenched his hand. He had a feeling it was a bad idea to let Adrian and Volka winter together. More and more, Volka was overstepping Adrian's authority as head of the council. Was it because Adrian was intimidated by the Wolf Clan leader? No, he hadn't been before, despite how easygoing Adrian was. He froze. Was there a chance Armand had put Adrian under an oath?

Was that possible?

A chill traveled down his spine, despite the warmth from the fire nearby. Could Armand whisper a vow and bind the hjars? From what he knew, the vow needed to be spoken and bound. But was there a way Armand could work around the agreement of the oath?

"Hjar Gurmund?"

Gurmund looked up to find Viessa studying him. "Thinking," he grunted.

"Of course, if you want to send some of your warriors with me, I would gladly use them."

Gurmund paused at her words and stared at her. *Never.*

But . . .

Was there a way to utilize Bard and keep an eye on Viessa?

"I could maybe send my son," Gurmund said after a moment. "Our stronghold is three days' hard ride north of Stelriden. Despite the war, neither side has engaged in battle."

Viessa turned her head. "Why is that?"

"I did not leave enough warriors to take a place like Stelriden. My son's duty was to keep the border and alert us to any troop movement in the north. What good is it to secure land here in the south, only to lose our home in the north?"

"That makes sense," Viessa murmured. "But once we take Stelriden, your son will no longer need to patrol the border. He can guard the north from the fortress."

"I will ask him in my next correspondence," Gurmund replied.

Maybe it was time to start making plans of his own. What those were, he wasn't sure yet. All he knew was the longer his people were under the thrall of Armand, the more would die. It wouldn't matter who won this bloody war if there were no Nordic people left.

But he—and anyone who joined him—would have to move very carefully so as not to rouse the suspicions of Armand and his companions.

Gurmund sighed and stared into the fire. Covert fights were not his specialty. That was for the Owl Clan.

But an old man could learn . . . if it meant saving his people.

26

Brighid hung the practice sword on the rack, then carefully placed the shield against the wall nearby. The training room felt warm and stifling, with the firepit burning bright behind her and the other warriors recovering from a full morning of exercise. Sweat trickled down her face, and her tunic stuck to her body. Maybe she would find a bucket of water and sponge off the sweat.

As she turned around, her stomach growled, reminding her she hadn't eaten since the first meal of the day. Brighid pressed a hand to her middle.

Vigi stopped talking to his brother a couple feet away and looked over. "Built up an appetite, eh?" he asked with a grin.

"Yes."

"There's smoked venison and cheese in the main hall."

"Thanks, I think I'll head that way."

Nora and Arngrim were arguing in the corner. They had sparred again today and Nora won, but she didn't believe Arngrim gave it his all. Brighid chuckled. Even she could tell there was something between them. Then she sobered as she approached the door. Their banter reminded her of Johan and Marta.

A dull ache filled her chest. She missed them. She missed the other clanless warriors. She even missed fighting. Not the killing and the blood, but the euphoria of rushing into battle with her comrades beside her and the red haze taking over, freeing her to fight.

Yes, she was safe here, and sparring helped a little. But it left a restlessness within her soul. Her hands craved more.

She grabbed her cloak from the peg, swept it over her shoulders, and left.

Outside, grey clouds filled the sky, threatening to cover the already existing mounds of white piled high along the stone and wooden buildings. Even the air smelled cold and crisp. Brighid breathed it in and felt her body finally cooling from the sparring.

This winter was different from the others she had faced in Ragnbork. No endless coughing, no shivering children in the shadows, no disease running rampant through the streets.

She swallowed. No icy chill as death flew by, reaping souls along the way.

She hadn't felt death since she had survived Armand's oathbinding, other than briefly before she passed out in the snow and arrived here. If she returned to the war, what would the battlefield be like with this feeling?

Would it paralyze her?

A figure came alongside her. "Hjaren Bard," Brighid said quickly, dispersing the darker thoughts from moments before. "I did not hear you approach."

"You seemed deep in thought. Care to share?"

She shook her head.

"Ah, I see. Not pleasant thoughts."

Brighid didn't respond. When they reached the main hall, Bard held the door open. Brighid entered, then stopped, trying to remember why she came.

"Food, I suspect," Bard said, seeming to read her mind.

Her stomach growled again in confirmation. They headed for the side table, where chunks of dried meat, rounds of cheese, and a barrel of watered down ale awaited those who needed something midday.

"How much do you remember of the day you arrived here at our stronghold?" Bard asked as he grabbed some venison.

Brighid looked up, surprised by his question. "Not much. I was barely conscious."

"Do you remember how you arrived?"

Brighid paused, her hand above the dried meat. "I recall you saying a bear carried me." She grabbed a piece of venison and tore into it.

"But do *you* remember?"

She chewed some more. Memories of snow, heat, and a dog bite filled her mind. A fever and darkness, and how she was determined to crawl to Nordica if she had to.

Brighid swallowed the food. "I never saw the bear," she said. "I was delusional from my leg injury. And it was dark. All I remember was a large beast coming upon me. I thought it was going to kill me, but it didn't. For some reason I took a chance and climbed onto its back and held on. And it brought me here."

Bard nodded slowly. "Yes. That is how we found you. Astride a large bear. Since then, I have wondered if there is Bear Clan blood flowing in your veins."

"*What?*" Brighid whirled around. "I can't be. I'm clanless. I always have been."

"That is not the normal behavior of a bear. But for some reason, he reacted to you. He sensed you—and the danger you were in—and he brought you to us. He felt the connection of our clan inside you."

"That . . . can't be right." Brighid turned toward to the table and placed both hands on the edge to keep her balance. "Are you sure the bear wasn't just rescuing someone within your lands?"

"I'm certain. Even some of those within our clan cannot connect with a bear. It is a gift we believe was given to us a long time ago. A gift within our blood. A gift I believe saved you."

The meat churned in her middle. Elphsaba said her father was a Rylander but had no idea who her mother was. Was it possible her mother came from the Bear Clan?

Brighid rubbed the side of her head. Given she was born in the Wastelands—their jurisdiction—perhaps it *was* a possibility. An illegitimate child born to a Bear Clan member. She glanced at Bard. What would they think of someone like that?

"What would you say to meeting that bear again?"

Brighid stood still. Why was Hjaren Bard telling her this now? Did it have to do with what Orest said a few mornings ago? Did it have something to do with this Kalla? "Is it possible?" she asked.

"I can try calling for him. The snow isn't so deep that he wouldn't come."

"But wouldn't he be hibernating?"

"I believe your presence has awakened him. He could even be waiting for you now."

That bear was waiting for her?

Emotions tangled inside her. Disbelief and shock at his words. But also a tiny flicker of hope. Could it be possible that she belonged to these people? But what if it all turned out to be a coincidence?

"Yes," she said before fear could take over. "Let us see if this bear comes."

Bard smiled. "Follow me."

Brighid grabbed another piece of dried meat and headed back outside, behind Bard. The two crossed the snow-covered area, bypassing the small log homes where other clan members lived. They passed the training hall, smithy, and enclosures for animals until they reached the gate to the stronghold. A small sloping shed stood next to the gate. Bard opened the door and retrieved what looked like the horn of an animal. "If the bear that brought you is still connected to you, this horn will bring him here."

"How?"

Bard held the horn up. It was the length of his arm, narrow on one end, then opening into a wide circle on the other with four holes along the side. "Our clan has had this horn for many generations. I can't explain exactly why the sound from it calls them, but the bears connected to our clan can hear this and respond."

"But not all bears?"

"No. Most bears are wild. That is why I was surprised at the manner of your arrival. And the bear that bore you was unfamiliar to us. That is also why, for a moment, I wondered if something had changed with our people's connection to bears and if this bear had simply brought you to us. Or as you said, rescued you because you needed help within our lands. But now I think there is something more."

Brighid waited, but Bard didn't elaborate. Instead, he opened the gate. Outside, towering pine trees surrounded the compound, with thick layers of snow piled across the deep green branches. The sky had turned darker, and a few flakes of snow began to fall. He stood in the gateway, took in a deep breath, then blew.

The sound that came from the horn was low, then moved up two pitches. Bard moved his fingers along the holes. The call echoed across the snow-laden forest. Then a moment of silence. A few seconds later, he repeated the sound. Then a third time.

"There." Bard lowered the horn. "Hopefully he heard and will respond."

"How long will it take the bear to reach us?"

"I don't know. It depends on how far he is. There is a chance he stayed close after he left you here, if there really is a connection between the two of you. My own bear, Amro, stays close, although I believe he is hibernating nearby for the winter."

They waited. Brighid pulled the hood of her cloak over her head. The sweat from earlier had cooled across her skin, but she wasn't cold. A wind blew through the pines in a soft, gentle way. Then a dark figure appeared deep in the forest.

From the corner of her eye, she saw Bard's face lift slightly with an expectant look. The figure lumbered toward them through the snow. A half minute later and the dark shape took form. A bear. Bard's face brightened even more. When the bear broke past the last line of trees near the compound, Bard spoke.

"There he is," he said softly. "The bear that brought you to us."

The creature was massive, with a glint of silver along the tips of his fur. Deep black eyes stared back at them. Then he lifted his snout and sniffed.

"What do I do?" Brighid whispered.

"Greet him."

Brighid hesitated, then stepped past the gate. Her gaze never left the bear. He lowered his head and his gaze was set on her. There was something . . . familiar . . . about the majestic beast. A sudden kindling in her soul, as if a part of her had been lost, and now she could see what had been missing.

Halfway across the space between them, she lifted her hand. At the movement, the bear lifted his head. He was beautiful and strong, with a keen intelligence in those dark eyes, and the silver sheen across his fur appeared as if he were standing in moonlight.

"My friend," she said before she realized what she was doing. He stepped forward and met her. There was no fear inside her, no hesitancy. She knew this bear. Her hand met his muzzle. "You know me, and I know you."

"How do you know the ancient tongue?" Bard asked.

"What?" Brighid glanced at him.

"You just spoke to him in our tongue. The tongue of the Bear Clan."

The bear nudged her, bringing her attention back to him. "I don't know how, but I know him, and I can speak to him. It's like I've always known him. Bjornfrost."

"Bjornfrost?"

"That is his name."

"He told you this?"

"The name just came to me. But it's his true name." Brighid walked along the side of Bjornfrost, letting her fingers trail through the thick fur along his neck and shoulders. "Thank you, my friend. For rescuing me that day."

Bjornfrost let out a snort as he turned his head toward her. Brighid smiled. "Yes, you found me. You were waiting for me for a long time." There were no words between her and Bjornfrost. Just impressions. Feelings. And knowing they were connected.

"Amazing," Bard said behind her. "This answers one of my questions. Bjornfrost did not rescue you just because you were in our lands. He connected to your blood."

Blood. Was that really possible? Brighid stroked his fur. Everything still felt unreal. "All I know is we are meant to be together."

"Then I will teach you."

Brighid glanced back again. "Teach me?"

"How to ride, speak, and fight alongside your bear." Bard's gaze returned to Bjornfrost with a look of admiration. "I will teach you the way of the Bear Clan. But for now, strengthen your bond with Bjornfrost."

"How?"

"Spend time with him. Commune with him. Get to know each other."

Brighid turned again to Bjornfrost. He watched her, and suddenly she knew what she wanted to do. She spoke words she had never heard, but they came to her, and Bjornfrost lowered himself at her command. She took a deep breath, then gripped the fur along his shoulder and heaved her way up. She settled along his back, her legs barely reaching his sides, then gave another command in the same strange language. He rose in one swift motion. She followed his movement, keeping herself steady with her hands deep in his fur.

"You really do know our language," Bard said in awe.

"I don't know how, but the words came to me."

"That is how the ancient tongue works. It awakens in the soul the moment we connect with our bear."

A smile spread across Brighid's face as she sat upon Bjornfrost. A fiery joy filled her chest. She leaned toward his head and whispered, "Let's go."

Bjornfrost let out a roar and turned. She could feel his muscles tightening in preparation as he twisted, then he burst through the snow and into the forest. They ran between the trees, Brighid staying in motion with the loping of his gait. Snow fell across them, melting at the heat of their bodies, and the powder sprayed up into the air at the pounding of his paws. A flock of crows took flight into the grey sky, leaving the evergreens and naked trees empty.

After a few minutes, Bjornfrost turned right and ran for the incline ahead. He climbed the hill, moving swiftly between the trees until he came to a clearing. Then he slowed. Ahead, Brighid spotted a cliff that overlooked the valley below. Carefully, Bjornfrost brought them to the edge and then stopped. The wind blew, sending her hair flying around her face. She felt like she was at the top of the world. Just her and Bjornfrost.

The fire burning inside her flowed from her chest and up her throat, until she lifted her head and let out a great shout. Her voice echoed across the valley. A second later, Bjornfrost followed her lead and let out a roar of his own. Then they roared together.

As their echoes died and silence descended on the land, Brighid heard a stirring behind her. There was no wind, but the pines creaked softly. And then the voice came. Like the deep humming of a man. Bjornfrost lifted his muzzle and sniffed the air.

"Do you hear it too?" Brighid asked.

Bjornfrost continued to sniff the air.

"Word, is that you?" Brighid whispered as she watched the snow fall around her and across the white valley below.

The humming changed into a low rumbling, so low she could barely hear. Then it was swept away as a wind blew across the cliff and over the valley, sending a flurry of snow out over the expanse. The sound from minutes ago had brought a yearning to her heart. It was a yearning she had carried for as long as she could remember, from the moment she first felt death and ran. These sounds, this song, this voice. Had she always heard the Word?

Bjornfrost snorted and shook his head, breaking her reverie. She patted his side. "Ready to return?"

As if in answer, he turned and started for the forest behind them. Instead of running, they took their time returning to the Bear Clan stronghold. Brighid leaned forward and pressed her face into Bjornfrost's fur. A musky, wild scent filled her nostrils. Yes, she remembered him from that night, when heat racked her body and she wasn't sure she would live.

"Thank you," she whispered, both to him and to the voice that was always with her. "Thank you."

Before long, they arrived back at the compound. Bard still stood in the gate's archway. Snow fell in soft white flakes. "How was it?" he asked as they approached.

"Breathtaking," Brighid said, her voice catching in her throat. Beautiful, awe-inspiring, and more words that filled her heart but refused to rise and be said.

Bjornfrost lumbered to a stop a few feet away from Bard. Brighid patted the side of his neck, then slid down his back. The snow gave way under her boots. Bjornfrost nudged her as she walked past him.

"He is a majestic beast," Bard said. "And will fight well beside you."

"So you will teach me how?"

"Yes. I have one more thing to ask of you. I know you've already practiced this morning, but I want to confirm something. Would you meet me in the training room later this afternoon? I wish to spar one more time."

Confirm something? Did it have to do with the possibility that she was part of the Bear Clan? "Yes, I can do that."

"Good. Then I will see you midafternoon. We can also talk about training with Bjornfrost." Bard swiped at the snow that had amassed at the top of his head. "Stay here as long as you like. And before you head inside, bid your bear farewell. He will return to the forest."

Brighid bowed. "Thank you, Hjaren Bard."

Bard frowned for a moment, then his face relaxed. "You are welcome, Brighid."

Brighid wondered at his look before turning back to Bjornfrost. "What do you say, my friend? Shall we take one more ride?"

Bjornfrost lifted his head in answer. A minute later, they returned to the forest.

27

Brighid entered the training room for a second time that day. Low light filtered through the windows, and the flames in the firepit had burned down to glowing embers. The room was warm and smelled of sweat from the previous occupants. Fresh torches flickered, and the practice sword and shield remained where Brighid had placed them that morning—before meeting with Bjornfrost and the revelation of her connection to the bear.

She crossed the room slowly, bypassing the firepit, and gently touched the hilt of the wooden sword. She still couldn't believe it. This connection she had to Bjornfrost. A connection that somehow meant there was Bear Clan blood in her. Blood most likely inherited from her mother.

Bard entered a few seconds behind her. "Good afternoon, Brighid."

Brighid bowed. "Hjaren Bard."

A reaction she couldn't read flickered across his face. "I called you here this afternoon because I have seen something in your fighting style, something I wish to discuss and confirm."

Brighid pulled her hand away from the sword, unease spreading inside her chest. Had he seen it? The times when she sank into the red haze? Was it possible he knew what that was?

Did she want to know?

Bard walked over and chose his weapons, two small axes. "Tell me about your fight style," he said as he turned and began to warm up with the axes.

"Fight style?"

"Yes. What is going on in your mind and body when you fight? Where did you learn to fight? Why the sword and shield?"

"Oh." How much should she share?

Brighid retrieved her own weapons, her heart suddenly thumping hard. She had never told anyone about the red haze. How it covered her vision and guided her body. She swung the sword a few times, then adjusted her hold on the shield.

Tell him.

They weren't audible or distinct words. More of an impression.

Tell him.

Maybe the red haze was also connected to Bjornfrost. And her unique and terrifying fight style was a secret of the Bear Clan.

Brighid paused and swallowed. Then she faced Bard. "I never really learned to fight. It came naturally to me. The first time I fought, I knew exactly what to do."

"Tell me about your first fight."

She took in another breath. "It was on a winter's day. I was surrounded by an eljun. The leader swung at me. I dodged, and then somehow I knew how to fight back. I not only took out the leader, but every member of the eljun."

Bard's eyebrows shot up. "Alone?"

"Yes."

"Is there more?"

Bard knew. He knew her secret.

Brighid looked away, toward the glowing embers in the firepit. "When I fight, I enter a red haze." Her heart pounded. "It's like I'm possessed by a red fog. I neither see nor hear anything. I feel only the fight inside me. And when I am done, I return to myself."

Bard stared at her. "Did my father ever see you fight?"

"Hjar Gurmund? Yes, I believe so. He was at the arena when the clanless battled for a place. I entered the red haze during my trial." Her heart clenched for a moment as she remembered Roldar. "I also saw him many times during the battles."

"Did he ever approach you? Or say anything?"

Brighid shook her head. She also recalled that one time she ran into Hjar Gurmund at the river's edge, when he and the other bear masters came to water their companions.

Bard stared into the fire. Brighid watched his face, noting the reflection of flames in his eyes. "Interesting," he said. "It would seem that not only have you bonded with a bear but you might also possess our Vilrik."

"Vil-what?"

Bard looked up. "Our fighting spirit."

"So this red haze I've experienced—"

"Is called the Vilrik. The bear's strength."

"Vilrik." Brighid tasted the word on her tongue.

"Very few inherit the Vilrik. The last woman to possess it was my great-grandmother."

"Who else has this Vilrik?"

"My grandfather did. Now only my father and myself. And apparently you."

Brighid's chest tightened as a shadow passed over her heart. Only the hjar and hjaren harbored this Vilrik. Was Bard saying what she thought he was saying? No, that couldn't be . . .

Brighid stood. "Shall we fight?" She swung her sword around. "After all, that is why you brought me here, correct?"

"Yes." The faraway look on Bard's face disappeared. "This is why I asked you here. To confirm if you indeed possess the Vilrik."

Brighid swung her sword again. "I will warn you. I can't command the red haze. It comes when it comes."

Bard brought his axes out. "Interesting. It must be powerful to be instinctual. Has there ever been a time when the red haze did not come upon you?"

Brighid thought back. "Yes. There was a time when . . ." Then she faltered, and her sword dropped to her side as heat crawled up her neck. It was when Roldar took her to pressure Havard, the blacksmith. The red haze never came.

Bard raised an eyebrow. "You do not need to share. Our Vilrik is honor-bound. It was given to us to protect our people and fight for what is right. It safeguards both us and our people from being misused."

Brighid looked away. That made sense. What Roldar had demanded of her was not for honor, nor did it protect the Nordic people.

"I know some of your past," Bard said. "And that you were clanless. I know what Ragnbork can be like for the clanless. How hard life is in that district."

Brighid snapped her head around. "If you knew, why didn't you do anything about it?"

He paused and a shadow of hurt crossed his face. "For a long time, the clans have been attached to their narrow way of thinking. Including myself. It wasn't until I visited Ragnbork and saw how the clanless were treated—our own people—that I realized how wrong we were. Ever since then, I have fought to change our ways. But it's an uphill battle, a battle against centuries of prejudice. But if I may, not all of us clansmen are like those in Ragnbork."

Brighid let out her breath. He was right. She and Elphsaba rarely experienced any bias due to their clanless status until they moved to Ragnbork. In fact, Elphsaba was set to marry into the Bear Clan until the man died during a hunt.

Brighid turned toward Bard. "So how do I bring forth this Vilrik by will?" she asked as she readjusted her hold on both the sword and shield.

"By practicing. You said you felt like you were possessed by a red fog when the Vilrik came upon you. It's kind of the same when you control it, but you remain aware. Think of how it feels when you sink beneath the warm waters of a wash tub. How you are surrounded by warm water. But you can still see and hear to some extent. That's what a controlled Vilrik feels like."

"So I'll be able to see through the red haze?"

"Yes. When I enter the Vilrik, there is a dim red fog, but I can still see and am conscious of everything around me. I can also hear, but it's like hearing through rushing water. The Vilrik is a powerful force, but with practice and time, it will come under your control."

"How do you enter it?"

"It's like an emotion. I feel it first, rising inside me. But before it takes possession of me, I hold it back. Like holding back my anger. Then I channel it. Same with anger."

Brighid frowned. "You can channel anger?"

"Of course. If I let my anger control me, I would end up hurting others. Instead, I hold it back, and if the cause of my anger is just, I channel it to bring about good. Anger over injustice and seeing innocent people hurt is not bad. But it must be directed, not allowed to run free."

Brighid nodded slowly. That made sense.

"However, our Vilrik will not ignite if it is not honor-bound or in service to our people, so unlike anger, we do not have to worry about it being out of control."

"If that's the case, why control it? Is it not better to let it run its course?"

"Which is more powerful? A raging, untrained warrior, or one who knows how to wield his weapon with a clear and steady mind?"

"The second."

"So it is with the Vilrik. Now, let me teach you. First, we need to bring it forth. Usually this would happen on the battlefield or during a confrontation, but we are training, so we will rely on memories. Close your eyes and picture a memory that triggered the Vilrik for you."

There was a hint of fear inside Brighid as she shut her eyes. What if the red haze came upon her and—despite what Bard said—she couldn't control it?

"I'm here," Bard said softly, as if answering her question. "Your brow is furrowed, so I can tell you are anxious. I won't let go of you."

Brighid nodded.

"Now, replay the memory. Let yourself sink into the feelings and images."

Brighid brought forth memories, remembering, then discarding each one as they came. The first time the red haze came upon her, she was ambushed after stealing bread. Fighting with the eljun. The night Roldar had been drinking and tried to make her stay. The arena when she fought Roldar with sword and shield. His taunting, and the sudden ignition of fury inside her—

She squeezed her eyes shut tighter. *No, I don't want to remember that.* But she couldn't stop that particular memory, and she saw Roldar lying on the ground, choking on his own blood. "No! Not that!"

"What? What are you remembering?"

Brighid opened her eyes to see Bard staring her. She quickly shook her head.

"You killed someone."

Her throat went dry at his words.

"And it was the first time."

She worked her mouth. "Yes," she whispered.

"Part of fighting under the Vilrik is to bring death to others."

"I know. I fought in the war. I killed many."

"But the first time is the hardest. Especially if you weren't trained in the Vilrik, and you feel like you lost control."

"I didn't mean to."

Bard smiled sadly. "I'm sure you didn't. That is why there is awe and fear for our clan and our power. You didn't have family to help you or train you. And life is both resilient and fragile. One inch and what would have been a simple injury can become a deathblow. Sometimes we can't control that."

He was right. She'd hit Roldar at the right place with the right amount of force to . . . to kill him. But it was never her intention. And even then, she had never been out of control.

Brighid breathed in deeply and, with the air she blew out, she let that memory go as well. Finally, she landed on a memory she could use: when she was fighting for all she was worth to protect Johan and Marta.

Yes, this one. She closed her eyes. It fulfilled everything Bard said about fighting for honor and for the Nordic people. She remembered the heat and sweat and the yells across the battlefield. The fire that filled her chest when she realized her friends were in danger.

The same heat began to fill her veins again. "I can feel it," Brighid said without opening her eyes.

"Hold on to that memory. And when you are ready, face me."

It took her a moment to feel like she had a hold of her body, then Brighid looked up. The world was red, but she could see. The rush flowed along her veins, across her arms and legs, pumping with every pulse of her heart.

"Let's fight," Bard said.

Brighid dashed toward him, her sword raised and a shout escaping her throat.

Bard met her sword and shield with his axes.

Instead of falling into the red haze, she moved through it, always retaining part of herself.

Bard kept up with her every movement. She could feel the same fighting spirit inside him, this Vilrik.

They clashed again. He caught the edge of her sword with his axe, but she was able to slam her shield into him and throw him off balance.

"You are strong," she heard him say, as if hearing through water.

She answered with a swing of her sword.

The red haze never enveloped her. But it did guide her, allowing her to see openings in less than a second and to take advantage.

Minutes went by. She barely felt the fatigue creeping across her body, or the drip of sweat along her cheek.

Bard hooked her sword again and brought his other axe down on her shield, sending a shudder along her arm and into her body.

"Enough!"

It took a moment for her to register his words. Then the red drained from her mind, sight, and body until she stood in the training room, panting, with her sword and shield hanging limply at her side.

"Very good," Bard said with a smile. He lowered his own axes. "Your instinct for the Vilrik is exceptional. I would think you were trained by how easily you brought it under your command, then banished it."

"What does this mean?" Brighid asked as her body cooled. Bard had said he wanted to confirm something. Had he found what he was looking for? Was it more proof that she was—indeed—part of the Bear Clan?

Bard brought his breathing down. "It means you have Bear Clan blood running through your veins. And more I believe."

"More?"

"Yes. But I would like my mother to be part of that conversation. Would you mind meeting us in her room this evening?"

What did Ana have to do with the possibility that she had Bear Clan blood? "Yes, I can do that," Brighid said.

"Good." There was a hint of emotion in Bard's voice and eyes. "I am—" His voice hitched. He cleared his throat. "I am looking forward to it." He turned around and headed for the weapons rack and hung his axes. Brighid returned her own gear.

"I'll see you tonight," Bard said after dousing the fire. Then he left the training room. Only a single torch remained. Brighid turned and stared at the door where Bard had exited. Thoughts and emotions swept through her like wind through the pine trees. The fact that she could control the red haze, that she was possibly part of these people, and perhaps even more . . .

"Elphsaba," she said quietly. "I might actually know who I am." Her throat tightened. "I just wish you were here to share in these revelations."

Then again, she had always known who she was. Elphsaba's daughter. And nothing would change that.

28

Brighid entered the main hall and turned right. Off to the side was a small room where she stayed with a couple other women, including Tola, who assisted Ana with work around the kitchen and hall. Five beds made of hay and fur. It was rustic, but there was a comforting feel to it. It reminded her a little of the hovel she shared with Elphsaba. Only nicer.

The room was currently empty, and the fire in the firepit had burned down low. A bucket of ice-cold water stood in the corner for washing. Brighid stripped off her outer clothing, then hunched down and splashed the frigid water on her face, flinching at the chill. A rag hung on a nearby peg, still damp from the previous user. She dunked the rag and quickly cleaned the sweat from her skin. Last, she redid her braid. Whatever this meeting was with Bard and his mother, she wanted to look presentable.

Cold from the quick washing, Brighid pulled her tunic on and grabbed Kaeden's old cloak from the top of her bedding and pulled it over her shoulders. She bunched the fabric under her nose and took a deep breath. Why did Bard want her to meet with Ana? She saw the hjar's wife almost every day. Did Bard want her there when he shared her connection with Bjornfrost and her possession of this Vilrik?

How would Ana respond?

A jolt shot through her middle. What if she wasn't happy? Sometimes illegitimate children were seen as worse than clanless. Perhaps in the case of the Bear Clan, clanless was fine, but not illegitimate offspring.

She mentally shook her head. No, that wasn't like Ana. And Bard seemed excited about their discussion this evening.

However, this question continued to plague her mind through dinner that night in the main hall. To make matters worse, Ana was absent. No matter how many times Brighid looked around, she didn't see the older woman.

"Everything all right?" Lodin asked as he came to sit by her. Unlike Vigi, Lodin was quiet and thoughtful. Meanwhile, Vigi sat two tables away, roaring with laughter over something Arngrim must have said.

"Yes," Brighid said without looking his way.

"You're not a very good liar." He dipped his wooden spoon into the venison stew. Brighid turned to him. His dark hair was pulled back, exposing his shaved neck and the bottom contour of his head.

"Do your parents live here at the stronghold?" Brighid asked, curious about the families of the others.

Lodin paused, his spoon halfway to his mouth. "Our mother died in childbirth." He sighed and lowered the spoon. "Unfortunately, it is common. And being twins, our birth was even more difficult."

"I see." Brighid knew only too well how common death was around birthings. It always hovered around both the mother and child, hoping to take a soul with it. "And your father?"

"He died last year when a group of Rylanders crossed the border. They were more bandits than anything, and he caught a stray arrow. The wound became infected and went to his heart."

Brighid looked down into her own untouched stew. "I'm sorry. I shouldn't have asked."

"There is no hurt in asking. Death happens. It is part of life." Lodin took a bite of his stew.

Brighid stared at him for a moment. How could he remain so calm when talking about death? Was there a secret he possessed that she didn't know about? Could she ever be as calm about death as he appeared?

Even when she felt death again?

She wanted to ask. The question made its way to the tip of her tongue, but she stopped. Fear of death was not a desired trait in Nordic society, although that didn't stop some warriors from breaking down in terror on the battlefield. She didn't want to let Lodin know her fear. She was gradually making a name for herself, and it was best to not reveal that.

Instead, she shoved a bite of stew into her mouth and listened to the conversations filling the rest of the hall. Lodin also remained quiet, tucking into his meal. For that, she was thankful.

As she used a piece of flatbread to sop up the remaining broth at the bottom of her bowl, Bard came to stand near her. "Whenever you are ready," he said quietly. "We will both be by the firepit."

Lodin looked questioningly at Bard, then at Brighid, who nodded. She watched Bard cross the hall and leave through the door that led to Hjar Gurmund and Ana's private quarters.

Her stomach tightened as she stared down at the bit of bread soaked in broth, then let it drop back into the bowl. She couldn't eat another bite and was now regretting even coming to dinner.

"Everything all right?" Lodin asked again, a concerned look on his face.

"Oh, yes. Just something Hjaren Bard and Ana want to ask me."

"You're shaking."

Brighid looked down at her hand. Sure enough, her fingers were trembling. *Bolva!* She clenched her hand and placed it down on her lap.

"Is there anything I can do?"

"No." The word came out firmer than she had intended, but she hated that someone was seeing her vulnerable. "But . . . thank you for asking."

Lodin bowed in reply. He went back to eating. Brighid grabbed her bowl and stood. Best to see what this conversation was about. She placed the empty bowl on the side table and made her way across the hall.

Each step brought more thoughts she hadn't pondered. Was it possible they were going to send her back? She had considered returning once winter thawed to find a way to free Johan and Marta.

Or did they want more information on the Shadonae? Brighid frowned as she reached for the door handle. She had shared all she knew. Or . . .

Her gut clenched and she faltered. Perhaps Ana had received word from Hjar Gurmund about Johan and Marta.

No. She shook her head. She swore the look on Bard's face at the end of their sparring session had been one of relief. And seeming happiness. None of these thoughts would cause such a look.

So what could it be?

Fear turned to caution as she entered Ana's living quarters. Three chairs were set around the fire. Ana sat in the nearest one, her back to the door, her silver hair braided around her head. She didn't turn as Brighid entered.

Her middle clenched hard at Ana's lack of response.

Bard stood behind the chair on the left, his hands resting along the backside. He glanced up and motioned toward the empty chair.

The room felt dark and stifling, despite the bright fire burning in the pit and the oil lamps lit around the room. Brighid rounded the chair and took a seat. Ana looked up, and a pained look clouded her face. Brighid sucked in her breath. Maybe Hjar Gurmund had died.

Then she looked at Bard. He returned her glance with a gentle smile. Wrong again.

Bolva! What in the Lands is going on here?

The door opened behind her, causing her to start.

"Well, well." Orest's voice boomed behind her. "Glad I'm not late."

He walked past Brighid and grabbed a chair that was leaning against the wall, then hauled it toward the firepit. The loud scraping filled the room as he shoved it near Brighid and dropped down into the seat with a loud huff. "Time to solve this mystery, eh?" he said, glancing at Bard then at Ana.

Ana looked down at her folded hands. Brighid did a double take. The hjar's wife, who had always appeared strong and capable, suddenly looked small and broken in the firelight. The change shook her.

"What's going on?" Brighid asked, tired of these confusing thoughts. She was never one to hold back in battle, and she wasn't going to hold back here. It was best to get to the point so she could react accordingly.

A single tear ran down Ana's face. Bard moved around the chairs and placed his hands on his mother's shoulders. "Let me share a little of our history with you," he began.

Ana lifted a hand and placed it on Bard's. That touch seemed to give her some strength.

"I had an older sister. She was full of life and passion. And headstrong."

"Stubborn, you mean," Orest said with a laugh.

"Yes. And beautiful. Her name was Kalla."

Kalla. The hair along Brighid's scalp rose at the name. Not long ago, Orest said she resembled this Kalla.

"She disappeared when she was eighteen winters, during the height of summer. We did everything we could to find her. But no trace of her was ever found."

Brighid gripped the arms of the chair, her heart beating faster with each second. "Why are you telling me this?" she asked, although she had a feeling she knew, and the very thought rose like a massive wave about to crash over her.

Ana raised her head and spoke. "You said your mother died during childbirth. Did Elphsaba tell you anything about her when you grew older?"

"A little." Brighid gripped Kaeden's old cloak between her fingers. "She had blue eyes. And no Marks of Remembrance."

Bard sat down in the empty chair while the three of them exchanged looks.

"And your father?" Bard pressed gently as he turned his attention back to her.

She gripped the cloth even tighter. This was it. Another dirty secret of hers. "He was . . . a Rylander. A Rylander captain."

At her words, Ana looked stricken. Bard let out a long sigh and glanced away. Orest nodded to himself. Her words seemed to mean something to the three of them.

"Well," Orest said seconds later. "I think that pretty much confirms what we thought."

Ana's head jerked up. "Orest!" she snapped.

"Come on, sister. The truth is staring at you plain as day."

Bard intervened. "Brighid, for a while now we have wondered if—" He took a deep breath. "We wondered if you might be my sister's daughter."

Brighid froze. Numbness took hold of her, like a protective shield from these words that now pounded across her heart and mind, threatening to shatter everything she had known about her life.

"It would explain many things," Bard continued. "When you first arrived, both my mother and I were struck by how much you look like Kalla. And you were delivered to us by a bear. I considered these all coincidences because every time we remembered Kalla—and her disappearance—it hurt."

Ana nodded but didn't say anything.

"Then I saw the Vilrik in you the day we first sparred. I still denied the possibility until Orest arrived and said what had been lurking in the back of my mind all winter: that there was something more to you." Bard leaned forward. "You see, only those with a direct blood connection to the hjar possess the Vilrik *and* a connection to the bear."

Brighid took in a deep breath. "And I have both."

"Yes. That is what I wanted to confirm today. Your story also seems to match many things about my sister's disappearance. How old are you?"

"Nineteen winters."

"Kalla disappeared twenty years ago. You are the right age to be her child. And the winter before her disappearance, we housed a dozen Ryland soldiers and captains. She was enamored by them, particularly one. Given her free spirit, she may have followed her lover when she discovered she was pregnant."

"But why wouldn't she have told you?" Brighid asked. The more she learned about this Kalla, the more she wasn't sure she liked the young woman. They seemed opposite in nature.

This time, Ana spoke. "Because my daughter was promised to another. A good, strong man from one of our main families. But when Kalla set her mind to something, nothing could stop her. In that way, she truly was the epitome of the bear spirit."

"That she was," Orest said softly, with a fond look on his grizzled face.

Brighid scowled. "So she would just run away?" No, she didn't like Kalla. Why would someone leave their family and clan, especially one like this?

"You must understand, for the longest time we had no idea what happened to her," Bard said. "One day Kalla was here, the next she was gone. For the first few days we thought she needed some time to cool off. My father and sister butted heads like the mountain elk in the fall. It wasn't the first time she'd gone off into the woods and returned later. But as time went on, and she didn't come back, my father sent out search parties. Nothing was found. Not a trace. Not even a whisper. I don't know where Kalla went that summer or fall. By winter, well . . ." Bard ran a hand through his short hair. "We thought she was dead. Or long gone."

Ana slowly shook her head. "It never occurred to me she might be pregnant, or trying to find the Ryland captain she loved—"

"Which we now believe is what happened."

"When were you born?" Orest asked.

Brighid glanced over at the older man. He looked like a true mountain man, with his unkempt beard, speckled grey hair down to his chest, and a gaunt look from living lean in the wilderness. His eyes and nose, however, were exactly like Ana's. "Winter."

The three of them looked at each other again.

"Everything adds up," Orest said. "Brighid even said her father was a Ryland captain. Do you know his name?" he asked, glancing at her.

Brighid shook her head. "No—wait. Elphsaba said the day I was born he arrived in his Ryland regimentals. And that he was tall, with dark hair, and a scar through his left eye."

Bard sat up. "It's him. The one Kalla was fond of in particular. I remember that scar. Tallest out of the group stuck here that winter. With thick, dark hair. Markus was his name."

Markus. Brighid turned the name over in her mind. Years back, when she wanted to know more about her parents, she had sometimes imagined their names and who they were. Then, when Elphsaba shared the bitter truth with her, they faded from her mind. Until now. Now she had their names. Like Bard said, there were too many coincidences. She was sure these strangers were her parents. This wild woman named Kalla. And a Ryland captain named Markus.

One died, one left. Both abandoned her.

The same torrent of feelings she felt that night Elphsaba broke the story to her began to swell inside her, rushing past her numb state.

"But Gurmund contacted Markus at Stelriden Fortress," Ana said. "And he knew nothing about Kalla's disappearance."

"That was shortly after she disappeared, Mother. Perhaps Kalla had not reached him yet."

"Then do we know if Kalla ever did? And if she did, why didn't Markus tell us?" She gripped her dress. "Still, so many questions."

"My father didn't want me."

All eyes turned toward Brighid.

"On the day I was born, Elphsaba told me my mother died and my father left me. Perhaps this Markus never told you because he didn't want to take responsibility."

Ana looked stricken in the firelight. "Oh, my sweet girl," she whispered. "If you believe you were never wanted, it was because we didn't know you existed."

"To the Abyss with that man," Bard seethed. "He could have at least told us he knew what happened to Kalla. Or that she had given birth."

"Do you know if he is still alive?" Orest asked.

Bard shook his head. "No. All communication ceased shortly after that winter, when the Ryland people started invading our lands. Stelriden Fortress refused to speak to us."

Ana stared at Brighid. "I'm so sorry you grew up clanless. I can only imagine what life was like." A tear rolled down her cheek. "All this time, I had a granddaughter—" Her voice caught, and she quickly rubbed her cheek.

Seeing Ana's anguish softened Brighid's heart. "I had Elphsaba," she said quietly. "And she was a good mother to me."

"Thank the Word for that wonderful woman," Ana whispered as another tear escaped her eye.

"She passed away two years ago." Brighid touched the area above her left eye. "I wear this mark for her."

"It is a beautiful expression of love," Ana said. "I hope you will come to forgive our family for the hardship you went through all these years."

Brighid left her chair, walked around the firepit, and knelt in front of Ana. She took the older woman's hands into her own and gave them a squeeze. "There is nothing to forgive. You did not know about me, and I did not know about you."

"You're right." Ana returned her squeeze. "I look forward to a future where you are part of our family and clan. And I will forever be thankful for Elphsaba for raising you in our stead."

Brighid felt the numbness inside her thawing. She still hurt from the actions of Kalla and Markus all those years ago, but she had also experienced love through Elphsaba. And it now seemed she had an unexpected new family. She looked up into Ana's shining eyes. A grandmother. Then she looked over her left shoulder at Bard. An uncle. *And even an eccentric great-uncle,* she thought as she looked to her right at Orest.

Then it hit her. Hjar Gurmund was also her family.

A wave of dizziness stole over her. The highly respected leader of the Bear Clan . . . was her grandfather.

Elpshaba, I wish I could tell you this, Brighid thought as she gripped Ana's hands again. *I discovered who I am. And I know what my hands were created to do.*

Bard walked over and placed a hand on Brighid's shoulder as well as his mother's. "Welcome to the family, Brighid."

29

Kaeden held his head in his hands, his elbows resting on the library table. Too many people, too many voices. The Healers Quarters were filled with patients suffering from sickness brought on by the winter cold. People crowded the hallways, seeking asylum in the White City. Even those of higher status were homeless with the desolation of villages along the northern border.

His dreams, too, swelled with voices and people. And Brighid. Always Brighid.

Kaeden glanced up, spotted Treyvar sitting at the other end of the table, and sighed. He had dreamed of Brighid again last night, and questions were starting to pile up in his mind about these strange occurrences. *Should I tell him?*

He tapped his finger three times on the table, then reached for the nearest book Treyvar had retrieved for him. He opened the leather binding and scanned the first page. Soft light filtered in from the nearby window, with a layer of snow along the sill. Silence filled the library, broken only by the soft whispers of pages turning every few minutes. Very few were permitted in this place, and for that he was grateful. It allowed him to hear his own thoughts. Or at least he was usually grateful. Today, all he could hear and feel was Brighid.

He looked at the page again. Beautiful calligraphy graced the parchment. The date at the top was two hundred years ago. His fingers hovered over the surface.

"The parchment is thick. It was made to endure," Treyvar said without looking up. "So feel free to read the book."

"All right."

Kaeden turned the page and stared at the next set of words but read nothing. His mind returned to last night's dream. Brighid was talking to an older Nordic man with matching warm blond hair and beard, wearing a fur-lined cloak. They sat near what looked like a firepit, and whatever he had told her had sent feelings of shock, disbelief, and a layer of hurt through her. He knew because he felt those feelings reverberate through him seconds before he awoke. Even now, they lingered inside his heart.

No other dreams affected him like this. And no other person showed up in his dreams so much, not even his parents or Mathias. And these dreams—could they even be called dreams? They felt almost real. Like he was there, with Brighid, watching her life, feeling her emotions, living her life—

"What's bothering you?" Treyvar closed his book and set it aside.

"What do you mean?"

"You've been staring at the same page for over ten minutes."

Kaeden tapped his finger on the wood next to the book. He opened his mouth, then closed it. Sighed. He would take the chance and ask. "I've been having strange dreams for the last several months. Ever since I became the Truthsayer."

Treyvar moved his chair until he faced Kaeden, then folded his arms. "Tell me about them."

Kaeden hesitated again. It wasn't like the dreams were wrong or lustful imaginings. But they were of a woman. Of Brighid. Part of him was hesitant to share. But something deep inside felt like they were significant. There was a reason for them. It couldn't be a coincidence that they started when he came into his power.

"I've been dreaming of the Nordic woman I freed. But they're not normal dreams. It's almost like I'm seeing her life. Not her past, or what I saw when I used my truthsaying power. Rather, what she is experiencing now, at least that is how it seems. I saw her traveling north. And during the snowstorm. It's like I'm catching glimpses of her life from here in the White City." Kaeden looked up. "Is that possible?"

Treyvar leaned back into his chair and tugged on his short beard. "Yes, it can be."

"It can?"

"It's possible you bonded with the Nordic woman."

"Bonded?" Kaeden's eyebrows flew up. He knew there were different bondings—from a simple term used for the relationship after lifelong vows were said, to the connection that could happen sometimes between couples who actually loved each other. But no such acts or expressions had occurred between him and Brighid. "How is that possible?"

"I've read that when a Truthsayer bonds, it is different from the human nature of bonding. For humans, most bondings are simply marriage. But for a Truthsayer, a bonding goes much deeper. It is a connection of the mind and spirit. It's different even from the connection between Eldarans." Treyvar paused thoughtfully. "I wonder if this bond occurs because of the unique nature of the truthsaying gift. You see inside people, their deepest secrets and desires. So it makes sense that when you bond, your bonding would be deeper than what others experience."

"Are you saying I may have bonded with her, with no vows or relationship in place?"

"Possibly."

"And that is why I'm dreaming of her? And you think those dreams are real? That I'm seeing her life?"

"It's possible. I could be wrong, but if the bond between you is strong, she might also be experiencing your life."

Kaeden ran a hand through his hair. Brighid might be dreaming of him and seeing his life as well? "That can't be. We were together for only a few days. How in the Lands could this bond have occurred?"

Treyvar folded his arms. "You said your power first ignited when you healed her."

"Yes. I never thought my Eldaran power would awaken. But that day it came alive." So powerfully it physically shook him.

Treyvar nodded. "The moment your power awakened, you brought someone back from the brink of death. I think it could create a bond of that magnitude."

Kaeden shook his head. "But I didn't give her my heart. And we didn't exchange any vows."

Treyvar looked at him "Have you ever loved a woman before?"

"No."

"Are you sure you don't love her?"

Love her? What did that mean? *Did* he love her? He certainly cared for her. Perhaps more deeply than he would admit. When he saw inside Brighid's soul, saw her hurt and memories, he resonated with her. Had that moment produced something more?

Like love?

Kaeden turned away. "This is a lot to think about."

"It's not a real bonding, you know."

Both Kaeden and Treyvar looked up as Selma stepped from the shadows and walked past the nearest bookcase. How long had she been standing there?

"What do you mean?" Kaeden asked.

"It's just a connection. Just like the connection we make when we touch a human." Kaeden caught Treyvar frowning at her words. She continued. "Like you said, no lifelong vows were made, like a true bonding would have. I'm not sure I would even call what you are experiencing a bonding. You simply made a connection with this woman. Nothing more."

"I'm not so sure about that," Treyvar said slowly. "Even for your kind, what Kaeden is seeing and feeling is unique."

Selma shrugged. "Do with it as you like, but I don't think it is helpful to lead Kaeden to think he has bonded with that woman."

Treyvar narrowed his eyes. "Are you threatened by the fact that Kaeden might have bonded with a human, Selma?"

For the first time, Kaeden saw a flash of anger in Selma's eyes. "As the only Truthsayer, he should be careful who he connects with."

"Those are some revealing words," Treyvar said.

"Our kind are dying out. If we are not careful, there will be no more Eldarans."

"Setting yourself apart from humanity is not the answer."

Kaeden raised his hands. "Wait, both of you. I am simply seeking answers. Treyvar, could you find where you read about the bonding of Truthsayers? Selma, was there a reason you came to the library?"

"Yes." The anger from moments ago vanished from her eyes. "Healer Weylin was asking for you. I told him I would find you."

"Does he need me now?"

"No, just sometime today."

Kaeden nodded. "Tell him I will head to the Healers Quarters within the hour."

Selma bowed. "Yes." She turned and disappeared beyond the bookcases.

Treyvar waited a moment, then he stood, walked over to the edge of the nearest bookcase, and peered down the aisle. Satisfied, he turned back around. "Selma's not the first Eldaran I've met who believes there should be a firm line between Eldarans and humans."

Kaeden glanced at his friend. "What do you mean by a firm line?"

"No bonding between humans and Eldarans. Keep the bloodline pure."

"Have there been Eldarans who bonded with humans?"

"Yes. And records show through the mingling of blood, the Eldaran power weakens. I suspect that is part of the reason for the community of Eldarans who live in the far northwest, near the land bridge. But in doing so, they are not serving mankind as they were intended. And I suspect the population of Eldarans is small. Sooner or later, the blood of the Eldarans will weaken anyway. Because of that, I believe your kind was supposed to eventually be grafted into humanity."

"That's an interesting perspective," Kaeden said.

"What do you think?" Treyvar asked.

"What I know is the example my parents left for me. They served and loved humankind the same way the Word does."

Treyvar sat down again. "Then you were truly raised in the way of the Word."

Kaeden huffed. "That way is not easy, though." *Loving people . . . touching people. Not easy at all.*

Treyvar let out a small laugh. "It's not easy for us humans either. But the Word gives strength to all, Eldaran and human."

Kaeden smiled back. "Yes, He does. Thank you for your wise words, my friend."

"It's all from my reading. I'm not an Eldaran, so there are mysteries about your kind that I am not privy to. Still, I don't think it was ever the Word's will for there to be a divide among our kind. Eldarans served during the Great Battle, and now you continue to live and serve among humans. I believe that would also mean bondings between our kind."

Kaeden shook his head. "I still don't know about Brighid."

"You don't need to. Right now you are each on your own path. She is in the north, and you are here in the south, fighting. But perhaps there will come a time when you will join again. After all, if your dreams are any indication, the bond between you is powerful."

Kaeden lay with his hands behind his head and stared at the ceiling. A slip of light poked through the bottom of the door to his right, where Treyvar worked in the main sitting room they shared in the guest quarters. Would he see Brighid again tonight? What had she seen of his life so far? Was she as confused as he was? Or did she dismiss these glimpses—as Treyvar called them—as dreams?

"Word, was this always Your plan?" he whispered in the dark. "To connect me to Brighid?"

He thought back to the moment he met her and her cry to live. When his power came to life. Was that the moment they connected? Or was it when he saw inside her soul? Either way, there was a connection now, whether Selma liked it or not.

Will I see you again?

Her last words to him.

I don't know, was his reply.

I hope we do.

Then she left. But not fully. Because apparently they were sharing their lives.

"Maybe we will see each other again, and it won't be just glimpses," he whispered.

Have you ever loved a woman before?

He had been so sure of the answer he gave to Treyvar that afternoon. A definite no. After all, how could he love someone without knowing it? But now . . .

Do I love Brighid?

He stared at the ceiling.

What is love?

Was this possibly the beginning?

And if it was, and they really had bonded like Treyvar thought, how would that work when they were on opposing sides of a war?

He didn't have an answer.

30

Brighid wiped the side of her face as she sat astride Bjornfrost deep inside the forest near the stronghold. It was still winter, but what had started early and harsh was now easing into a gentler season, if winter could ever be called that. A few days of clear skies and warmer weather had caused the pine trees to shed their white coats, and a large amount of snow had melted. It didn't mean winter was done, but it allowed space for her and Bjornfrost to train. Three dummies of hay and wood were set up for practice in the middle of the clearing.

"Again," Bard said as he sat astride Amro, his own bear. "You must become used to mounting and dismounting from the saddle. You can only fight with your sword from Bjornfrost's back for so long. And he cannot use his front paws when you are on his back."

Brighid nodded. Then she grabbed the upper lip of her saddle with her left hand, hefted the wooden sword aloft with her right, and shouted in the ancient tongue. With a burst of strength, Bjornfrost shot forward, sending snow flying into the air. With her knees and words, Brighid guided Bjornfrost through the trees, turning right, then left, then coming around to attack one of the dummies.

Bjornfrost roared as he charged forward. Brighid held on to the saddle, her body coiled and ready to attack. As they passed the dummy, she swept out with her sword and caught the figure along the chest. Not quite where she wanted to land the blow, but it would do.

She brought Bjornfrost around and leapt to the ground, then ran for the figure. Bjornfrost let out a roar and followed. This time she sliced along the neck. Bjornfrost rose on his hind legs and swiped at the other dummy.

With a splintering crack, half of the figure fell to the ground in wooden shreds. Bjornfrost snorted over the broken pieces, then looked over at Brighid. "Well done, my friend," she said, although she was slightly horrified by the damage one paw had done. What would that kind of force do to a human?

Bard rode up. "Very good, both of you. Now let's see you mount up."

Brighid turned, grabbed the saddle, and hefted herself up in one movement.

"Let's do that one more time. Come around, attack, and mount back up."

Brighid nodded. She gripped the saddle, spoke to Bjornfrost, and away they went, her hair flying in the wind and his massive paws sending snow into the air. Around the trees they went, then turned and charged for the clearing. Instead of attacking as they dashed by, Brighid slid from his back and slashed the target, swiping the neck and sending the imaginary head off into the woods.

Bjornfrost swerved around and lumbered to her side with a huff.

"You shredded your target," Brighid said.

He huffed again.

"There aren't anymore."

She swore she heard the beast whine and laughed at his response. Then she sobered as she realized fighting wooden dummies and real humans would be vastly different. Those hit by Bjornfrost most likely would not live long. She raised her sword and stared at the blade. Then again, those who met her blade also did not last long.

She let out her breath and dropped her arm as Bard came riding up.

"You and Bjornfrost fight well together. He will complement you in battle."

In battle. Would she be returning to battle? If she hoped to share of their allies' duplicity, she had to return to those who needed to hear. This mission wasn't given to Bard or anyone else. It was given to her.

And she was made to fight. To protect those she loved. The Vilrik and Bjornfrost were evidence of that. There was still a war going on, and Nordica needed her.

But . . . she could feel death. Would that change how she fought? Or would she freeze like she had in the past?

"I think I'm going to spend a little more time with Bjornforst before I head back," Brighid said, glancing up.

"Don't forget the feast tonight." Bard looked at her proudly. "We will be announcing your connection to the Bear Clan."

"Don't worry, I will be there." She mounted Bjornfrost and directed him into the forest. As they entered the woods, she felt her uncle's gaze on her back.

A jumble of emotions filled her chest. She knew who she was now, but instead of replacing her previous identity, it felt like both lived inside her. She was Hjar Gurmund's granddaughter—and Elphsaba's daughter. She was part of the Bear Clan—and yet she still felt a connection to the clanless. She was a simple woman trying to survive in the harsh north—and she'd been given a mission to save her people.

Truth be told, she wasn't sure how she felt about all of this. And who she would be at the end of this journey.

Twenty minutes later, she and Bjornfrost arrived at the edge of the cliff that overlooked the Rokr Valley, the same place they came the first time she rode him.

Bjornfrost lifted his nose into the air and sniffed.

"Smell something?" Brighid asked and patted his side. She wasn't sure if she would ever get used to riding a bear. She had never even ridden a pony or horse before.

He sniffed again.

She then spotted a small, single wisp of smoke rising into the air. It was probably nothing, but she would still let Hjaren Bard know about it.

No, not Hjaren. Uncle.

Brighid shook her head and took in a deep breath. Yes, there was a lot to get used to.

"Come on, my friend. Let's head back."

Somehow Bjornfrost understood her words and slowly turned around. What did the ancient tongue sound like to others? The words slipped easily from her lips, as if she had known them since the day she was born. She didn't even know she was using them sometimes. To her, the ancient tongue was the same as her mother tongue.

Just another one of the mysteries of the Bear Clan.

Did the other clans hold as many mysteries?

Instead of racing to the stronghold, Brighid let Bjornfrost lope through the forest. This was her time, before everyone knew who she was. A time to listen.

There wasn't a bird in the sky, nor any other animal. Just the silence of snow and winter. And yet . . .

Brighid closed her eyes. There, the softest whisper on the barest breeze. That voice. Always that voice. Was it possible that just like she could feel the presence of death, she could hear the words of the Word?

You feel that which cannot be seen. And someday you will hear the words that cannot be heard.

That was what the deathkeeper had told her when she went to the sepulchers to arrange Elphsaba's pyre. Had it been a prophecy? Or something more?

Why am I different?

Brighid leaned forward and pressed her face into Bjornfrost's fur. If she had ever asked Elphsaba that question, she probably would have said, *"Why not?"*

That thought brought a smile to her face.

What would Ana say if she asked the same thing?

Brighid sobered. She was still getting to know her new family.

Family. The very word still felt foreign.

She didn't know what Ana would think. But . . . she had a feeling her answer would be similar to Elphsaba's.

Brighid arrived back at the stronghold as evening fell. Thorald met her at the gate. His brown beard hung to his waist and thick eyebrows overshadowed hazel eyes. Brighid had heard his story—that he was crippled from birth—but Gurmund gave Thorald care and purpose through assigning the job of overseeing their stronghold.

Thorald leaned against his walking stick. "Brighid," he said, his breath making puffs of steam in the cold air. "Everyone is gathering in the great hall. It appears Hjaren Bard has something to share."

"Yes. He told me. Thank you for letting me know, Thorald."

Brighid dismounted Bjornfrost, removed his saddle, then bid him goodbye. Konal, one of the stableboys appeared and took the equipment from her. Bjornfrost shoved his head into Brighid's shoulder as the boy disappeared into the storehouse. The act surprised her for a second, then she closed her eyes and brushed the side of his neck. "Go," she whispered. "I will call you again."

Bjornfrost turned and lumbered into the forest. Brighid watched him until he disappeared into the trees.

"You remind me of Hjaren Bard when he connected with his bear, Amro," Thorald said. "He was eighteen winters when Amro came and found him."

"It still amazes me," Brighid said quietly.

"It amazes us all," Thorald replied. "Very few have the honor of being chosen by our clan animal."

Brighid glanced at him from the corner of her eye. Did he already know? It wouldn't be surprising. Rumors had been circulating of her connection to the clan ever since her arrival. "I am flattered."

Thorald glanced past her. "He is a fine bear and will make an excellent companion. Come, I will escort you inside."

He invited Brighid to walk beside him. She obliged and matched his gait as they crossed the stronghold and headed for the great hall.

At the doors, Thorald opened the left one and stepped back, letting Brighid enter first.

The interior blazed with light from oil lamps set around the cavernous room and the fire burning in the firepit. Every clansperson was gathered at the tables that lined each side of the hall. A hundred voices conversed, and laughing filled the area. Frothy mugs were lifted and drained, then placed down with loud thumps. The scent of meat and bread permeated the air.

Bard stood near the front with his mother. Both spotted Brighid and beckoned her forward.

Her stomach tightened. This was it. Soon those gathered here would know.

As she crossed the room, gazes followed her. Perhaps they already knew why the feast was being held. She spotted grins and bright smiles, all directed toward her. As she passed by the twins, Lodin smiled softly, while Vigi grinned and gave her a wink.

Each welcoming face made her insides uncoil until she finally stood beside Bard and Ana. Brighid's excitement replaced the nervousness from minutes ago.

"As the Hjaren of the Bear Clan, I have an announcement to make. Over the winter months, we have come to know the young woman Brighid. As she joined us for our meals and sparred with our warriors, I realized there was something more to her. I believe many of you have as well, so what I'm about to share is probably not a surprise."

"Get on with it!" Arngrim shouted from a nearby table.

"Yeah, we already know," Vigi said with a grin.

Bard shook his head, but a smile graced his lips. "Then I shall. After trials and testing, we have discovered Brighid is a long-lost daughter of the Bear Clan. Even more"—he reached out and gripped both Ana's and Brighid's hands—"she is Kalla's daughter."

The great hall erupted in roars and hollers. As she thought, most suspected the connection, although there were a few surprised faces, but they were quickly replaced with smiles.

"I knew it," she heard Galt say from the front table.

"I thought so too," Nora agreed with a nod.

"I knew it first," Orest yelled and pointed to those around him. "You all needed me to tell you."

"Welcome to the clan," Lodin said, his voice rising above the clamor filling the room.

Brighid stood there, her hand in Bard's. She felt such a warmth rising in her chest that she thought it would burst from her. Never did she think she would receive such a welcome. Overwhelming. All-encompassing. Completely wanted by these people.

She was sure some wondered how she was Kalla's daughter, and there would be questions. But for now, she would soak in this love and sense of belonging. She gripped Bard's hand tighter as a realization washed over her. This belonging needed to be extended to all Nordic people. Clan and clanless. Together, all of them were the people of the North.

Her people.

I am the Stryth'Viezla. And I am a daughter of the Bear. Tears glistened in her eyes as she looked over the crowd.

I am a warrior of Nordica.

Her heart pounded, and a red haze slowly spread across her vision. But as Bard had taught her, she took hold of it and let it encompass her without allowing it to take over.

And I will not let the Shadonae annihilate my people.

Vigi started chanting, "Til Val! Til Val!" Soon others began to chant it too, until the hall shook with their voices. It was the chant of her people that meant cheer and victory.

Then someone started singing an old song about the first bear. Others joined in while ale and mead were passed around, along with long wooden platters of steaming meat, bread, buttered root vegetables, and dried fruit.

Bard led his mother and Brighid to the closest table. The rest of the evening was spent in good spirits, with much food and drink. Never in her life had Brighid been part of such a celebration. And she would remember it long afterward. A feast to celebrate that she existed and was wanted.

31

Weeks later, Brighid returned to the stronghold after running drills with Bjornfrost. The sky was an icy blue, and the air as chilly as a mountain river, but the exercise had left her invigorated and warm. She removed the bear's saddle, patted him down, and checked for any injuries, then she gave him a piece of pamon from storage. Afterward she sent him into the woods.

As she watched him disappear among the evergreen trees, she thought again of war. There were hints that spring was coming, despite the cold and latest snow. Winter didn't last forever, and that meant the conflict down south would commence again.

Would she return? The thought lay heavy on her mind. Suddenly, she saw Johan's and Marta's faces in her mind, and her heart twinged. She missed them. What would they think when they found out she was no longer clanless but the granddaughter of Hjar Gurmund and one of the bear fighters?

That is, if they were still alive . . .

Brighid turned and headed for the main hall ahead. Perhaps there would be news from Hjar Gurmund. Ana had said she would inquire about her friends in her next letter. Brighid didn't know how long it took messages to come and go between the couple, but it had been a while, and she hoped she would hear soon.

As Brighid opened the door to the main hall, she found many of the clan warriors gathered along the tables closest to the firepit. Bard stood in the middle of the hall, a piece of parchment in his hand.

He glanced up as Brighid closed the door softly behind her. "Brighid, you are just in time. We have news from my father and the war."

It was as if her thoughts had taken form. Brighid drew in a deep breath and crossed the hall. She spotted Vigi and Lodin sitting to the right and decided to join them.

Bard began. "First, our fellow warriors are doing well. Our hjar has seen to their well-being and even found a clanless man to help them heal." A few voices murmured at that news. Brighid gripped her hands in her lap. Of course, she wasn't the only one with loved ones caught up in this war. There were people here with fathers, brothers, sisters, sons, daughters, and lovers who were far away from home, in a foreign country, stuck in a fortress for the winter. And some—she cast a side glance at the twins—who had already lost a family member to this conflict.

Bard shared a few more things. "Lastly, our hjar has received word that our clan will be sent south come spring. However, the Wolf Clan will be heading to Stelriden Fortress under the command of one of our allies."

"What do you mean, 'sent south'?" Arngrim asked from the other side of the hall, his arms folded across his chest. "We are the most familiar with Stelriden Fortress. Shouldn't our clan be the ones leading the charge?"

"Perhaps that is why." Bard folded the note.

"What do you mean?" called out another warrior.

Bard tucked the note away. "Long before this conflict, we were once friends with those in Stelriden Fortress."

"That was years ago!" someone else shouted. "Then they allowed Rylanders to cross our border, steal from our people, and encroach on our land. They are no friends of ours."

More voices rose in agreement.

"Well, you might just have your way," Bard said. The hall quieted down. "While Hjar Gurmund and our comrades are sent south, we here at the border might be asked to assist with taking Stelriden Fortress."

Heads turned toward one another, and murmurs rose.

Vigi growled. "Help the Wolf Clan? So they can take the credit? This sounds like something Hjar Volka would do. Send in his warriors, ask for our help, then shove us aside when he is done."

"I agree," Lodin replied.

Bard raised his hands in a gesture to silence the room. "I don't like it any more than you do," he said as voices dimmed. "And Hjar Gurmund asked why he is not leading this battle. I can only surmise it is because of our history with the people and the fortress. However, I can tell you this: It is not Hjar Volka who will be leading this charge, but one of our allies."

"Allies? You mean those strangers?" Arngrim asked.

"Yes."

A shot of ice tore through Brighid's body. One of the Shadonae would lead the charge? Which one? Not Armand. And probably not the other male. He was always with Armand.

Was it the woman? The one named Viessa?

The room came back into focus, along with the murmurs and complaints of those in the hall.

"We need to be ready if we are called upon," Bard continued. "More training, more practice. We will continue to patrol the border as we always have. And we will be ready. You are dismissed."

Brighid continued to sit while the others stood, talking among themselves.

"I don't like it, not one bit," Arngrim said nearby.

"I agree," Nora said.

"And I never liked that we allied ourselves with those strangers. We are Nordics, we didn't need their help."

"I heard," Vigi started, then he looked around. Brighid watched him from the corner of her eye. "I heard those strangers killed a handful of our warriors during training, before they marched to war."

"I heard that too," Lodin said.

Arngrim huffed. "From whom?"

"I overheard Hjaren Bard talking to Heming about it last spring."

"Why didn't you say anything?" Nora asked.

Vigi and Lodin looked at each other. "I told him not to," Lodin finally answered. "If Bard wanted us to know, he would have said something then."

"So why are you telling us now?" Arngrim asked. He saw Brighid and walked over. "You know about these strangers. You fought in the war. What do you know about them?"

Brighid spotted Bard looking her way with a frown. "I do. They are powerful."

"Did they kill some of our warriors?" Arngrim pressed.

Brighid hesitated. How much did she share? If Bard hadn't told them, maybe she shouldn't either. At least, not yet. "All I know is a group of Bear Clan warriors no longer wanted to be bound to the oath they took before the war. They disappeared days later. And Gurmund was furious."

"It is not the way of our people to renege on our word once it is given," Lodin said.

Vigi shook his head. "Why would they do that? I heard the oath made them more powerful. What about you? Did you take the oath?"

Brighid stiffened. Bard and Ana knew the truth behind the oath. But so far, it was only the two of them. If Bard hadn't told them about the strangers, should she? Perhaps he had a reason—

Bard appeared beside her. "There is more in the letter. For you. If you would follow me . . ."

Brighid bowed. "Yes, Hjaren Bard." She would ask him in private.

Bard led the way to the back where his parents' rooms were. "It feels odd now to have you call me Hjaren." He opened the door. "Feel free to call me Bard or Uncle in private if you wish."

"Yes, Hjar—Bard," Brighid amended.

The room was dark, with just a trickle of light from the oiled skin windows and the glowing embers from the firepit. "My mother wanted to let you know that she inquired about your friends, and my father answered. Of course, that letter was sent before we fully knew who you were, so my father doesn't mention you in that regard. The clanless warrior who has been assisting him with the sick and injured is Johan."

"Johan!"

"My father has never liked the deathkeepers or their ways, so when he discovered Johan knew about herbs and healing, he asked for his help while they stayed at Dallam Fortress. Apparently, the man is as knowledgeable as my mother in such things. He even knew of Ammelica and had some on his person. And he knew you."

Brighid nodded. That made sense. Johan always had a pouch of herbs on him, and he helped her and Marta when they were injured. "What about Marta?"

"The red-headed warrior? Also stationed at Dallam. Most of the clanless are there, under my father's watch."

"What did they say when they heard I was alive?" Brighid asked.

"My father asked them to stay quiet about it. It wouldn't do for others to hear that you were the only survivor of those captured during the Battle of the Plains. Or that you were in the north again. It could be construed as desertion if others heard. Like Hjar Volka. But he did say your friends were relieved."

Brighid smiled. Her friends were still alive. An aching filled her chest. If only she could see them again.

"May I ask what you were talking to the twins, Arngrim, and Nora about?"

Brighid looked up. "Our allies. Or as you and I know them, the Shadonae. But they don't seem to know much."

Bard nodded and crossed his arms. "I haven't shared a lot about them. My father was opposed to joining hands with them from the very beginning—"

"Hjar Gurmund was against allying with the Shadonae?"

"Aye, but the other hjars voted him down. However, he kept me here, along with a fourth of our clan, to keep us away from their power. I never told our warriors about that, only that it was our duty to protect our border and country while the rest of Nordica fought for us. A few complained, but in the end, they stayed. And I'm glad. That means there are some of us left who are not under that accursed oath."

Silence spread between them as Brighid took in this information. "Bard, I have a question." She looked up.

"Yes?"

"After the Battle of the Plains, I was set free. My mission was to share what was really happening to our people, how we were manipulated and brought under the power of these Shadonae. And that the war wasn't what would eventually kill us off, but these strangers."

"Yes. I remember."

"If one of these Shadonae will be leading our forces to Stelriden Fortress, perhaps—" Brighid stopped. What was she thinking? It was one thing to kill in battle and another to look ahead at the prospect of taking a life. But how else were they going stop these beings? Could they *even* be killed?

"You're wondering if it might be an opportunity to turn on one of our allies. To assassinate them."

Brighid felt sick at the thought but nodded. She was a warrior who fought for her people and country. And in her eyes, Bard's, Hjar Gurmund's, and others', the Shadonae were the real enemy.

"It's an idea, one I've already thought about. It's not our way to covertly take life. It feels dishonorable. But I have a feeling if we went face-to-face with these beings, we would lose." He sighed. "It might be the only way."

"I agree," Brighid said.

"For now, we wait and see what happens. Things could change. The woman may not come. Perhaps another will lead. Or we could be asked to take Stelriden ourselves."

"So it's Viessa they are sending," Brighid said.

"You know her name."

"Yes."

"Do you know her power?"

Brighid paused. "No, not fully. I remember she was the one in charge of clearing Ryland villages for supplies. A warrior named Hagen spoke about it one night. Said that when the clanless sent to assist entered the villages, they found everyone dead. But there were no wounds or blood. It was as if everyone had died in their sleep."

Bard frowned. "Are you saying Viessa took out these villages by herself?"

"I believe so, yes."

"I don't like it. I wonder if that is how she plans to take Stelriden Fortress. With whatever power that is." Bard rubbed his beard. "I will see if my father has more information and find out his thoughts on the matter. If we move against Viessa, our venture could be construed as treason. That is not an action I want to consider lightly. However, communication has been very slow, so I don't know if we will hear back in time. We may ultimately have to decide if it is worth it."

Brighid shivered. Could there be something more powerful than Armand's oath? Or Viessa?

Yes.

Kaeden's power.

Bard moved to walk past her and back out in the main hall.

"Wait." Brighid held out her arm.

"Yes?"

"There might be another way. As powerful as Armand's oath is, and whatever this ability Viessa possesses, I believe Kaeden is more powerful."

"Kaeden. The Truthsayer you mentioned to my mother. Yes, I remember."

"Kaeden said it was his job to stop the Shadonae. It's like when a warrior goes rogue—it is the duty of the clan to bring the warrior in. I believe it's similar with them. They are the same race. But Armand and the other two no longer follow the way of their people. I think that's why the marks on their palms look like decaying flesh. It's like a physical sign they have turned away."

"So we wait for this Kaeden to deal with the Shadonae?"

"More than that. We find a way to ally with him."

Bard frowned. "I'm not sure how. He is in the south, as part of their alliance. In the eyes of our people, he is the enemy. It also feels like we would be trading one pact with a powerful ally for another. I'm not comfortable with that."

"I don't know if we have a choice. Too many of our warriors are under the oath. They are bound to stay with Armand whether they like it or not. We need help. Kaeden said he will stop the Shadonae."

Bard waved his hand. "So let him."

"In order to reach them, he will need access to them. A way forward through our forces. He is also part of the south, as you pointed out. That could be to our advantage."

"How so?"

"Even if Armand and Viessa are stopped, the war will continue. We will need people to help broker peace. He could be one of them."

Bard remained quiet. Brighid could almost see her words swirling around his mind. "You make a couple of good points," he finally said. "But there are many difficulties in what you propose. And we still have the issue of what will happen to all the Nordic warriors under the oath once Armand is no more. Does Kaeden know how to negate the withdrawal symptoms? Can his power do that?"

Brighid blinked. Bard was right. "I don't know. He became the Truthsayer during that time."

"You keep saying Truthsayer. What exactly is that?"

"It's Kaeden's power." Brighid looked away, toward the firepit. "Armand uses words to bind people, but Kaeden can reach inside the heart and mind with one touch of his hand. It is far more powerful than the oath. When he used his ability on me, he was able to see inside me—*all* of me. Everything I have ever thought or did. As if I my soul had been laid bare before the brightest light."

"Bolva," Bard said with his eyes wide. "That sounds more terrifying than the oath."

Her uncle was right. If simple words spoken by Armand could bind the fiercest Nordic warrior, what could the all-seeing power of Kaeden do? More than bind their words, but also their minds and souls?

She shuddered at the thought. She hadn't considered the greatness of that power until now. But . . . that wasn't Kaeden. And that wasn't Mathias before him. She couldn't put her finger on it, but there was something different about those men. A humility and servanthood lacking in Armand and his companions. As different as the marks on their palms.

"In any case, we may his need help," Brighid concluded. "And he will need ours if he is to reach the Shadonae."

Bard let out a long breath. "This is a lot to think about. I will need time to consider your words and weigh what is best for both our clan and the Nordic people." Then he raised his arm and placed a hand on Brighid's shoulder. "Thank you for sharing your thoughts with me. You think like a true hjar. One who must make hard decisions for one's clan. I look forward to seeing how you grow in your role as an honored member of our clan. And as my niece."

Brighid's throat tightened. "Thank you."

32

The first signs of spring brought a sense of foreboding to those in Celestis Castle. That feeling intensified when a message came for the fighters and healers to return.

Kaeden stood before the window inside the guest quarters he shared with Treyvar, who was reading a letter from Avonai, while Kaeden watched people scurry like ants across the courtyard below. Beyond the castle walls, the White City slowly stirred as morning took hold. There was no longer snow on the ground, but the air froze each night, and a thin layer of frost appeared in the mornings. However, a few more weeks and spring would fully be there. And the return of war.

Treyvar cleared his throat behind Kaeden. "I've been asked if I will serve again as a healer for the southern forces."

Kaeden turned around and left the window, his soul heavy.

Treyvar lowered the letter and looked up. "I was also asked if you would be joining us once more."

"That depends on where you are heading." Kaeden moved toward the seat opposite Treyvar. "I have my role to fulfill as the Truthsayer. But if that coincides with where you are going, I will continue to serve alongside you and the other healers. I believe the upcoming conflict will lead me to the Shadonae. They will be there, somewhere, on those battlefields."

"And then what will you do?"

Kaeden sighed as he sat down. "Mathias told me before he died that it was his responsibility to pass judgment on them. And now it is my responsibility."

Treyvar scowled. "Will mere words stop such beings? They've already proven they are willing to twist their gifts for power."

"I've had all winter to think about it, and I don't think Mathias had words in mind when he said he would pass judgment."

"You would physically punish them? You? A pacifist? How?"

Kaeden shook his head. "No, not that either. I will hand them over to the Word after denouncing them and let Him mete out their punishment."

Treyvar gave him a dubious look. "Forgive me, but I don't see how words, even harsh words, can be so terrifying."

Kaeden glanced at the window nearby, recalling the verses from the last tome he read. "The voice of the Word creates and destroys. Brings the spring rain and the winter snow. Life begins and ends at His command. I have a feeling it is a terrifying thing to be denounced by the Word. Our words hold some power, but His words hold our very existence."

"You mean, they would disappear?"

Kaeden turned around. "Maybe. Despite all I've read, I found very little about dealing with those who have completely abandoned our ways."

Treyvar's face grew dark. "Why does the Word need you to do anything? Couldn't He have already judged them? Why doesn't He speak and take the Shadonae out of existence? It's not as if He needs you to do it. And if He had done so, there would be no war now."

Kaeden let out his breath. At moments, he secretly wondered the same thing. But he had a feeling he knew why. "Because all life is given a chance to return to the Word. Even the Shadonae. When I judge them, it will be their last call."

Treyvar huffed. "You think they'd really come back? I've seen what a taste of power can do to a man, let alone an Eldaran."

Kaeden paused. Did Treyvar just reveal a hint about his family?

Treyvar crossed his arms. "What about those whose lives were snuffed out by the Shadonae? Were their lives not as important? As precious? Why weren't they given this extra chance you speak of?"

Kaeden looked away. Treyvar wasn't wrong. But they were also not privy to all the times the Word called each person. To every human. Through song and silence. Through the constant voice holding the world together. In the rain and the wind and the sound of laughter. If one was quiet long enough, one could hear the Word. "That, I cannot answer," he finally said. "All I know is this responsibility that has been given to me."

Treyvar shook his head. "Forgive me, this war makes me angry sometimes."

Kaeden snorted. "It should make everyone angry. But there are those who relish the fight. And some who are benefiting from this conflict. And worst, there are those who let this happen and leave it to others to dirty their hands."

"You're talking about our leaders, aren't you?"

"Yes," Kaeden said softly. "You are the only noble I know who is actually fighting. Those who lead should lead by example. Instead, they stay hidden within their castles and direct this war like pieces on a board."

Treyvar laughed darkly. "This war might have been over after the first battle if Lord Rayner and my father had joined the fight. Or even my brother or Teduin. The horrors might have sent them to the peace tables. Instead, it might take Nordica reaching the White City or Avonai to finally convince those in power to end the bloodshed." He let out another heavy breath and stood. "Captain Reginar has asked if I will go with him to Stelriden Fortress. We don't know all the movements the Nordics might take, but that is the last bastion we hold in the north along the boundary. A contingent of soldiers and captains will be sent there to solidify our hold. It was once Captain Reginar's post, so he is familiar with the fortress."

North. Kaeden furrowed his brow. That might be a good route to go. The Shadonae were hiding somewhere behind the Nordic forces. Crossing the entire might of Nordica on a battlefield to reach them was not an option. But perhaps, if he headed north, he might find a way to circumnavigate the Nordics and discover where the Shadonae were staying. The faster he could confront his kin, the faster this war could resolve itself.

And there was the possibility of meeting Brighid again. Slim, but a possibility.

"Go with me?"

Kaeden tuned back into the conversation. "I'm sorry, I missed what you said."

"I asked if you would want to go with me."

"Yes." His mind was made up.

"That was a fast answer."

"I believe it's my best chance of reaching the Shadonae."

Treyvar paused. "I hadn't thought of that. You could be right." He held up the letter in his hand. "I will let Captain Reginar know your answer. He will be pleased."

Treyvar crossed the room and left, shutting the door softly upon his exit. Kaeden sat in the silence for a moment, then leaned forward and placed his head in his hands. The heaviness returned. "Word," he whispered. "I don't know what I'm doing, or if this is even the way to do it."

Then his words dried up. He felt like he was standing before a towering snow-capped mountain with an avalanche rushing toward him. *I am but one person. How can I accomplish this?*

His heart beat faster and he gripped his hands. *Please don't let me be alone in this endeavor. Give me wisdom and strength of heart for what is ahead.*

He swallowed. *Please.*

There was no answer. No sudden peace. The avalanche was still there in his mind, barreling toward him, ready to swallow him up.

All I can do is take the next step before me.

Kaeden raised his head.

Take the next step.

His next step would be accompanying Treyvar and Captain Reginar to Stelriden Fortress. "And then I'll take my next step, whatever it will be, until I finally reach the Shadonae and judge them."

Kaeden organized his few belongings and hefted the pack onto his back. He decided to leave his white cloak behind, choosing instead a less flashy and more durable grey, the same grey as his previous one. However, this one felt different, and it made him wonder if Brighid still had the cloak he had given her last fall.

Then he left the guest rooms for the final time. As he headed down the stone corridor, he gripped the straps of his pack. He would stop by the Healers Quarters first and bid Healer Weylin farewell. Then the training room where he had spent all winter with the guards, keeping his body in shape.

There was a bitter sweetness in his soul as he descended the first flight of steps. He had found purpose and camaraderie at Celestis Castle, not something he had thought would happen. And he would miss them once he left.

Down another hallway he went, acknowledging the bows of respect sent his way as he passed, until he reached the Healers Quarters. Inside, he found the room bustling with healers dressed in white robes as they packed supplies for the battles ahead.

Kaeden stood in the doorway for a moment, taking it all in. The familiar scents of herbs, especially mint this morning. The bookcases filled with scrolls, pestles and mortar, books, and dried plants. The long windows against the far wall that overlooked the garden outside. And his fellow healers. Most of them would be heading out with the rest of the southern forces, including Selma.

The moment he thought her name, she came around the corner and spotted him in the doorway.

"Master Kaeden," she said as she approached him. At her respectful voice, most of the healers stopped and glanced his way. She stopped and bowed, her dark, wavy hair falling along her shoulders.

"Master Kaeden," the others murmured and mimicked Selma's behavior.

Kaeden crushed his hands into fists, feeling the leather glove across his right hand give under his strength. He wasn't sure he would ever get used to admiration. And Selma seemed to encourage it frequently with her own actions.

"Thank you." He released his hands. "I came to wish you all a farewell as we part on our different assignments."

"Different assignments?" someone whispered as his head came up.

"I heard the Truthsayer is heading north to Stelriden Fortress," his companion muttered.

Selma's face tightened at the words. He had heard she asked to accompany him but was turned down, stating it would do well for an Eldaran to travel with the other troops.

"Master Kaeden!" Healer Weylin boomed as he emerged from one of the side rooms. His grey hair seemed frizzier today and his beard full. He smiled as he crossed the room, his brown eyes full of warmth. Healer Weylin was the cheeriest person Kaeden had ever met. He would miss working with him. "I heard you would be departing today."

"I am." Kaeden stepped into the large room and toward the older man. "I wished to say goodbye and thank you for everything you taught me over the winter."

Healer Weylin stopped before him and bowed. "I am glad I was of help to you. I wanted to give you something for your journey." He turned and headed for one of the bookshelves while the other healers watched. "It's not much, but I think you will find it helpful in the north." He turned back around with a small bag in his hand. "Mint leaves. Steep in hot water for five minutes. Helps clear the head, aids in digestion, and calms the spirit."

"Thank you." Kaeden brought his pack around and stuffed the

small gift inside, touched by Healer Weylin's kind gesture. They spoke for a few more minutes, and some of other the healers chimed in. Then Kaeden bid them farewell one more time and left. For a moment, he wondered what the future held for all of them. Healers usually survived the battles due to their job and location, far from the heat of the fight. But that didn't guarantee all would live.

"Wait, Kaeden!"

He stopped halfway down the corridor and turned to find Selma rushing his way. "I wish I was going with you," she said in a hurried breath. "It would be better if we served together."

"You know the real reason I am heading north."

"Yes, to find the Shadonae."

"It will be dangerous."

"I know. I could protect you."

Kaeden frowned. "How?"

Selma lifted her hand. Her mark glowed dimly in the torchlight. "You know our blood makes us powerful. I might not be a fighter, but I am strong. Are you sure you don't want me to accompany you?"

Kaeden gently gripped her shoulder. "Thank you for your offer, but I agree with the commanders. You are needed with the rest of the healers heading south."

Her face darkened. "I am needed with you."

"I will have Treyvar."

Shadows covered her features more.

"And I have the Word. Each of us has been asked to walk our own path. Mine is north. Yours is with the south."

"I believe my path is with you, a fellow Eldaran."

A chill went down his spine. Selma's devotion to their race, and to him in particular, made him uneasy. It felt misplaced. "We will meet again. I won't be north forever." Selma looked away and Kaeden dropped his hand. "You have friends among these healers. Protect them. Watch over them. Just like Mathias taught us."

She let out her breath. "Yes. I will." But her heart didn't seem to be in her words.

"I must go now. I have one more place to visit before I leave."

His heart felt heavy as he left Selma behind. Was she the future of the Eldarans? Closed off, with a desire to be only with their own kind and gradually forgetting why they existed? Or were Armand and the other Shadonae their fate? He didn't know why they had turned, only that they had, and the Lands were paying the price for their choice.

Kaeden sighed as he turned the corner. Once again he found himself missing Mathias—their talks, his wisdom, his laughter. His carefree way of life and devotion to the Word. How he cared for both human and Eldaran. The desire to be like his mentor flared in his heart. "I want to be like you," he whispered. "Word, help me."

Minutes later, he arrived at the training room and found only a handful of guards. Most were out on patrol. They already knew he was leaving, but he still wanted to visit this place once more before he left. He wished he could go to the Sanctuary and bid Mathias farewell, but time prevented him from one last visit. When he returned to the White City, he would do that.

Grey sky filled the glass dome above the room. At least it wasn't snowing. The sound of practice swords clacking against one another stopped and a deep "Hello" followed.

Kaeden smiled as the guards came forward. Most were stripped down to their inner tunics, and sweat trickled down faces and necks. The scent of perspiration and musk followed in their wake. They all took turns slapping him on the back and wishing him a safe journey north.

"Thanks for teaching me those moves," one of the younger men said, flexing his arm and laughing.

"If you ever return to the White City, come see us again."

"Yeah, I'll be your opponent in your next match."

The heaviness fell away and Kaeden smiled, assuring them he would eventually return. They bid him farewell and Kaeden found himself back in the hallways, heading toward the front doors of Celestis Castle. This place never became home, but he would have fond memories of his winter here.

Then he shook his head as he remembered Selma. Perhaps he was being too tough on her in his thoughts. After all, she still might have friends around the castle—human friends. And from what he had observed, she communicated and interacted well with humans. And she could touch them, which was more than he could do.

But I am getting better, he thought and glanced at his gloved right hand. He was less repulsed than when he first arrived. But those were controlled actions when he was assisting in the Healers Quarters, concentrating on his movements. What would happen when he was unexpectedly touched? Would he react violently and push the person away? Or worse, what if they accidentally touched his mark, like Teduin had?

His stomach tightened. He might never be able to touch others freely.

As he reached the entryway, a guard bowed and opened one of the massive doors. Kaeden stepped outside into the cold, grey morning. Not quite cold enough to see his breath, but not comfortable either. He tugged the cloak closed and headed down the wide stairs to the courtyard where Treyvar waited.

"Captain Reginar went ahead into the city and asked us to meet him at the main gates."

"I guess that means we have a bit of a walk." Kaeden readjusted his pack. He looked ahead, through the castle gates to the street that led into the White City. Who knew what lay beyond? He had never been that far north. Stelriden Fortress lay near Nordica's border and Brighid's homeland.

Interesting. He might get a glimpse of what her world was like. And by seeing her homeland, maybe he would understand the warrior woman a little more.

Captain Reginar led a contingent of Rylander soldiers and scouts. Kaeden, Treyvar, and a couple of healers accompanied them. The main goal of their mission was to reinforce Stelriden Fortress with both manpower and support. That first night, as Kaeden sat near the fire with Captain Reginar, the older man commented how lucky they were the Nordics hadn't taken the fortress.

"I'd have thought Hjar Gurmund would have sent his warriors down the valley and past the border, but the man chose to guard the Nordic border instead," Reginar said.

Kaeden looked up, surprised. "You know this Hjar Gurmund? Which clan does he lead?"

"He's the head of the Bear Clan. Long ago, I was stationed at Stelriden Fortress. One winter, I was out on patrol with my captain and a few others. We became lost during a terrible blizzard and didn't realize we had wandered into Nordica. Hjar Gurmund and his warriors found us on the brink of death and brought us to his stronghold. The blizzard and heavy snowfall caused an avalanche in the Rokr Valley, so we were unable to return to Stelriden for many weeks. Lucky for us, Hjar Gurmund was not only a Nordic warrior, but a man of integrity and hospitality. He and his family took care of us."

Kaeden furrowed his brow. "So Hjar Gurmund doesn't live far from the border?"

"No."

He stared into the fire. When he freed Brighid, her goal was to head north toward Nordica. It seemed possible, then, that when he dreamed of her wandering through the snow, she was crossing the Rokr Valley. And the people caring for her in his most recent visions matched what Reginar shared of the Bear Clan. Was it possible she ended up in Hjar Gurmund's home?

The next few days were spent heading east through Anwin Forest. Spring had not yet touched the thick, dark forest. No green buds appeared on the ancient trees, and the ground was littered with years of fallen leaves. Between the naked branches and the overall haunting feeling of the forest, Kaeden felt his spirits spiraling downward. And he didn't seem to be the only one. As each night passed and fires were lit, fewer people spoke.

"What's with this place?" Treyvar said four nights in as he clutched his cloak around his neck.

"Feels like it's going to snow," one healer murmured beside him. A young man named Rosk.

"So dark," said Sumar, another healer, as she glanced up. "I can't even see the stars."

It wasn't just the thick branches above blocking the sky. There was nothing beyond. Most likely, heavy clouds were obscuring the view. Kaeden burrowed deeper into his cloak. He hoped it wouldn't snow.

He was wrong.

The party woke to large, white flakes falling. Thanks to the trees, most of the snow came down only where it could bypass the branches. Still, the sudden change in weather did not help those with waning spirits.

Even Treyvar seemed affected. With his hood over his head and his cloak clutched beneath his chin, only his nose was visible as he trudged along the path. The one seemingly unaffected was Captain Reginar. He led the group, his shoulders straight, his gait firm, unhindered by the weather or cold.

It took longer to light the fires that night. Most of the gathered wood was wet, along with any kindling. Kaeden's fingers felt frozen as he coaxed the flame to life beneath the wood he had set up as a cone. It took three tries before the leaves and thin branches took, and a little longer before the logs finally burned.

He held his fingers to the flames. How did Brighid survive out in this wild country alone? Granted, her path didn't take her through Anwin Forest, but the forests and hills along the Northern Ari Mountains couldn't have been easier.

He closed his eyes, feeling a little bit of warmth creep across his body. If he hadn't seen later glimpses of her life that assured him she had survived the trek, he would worry she had died along the way. Still, he knew from those same visions that it hadn't been easy.

He recalled Brighid's journey. The towering Ari Mountains, the thick forests, the day he woke up and felt his leg on fire. Not only had she traversed north alone but she had been injured.

Kaeden shook his head and opened his eyes. The Word had been watching over her. He didn't know how she made it to where she was now, but she had made it back to civilization. He knew from his dreams. And that bolstered his spirit.

A week later, they left Anwin Forest. A heavy sky of grey hung over the vast plains that spread out before them, with the Northern Ari Mountains rising in the distance. Kaeden stopped at the forest edge and wiped his brow. Despite the chill in the air, he was warm now from walking every day. What he wouldn't do to rest and let his body soak in hot water. Every muscle ached, despite training his body during the winter.

But they still had more than a fortnight before they reached the fortress. He readjusted his pack and started forward again.

"This is worse than a battle," Rosk grumbled.

Kaeden glanced toward the young healer. "Which battle were you at?"

"Battle of the Plains."

"And you think walking is worse?"

"At least it wasn't cold," he muttered and pulled his cloak tighter.

Kaeden shook his head. Did the man not remember all the blood and screams and death?

"This is my first time leaving the White City," Sumar said. She was the only woman healer in their group. Two light brown braids stuck out from beneath her hood and hung over each shoulder. "I heard the north is wild and vast."

"Of course it is. Look at the barbarians who live there," Rosk said.

"They're not barbarians," Kaeden replied as he kept walking.

"Then explain the way they fight, and those strange marks on their faces. I heard they eat their young."

Kaeden glanced at him again. Rosk was short and thin, with dull brown hair and only a hint of facial hair. He couldn't be more than eighteen or nineteen years old.

"Do you believe everything you hear?" Kaeden asked.

"What?" Rosk looked up. "No," he said sullenly.

"Just because someone is different doesn't mean they're not human. And they don't eat their young," Kaeden said. "They eat the same food we do."

"How do you know?"

"Because I cared for some of them during the Battle of the Plains and came to know them."

"Then what about those marks?"

"They're not for kill counts." Kaeden recalled the half-sun tattoo etched around Brighid's eye and the day she received that mark. He felt the deep love she held for the elder woman the mark represented.

"The Nordics wear tattoos in remembrance of those they love, their clan, and sometimes remarkable feats of strength."

Kaeden glanced back to find Treyvar had caught up to them.

"Really?" Sumar said. "That's surprisingly human."

"They're not that different from us." Treyvar began to share all he knew about the Nordic people with Sumar, while Rosk listened reluctantly.

It's possible you bonded with the Nordic woman.

Kaeden recalled Treyvar's words as the young prince continued to speak with Sumar. He knew Brighid better than anyone else, but what about her? What did she know of him? Those few days they shared—and these intermittent dreams—didn't count as the day-to-day living a true bonding would require. She was Nordic and part of a culture he was still learning about. And he was an Eldaran—and the Truthsayer.

How could she bond with someone she knew so little about?

He sighed. Their worlds were as different as the sky and sea.

Then again, Selma could be right, and it was just a temporary connection that would eventually fade away.

How would they know?

34

Stelriden Fortress.

Kaeden stared up at the massive stone structure set in the side of the mountain. A wide stone staircase led from the main gatehouse down the mountain to the forest floor below. High battlements surrounded the fortress, connected by thick stone walls and towers at each corner. Arrow slits were placed along the wall and within the towers. Banners of blue waved in the air against a sky of even brighter blue.

Did they really need to reinforce such an intimidating structure? With the gates closed, he wasn't sure anyone could take the fortress. The only place possibly more secure was the White City itself.

"My word, I had no idea Stelriden looked like this," Treyvar said beside him. "I thought it was like all the other fortresses and garrisons along the Ryland Plains and coast. Simple, plain, and small."

"I thought the same." Kaeden still craned his neck to look up at the fortress.

"It was built near the same time as the White City," Captain Reginar said, coming to stand beside the men. "A bastion against the North back when Nordica was more aggressive, and their clans were not united. Stelriden has seen many battles over the years."

"I don't know how the Nordics can possibly take this place," Treyvar said. "It truly is remarkable architecture."

"Wait until you see the inside." Captain Reginar raised his hand and glanced behind him. He shouted out a command, dropped his hand, and started toward the stairs. It took ten minutes to ascend to the front gates.

"The stairs alone would take out an army," Treyvar panted as he leaned forward.

"I invited you to exercise with me over the winter," Kaeden replied with a laugh.

Treyvar looked up with a scowl. "And I told you I'm more of an intellect."

"The stairs will kill you."

"Humph."

Once at the top, Captain Reginar called up to the gate guard. "Reinforcement from the White City," he shouted.

The guard disappeared, and moments later a deep groan sounded through the gate. A crack appeared, then the gates slowly drew open. By then, Treyvar had caught his breath. "See?" He flashed a grin at Kaeden. "I'm fine."

Kaeden smiled and shook his head.

Minutes later, they were escorted into the fortress. The inside was just as impressive as the outside. Thick stones made up the inner walls and buildings surrounding a courtyard that could accommodate hundreds of soldiers. Past the courtyard stood the main hall. A semicircle of pillars held the roof high above a porch, and wide doors led into the building. The scents of smoke and pine filled the cold air.

As Captain Reginar spoke with the gatekeeper, Kaeden wandered up the stairs. At the top, he stood beside the rampart and his breath caught in his chest. The view beyond . . .

"That's something else," Treyvar said, coming to stand beside him.

Over the ramparts, Kaeden could see the Rokr Valley stretching into the distance toward the snow-capped Ari Mountains. It was a wide basin full of pine trees, covered in a thin mist that was currently golden as the sun's rays hit the haze, creating an ethereal view. "I could look at this all day," Kaeden murmured.

"I'm still partial to the coasts of Avonai, especially when the sun rises over the sea, but I have to admit, this comes close." Treyvar made room as others joined them, all expressing their appreciation for the view.

"Is that Nordica?" Sumar asked, pointing north.

Kaeden glanced that direction. All he could see were forests, foothills, and towering mountains.

"Yes, I believe so," Treyvar said.

"I would love to visit there someday," Sumar said quietly. "My grandfather was a bard and spoke a little about his travels."

"A bard?" Treyvar glanced at the young healer.

"Yes. Before he bonded with my grandmother. He traveled all over, even west to Thyra and the lands of Kerre. Hearing his stories always made me want to travel."

"What tales did he share?" Treyvar asked.

"His favorites were tales of the Great Battle. And the Eldarans." She glanced shyly at Kaeden.

He fought the urge to rub his neck and look away. He knew, to some people, he was someone special. But he didn't see himself that way. Instead, he gave her a small smile and a nod. His parents accepted admiration with grace and humility. He would do the same.

Not long after, the weary travelers were treated to food, then shown to their living quarters. Despite its magnificence, the fortress was still a military structure and, as such, there were only a handful of rooms for those in leadership. The rest were directed to the barracks. Kaeden chose to stay with the other healers.

One large room to the left of the main hall served as storage for healing supplies, recovery for those in need of it, and a place for healers to prepare their poultices, bandages, and tinctures. Next to it was a smaller room with rows of beds and chests. Kaeden took the bed at the far end, sat down, and let his bag drop to the ground. Treyvar chose the one next to him.

Kaeden looked up. "You could probably get your own room."

"So could you," Treyvar replied as he opened the wooden chest and deposited the items from his pack inside. "But these are the people I will be working with. I will also live with them."

"I feel the same way." Kaeden relaxed a moment longer, then started unpacking. He made sure to keep out the small pouch of mint leaves Healer Weylin had gifted him.

Treyvar eyed the pouch. "Mint leaves?"

"Yes."

Treyvar held up his own pouch. "It appears Healer Weylin sent all of us with a small gift."

"So he did," Kaeden said with a smile.

The next morning, everyone was called to the main hall: both those newly assigned to Stelriden Fortress and those already serving there. Bright sunlight trickled in through the long, narrow windows that lined the front of the room. Despite the cheery light, the room was chilly, and many of the occupants rubbed their arms vigorously or blew into their hands.

The handful of healers who had accompanied the military reinforcements stood in the corner of the main hall near the large stone fireplace, their white robes setting them apart from the soldiers gathered.

"So cold," Sumar chattered as she clutched her arms across her body and stood as close as she could to the fireplace.

"I already hate this place," Rosk mumbled beside her.

"Then why did you come?" she asked.

"I didn't want to be sent to battle again."

"But you said the trek here was worse than the battle."

"It was, but that doesn't mean I want to return to the war." He shuddered and looked away.

"War may still come," Treyvar replied. "After all, that is why we were sent here."

Rosk's face darkened.

A man dressed in white approached them from across the room. He wove his way through the soldiers until he stood before the healers. "Welcome," he said in a tenor voice. He was a middle-aged man, medium build, with sandy brown hair and a short-cropped beard. "Healer Aspar, at your service. I have been the sole healer here all winter. It will be nice to have the company of other healers." He turned, then motioned to them. "Let me show you around so you can become familiar with the fortress."

Treyvar, Kaeden, and the two young healers followed Healer Aspar. They were already familiar with the room set aside for the healers and the main hall. He pointed out the collection of rooms to the right of the hall for the captains, the barracks, stables, kitchen, and other facilities needed for Stelriden Fortress to function without a town nearby.

"Stelriden has a long and rich history," Healer Aspar said as he led them back to the main hall. "But it has a few dark secrets as well." He took them to the right and into the soldiers' barracks. After a short hallway, the corridor opened into one long room. On the right were half a dozen doors, each leading to smaller rooms filled with bunks. At the end of the narrow room sat a desk, cupboard, and another door.

Healer Aspar pointed at the door near the desk. "Here is where prisoners would be kept." He withdrew a set of keys and a lamp from the cupboard. He tied the ring of keys to the cord around his middle, then lit the wick of the lamp and walked toward the door. After the faint rustle of metal and a quiet click, the door opened, exposing a staircase leading down into darkness.

"Do we really need to know where prisoners are kept?" Rosk asked.

"Yes, because if there are prisoners who are injured, we care for them as well," Kaeden replied. The young man said he was at the Battle of the Plains, but he seemed ignorant of what went on in the healing tents. Perhaps due to his age, he had been only an assistant at that time.

Down the staircase the five of them went, with only the flickering flame of the lamp lighting their way. At the bottom, Kaeden detected a dim blue light. Apparently, fre stones had been imbedded in the stone walls. Healer Aspar led them along the corridor. On each side were metal bars, enclosing rooms of varying sizes. There were no windows, just the blue light from the fre stones and the lamp Healer Aspar held.

At least the place doesn't smell, Kaeden thought as he looked past the bars. "When was the last time this place was used?" His voice echoed along the walls.

Healer Aspar paused and glanced back. "Two years ago," he said.

"We held a handful of Nordics who had crossed our border and raided a village."

"Barbarian rot," Rosk murmured.

"It's not like we didn't do the same," Treyvar replied.

"What do you mean?" Rosk looked back. His face appeared cold and gaunt in the blue light.

"What do you think caused this war? Broken treaties and broken trust. Our people have been crossing the border for years, stealing from the Nordics and encroaching on their land. We also refused to trade with them after the bitter winters."

"How do you know that?" Rosk asked.

It seemed the other healers were not informed of who Treyvar was. Whether that was by Treyvar's command or someone else's, Kaeden didn't know.

"I'm Avonain, and I am familiar with the Nordic envoy that arrived over a year ago."

"Well, they should be able to take care of themselves," Rosk huffed.

"Their people were starving," Treyvar replied. "And we refused to help them."

Healer Aspar remained silent during the exchange as they continued down the corridor. Kaeden wondered what the man thought.

They reached another door. Once again, Healer Aspar used the ring of keys and unlocked it.

"More cells?" Treyvar asked.

"Yes, and no," Healer Aspar replied.

Kaeden frowned at his cryptic words.

Healer Aspar led the way down another set of stairs. Despite the lack of windows on the floor above, it hadn't felt as suffocating or dark as this next level did. As they reached the bottom step, Kaeden's heart beat erratically. He clenched his hand. Why was he reacting so strongly? There was nothing to fear here.

"This particular place has a dark history."

The hair prickled along the back of his neck.

They walked down the corridor. Instead of cells with metal bars separating the space, five wooden doors lined one wall, each with a tiny opening at eye level. Healer Aspar stopped in front of one of the doors and placed a key inside the barely visible hole near the handle. A soft click, then he pushed the door open.

A small room with chains hanging from the wall. Another set of chains was attached to the floor. Each chain ended in a manacle.

"Solitary confinement," Healer Aspar said.

Kaeden stared into the room and shuddered. He felt a sudden need to run upstairs and out into the sunshine. This place was darkness. This place was death. He could feel it in the chill of the air.

Healer Aspar shut the door and led them to the last door at the end of the corridor.

"Another room?" Treyvar asked.

"Yes. This is where prisoners are taken when we need information." He unlocked the door and let it swing inward with a long groan. The light from the lamp didn't reach the far wall. All that could be seen was a single chair nailed into the stone floor with manacles along the arms and legs.

"You mean interrogation."

"Yes."

"And torture."

"Hence the dark history," Healer Aspar said.

There was a moment of silence, then, "I hate this place." Sumar's soft voice sounded wrong in the space.

"I hope we never have to come here," Kaeden said and turned around. He would care for those brought here, but he would not participate in the actions of those who chose to use physical force to get answers.

As he headed toward the staircase, he suddenly pictured Brighid in such a room, chained to the chair, with a bloody visage and gaping wounds. That was probably what would have happened to her—or worse—if he hadn't freed her last fall. The Nordic warriors might be brutal on the battlefield, but the southerners could be just as brutal outside of battle.

He quickly ascended the stairs. No matter how cold it was outside, it couldn't compare. Better the fresh air and sunlight than this dark place.

"Kaeden, wait!" Treyvar's voice echoed behind him. He slowed a little. "Where are you going in such a hurry?" Treyvar asked as he caught up. Kaeden could hear the heavy breathing of the others behind him.

"I need fresh air."

He bypassed the cells on the next floor and hurried toward the second set of stairs. A couple minutes later and they were in the barracks. Kaeden crossed the narrow room and escaped out the door that led to the courtyard.

Icy mountain wind hit his face the moment he exited the fortress. Yes, it was cold. But the chilly air worked as a shock to his system, cleansing the darkness and suffocation from earlier. He closed his eyes and faced the sun, then took in a deep breath.

"Are you uncomfortable in tight spaces?" Healer Aspar asked from behind him.

"No," Kaeden replied without turning around. "Well, maybe. I've never been in a dungeon before." He wasn't about to explain how the darkness had pressed down on him, or how he could almost feel the pain and despair of that place.

He lifted his right hand, covered in a fingerless glove. That revulsion for humanity he had been fighting over the last year suddenly rose past his chest and into his throat, leaving a trail of burning bile. He clenched his fist and looked away. Once again, he wondered how he could love and serve humanity when they could be so evil to one another.

35

"Captain Reginar, an army approaches from the southeast."

Captain Reginar stood from the table where he sat in the main hall. The boisterous noise from dinner quieted at the scout's words. "So Nordica is finally coming for us." He let out his breath and glanced up again. "But why now?" He frowned, then started giving orders.

For the last few weeks, those who had arrived from the White City worked together with those stationed there to reinforce the structure, fill gaps, check the foundation, go through drills, and devise defensive plans. All for this day.

At Captain Reginar's words, the main hall became a flurry of activity. Soldiers ran to retrieve their weapons, while a few new recruits quickly cleared the tables. Kaeden followed Treyvar and the other healers outside. The room that would be used for healing was already organized, with cut and folded linen bandages, prepared herbs, and a dozen beds ready to receive the wounded.

Outside, the sun sank into the west as evening approached. The mountain wind blew cool air across the fortress. Shouts echoed throughout the wide stone courtyard as archers scurried up the stairs to the battlements with bows in hand. A few soldiers lit torches around the area and along the wall. Captain Reginar was already at the top. He approached the ramparts and stared out beyond the trees toward the southeast. One scout handed him a looking glass.

"There," the scout said. Kaeden struggled to pick up his words as he reached the top. "You can see movement within the trees along the road."

Captain Reginar held the glass to his eye. "Yes. I see. They even have torches lit. Why in the Lands are they not masking their approach? They could have spread between the trees and hidden their movement. Or better yet, come during the night and caught us unawares in the early morning. Why now? At dusk?"

Captain Reginar lowered the glass. "I don't like this. Unless they truly think their superior strength and numbers will take this fortress, whoever is leading them is being foolish—"

"Look!" an archer shouted, pointing toward the forest below.

Kaeden reached the wall at the same time as the others.

"I don't see— Wait . . . what is that?" one of the other archers asked. "Is that smoke moving?"

"Could it be a fire?" said another.

"But I don't see any flames, and smoke doesn't move like that, like a snake across the ground. It rises into the air, right?" the first one replied.

The hair along Kaeden's neck rose. He had never seen them in his lifetime, but the moment he spotted the barely visible smoke weaving through the trees and toward the stairs that led up to the fortress gates, he knew what it was.

The Mordra. The shadow-wraiths from beyond the veil.

His heart stopped. Just as Mathias had no power to free the Nordic people from Armand's oath, he had no power to banish the Mordra. That was the jurisdiction of the Guardian.

If the Mordra were coming, that meant one of the Shadonae was leading the assault.

"Oh, Word," he whispered.

"What is it, Kaeden?" Treyvar came to stand beside him and looked down.

"Mordra." Kaeden curled his fingers over the edge of the wall, his blood speeding through his body.

"Mordra? You mean the shadow-wraiths that were taking out the villages last summer?"

"Yes," Kaeden said, his voice hardly above a whisper.

One of the archers took aim and shot at one of the shadows, almost invisible in the dusky light and trees. The arrow went straight through its incorporeal body.

"Do not shoot!" Captain Reginar shouted, his eyes blazing as he glanced at the offender. The archer ducked his head, but it didn't stop the murmurs and whispers of fear sweeping along the top of the wall.

"Did you see that?"

"Did that arrow go right through that creature?"

"Captain! What are your orders?"

Captain Reginar stood very still in the torchlight, his face rigid, without a trace of emotion.

"Captain!" the soldier yelled again.

Seconds ticked by. Then he finally answered. "Remain at your post and prepare for the Nordic assault." Captain Reginar turned toward Kaeden and walked firmly in his direction. There was still no trace of fear on the man's face.

"Master Kaeden, how do we fight these shadow-creatures?" Captain Reginar asked once he was close, his voice lowered.

"We . . . can't," Kaeden replied.

For the first time, a crack appeared in Captain Reginar's visage. "What do you mean?"

"They are creatures who have been brought over from the other side. I cannot banish them."

"But what about your power? Your mark? Can that help us?"

A wave of frigid air hit the fortress, colder than a winter wind, leaving everyone's breath like wisps in the air.

"What in the Lands?" one of the soldiers said as he clasped his arms in front of his body. Others shuddered and one man whimpered.

"Look!" Another soldier shouted and pointed down. The shadows made their way up the wide stone stairs and reached the outer gates. For a moment, the Mordra paused in front of the gates, their smoke-like bodies swirling. Slowly, one rose as if lifting its head. Small, red eyes emerged from the fog, faint in the dying light.

Kaeden stared back. *Word, what do I do?* The words barely formed in his panic-filled mind. He couldn't banish them, but was it possible the light from his palm could protect the people in the fortress?

His mind snapped into action. He would try.

"They're coming!"

Kaeden grabbed the edge of his glove and began to pull. "Everyone, to me!" he shouted.

Down below, the first shadow-creature sank to the ground and slid beneath the gate.

The temperature dropped again with a chill so cold it made his skin hurt. "To me! To me!" Kaeden commanded.

Captain Reginar began to shout the same thing, but then screams emerged from the area below the wall, and those around him began to scatter in panic.

Kaeden threw his glove to the ground and held his palm aloft. Light blazed from his hand, illuminating most of the battlements and part of the courtyard below. "If you want to live, come to me!"

Treyvar moved between the archers along the wall, shouting the same thing.

Kaeden glanced to his side over the edge. The second shadow now flowed beneath the gate. More shouts and cries filled the fortress. Meanwhile, about half a mile away, the torches of the Nordic forces advanced on them.

The sun set beyond the mountains.

A few soldiers regained their thoughts and hurried toward Kaeden. The light from his palm reached from the battlements, across the courtyard, toward the main hall. Soldiers spilled out of the double doors, running toward the light.

Captain Reginar instructed the archers to remain by the wall and be ready with their bows. Some moved forward. Others stared back at the main hall as terrifying screams came from within.

"Focus!" Captain Reginar shouted. "The enemy approaches!"

Kaeden's arm grew weary. He faltered. The light drew away from the main hall, and one of the Mordra emerged at the same time as a soldier.

Before the soldier could dash across the courtyard toward the circle of light, the shadow-wraith shot over the empty space and fog swirled around the man. Both the wraith and the shadows were so dark, Kaeden could no longer see the soldier until a body dropped to the ground.

Kaeden shot his hand into the sky again. He took a few steps away from the battlements until his light reached almost the entire courtyard. If only he had done that sooner.

The Mordra glided past the corpse and faced Kaeden. It stayed just beyond the edge of the light, its ruby red eyes peering across the courtyard and up at him.

"You will come no closer!" His words sounded brave, but his hand shook as he held it high.

"Here, I will help you." Treyvar grabbed his arm above and beneath his elbow and kept Kaeden's hand in place.

The wraith began to weave back and forth like a caged animal. The soldiers quieted a little, but sounds still came from within the fortress.

Kaeden's teeth chattered from the chill and morbid thoughts in his head. How many had the shadows taken out? Who was left? Did they even stand a chance?

He shook his head and focused on his hand. The light almost burned his palm now, as if sensing the dark creatures. He would stand there all night if he had to.

Another pair of hands bolstered his arm. He glanced over to find Sumar, the young healer, assisting Treyvar. Her face was pale and her eyes wide and dark. She glanced at his face, then at his hand. "I can help too."

Kaeden concentrated on holding his arm up, keeping his fingers spread so the light of his mark could protect those around him. His face grew hot from the exertion, but his fingers were freezing, along with the rest of his body. Every few minutes, he glanced around. The shadows could not pass his light.

He closed his eyes for a moment. *Thank you, Word.*

Dusk faded into the night sky.

Sumar and Treyvar took turns holding his arm up. Time passed as if through water. All Kaeden could think about was saving as many as he could. Somewhere in the back of his mind, he could hear Reginar giving commands and the twang of bow strings as they loosed arrows.

"What's happening?" he asked at one point, his fingers numb.

"The Nordic forces have reached the gate," Treyvar answered.

"Our archers are keeping them at bay, but they are returning our shots with ones of their own."

Even as he spoke, Kaeden heard a thump, then a cry. He glanced over his shoulder to see an archer fall to the stone floor, an arrow protruding from his eye.

He turned away. Was this all for nothing? Was he simply prolonging the inevitable? His heart thudded dully and his hand trembled.

"Steady, there," Treyvar said. "You are all that stands between us and those creatures." He glanced at Sumar. "You go help the wounded."

Sumar nodded and dashed away.

Kaeden stared up at the night sky. A dozen lights twinkled against the inky blackness.

Persevere. Survive.

A loud thud sounded along the walls. Followed by another, and another.

"Target those carrying the ram," Reginar shouted from behind him.

More twangs. More thuds. Time dragged on.

If not for Treyvar helping him hold his hand up, he would have dropped it long ago.

A loud burst echoed across the area, followed by shouting and cursing.

"They're through!"

"Captain, what now?"

Reginar ordered something, but Kaeden couldn't hear the words past the sudden rushing in his head.

This was it. The light from his hand might keep the Mordra away, but it could not stop the Nordic forces.

They had lost.

That thought pierced his soul—

Thud.

His mind registered the arrow before his senses did. Right at eye level, above his elbow, in the arm he currently held aloft.

Then pain. First like a razor blade when he nicked himself while shaving, then spreading to a burning sensation.

Treyvar cursed for the first time as he held Kaeden's arm in place.

The weight of the arrow bore down, tearing his skin as gravity pulled on it. Someone bumped into him, causing the arrow to jostle and he cried out.

"Careful!" Treyvar shouted.

"The shadow-creature is retreating," someone else yelled.

Kaeden clenched his jaw and glanced toward the main hall. Sure enough, the Mordra that had been watching him had slipped along the wall and disappeared below, where the main gates stood. "Their master . . . must be calling them back," he said.

Dizziness washed over him as a familiar heat began to burn deep inside his chest. His power was awakening to the injury he had sustained. But—he panted as Treyvar continued to hold his hand aloft—it felt sluggish.

Kaeden blinked. "Treyvar," he said, hardly able to speak. His vision was slipping away. "I think—I think the arrow was poisoned."

Treyvar was looking toward the courtyard and didn't seem to hear him. "Here they come," he said.

"It-it's poison—" Kaeden's knees buckled, and he slipped through Treyvar's hold. His body slammed into the stone, and the arrow tore through his arm.

"Kaeden!"

Kaeden heard Treyvar yelling his name but couldn't see him. He couldn't see anything. Not even the light from his palm. All he could feel was the arrow in his arm and the battle between his healing power and whatever toxin had entered his body.

Was it possible a poison existed that could overcome his Eldaran healing power?

Fire swept over his body, surging through his bones. Whether it was his blood cleansing him or the poison taking him, he didn't know.

Everything faded to black.

36

"So, you finally woke up."

It was a female voice, low and sultry.

Kaeden blinked, then fully opened his eyes and the room came into focus. First thing he noticed was a woman sitting in a wooden chair in front of him.

She was petite with bright green eyes, pale skin, and black, silky hair with a single white stripe running along the right side of her face. She wore a simple tunic and dark pants and boots. Her legs and arms were crossed as she stared at him with a hungering curiosity.

Where am I? And who is she?

Faint light streamed in on his left from long, narrow windows. A single candle burned on the nearby desk, which sat against the far wall with a bookcase full of scrolls next to it. He recognized the room. It was a smaller room off the main hall that Captain Reginar had been using as his headquarters. If it was dusk, almost a full day had passed.

Suddenly, the woman leaned forward. "You were not what I was expecting."

Kaeden felt her eyes trail his form, and he stiffened under her perusal. He took stock of his body. His hands were bound tight behind him, but the pain from the arrow was gone, along with the sluggish feeling from the poison. Either she had administered an antidote, or his healing blood had won out. Probably his blood. Explained why he had been unconscious for almost a full day.

She tapped her chin. "I think I know the answer, but I want to hear it from you. What is your power, Eldaran?"

Kaeden struggled from the floor and sat upright. "It is usually polite to introduce yourself first," he retorted.

A spark of anger flashed across her eyes, but she schooled her features. "Fine. I am from the lands to the west and a fellow Eldaran—"

"No, you're not."

Another flash of anger. "Former Eldaran."

"And what is your power?" Kaeden asked. Already he was learning a few things about his captor. First, she was easily incited.

She crossed her arms. "I am—*was*—a Guardian."

"You are the master of those Mordra who attacked us."

"Yes."

"You tore the veil and brought those creatures into our world."

"Yes."

"And went against everything that was fought for in the Great Battle."

Her fingers dug into her arms. "That was a long time ago. Things have changed since then."

"To the point that you chose to free what the previous Guardians had *banished*?"

Instead of anger, she chuckled. "I think I know your power. You are the Truthsayer. Even without using your mark, you were able to get me to share the truth."

"Just something I learned from my mentor," Kaeden replied.

"The previous Truthsayer."

Kaeden nodded.

"Was he your father?"

Second observation: She was unaware of who he was. Or Mathias. And probably didn't know about Selma. That could be an advantage. "No."

"So how did you become the Truthsayer?" That same hungering curiosity returned to her eyes.

Kaeden remained silent. What was she searching for? What was it she wanted?

"Did you kill him?"

Kaeden watched her face. "What is your name?"

She returned his stare. "Viessa," she finally answered. "I guess we haven't exchanged names. As you said, it is the polite thing to do."

"I am Kaeden."

"Kaeden." She rolled the word out. "Kaeden. A strong name that means fighter. It certainly fits you." Her gaze passed over him again. "Now, how did you become the Truthsayer?"

Third revelation: Viessa was curious about the Truthsayer. But for what purpose? "As a former Eldaran, you should know how our gifts are passed on."

"Yes, but there can be discrepancies. I inherited the Guardian gift, while my brother did not."

Brother. Was it possible he was one of the Shadonae? But which one? The Oathmaker or the other?

"Hmmm. Not inherited. If you had received the gift from your father or mother, I don't believe there would have been a shaking."

"Shaking?" Kaeden frowned.

"Oh, something you don't know?" Viessa grinned.

There was a lot he didn't know.

"We felt the tremors when you came into the truthsaying power. That was how we knew one had died and another had taken their place."

Kaeden blinked. He had no idea such a thing had occurred. He wanted to ask what it was like but held back. The more connections he made with Viessa, the easier it could be for her to manipulate him. Best not to let her know his ignorance and curiosity about their people.

"So." Viessa stood and started walking around. "You did not inherit the power. Instead, you came into it when the other Truthsayer died. The Truthsayer was your mentor. Which means either proximity or your relationship could have been the reason the power transferred to you." She stopped in front of him. "One way to find out. I think I'll start tomorrow." She looked over his head. "Hauss!"

The door opened behind him. "Yes?"

"Take this man and lock him up with the others in the cells below. Wait, no." Viessa glanced down at Kaeden, and her lips parted in a wide smile. "Take him to solitary confinement."

Solitary... confinement?

"Solitary confinement?" Hauss asked, echoing Kaeden's thoughts.

Kaeden glanced over to find a brutish man with long, dark brown hair gathered in a dozen braids and short facial hair. A single rune was tattooed along his neck. Beside him entered a long, lean grey wolf. The wolf peered at Kaeden but didn't seem hostile.

"Yes."

"Is there a reason?" Hauss asked as he approached.

"You saw what he did last night and the light from his hand. His power will thwart what I have planned for the other prisoners. He needs to be confined alone in the lower depths."

Depths? Kaeden's head shot up. Did she mean the level beneath the dungeons? Where only a handful of tiny rooms and darkness dwelled?

"All right," Hauss muttered. He grabbed Kaeden by arm and proceeded to lift him.

Kaeden jerked back and twisted his wrists, but whoever bound him made sure the thin ropes were tight.

Wham.

Stars popped across his vision as blood trickled down the side of his face.

"It'd be better if you came along nicely." Hauss hooked the end of his axe into his belt loop. Kaeden reconsidered fighting, but his sight went dizzy again as his blood rushed to the wound.

Hauss pulled. "Bolva," he grunted a second later. "What kind of man is he?" He heaved one more time and brought Kaeden to his feet.

Viessa laughed. "Not your typical kind. But more dangerous than any of your greatest warriors."

"Is that so? But he's dressed like a southern healer."

"Don't let his clothes deceive you. Remember that light."

"As you say." Hauss shoved Kaeden around. "Down into the depths you go." He pushed Kaeden toward the door.

"Don't forget, never touch his hand!" Viessa called out.

Hauss growled as they left the small room and entered the main hall. "What are you? Contagious or something?" Kaeden caught him peering at his bound hands while his wolf companion loped along behind them. "Do you have a mark like Viessa?"

Kaeden didn't respond. All he could think about were those tiny, dark cells with no light.

The main hall—once filled with the forces of the south—now held Nordic warriors. They stood or sat at the long tables, chatting away and drinking. However, their numbers didn't fill even half the hall. That took Kaeden by surprise as Hauss shoved him toward the soldiers' barracks. It would have been impossible for such a small number to take Stelriden. The only way it was doable was because of the Mordra. He glanced around. Where were those creatures now?

Hauss pushed him to the end of the corridor and into soldier's barracks. With a grip on his arm, Hauss directed him left, where a desk, bookshelf, and doorway stood at the end of the narrow room.

Kaeden swallowed. "You can just place me with the other prisoners," he said as they approached the door. Viessa had mentioned the prisoners were in the cells below.

Hauss grunted. "The lady said to put you away. Alone."

"Why? What does she have planned for the others?"

Hauss didn't answer as he grabbed the ring of keys from the desk and opened the door.

The inky darkness beyond appeared like a gaping maw. Kaeden balked, but Hauss pushed him forward. It felt like the walls were closing in on him as he descended the stairs. He twisted his hands, hoping to loosen the rope, but the cord held tight, so tight his fingers began to tingle. No use.

As they approached the bottom, Kaeden could hear voices and spotted the dim, blue light from the fre stones mingled with a hint of orange from a torch beyond.

When he reached the bottom step, Hauss shoved him from behind. "Move it."

Kaeden staggered forward into the corridor between the cells. For one moment, he contemplated kicking Hauss and making a run for it. But he wouldn't get far. Not with his hands bound and an entire room of Nordics waiting up above.

"Kaeden, is that you?"

Kaeden peered beyond the bars. In the dim, blue light, he could see people gathered within the cells on each side. A figure moved to his left and stepped toward the iron rods. Treyvar.

"Treyvar, you're here."

"Yes, all of us who are left—"

Hauss slammed the bar near Treyvar's face with the side of his fist. "Shut it, Rylander filth." His wolf companion followed up with a low growl.

Treyvar didn't even flinch. He stared boldly at Hauss. The Nordic glared back. "We are all here," Treyvar continued. "Including Captain Reginar, but he's—"

Slam! "I said shut it!"

Treyvar took one step back but kept his gaze on Kaeden.

"That's better." Hauss shoved Kaeden. "Move."

The prisoners murmured as Kaeden walked between the bars toward the archway at the other end, where a torch was lit and hung in an iron ring.

"Where are they taking him?" he heard someone whisper.

"Looks like down the stairs."

"Where they torture people?"

"I'll be all right," Kaeden said as he glanced left and right, thankful his voice didn't crack. Then he opened his marked hand as wide as he could, despite the cord around his wrists, and let the faint light spread across the cells. He would leave hope for these people.

The crowd hushed. Even Hauss seemed stunned for a moment. Then he came out of his reverie and shoved Kaeden toward the doorway ahead. "She won't like this," Hauss muttered as they reached the end of the corridor. Hauss grabbed the torch. "Down you go," he barked.

Kaeden didn't risk a glance back. He had given them something to cling to. As for himself . . .

With each step, the darkness consumed what little light he had left inside, until all that remained was the orange glow from Hauss's torch. He could feel it now: the death and despair of this place. It seeped into him like a bone-chilling fog, permeating every part of him, stealing his breath and leaving his heart pounding.

"She must really hate you to place you down here," Hauss said. There was no humor in his voice. "Or maybe she plans on torturing you. All I know is she was excited when she realized you were here at the fortress."

Kaeden barely heard him over the rushing in his ears.

At the bottom, Hauss guided him roughly down the corridor.

Cold sweat broke out over his body. He suddenly wanted to plead with Hauss to take him back upstairs. The words were already forming on his tongue when he pressed his lips together. No. That would be weakness. A weakness Viessa would hear about and no doubt use.

Instead, he clenched his hands behind him, so tight his fingernails dug into his skin and mark. Viessa wanted him here, away from the others. She wanted to know more about how he became the Truthsayer. She was easily incited, and although Hauss listened to her, he did not seem to respect her.

How can I use this knowledge? he thought as Hauss opened the last door before the torture area.

Persevere. Survive.

They were the same two words that came to mind as Kaeden held his hand aloft last night to save the southern soldiers from the Mordra. He would need to live by those words again.

Hauss pushed him into the small room. "Next to the wall," he barked.

Kaeden walked to the wall.

"Turn."

He did as he was told. Hauss pulled the chains from the wall, first setting the manacles around his feet, then around the area above his wrists, while his wolf waited out in the corridor.

Hauss sighed as he clasped the last manacle. "Listen, I don't like doing this. This isn't our way."

"Our way?" Kaeden's heart was still thumping, but he had been able to harness the fear pulsing through him. It would do no good to panic. He needed his mind intact.

"My people. We aren't like you, invading land that isn't ours and starving people. Well, not all of us." He rubbed the back of his neck. "Hjar Volka can be a bit harsh."

"Then would you leave some light for me?"

Hauss looked up. "Aye, I can do that. I can't leave your door open, but I'll hang the torch just outside."

"Thank you."

Hauss squinted. "You're an interesting man. Most would be yelling or crying at the thought of being left down here."

Hauss had no idea how much he was holding back.

"Well, I best be going." Hauss left the cell. A loud creak filled the area as he shut the door. It latched with a thud. Kaeden swallowed the panic rising in his throat. Only a small square of light remained in the dark cell.

The orange light moved across the tiny opening and for a second, Kaeden thought Hauss had changed his mind and was going to take the torch with him. But then he heard a scraping noise and the light stopped. The sound of boots slapping against the stone faded until all that remained was nothing.

Kaeden sank to his knees, his hands still bound and now chained behind him. He wanted to let loose all the fear and hopelessness building up inside. Was this how his parents felt when they were captured during the Khodath uprising? Imprisoned, awaiting their fate?

He bowed his head. Slowly, he opened his palms behind him. The barest light filtered into the room. Light from his mark. Light passed down to him from his parents and their parents. Generations of Eldarans who fought in the Great Battle alongside the Word and remained behind to help mankind.

They, too, had faced darkness. Like his parents.

He wasn't alone.

He closed his eyes. The fear of this place seemed to lessen, but it was still there, lingering along the edges of his mind. "Here I am, Word," he whispered, his voice breaking the silence. Nothing more came. It seemed the words were twisted inside his heart. But he knew one thing. He had come north. And now he was near one of the Shadonae. One who had released the Mordra back into the Lands.

She had to be stopped.

"I don't know how I'm going to do that," Kaeden whispered. He might still harbor distrust and reluctance toward humanity, even revulsion at their touch. But that wouldn't hinder him from fulfilling Mathias's mission. To fulfill the role of a Truthsayer.

Someway, somehow, it was his responsibility to pass judgment on Viessa.

37

The moment Viessa saw that beam of light shoot from the ramparts of Stelriden Fortress, she knew an Eldaran was stationed there. But never did she imagine it was the Truthsayer himself. The light from his palm had held off the Mordra, something she didn't think anyone but another Guardian could do.

His power was glorious to behold, and to think she had found him—and Armand had not.

Viessa smiled to herself as she held her torch aloft and descended into the dungeons. Armand, with all his plans and wisdom, never considered the Truthsayer would come to this northern fortress instead of heading out with the main southern forces.

Now, to keep this information to herself and figure out how to make his power her own, and never Armand's.

Viessa bypassed the cells filled with southerners, ignoring their shouts and derisions. They were nothing but mewling weaklings, whose lifeforces would be used to refuel her and the Mordra. One of the Nordics following her yelled at the prisoners, while Viessa reached the end of the row and began her descent to the second level.

As she stepped off the last stair deep within the dungeons, she spotted a single torch burning at the end of the corridor. It appeared Hjar Volka's skal was soft. Hauss and another Nordic accompanied her down the corridor, bypassing the other enclosed cells. "Which one did you put him in?" Viessa asked, her voice echoing along the stone.

"The last one before the torture room," Hauss replied.

"And you left a light for him?"

"He asked. I didn't see any reason why not."

Viessa shook her head. She had assumed Volka's clan would be as ruthless as he was, but apparently there were a few who held back. Even Hauss's wolf seemed tempered. "Is the door locked?"

"No. He's chained inside. I saw no reason to lock it."

She stopped before the door. A small square stood at eye level, but she could see nothing within. She didn't want Kaeden to see her use the prisoners to replenish her strength. That, and she believed he would be more pliable in her hands after a night alone in the darkness. However, Hauss had left him a torch.

She would make sure that didn't happen again.

Pressing down on the latch, she opened the door. Dim light spilled into the tiny room and across Kaeden's bent figure. He slowly lifted his head, his thick dark hair parting to reveal his face. It was a handsome face and complimented his nice physique. She could appreciate that about him, but that was all. What she really wanted was his ability.

"How was your evening?" Viessa asked as she entered. "Sleep well?"

Kaeden simply watched her with a wary gaze.

"Hopefully you've rested enough. Hauss, unshackle him and take him into the next room."

"Fine."

Viessa narrowed her eyes but didn't say anything. Unlike the clanless she usually worked with over the last few months, Hauss and the others from the Wolf Clan did not treat her with respect. They were here only under Volka's orders and never failed to remind her, by their words and actions, that she was not worthy of their regard.

Hauss undid the manacles while the other warrior held Kaeden in place. Once he was free, Hauss hauled Kaeden to his feet. "Out you go," he said and directed Kaeden through the door.

Around the corner they went, and into the next room. Viessa instructed the other warrior to bring two more torches while she held her own up to illuminate the chamber. It was bigger than the tiny cells, with a single chair in the middle of the room complete with restraints.

"Place him in the chair," she said.

Hauss shoved Kaeden into the chair.

"Lock him in."

He did as he was told.

Viessa watched Hauss work. If Kaeden had received this power through the death of the previous Truthsayer, then it was possible she could obtain it through the same means. At least that was what she had conjectured last night.

However, there were a few problems with that idea. One: If that was how gifts were transferred, then her brother, Peder, would have killed a more powerful Eldaran a long time ago. Perhaps even Armand. But Eldarans died all the time, and their gifts with them. Even if that wasn't the case for the Truthsayer, there had to be protective measures in place for the leader of their kind.

So taking Kaeden's head with one stroke was not an option—at least, not at this point.

But perhaps there was a work around. A way to wheedle down his lifeforce until it gave out. It would be difficult. His Eldaran blood would continue to heal him. And he was young, which meant his power was at its peak. What would it take to bring him to the edge of death?

She tapped her chin. She would just have to try.

Hauss finished restraining Kaeden, while the other warrior returned with more torches. "Need anything else?" Hauss asked as he stepped back.

Viessa pursed her lips. She would rather have these men do the dirty work, but she had a feeling Hauss would refuse. There was still a sliver of that Nordic honor in the man. And he would probably use that honor to stop her from employing the other warrior.

She was on her own. Well, she had ways. She listed out a few weapons, including a dagger and axe. Hauss crossed his arms and frowned at her demands but, in the end, obeyed.

"After you deliver them, I'll have you wait outside in the corridor."

Hauss's scowl deepened.

Viessa lifted her lips into what she hoped was a smile. The Nordics were easy to manipulate, up to a point. Then their accursed honor stepped in and stopped them. Except Volka and his closest warriors.

They had no problem killing. They even took glee in it. She should have asked for someone other than Hauss and his men to accompany her. Too late now.

An hour later, Viessa leaned against the wall, sweat running down her face and body. All she could smell was blood. She raised her head to find Kaeden staring at her. His lips twisted into a ghastly smile.

"*What?*" she yelled.

Kaeden laughed, the blood around his mouth coating his lips. "Is this all you can do?"

Viessa covered the ground in three strides, grabbed a fistful of his hair, and jerked his head back. "No, I can do more. *A lot more.*"

She began to circle him like a cat.

"It won't work," he said.

"What won't?"

"What you're trying to do."

"And what am I doing?"

"Take my power."

So he had figured that out. "Yes, I am."

"And what will you do with it? Do you know what it's really like? To see inside people?"

"I can handle that."

Kaeden craned his neck and looked at her. His visage was bloody and gruesome, along with the shreds of his robe hanging from deep wounds inflicted by her. His gaze held such an intensity that it sent a shiver down her spine. "No, you can't."

She froze. She had heard stories of the Truthsayers and the immense power they wielded. So much that only one of their kind ever possessed that power at a time. The ability to see everything and to hold both the mind and soul of a human in the palm of his hand. More powerful than Armand's words. More powerful than command of the Mordra. Just the thought of that power erased the sliver of fear and replaced it with an intense warmth in her middle.

No, she wanted that power. *Needed* that power. More than anything.

Armand had promised a better life if they left. Instead, she had become one of his puppets. Viessa bent over and grabbed his chin. Not anymore. She would forge her own way. "I want it," she whispered.

For a moment, Kaeden appeared solemn in the light. Then the look on his face changed. He spread his lips into a grin, with blood staining his teeth. "Then take it. Take my hand. Take my arm." His grin spread wider. "Take whatever you like."

Viessa drew back and narrowed her eyes. What just happened to him? Was the Truthsayer secretly crazy? This sudden change was unnerving.

"Maybe I'll do that." She had done many things in life. She wasn't afraid to cross lines. Not after she crossed the ultimate line when she denounced her people. She reached for the dagger. But she wasn't ready to take a limb. Better to see how long he would bleed.

Kaeden never lost consciousness. He would pant and cringe, but he never cried out. And his body repaired itself, almost in a mesmerizing way. This. This was the power of the Truthsayer. Beyond what she held in her own blood. Beyond what Armand possessed.

And yet it angered her as well.

"Why. Won't. You. Die?" she yelled and threw the knife across the room. It hit the wall and clattered to the ground.

Kaeden didn't look up.

Viessa paused. Had she done it?

His fingers curled over the edge of the chair. No. He was still here.

Primal rage filled her chest, and she took a step toward him. No more playing, no more testing. It was now time to end him—

Wait.

Viessa froze as a horrible thought entered her mind. She stared at Kaeden, barely conscious, save for the subtle movement of his hand. Drops of blood were scattered around his feet. As she watched, his shoulders slowly rose and fell. He breathed. He was still alive.

She twisted around, clutching a hand to her chest. What if—what if he died by her hand . . . and his power passed to another? Perhaps distance wasn't the only thing that influenced the transition of the truthsaying power. Was it possible that if she inadvertently delivered the deathblow and he didn't just bleed out, she could be passed by?

Viessa gripped her head with her hands. "No," she whispered. "I can't let that happen. Armand took everything else. If I don't find a way—" she lifted her hand and stared at the black mark across her palm, faintly visible in the torchlight. As if the fires of the Abyss had burned a hole through her hand, leaving the surrounding skin charred and dead. "I must never die. But the Mordra are not enough." She glanced at Kaeden. "If I accidentally kill him, Armand might receive that power."

Viessa straightened. Armand. Once she had admired him, but now she hated him. Perhaps more than she hated the Eldarans. He made so many promises back then to both her and Peder. His words were like honey, pleasant and addicting. Then the light disappeared from her palm, leaving behind this revolting black hole. If she had any regrets, it was that. The others lived like hypocrites, and yet she had been cursed with this necrotic mark. "I despise you, Armand. I would rather lose everything than see you obtain the Truthsayer's ability."

Viessa clenched her hand. "I need more time to think." She crossed the room and opened the door. Outside stood Hauss, his wolf companion, and another warrior. "Lock him up in his cell. And be sure to secure his hands, especially his right one."

Hauss looked inside and muttered, "Bolva." The other warrior grimaced. The fur rose along the wolf's back and she growled.

Viessa ignored them as the men entered the room. She waited in the hall, watching them undo the restraints. *Yes. I need to revise my plan. And think carefully before I accidentally give Armand what he wants. Maybe poison. A slow-acting poison . . .*

The warriors roughly pulled Kaeden to his feet. His head lolled forward. He was passed out. But he wasn't dead, right? As the two men dragged him toward the door, Viessa stepped forward. "Wait." She reached up and placed two fingers along Kaeden's neck. Barely a pulse, but it was there. She let out her breath. He still held on to life. Amazing, after all she had done to him. "Take him away."

She stepped back and the men proceeded. Outside the room, they dragged Kaeden to his cell. Viessa watched them struggle under his weight and height. His body was probably another reason he had kept from succumbing to her torture. A lesser Eldaran would have perished, but he persisted. His size and health. And his power. The perfect combination to make him almost immortal.

"I will find a way," she murmured as they disappeared around the corner. "You will die. And I will inherit your power, one way or another."

※○※

Kaeden blinked. Darkness. And pain. Wait, no, there was a small light just above him. He lifted his head, then grimaced. Even that hurt. He took in a couple breaths, then more slowly lifted his head again. A small square of light.

The feeling in the rest of his body returned in stabbing pain and agony. And burning as his power flowed toward the wounds and began to heal. How much longer could his body sustain this? And how long would he be unconscious afterward to replenish his strength?

He ran his tongue along his teeth and lips, then spat. Blood. So much blood. Maybe he shouldn't have pushed Viessa over the edge like that. After all, as he had seen, she was easy to provoke. But it did help him to figure out a few things. She had spoken the words out loud.

She wanted the truthsaying power.

She never wanted to die.

She despised Armand.

The last one was interesting. At first, he thought she was power-hungry to the point of being unhinged. But then those words. And the way she had looked at her hand. Although he didn't see her mark, Mathias said the Shadonae lost all light in their palm, turning it into something grotesque.

And she seemed to blame Armand for it.

Kaeden let out a painful breath. Did Viessa not know that, even with the truthsaying power, she would eventually die? Mathias died. The previous Truthsayers died. Nothing could stop death but the Word.

He shifted his body, and the chains bound to his hands and feet rattled against the stone floor. His knee knocked into something. A bucket hardly visible in the faint light. Kaeden opened his palm, letting more light into his cell. It was a bucket of water. There was also a wooden platter with what looked like a small loaf of bread close by.

Who had left those? If Viessa wanted him to die, hunger was one way to do it. It must be the Nordic. He had also left a torch in the corridor again.

"Thank you," Kaeden whispered as weight began to settle along his shoulders and chest. Now that his body had healed, it would force him into an unconscious rest. Better eat and drink while he could. He stared at the bucket, then dipped his head down and lapped like a dog.

After quenching his thirst, he strained his neck forward and caught the bread between his teeth, pulled it toward him, and consumed what he could. It was difficult without hands, but he managed.

The weight across his body increased until Kaeden was forced to stop. His head lolled forward, and his eyelids drooped. At least he was able to eat and drink.

Thank you, Word, he thought as he closed his eyes. Never had he thought he would end up in such a place. Anxiety would have taken him if not for the fact that he was not alone, evidenced by the wavering torchlight outside his cell and the knowledge his parents had instilled in him at a young age—that the Word was everywhere.

Even in the darkness.

38

"Kaeden!"

Brighid sat up and clutched the blanket to her chest. Cold sweat covered her body. She could still see the dark cell and almost smell the blood that pooled around his boots. And that woman. Dark hair with a stripe of white, blazing green eyes, and a dagger in her hand. A dagger she used to carve Kaeden's body.

It was Viessa. One of the Shadonae.

Brighid tossed the blanket aside and swung her legs around. Was this dream real? Or a nightmare?

She leaned forward and held her head in her hands. These dreams she had of Kaeden were so confusing. More like glimpses of actual events rather than the vague images of her other dreams.

If these dreams were real . . . what did she just see? Had Kaeden been captured—and tortured—by one of the Shadonae?

Brighid looked around the room. Rows of beds lined the walls, each with a sleeping figure. She quietly let out her breath. Her yell hadn't woken the other women she shared this space with, including Tola, who snored softly.

Through the nearby window, the faint rays of dawn shone. Early, but still morning. She got up and dressed. She needed to do something. Anything. Bjornfrost came to mind. Yes, she would take him out on a run.

After securing her boots, she snatched her cloak. The old grey one Kaeden gave her months ago when he freed her. She pressed the faded fabric to her face. Restlessness filled her, and she gripped the cloth tighter between her fingers.

Was he really being tortured? But where? Had he been captured? And why was Viessa torturing him?

Brighid silently left the room and ventured into the great hall. No one was there this early in the morning. She crossed the cavernous space and headed out the door. Dawn filled the sky with rosy colors that caused the trees around the stronghold to appear as if they were on fire. For one moment, she stopped and stared in awe. Rarely was she out this early. Then the restlessness hit her again.

She used the horn by the gate to call Bjornfrost. Almost as if he anticipated her need, her bear companion appeared a minute later through the trees.

"Bjornfrost," she cried and ran toward him. He lifted his head and regarded her as she approached. Brighid went to his side and mounted him with no saddle. Although one had been made for the pair, Brighid didn't want to take the time to retrieve it. She needed to feel the wind in her face and let nature fill her. The same way it always did when she felt death.

"Go," she said in the ancient tongue. He turned and ran for the forest. Most of the snow was gone, with only a few muddy patches remaining beneath ancient pine trees where the sun never shone. The air was still cold, but today it felt good against her skin.

They raced through the forest until they reached the cliff that overlooked Rokr Valley. The sun was swiftly rising to the east, casting its rays across the forests and valley below. Brighid remained on Bjornfrost's back and watched the world come to light. Slowly, her gaze turned toward the southwest. At the other end of the valley stood the border between Nordica and the Ryland Plains. And Stelriden Fortress.

She frowned. Over a month ago, they had received a message that there would be an attack on Stelriden Fortress led by one of the Shadonae. The message also said that Bard and the warriors here might be asked to help.

Was it possible Viessa had already led the charge and held the fortress? And somehow Kaeden was there during the attack and had been taken captive?

Or was it just a nightmare? A figment in her head?

"I don't know," she whispered. She patted Bjornfrost's neck and he huffed.

A wind sprang up. First, soft and gentle. Then it turned into a strong gust that tore across the cliff, forcing Bjornfrost to back into the tree line. Brighid held her arm to her face to protect her eyes.

Go.

Brighid pressed her arm closer.

Go.

Was she really hearing that?

The gust moved on, leaving behind that soft, gentle breeze.

Brighid lowered her arm. Go? Go where—

She looked across the valley. Go to Stelriden?

She gazed in that direction, and her muscles tightened as if preparing for battle. Her jaw clenched and she pressed her lips together. Yes. If Kaeden was there, she would go to him. He rescued her months ago from the southern forces.

It was her turn to save him.

When Brighid arrived back at the Bear Clan's stronghold, she searched out her uncle. She found Bard inside the main hall and went directly toward him. A fire had been lit in the large firepit, and he stood along its edge, warming himself. At the sound of her approach, he looked up. "Brighid? What are you doing awake this early in the morning?"

"Do you know if the attack planned for Stelriden Fortress has taken place?"

"Not that I know of. Nor have we been summoned to assist."

"Is there any way you can find out?"

Bard frowned. "Why are you asking?"

Brighid paused. She still held secrets. That she could feel death and had strange dreams of Kaeden. She wasn't sure if they were real or just a lingering connection she had made with him.

"I had a strange dream last night."

Bard crossed his arms. "Go on."

Brighid glanced around to make sure they were alone, then told him what she saw.

Bard shook his head. "I don't know what to think. On the one hand, we all have nightmares. But the details you were able to see, and the fact that we know one of those strangers would be leading the attack, are unique. Those powerful within the Owl Clan can have similar visions of real places, people, and events."

Brighid's eyebrows shot up. "They do?"

"Yes, after all, they are tied to the mystical. But you're not of the Owl Clan. However, this Kaeden is not human but something greater. Perhaps there is a connection between the two of you, and he reached out to you in a moment of suffering."

"Is that possible?"

"There are many strange powers in this world. Given that you said his mission was to seek out the Shadonae and judge them, it's possible he is at Stelriden Fortress. He would need to find a way to get close to them. Placing himself in the north is one way."

"If what I saw is real, is there a way to save him?"

Bard grew quiet. "You know my thoughts. Moving against Viessa could be considered treasonous by the rest of Nordica. And we are already paying the price for allying ourselves with powerful beings."

"That is true. But Kaeden might be the only one who can stop Armand and break the hold he has on us."

Bard glanced away and let out a long breath. "If we are to survive as a nation, we will need to stand against our so-called allies." He turned back to Brighid. "Perhaps an opportunity has finally come to eliminate one of them. But before I commit our clan to such an act, there are things we need to consider. If we fail, and word gets back to Armand, all of the Bear Clan will be in danger."

Bard was right. Brighid squeezed her hand shut. But how much longer did Kaeden have?

"If your vision is true, we don't have much time. Stelriden Fortress is a three-day march from here. We would need to leave today."

Brighid glanced up. Did this mean Bard was considering rescuing Kaeden?

"We will need to determine the situation once we reach the

fortress. Has it been captured by our people? Who is in charge? Viessa? Or one of our leaders? And how do we save this Kaeden without hurting our own people? And Brighid"—Bard paused and looked at her—"there is a risk he might not join us afterward."

"Because he is allied with the south."

"Yes. If he is imprisoned, there's a good chance his comrades are also prisoners. I don't think a man like him would leave his friends behind, even if he remembers you."

Brighid nodded. "You have a point. But his mission is to judge the Shadonae. We are his best means to do that. However, I understand not wanting to leave comrades behind. As a gesture of goodwill, we could offer to treat the prisoners well."

Bard sighed as the door at the far end of the hall opened. "I hate this. I wish things were simple, but that doesn't seem to be an option." Then he huffed and smiled. "You're already thinking about a way to end this war. Those thoughts remind me of a banrok player. Planning multiple moves ahead. That is the way a hjar needs to think. Like a leader."

Brighid paused as warmth filled her from her uncle's praise. "But none of this will be possible if we don't save Kaeden," she said. "Without him, we have no hope of stopping the Shadonae and freeing our people."

Bard let out his breath. "We need him."

"We need him," Brighid repeated.

"Then that's it. Whenever there is danger against Nordica, it is the Bear Clan that has always led the charge. The time has come for us to move against the Shadonae and eliminate our true enemy."

"What are you two talking about?" Vigi asked as he approached the fire, shutting down their conversation.

"War, Vigi. War," Bard answered with an annoyed look.

Vigi grinned. "We're going to join the fight?"

Bard glanced at Brighid, then turned back. "Possibly. Pack your bags. We're heading to Stelriden Fortress."

39

"Hjaren Bard."

"Hauss."

Hauss crossed his arms as he stood inside the gateway of Stelriden Fortress. Evening descended upon the land. His wolf companion sat on her haunches next to him, warily watching the crowd ahead. "What brings you to Stelriden Fortress?"

Amro let out a snort next to his master. Bard placed a hand on the bear's shoulder. "My father sent me. We received a message near the end of winter that Nordic forces would try to take Stelriden at the beginning of spring. He said you might need help. So here we are." Bard waved behind him at the Bear Clan warriors who had accompanied him, over twenty in all.

Brighid stood near her uncle with her hood pulled over her head, her shield strapped to her back, and her sword at her side. Bjornfrost huffed behind her, his presence reassuring. Heming remained nearby astride his own bear companion, Uthun,

"You're late. We took the fortress a few days ago," Hauss replied.

"You know how long messages can take by bird. But now we're here." Bard looked up at the walls and nodded appreciatively. "Looks like you did a good job."

"We were never told you were coming."

Bard glanced at Hauss. "Does the leader of this expedition tell you everything?"

Hauss scowled. "No, she doesn't."

"She knew. At least, she should have known. Now, are you going to welcome us in or send us back north?"

Hauss rubbed his neck. "That is not for me to decide."

"Then go ask your mistress."

Hauss's head snapped up and he glared at Bard. "She is not our mistress. We serve Nordica alone."

"That's not what it looks like."

Brighid frowned. Why was Bard baiting the skal of the Wolf Clan?

Hauss clenched his jaw and looked over the rest of the bear company. His gaze stopped at Brighid and his eyes went wide. "What is *she* doing here?"

"Who?" Bard glanced around.

Hauss pointed at Brighid. "Her! The Stryth'Viezla."

"The who?" Vigi asked and glanced around. The others did as well. Brighid remained silent. Only Bard knew of her moniker from the war.

"I heard everyone captured during the Battle of the Plains died. How is she here? With you?"

"You mean Brighid?" Bard pointed at her.

Everyone looked her way. Heat crawled up her neck, but she remained rigid and quiet.

"Yes." Hauss stepped past Bard and stood in front of Brighid. At his movement, Bjornfrost let out a warning huff. Hauss glanced at the bear, then back at her. "How are you not dead? Wait, did you fight your way out of their camp?" There was a look of awe on his face.

Brighid felt the stares of her comrades. "No," she said finally. "I escaped."

Hauss shook his head. "But how? We were told everyone taken prisoner had died." Then he grinned. "Count on the Stryth'Viezla to survive."

"Stryth'Viezla?" Vigi asked.

Hauss glanced at him, then the others. "Wait, they don't know who you are?"

"We know exactly who she is," Lodin said, folding his arms beside his brother.

Bard stepped between Hauss and Brighid. "Brighid escaped her southern captors and fled north. Snow came early and she was caught in a blizzard. We found her injured and very sick. My mother nursed her back to health, and she has been with us ever since."

"That explains why you didn't return to your company," Hauss said, glancing past Bard. "I knew you weren't the kind to desert your own."

Brighid folded her arms. "No, I'm not." He had no idea that was why she was there. To rescue all of them if she could.

Hauss grinned. "I don't care what Viessa says, come on in. You are welcome at our fire. A few of our warriors went hunting and we have fresh game. Come celebrate our victory."

Bard bowed. "We accept your invitation. It's a pity we weren't here to assist with the battle."

Hauss shrugged. "It is what it is."

Brighid stared at the burly warrior with dark brown hair and a rune tattoo that ran along the length of his neck. This Hauss was nothing like Hjar Volka. A bit brusque but good-natured. What would happen if he discovered why they were truly there? Whom would he side with?

Hauss yelled up to someone along the top of the wall, and seconds later the damaged gates widened. When they had first arrived, Brighid was impressed with the fortress. The long stairway that led up to the main gates. The thick stone walls. It was a solid stronghold built into a mountain cliff. Much more secure than Dallam had been.

How had these Nordics taken it? There were signs of a recent battle: cracks and splinters in the gates and loose hinges. However, there should be more, like broken walls and scorch marks. But all she could see was damage to the wood, which meant they probably entered through the gates.

How was that possible? Archers would have rained down arrows on the bearers as they heaved the battering ram up the stairs, stopping them from breaking the gates.

Bard seemed to be thinking the same thing as they entered the massive courtyard. Dark shadows spread along the wide space with only a long patch of sunlight along the east wall. Ahead stood a large building, with smaller ones jetting out from the main one. The only warriors present besides the newly arrived Bear Clan were the two guarding the top of the gate.

Bard glanced around. "It appears it was an easy battle. I'm familiar with Stelriden Fortress. This place is heavily fortified, both by stone and the mountain. How did you take it with so little damage to the fortress?"

Hauss appeared uncomfortable as he led them across the courtyard, his wolf loping alongside him. "We had help."

"Help? What kind of help?"

Hauss tightened his jaw. "Viessa used her power."

The hair raised along the back of Brighid's neck. She was unfamiliar with Viessa's power and even less so with Peder's. The only one she had witnessed was Armand's.

"Can you share what that power was?" Bard asked. Amro stayed a few steps behind his master.

Hauss glanced to the left, then right, and Brighid barely overheard his next words. "She controls creatures from the other side of the veil. But don't say anything. My warriors are already spooked by the apparitions."

"You mean spirits—"

"Shh!"

Bard nodded. Another chill went down Brighid's back. If Hauss and the warriors from the Wolf Clan were afraid, it meant these creatures Viessa controlled were terrifying.

"What did you do with those who were captured?" Bard asked a couple seconds later.

"We placed them in the prison cells below."

Prison cells.

Suddenly, images of Kaeden tortured and bloody inside a small, dark cell filled her mind. Her heart beat faster. That vision . . . was real. He was here, locked away somewhere below.

"You kept them as prisoners of war?" Bard asked. "I heard Hjar Volka made sure there were never survivors after a battle."

Hauss turned around. "Viessa wanted them alive."

"What for?" Bard continued. "To trade?"

Hauss pressed his lips together and silently shook his head.

Brighid didn't like the way he chose not to answer. She was barely restraining the urge to run ahead and search for Kaeden. Even now he could be on the verge of death.

Patience, she reminded herself and breathed in through her nose. They had made multiple plans last evening, depending on the situation at Stelriden Fortress. Heming had scouted ahead with Uthun and confirmed Nordics held the fortress. But there was no news of strange creatures lurking around. What should they do?

"Where would you like our bears housed while we are here?" Bard asked.

Brighid tensed. This was it. This was the cue for a few of them to break away and search the area. And now they knew where to look: below.

Hauss stopped by a double set of doors that seemed to lead into the main part of the stronghold. Light spilled out from windows on each side across the darkened courtyard. "There are some stables to the east, near the soldier's barracks, with hay for bedding and water. Is that all you need?"

"Yes, thank you. Vigi, Loden!" Bard hollered. "Can you lead Amro there?"

"Yes, Hjaren," the men replied.

"Brighid, go ahead and follow them with Bjornfrost."

Brighid dipped her head. "Yes, Hjaren."

"Uthun and I will walk the perimeter," Heming said as he dismounted. "His muscles are tight, so I want to work them out. Arngrim, Nora, I wish to speak with you. Mind joining me?"

The two broke away from the group and joined Heming. Together, they headed toward the western wall.

Hauss glanced at Brighid, then Bjornfrost, with a questioning look, but he didn't say anything. She turned and spoke to Bjornfrost, while Vigi and Loden retrieved Amro. The bear let out a snort after Bard spoke to him, then slowly turned and followed the twins.

Bard subtly glanced over his shoulder at Brighid and gave her the smallest nod.

Brighid returned his gesture and walked away with Bjornfrost beside her. In the dusk light, she saw a wooden structure next to the wall that appeared like stables. With quick steps, she caught up to Lodin and Vigi.

"Hauss said the prisoners were down below," Lodin whispered. "I suspect the man we are rescuing is located there. He also said these stables are next to the soldier's barracks. If I were designing a fortress, I would place holding cells near the barracks. We should look there first."

"So, this southerner can really help us?" Vigi replied quietly.

Lodin glared at his brother. "You heard everything Hjaren Bard said before we left. About our allies, and what this man can do."

"It's hard to believe it all—that the hjars allowed our people to be bound in such a way, and that power like that exists."

"It does," Brighid said quietly as they approached the stables. Twilight began to turn to night, and the first star appeared overhead. "I would not be alive if it didn't."

"This man saved you," Vigi said.

"He did."

"Well, that's good enough for me," Vigi whispered. "Now we need to find him."

Brighid's lips twitched. While others needed more convincing, Vigi was simple.

They led the bears into the stables. Usually, they would have left them outside the fortress and let them roam the forest, but Bard had seen them as a good excuse to separate Brighid and the others to search for Kaeden.

At least the stalls were large. A horse stood in the farthest one and didn't seem happy about her new stablemates. The bears ignored her and settled down.

"I'll be back," Brighid whispered after removing his saddle.

Bjornfrost nudged her with his nose.

She patted him on the side of his neck, then turned and walked away. Outside, she met up with Lodin and Vigi.

Lodin pointed to a door that led into the side building. "Should be the soldier's barracks. Let's go."

The other two nodded. Silently they hurried toward the door, using the shadows from the wall to hide their movement. At the door, Vigi pressed down on the latch, and the door opened without a sound. "No one is inside," he said a moment later.

"Makes sense, everyone is eating. And they don't expect an assault from their own kind," Lodin said.

"Hopefully it won't come to that," Brighid replied. "Just retrieve Kaeden and leave."

The three of them slipped into the barracks. The first room was long, dark, and narrow, with additional rooms on the right, each filled with rows of beds. At the opposite end rested a desk, cupboard, and the faint outline of a door.

Brighid wiped her sweaty palms along her pants. This was it. Bard had taken a chance on her and brought the Bear Clan here. All to rescue a man who had once rescued her. No, more than that. A man who might just be able to rescue all of Nordica. Her heart began to pound at the thought as she neared the stairs, along with a strange fluttery feeling in her stomach.

Vigi approached the door and tried the latch. "Locked."

"I'm not surprised." Lodin looked around the desk. Seconds later, there was a jingle as he held up a ring with a handful of keys. "These might work." He walked over and tried a few. The third one worked as a click sounded and he opened the door.

Lodin glanced back. "I see stairs and a faint blue light. There must be fre stones below. Be careful going down."

As they started their descent, Lodin spoke again. "I heard stories about this place," he said, his voice an eerie echo between the stone walls. "A couple of years ago, a handful of Nordics decided to cross the border and raid a village. Their bodies were returned to us after they had spent a fortnight here."

"Ugh, I remember that," Vigi replied behind Brighid. "This is where they came from?"

"Yes."

They reached the bottom. Dim blue light revealed a long corridor with barred cells on each side.

"There are people here," Lodin whispered over his shoulder.

Vigi whispered a curse. "What do we do? Can we find a way around them?"

Too late. One of the shadowed figures stood. "Is someone there?"

Lodin paused, then stepped forward. "We are here for Kaeden," he said as he stepped into the space that ran between the barred cells. "Is he here?"

Other voices murmured as more prisoners stood, grabbed the bars, and pressed their faces between the gaps. Brighid heard Vigi gasp nearby and understood the young man's surprise. Their eyes were sunken and their faces gaunt in the cold blue light.

"You're not one of those other Nordics," a prisoner said. "Or you would know where Kaeden is."

"Is it possible they are here to help us?" someone whispered.

"They're Nordics," another said sullenly and stepped back. "They don't save anyone."

"Please," a young woman in white robes pleaded, her fingers curled around the bars. "Don't leave us here." Then she began to sob.

Brighid's heart constricted. She knew what it was like to be taken prisoner. And how tenderly Mathias and Kaeden had treated her. Then a cool wave passed over her. She also remembered how the other Nordic prisoners were treated. Hung on poles and left to die.

No, she was here for Kaeden. Not for them. But would he come with her and leave his friends and comrades behind? She would figure that out later.

She searched the cells. Kaeden was a head taller than most men. If he was here, he would be towering over those gathered.

"Where is he?" Lodin asked again.

No one answered.

Brighid closed her eyes as she recalled her dream. A dark room with only a few torches for light. Kaeden chained to a chair. Blood splattered around his feet.

She observed the space again. None of these cells looked like that room. Her heart faltered. Was it possible she was wrong?

No, he must be here. Not only had she dreamed about him but that familiar voice on the wind had whispered, *Go*. She clenched her hand. *I believe You sent me here. I just need to keep looking.*

"I know you."

Brighid stiffened. She turned slowly. In the blue light she spotted a man beyond the bars. He made his way forward. His light hair was matted, his eyes rimmed in shadows, with scruffy facial hair and a gash along one cheek. But there was a familiar air of intelligence about him. A second later, she knew why she recognized him. He was there the night Kaeden freed her.

"Are you here for him?" he asked.

"Yes," Brighid answered, horrified by the change in his appearance.

"You're here to repay your debt."

She hadn't thought about it that way. "I need him."

The man nodded. "They are keeping him down below."

There was another level?

"Get him out of here. I don't know what they've been doing to Kaeden, but he needs to live."

"Yes."

Brighid turned and sprinted to the end of the corridor, her sword and shield slapping against her body. Through a doorway, another staircase descended. She paused long enough to see the faintest hint of light at the base, then placed a hand on the cold, uneven stone and started down.

At the bottom was a long corridor lined with doors. A single torch burned at the end. There was no sound in this place. She couldn't hear her comrades anymore, or the voices of the prisoners. Just a dark abyss of silence. She swallowed the lump in her throat as she started along the narrow hall. Was Kaeden really in this awful place?

Each door had a small square cut into the wood at eye level. Brighid glanced inside every cell she passed. Nothing. Just tiny, empty rooms with chains set in the walls. She stopped near the torch that hung from an iron ring set in the wall. Two doors left. One on the side and one at the end. Heart pounding, she peered inside the square opening.

There was a hunched form.

Brighid took a step back and studied the door. A single latch. She pressed down on the metal and the door gave way before her.

Within the cell, a man knelt on the ground, his head bowed. His hands and legs were chained to the wall behind him. Thick, dark hair fell across his face, and wide shoulders barely moved with each breath. His dingy white robes were torn and covered in blood. A water bucket lay near his knees beside a half-eaten loaf of bread.

She knew that build and that thick dark hair. This scene was like her dreams.

Brighid entered the cell, ignoring the pungent smell, and pulled back her hood. "Kaeden?"

The word echoed within the room, breaking the silence.

At her voice, he raised his head. Sunken eyes stared at her from a haggard face covered in dark stubble. There was a flicker of recognition in those grey orbs. He attempted to speak, but it only came out as a croak. He tried again. "Brighid?" he said hoarsely.

Something broke loose inside her at his look and voice. "Yes, it's me." A strange feeling swirled in her middle as she knelt in front of him. "I'm here."

He lifted his head higher. "How is that possible?"

"I dreamed of you."

Her gaze moved across his face, taking in every detail. Then the rest of his body. His robes hung in tatters along his frame, revealing his scars. So many scars. Across his chest, his middle, his arms. Everywhere. Aged, but also new. What kind of torture had Viessa put him through? And why hadn't he healed from them, like he had healed her?

Brighid reached out her hand and touched the scar that ran across his chest. His muscles tightened under her fingertips, and he sucked in a breath.

"Did that hurt?" she asked, looking up.

"No. It's already healed."

She pulled back. "All of these have healed?"

"Yes."

"But there are scars . . ."

He frowned. "There are always scars."

Wait, did that mean there were scars from when he healed her? Her heart clenched as she looked back at his face. "Why did Viessa do this? Was she trying to kill you?"

He paused, then, "Yes."

A fire burst inside her chest, taking her breath away. Her fingers curled beneath her and her body flushed with heat. The red haze. Brighid breathed harder as she stood. "I'll be back." Before he could say anything, she left.

As she ran toward the staircase, the red haze flooded her body until all she could see was crimson.

No, I need to get ahold of myself.

Brighid stopped halfway up the stairs and took in a couple deep breaths. *You control the Vilrik. The Vilrik does not control you.* She recalled her uncle's words and closed her eyes. Yes, this anger in her was righteous. And it was honorable. But this was not the time to fight. She needed to free Kaeden.

She took in a couple more breaths, then ascended the rest of the stairs. But her thoughts still churned. How could they do that to him? Let Viessa torture him to near death, then chain him like an animal to the wall and leave him in the darkness and filth? Her own people?

No, she could believe it. She had seen the ruthlessness of the Wolf Clan and how little the Shadonae seemed to care for life. There was no honor in their actions. None.

This was brutality.

40

"Kaeden?"

Kaeden lifted his head . . . and his heart stopped. Although he could see only part of her face in the torchlight, he knew those features from his dreams. It was like light itself had taken form and stepped into his cell. He tried to say her name, but his voice came out like a croak. Then he tried again. "Brighid?" he said hoarsely.

"Yes, it's me." She crossed the cell and knelt in front of him. "I'm here."

He lifted his chin. "How is that possible?"

"I dreamed of you."

He watched her gaze move across his face, then along his body. She had dreamed of him. Like he dreamed of her. And she came for him—

He sucked in his breath as her fingers grazed his chest. It didn't hurt. Instead, her touch was hot and sent a tendril of heat across his skin.

She drew her hand back. "Did that hurt?"

"No. It's already healed."

Her eyes widened. "All of these have healed?"

"Yes."

"But there are scars . . ."

Didn't she know? "There are always scars."

She appeared both surprised and distressed by his words. When she asked if Viessa was trying to kill him, he paused. "Yes," he finally answered.

Then he saw it. Like a fire rising in her eyes. She breathed harder. "I'll be back." She jumped to her feet and ran from the cell.

A chill replaced the warmth her brief presence had brought. What if Brighid didn't return? What if something happened to her? He paused. How did she even get down here?

Was he hallucinating?

He stared at the open cell door and the torch that burned brightly in the iron ring. No. Brighid was real. She spoke to him. Touched him. Another wave of heat washed across his chest as he remembered the feel of her fingertips. Unlike his usual reaction to the touch of a human, this was different. It was something . . . more.

Kaeden waited in the darkness, straining his ears for the sound footsteps. Minutes went by. The torch burned in the hallway.

Then he heard boots on the stairs.

"Down here," Brighid said.

"I hope one of these keys work," a man replied. The sound of hurried steps and the jangle of metal echoed out in the hallway. "What made you search for another set of stairs?"

"One of the prisoners told me."

"And you trusted him?"

"I recognized him. He told me to rescue Kaeden."

Seconds later, Brighid appeared in the doorway, accompanied by a man slightly taller than her, dressed in leather and fur, with long dark hair.

"So this is the man we came to save," the man said, looking in.

"Yes."

His face scrunched up as he entered with a ring of keys in his hand. "Ugh. It smells terrible in here."

Kaeden gritted his teeth. Of course it did. He had been chained like an animal and left to rot. Why hadn't Brighid reacted to the smell when she first arrived?

"Who cares?" Brighid replied, answering his unspoken question. "Hurry up and free him. We don't have much time."

"Why did they lock him up away from the others?" the man asked as he moved past Kaeden, bent down, and began to fit keys into the clasps around his wrists. There was a clunk and Kaeden felt air across his skin. He twisted his hand, relishing the motion, then opened his palm.

The man gasped and took a step back as a soft light filled the cell. "You said he was like our allies, but his hand . . . and the scars across his body . . ."

"That's why we are rescuing him. If he stays here any longer, he might die."

The man glanced back at Brighid. "Are you sure we can trust him?"

Brighid stared at Kaeden. He could barely see her face with the torchlight behind her, but he heard the conviction in her voice. "With my life, Lodin. With my life."

Lodin let out a long breath. "All right." He approached Kaeden again, knelt behind him, and seconds later, the right manacle released from his ankle. The left one fell shortly afterward. His legs were free.

Kaeden pressed his hands against the stone floor and went to stand. He faltered and caught himself. Brighid rushed into the cell and grabbed him beneath his arm. "Can you stand?"

"I think I can." Kaeden struggled again and found the man named Lodin on his other side, assisting him. Together, they brought Kaeden to his feet.

"Lean on me if you need to," Brighid said and proceeded slowly toward the cell door. As they stepped into the corridor, Kaeden realized that even though Brighid barely reached his shoulder, her strength was unbelievable as she gripped his side.

Down the hallway they went, sideways to fit. When they reached the stairs, Brighid looked back. "We won't fit. How are you feeling now?"

"Stronger," Kaeden replied.

"I'll lead, you follow. Lodin, be ready to catch him if he stumbles."

"I'm not sure about that," Lodin replied from the rear. "He's bigger than most of our berserkers."

"Do what you can. And be careful, it's dark until we reach the top."

"I can help with that." Kaeden held out his palm. His mark wasn't as brilliant as it was minutes ago, but it emitted enough light for them to see.

Soon, the faint blue light from the fre stones beyond added to their visibility as the three ascended the stairs. With each step, Kaeden felt his strength returning. It was as if Viessa had never tortured him. Was this truly the doing of his Eldaran power and body, or had the Word infused him with His own strength?

Kaeden had a feeling it was both.

At the top, his eyes adjusted to the dim light. Brighid was already making her way between the wide cells that lined each side. Kaeden took one step forward, then stopped as figures took shape behind the bars.

His friends and comrades. He hadn't seen them since he was dragged down into the depths of this place. The light from his hand seemed to alert them to his presence, and their voices rose.

"Truthsayer!"

"Master Kaeden, free us!"

Sumar appeared to his right and gripped the bars, her face pale and tear-streaked in the blue light. "Don't leave us! That woman is consuming us."

"What do you mean?" Kaeden asked.

Treyvar appeared beside Sumar. His eyes were sunken with dark circles beneath, his hair matted, and there was a gash along his cheek. He raised one hand and grabbed the bar between them. "Sumar is right. I don't know how, but the woman who controls the Mordra visits us every day and uses the mark on her hand on a prisoner. Then—" He pressed his lips together and took in a deep breath through his nostrils, while Sumar backed away from the bars, gripping her hands together. Treyvar leaned toward the bars. "Kaeden, she seems to be able to steal life. Instead of healing with her mark, she takes it."

For a moment, Kaeden couldn't breathe. Then his mind rushed to catch up to Treyvar's words. In a twisted way, it made sense. Everything about the Shadonae and their power was perverted from its original use. It would make sense that, instead of healing and providing life, they stole it.

Kaeden turned away and held a hand to his lips.

"Why aren't you moving?" Lodin said.

Kaeden held his other hand toward Lodin without turning his direction. Brighid had come to rescue him. But—

He lifted his head and found her walking back toward him between the cells. He doubted she came to rescue the rest of these people.

"I can't go with you," he said as she stopped before him.

She opened her mouth, then looked around. She let out her breath and her shoulders sagged. "I know." She gave him a small smile that warmed him and broke his heart. "I will do what I can. But first, do what you came here to do. Take out Viessa. I cannot speak for the others who came with me, but I give you my word that I will help your people, as long as you can assure me they will not turn on my own."

Kaeden understood what Brighid was saying. Despite the connection they shared—one she didn't know about yet—they were still on opposite sides of a war. But perhaps this moment and this event could trigger the beginning of a partnership, not only between the two of them, but among those gathered at this fortress. A joining of forces that could not only stop the Shadonae but perhaps even end this war.

"Then I place myself and my people in your hands," Kaeden replied.

Brighid nodded. "Your trust will not be misplaced. Follow me." She led the way between the cells and toward the staircase ahead.

As Kaeden passed his comrades, he made a promise to himself. He *would* be back.

Minutes later they reached the main floor. They dashed past the small rooms filled with beds toward the door ahead.

With each step, Kaeden felt his heart pumping one word. Freedom. He could almost taste the cold mountain air and feel it on his face. He had been trapped in the darkness for what felt like eternity, only to be broken up by torture and healing.

But now he was almost free. The Word hadn't forgotten him.

They reached the door and stumbled outside. A thousand stars filled the sky above, and the air was cool and sweet. Kaeden pulled in two deep breaths, then froze as a voice rang out across the area.

"I was wondering why more Nordics had appeared."

A solitary figure stood in the middle of the dark courtyard with her arms folded across her chest. Despite her lithe frame, there was a dark and foreboding presence to her.

Viessa.

41

Brighid stood a few feet from the door she had just exited with Kaeden, Lodin, and Vigi. She recognized the woman the moment she made her presence known. Torchlight from the surrounding walls cast a harsh orange light across her beautiful and fierce face. A single white stripe of hair followed the curve of her cheek, a contrast with her silky black waves. Eyes as dark as night peered across the courtyard straight at Brighid.

Without a second thought, Brighid moved forward and placed herself between Kaeden and the Shadonae. This woman had tortured Kaeden. Left him covered in scars. That wasn't something he would get over anytime soon. She wasn't even sure if he had the strength to face his tormentor. What she did know was that she would protect him and give him the time he needed.

Viessa's face grew vicious as she crossed the stone slabs that covered the ground. "You thought you could sneak in here and take my prize?"

Brighid drew her sword and pointed it at Viessa. "He is no one's prize."

"Certainly not yours, *Stryth'Viezla*." She snickered. "Yes, I know who you are. But your fighting prowess will not help you in a battle with me." She lifted her hand, palm up, but instead of light there was only darkness. The air around them suddenly dropped in temperature.

"Who is she?" Lodin asked as he flanked Brighid's side. His teeth began to chatter.

Brighid kept her sword trained on Viessa, despite the cold. "She is one of those who deceived our people."

The double doors that led into the main hall burst open, flooding the courtyard with firelight. "What in the Lands is going on?" Hauss bellowed as he emerged, followed by dozens of warriors. He spotted Viessa, then turned to look in the same direction she was looking. He stiffened as Bard came to stand beside him.

"What is going on, Hjaren Bard?" Hauss asked coolly.

Brighid kept her eyes trained on Viessa.

"We're here for more than just the fortress," Bard replied.

Viessa turned her gaze from Brighid to Hauss. "They are traitors and are freeing the enemy. Seize them!"

A few of the Wolf Clan warriors drew their weapons, but Hauss hesitated. Viessa narrowed her eyes. "Should I send a message to Hjar Volka about your lack of loyalty?"

Hauss drew his sword at the same moment Bard drew his axes. The two men faced each other within the doorway to the main hall as the rest of the warriors reacted to their leaders' actions. Hauss's wolf arched her back and snarled at Bard. Tension filled the area like a frayed rope, taut and ready to snap.

"No, you're the traitor." Brighid stepped forward. She needed to stop Viessa from turning Hauss and the others against them. And they needed to hear the truth.

Viessa turned back toward Brighid and sent her a scathing look.

Brighid kept walking forward, her sword steady. Slowly, she began to draw upon the Vilrik inside her, letting it seep into her limbs, her mind, her vision. "I condemn you as a warrior of Nordica."

Another step forward.

"I condemn you as the sole survivor of the Battle of the Plains."

Viessa folded her arms. "Your condemnation means nothing. You might be the Stryth'Viezla, but you are also clanless and have no voice."

"You are wrong. Every Nordic fights for Nordica. Therefore, every Nordic has a voice. Even the clanless. Today, I speak for them."

Bard raised his voice. "Let it be known that Brighid is also the lost daughter of the Bear Clan."

"What?" Hauss took a step back and his sword lowered slightly. More exclamations filled the area, and Brighid heard a muffled roar far behind her. Bjornfrost.

"I also condemn you." Kaeden's deep voice rang out across the courtyard, silencing everyone. Goose bumps rose along Brighid's skin at the authority in his tone. From the corner of her eye, she watched him approach from the left. Was he ready to do this? "As a fellow Eldaran and the Truthsayer of these Lands. Your actions go against everything we stand for."

"You will never take me!" Viessa shot her hand into the air again and shouted out an unintelligible command. At the same moment, Vigi let out a battle cry and ran past Brighid toward Viessa, his sword raised.

"No, wait!" Brighid yelled. Something was here, something summoned by Viessa's mark—

Two shadows burst from separate corners where the shadows were deepest. They rushed toward their mistress, the smoke from their shadow bodies streaming behind them in their haste.

Kaeden rushed past Brighid, his hand thrust into the air as the light from his palm flared across the courtyard. Brighid turned her head away and closed her eyes for a moment. Bright spots appeared in her vision where the light from his palm had pierced it.

She slowly opened her eyes as the sound of clashing weapons filled her ears. Twenty feet ahead of her, Kaeden held his hand aloft, the light from his palm lighting the area like a torch. Viessa held a dagger in one hand while she held her own dark palm up. Along the perimeter of the light, the Wolf and Bear Clans fought. Wood splintered behind her, accompanied by a bellow. She could feel it in her soul. Bjornfrost was fighting his way to her side.

Viessa took a swipe at Kaeden, but he dodged it.

"To me!" Kaeden yelled, keeping his hand up while he dodged another jab.

Brighid realized the light was keeping the shadow-creatures at bay. "Bear Clan! Step into the light!" she shouted as she tore her shield off her back.

Most heard her yell and entered the perimeter of light. Bard and

Hauss fought near the entrance to the hall, along with a dozen Bear Clan warriors. To her right, Lodin engaged two more. Galt rushed for the light and Arngrim followed with a Wolf Clan warrior close behind him.

Vigi stood to the left of the circle, holding his own along with Nora. The shadows weaved back and forth just beyond the light, then started for Vigi.

"Vigi, move!" Brighid yelled. She didn't wait to see if he heard her. She needed to stop Viessa now.

Brighid raced across the stone slabs. Kaeden could dodge Viessa's dagger for only so long. Just as she moved in to strike at his chest, Brighid caught the dagger with the tip of her blade and knocked it away, then stepped between Viessa and Kaeden, her shield in place.

"You vixen!" Viessa shouted and brought her dagger down. Brighid caught it with her shield, then slammed her shield forward into the woman.

Viessa stumbled back, dazed.

Something big rumbled up to Brighid's side. Bjornfrost rose to his towering height and let out a deafening roar. Strength poured into Brighid as she approached Viessa, her sword out and ready. She didn't know what it would take to stop Viessa. Perhaps not even a bear. After all, Viessa possessed the same powerful blood as Kaeden. But she would try.

Brighid swung her blade and Viessa dodged. She moved in again, but Viessa was fast. Bjornfrost bound to the other side and took a swipe at the woman. Like the shadows that followed her, Viessa seemed almost incorporeal with the way she could slip away from danger.

"I may not be a warrior, but don't underestimate me, Stryth'Viezla," Viessa cackled.

Brighid moved faster, letting the Vilrik fill her vision with red, but holding back enough so she could focus on Viessa. As if sensing he could hurt his mistress, Bjornfrost moved to the outer the edge, letting out occasional growls.

Viessa matched Brighid's movements until they were engaged in a deadly dance.

All Brighid could see was Viessa, a silhouette against a shadow and crimson background. When she reached out with her sword, Viessa dodged. When Viessa dove to her side, Brighid jumped away from her deadly blade.

Someone shouted her name, but she couldn't decipher it over her rushing blood. Her entire being was centered on Viessa.

It wasn't until she felt a strong wind on her face that Brighid began to pull back.

Viessa dove for her right and slashed out. The tip caught her along her upper arm, and blood began to flow freely. Then Viessa dashed away. Bjornfrost let out a roar and rushed after her.

"Brighid!"

She finally registered her name as she twisted around.

Something chilling swirled between her legs. Brighid glanced down to find smoke gathering at her ankles.

She was outside Kaeden's light.

As if sensing another danger, Bjornfrost shuddered to a stop and whirled. A second later, he hurtled back toward her. Brighid gritted her teeth. Not today. Gathering all her strength as the smoke began to rise, she threw herself toward the middle of the courtyard and the light.

Her foot caught and she crashed down onto the stone, her knees hitting at the same time as her right hand. Her sword flew from her grasp and slid a few feet away. Bjornfrost swatted at the smoke, but it dissipated between his massive paws, only to reappear and trap the bear between the smoke. Bjornfrost bellowed at the monster and tried to break free.

"Bjornfrost!" Brighid shouted as she lifted her head. From the corner of her eye, she spied Viessa pull something from within her tunic as Kaeden approached with his hand still lifted high.

Death. She could feel it. A chilling tendril reaching out from the item in Viessa's hand.

Something told her that whatever it was, it was enough to kill even a Truthsayer.

With one last burst of strength, Brighid threw her shield aside and bolted from the ground. Pain blossomed throughout her ankle, but she shunted the feeling to the back of her mind.

Viessa raised her hand, and a glint of glass twinkled in the light.

Brighid dove for her. She caught Viessa's wrist and twisted. The glass flew into the air, hit the ground, and slid into the darkness.

Brighid crumpled to the ground as seething pain erupted around her ankle.

Air rushed around her. Brighid lifted her head. Lightning flashed in the sky, and the wind began to howl across the courtyard. A loud boom shook the fortress.

Brighid planted her hands on the stone slab beneath her.

When had a storm moved in?

Along the rim of light from Kaeden's palm, warriors were being pushed back by the wind.

A scream filled the air behind her. Brighid whipped her head around to see the last vestiges of the shadow-creatures whirl upward into the dark sky, then disappear. Bjornfrost stomped the ground, then shook his head, free of the smoke that had held him.

Seconds later, she held her arm across her face to keep debris from flying into her eyes.

Kaeden spoke. At first, she couldn't hear the words over the roar of the wind. Then she caught his voice.

"You captured me the first time. And you tortured me. You hoped to steal my power. But you still don't understand what it means to be the Truthsayer."

Brighid leaned forward and brought her arm away from her eyes.

Before her stood Kaeden as she had never seen him. Light not only shone from his palm but his entire body. As she watched, Kaeden moved his hand and cupped Viessa's cheek with his marked palm. "This is what it means to see inside another."

He bowed his head and closed his eyes, his hand still on her face. "As the voice of the Word, I bring your final condemnation."

Brighid's heart stopped. She remembered that touch and knew what was coming.

As she watched, Kaeden's face twisted in pain. Seconds later, Viessa screamed. Then they both fell to their knees, Kaeden's hand still planted on her face.

Brighid dropped her head and clenched her hand on the ground.

Viessa screamed again.

"Kaeden," Brighid whispered. Viessa was revisiting her life . . . and so was Kaeden. What terrible things was he being forced to watch?

Brighid went to move. She wanted to do something to help. Place a hand on his shoulder, reassure him. But her ankle continued to throb, and deep down she had a feeling this was something he had to do alone.

Viessa twisted her head to escape Kaeden's touch.

Brighid sucked in her breath. Viessa's eyes were so wide that Brighid could see the whites. Her mouth opened with no sound. Such fear. As if death were here.

But . . . Brighid didn't feel death, except a tiny sliver against the far wall.

What was Viessa afraid of? What could be more terrifying than death—

Slowly, Viessa's body began to disappear. Like she was turning into dust.

Brighid pulled away, both fascinated and terrified. Viessa's body shimmered for a second, then disintegrated in the light from Kaeden's palm. A sudden rush of wind blasted across the courtyard, sending the last specs of her body flying into the sky. Then she was no more.

Lightning flashed and thunder boomed, shaking the fortress again.

Kaeden collapsed across the stone slabs and his light went out.

42

Chaos erupted across the courtyard. There were shouts for torches, and both Hauss and Bard yelled for everyone to put down their weapons. Hauss's wolf and Amro stared at each other with bared teeth.

Brighid heard the commotion, but she had eyes only for Kaeden, his prone body a dark figure in the light coming from the main hall. And the empty space near him where Viessa had been.

Wake up, her mind commanded. But her body wouldn't respond. *Wake up!*

Brighid blinked and felt a breath of hot hair brush the top of her head. Seconds later, Bjornfrost nudged her with his nose. She moved one finger, then another. Gradually, her body emerged from its shocked state. She bent forward and began to crawl toward Kaeden. Each jostle of her ankle made her wince, and once she bit her lip to keep from crying out. But even stronger than the pain was the need to check on Kaeden.

Torches appeared and people ran across the courtyard.

Brighid reached Kaeden. In the low light, she made out his face. It was tight, and his eyes moved rapidly beneath his eyelids.

"Kaeden," she said, and placed a hand on his arm. "*Kaeden.*" He didn't stir.

"Brighid!" She heard Lodin's voice, then felt his hand on her shoulder. Bjornfrost let out a warning huff nearby.

"It's all right, my friend. I'm just checking on her."

She opened her mouth to speak, but nothing came. Instead, her body seemed to be settling into a numb state, too full to take in everything that had occurred over the last few minutes. All she could do was grasp the sleeve of Kaeden's torn robe.

More people ran up to them, all shouting different questions.

"What happened?"

"I couldn't see anything!"

"Where did that strange storm come from?"

She heard the questions around her, but she couldn't pull herself away from Kaeden until Bard bent down beside her and spoke her name. "Brighid."

She swallowed. Kaeden still hadn't woken up. "Yes?"

"Everything is all right. We've subdued the Wolf Clan. We're safe."

His words were like water, moving and sloshing within her mind. What did it matter if they were safe if Kaeden stayed like this?

Her lower lip began to tremble as a couple torches appeared and she could see the entirety of Kaeden's body: his shredded clothing, blood stains across the white cloth, the scars beneath, how much pain he must have gone through. She hadn't seen the extent of it in his cell. But now . . .

"Bolva! What happened to him?" Arngrim said from nearby.

"He's the man we came to rescue," Lodin replied, his voice subdued. "I believe he was tortured."

Vigi let out a curse. "Did the Wolf Clan do that?"

"No," Brighid replied. "That woman did."

Vigi looked around. "Where did she go? And those shadow-creatures? I couldn't see anything because of the storm."

Brighid squeezed her other hand shut. She was going to snap at Vigi if he didn't stop all the questions!

Bard stood and started giving directions. Brighid let out her breath, thankful to her uncle. Bjornfrost came to stand beside her, one giant paw near her hand. She reached out and touched a claw. "Thank you for coming to my rescue."

Bjornfrost let out a grunt and continued to watch everyone around them.

A minute later, Bard bent down again. "Let's move you and Kaeden inside. It looks like it's going to rain."

As if in answer, a drop fell across her face and a dozen more along the ground. Brighid looked up. The wind was gone, but this strange storm remained. Her hand still gripped Kaeden's sleeve.

"You can let go now. We have him," Bard said as Lodin came around Kaeden's other side.

Brighid nodded and released her grip. Kaeden still hadn't woken. She watched as her uncle and Lodin carefully lifted him, grunting as they did so. "He's big," Lodin said under his breath. Then they started for the main hall with Kaeden between them.

Brighid went to stand, then cried out when she moved her ankle. She grabbed Bjornfrost's side and took her weight off the injury.

Nora appeared next to her. "Did you hurt your leg?"

"My ankle. I think I twisted it when I escaped those creatures."

Nora didn't respond. Instead, she helped Brighid up. With Bjornfrost on one side and Nora on the other, she hobbled across the courtyard toward the main hall. More rain fell. Gentle at first, then harder. Brighid glanced back to where Kaeden and Viessa had stood. Nothing remained.

She turned around, feeling her body soaking from the rain. What happened to Viessa? Did she die? Or just disappear?

As she neared the hall, she spotted Hauss and the Wolf Clan warriors inside and to the right. Heming was talking to Hauss, as a few of the Bear Clan warriors gathered weapons from the Wolf Clan.

Brighid frowned. What caused the Wolf Clan to withdraw? Had her words made a difference?

Nora helped her into the hall just as the skies behind them opened and the downpour began. Knowing he could not enter the fortress, Bjornfrost stopped outside the doorway where Amro and Uthun also waited. Vigi ran up to her and brought her arm across his shoulders. "What happened to you?" he asked.

"Twisted my ankle." Although when she thought back to that moment, she had a feeling one of the shadow-creatures had held her in place. She shivered. What were those monsters? The only thing that seemed to keep them away had been the light from Kaeden's palm. She glanced over her shoulder at the rain and darkness that covered the courtyard. Would they return?

"That was some speech you gave," Vigi said as he and Nora led her toward the closest bench inside the main hall.

Brighid pulled back. "No. Take me to where they are placing Kaeden."

Vigi and Nora glanced at each other.

"All right," Vigi said, and they turned left toward the doorway where Bard, Lodin, and Kaeden had disappeared.

Brighid winced every time her boot touched the ground, but given how her foot was straight and she could place some weight down, she was sure it wasn't broken.

They walked past Heming, Hauss, and the Wolf Clan warriors, who were being restrained. Brighid lifted her eyes and caught Hauss glancing her way. Unlike the glares his fellow warriors were sending, he appeared stiff and cold. Bard said they had subdued the Wolf Clan, but what would happen next to Hauss and his men? Even worse—her gut clenched—how much time did they have before their oath unraveled?

Brighid looked away. As far as she knew, nothing could be done for them. At that thought, a burning filled her middle. Viessa might be gone, and perhaps her shadow-creatures, but the influence and power of these beings remained, imprisoning the Nordic people. How many more would suffer and die at their hands?

She clenched her jaw. At least Viessa was gone because of Kaeden.

I'm glad we came, Brighid thought as she hobbled between Vigi and Nora toward the doorway ahead. She doubted they could have taken out Viessa without him. Not with her strange power that commanded creatures from the shadows and her powerful blood. Brighid still didn't know why or how Viessa had disappeared, only that she was no more.

Now there were only two left. Armand and Peder.

And an entire war.

Brighid shook her head, while Vigi and Nora led her into a large, dark room. As her eyes adjusted to the gloom, she spotted shelves along one wall, two long tables set up in the middle, and crates and barrels stacked on the opposite side. Subtle hints of lavender and mint hung in the air.

"Looks like a storage room," Vigi said as they turned left and headed for another doorway.

"I think it's more than that," Nora replied. "Unlike our deathkeepers, the south employs healers to help those who are injured and sick. I recognize a few of the smells in here, and if you look on the shelves, there seem to be bandages."

"You mean what Hjar Gurmund's wife does for our clan?" Vigi asked.

"I believe so. Ana is like a healer of the south. I know she learned from them a long time ago. Vigi, can you take Brighid to the next room? I'm going to grab some of those bandages for her ankle."

"Yes," Vigi replied and assisted Brighid toward the doorway, where a slip of light shone. Nora headed for the shelves.

A single row of beds lined the wall of the next room, with two windows above. Bard and Lodin were placing Kaeden in the bed on the far right. A small table with a lit lamp stood in the corner. The sound of steady tapping filled the room as the rain continued outside.

Bard looked up as they entered and spotted Brighid. "He hasn't woken yet."

"I'll watch him," Brighid replied. "It would be best for him to see someone he knows when he wakes up."

"I agree. And I need to speak to Hauss."

Brighid instructed Vigi to place her on the bed next to Kaeden's. Once seated, she looked across the small gap between the two beds. Kaeden's eyes were still closed and his face tight, as if fighting some hidden battle within his mind.

Bard and Lodin left, leaving Vigi behind. The warrior stood beside the bed, studying Kaeden. "So he's the one who rescued you," Vigi finally said.

"Yes," Brighid said without looking up.

"And he's the reason we came here."

"Yes."

"He's not human, is he?"

"No, he is not. But he is good."

Nora arrived a minute later with bandages. She worked Brighid's boot off and felt the area. Brighid flinched but didn't say anything.

"Nothing is broken," Nora said, then began to warp the long cloth around her foot. There was noise out in the large storage room. "Bard instructed those who were injured to be brought to the room beyond. We should be able to find what we need to help them. The southerners were well prepared."

"Were many hurt?" Brighid asked.

"No, just a few cuts and bruises. The Bear Clan can hold its own against the Wolf. There." Nora tucked in the last bit of cloth. "Need anything for the pain?"

"No. But I would like a chair. And could someone place a blanket over Kaeden?"

Nora looked above her head. "Vigi, can you bring a chair and water for Brighid?"

"Yes," he said behind her.

Nora took the blanket at the foot of the bed and spread it over Kaeden's body. Then she grabbed another and handed it to Brighid. "You need one too."

"Thank you, Nora."

"I'm going to attend to the others now." Then, in a quieter voice, she said, "Arngrim is among them."

"I understand."

Nora turned and left the room.

Brighid watched Kaeden's chest rise and fall. One arm had slipped out from beneath the blanket and hung along the side of the bed. A glimmer of light shone from his palm. *I wish I knew what you were going through*, she thought as she brought her gaze back to his face. *I wish I could help.* But how could a mere human help someone who was the literal voice of the Word?

The rain outside provided a soothing sound, and soon she found herself tired from the day's events. But she didn't want to fall asleep. Not yet. Not until she knew Kaeden would awaken.

Vigi returned with a chair and placed it in the gap between the beds, then helped her into the seat. "Are you sure you don't want to rest in bed?" he asked as he handed her the cup of water.

"No. I'm not that injured, and I'm afraid I will fall asleep if I lay on the bed." She drained the cup and handed it back.

"Need anything else?" Vigi asked. "I can find food if you need it."

Brighid shook her head. "I'm not hungry."

"I'll be helping Nora in the other room. Yell if you need anything."

"I will," Brighid replied.

Vigi hesitated, then finally left. The light in the oil lamp flickered for a moment before resuming its burn.

Brighid reached over and gently brushed Kaeden's sleeve. She wasn't sure if he could feel her touch, but in any case, she wanted to reassure him. "I'm here," she whispered. "And I'll be here when you wake up."

Maybe she was seeing things, but his face seemed to relax just a little.

Then Brighid let out her breath, sat back in the chair, and waited.

43

Kaeden woke to the first rays of dawn streaming through the window above him. His body felt sluggish and cold. And his mind was still filled with Viessa's thoughts and memories. He blinked, letting those heavy impressions sink back into his conscience. But they would remain there, like Brighid's. And Teduin's. Probably like every person he would ever use his power on. Such was the burden of the Truthsayer.

As his body became aware, he felt a heavier weight along his right side. He turned his head and found someone laying near him. As his eyes adjusted to the faint light, he realized it was Brighid.

She was seated in a chair next to the bed. Her head lay across her arms with her face turned toward his. He could see the half-sun tattoo that circled her eye, the intricate braids in her hair, her small, slightly upturned nose, and full lips.

Instead of sitting up, he remained where he was, not wanting to wake her from her sleep.

Brighid.

From this vantage point, she appeared a young woman. That same young woman from the Battle of the Plains who, in a moment of desperation, asked for her life. It was hard to believe that such a beautiful creature could be so deadly.

But he knew of her strength. How she had made her way north, even during a snowstorm with an injured leg. He saw glimpses of her life over the winter: her training, her discoveries, her determination to fulfill the charge given to her and save her people from the Shadonae.

And more than that, she came to rescue him.

As he watched, slips of morning light spread across her face, accentuating the peace painting her features.

Something shifted inside him. He turned his gaze to the ceiling. Was it possible that Treyvar was right? Had he somehow bonded to this warrior woman?

He couldn't deny there was a transcendent connection between them. They had spent the winter visiting each other's lives. Knowing each other. Seeing what the other saw. And in those few months, he felt like he had come to not only know Brighid more, but the people of Nordica.

But what did that mean for their future? And would Brighid want such a connection?

Kaeden let out a long sigh.

The sound must have caused Brighid to wake up because she began to stir. She lifted her head and blinked a couple times before recognition entered her eyes.

"Oh." She sat up and brushed away a few errant hairs. She blinked again. "I must have fallen asleep."

Kaeden pushed up from the bed and sat against the wall. The blanket slid down across his lap. They stared at each other for a moment. "How long was I out?" he asked, breaking the silence. His words seemed to bring them both back to reality.

"Just a night. I offered to stay and watch over you. I thought it would be better for you to wake up to a familiar face."

"I appreciate that."

Silence again. Her gaze moved down his chest. Kaeden was still dressed in his healing robes, which were torn and bloody, leaving his skin and newly acquired scars exposed.

Brighid stood. "Let me see if I can find some new clothes for you."

Before he could respond, she was gone.

He took a moment to look around. They had placed him in the room adjacent to the storage and healer's area. The rest of the beds were empty. Did that mean he was the only one injured from last night?

"I hope so." He drew back the blankets and swung his legs around.

His boots hit the stone floor with a soft thud. Discolored patches were scattered along the leather. Blood. His blood.

He glanced down again. What at first appeared to be random slashes were specifically placed. Two slashes across his heart. One along his side. A gash along his arm. Others were created when Viessa lost her temper and simply carved into his skin. Yet none were deep enough to kill within minutes. Just deep enough to cause pain and bloodletting.

What exactly had been Viessa's goal? She could have killed him outright, but she wanted his gift. Had she hoped he would die slowly without her delivering the final blow to bypass any safeguard that kept his kind from killing one another for power?

The idea was gruesome.

He felt a presence and looked up. Brighid stood in the doorway with an armful of clothing, watching him. She entered and approached him. Her eyes moved across his body, then rose to meet his gaze. "I've seen a lot in battle," she said quietly. "But never something like what you went through."

"You saw what happened to me?"

"Yes." She didn't elaborate. Instead, she handed him the clothes. "Hopefully these fit. They are the largest I could find." A hint of pink colored her cheeks. "After you are dressed, I will meet you in the next room over."

Kaeden took the clothes. "All right."

After she left, he removed his torn robe. Her comment seemed to confirm that she had seen glimpses of his life. Including the moments Viessa tortured him. Yes, there was definitely a connection between them.

He dropped the robes on the floor and pulled the grey tunic over his head and across his chest. A bit tight. The trousers were wider but ended above his ankles. He grabbed his golden cord and wrapped it around his waist, securing it in a loop. Lastly, he slipped his boots back on. At least the boots hid the fact that the pants were a bit short.

He brought a hand along his face. Perhaps he would find a way to shave and bathe later. Of course, his freedom might be short-lived.

After all, the fortress still belonged to the Nordics, and he was a southerner.

Kaeden left the bloody robes in a heap in the corner and exited the room. The storage room had been turned into an infirmary, with a dozen wounded warriors laid out on blankets and resting. A hint of morning light filtered through the windows. Brighid stood by the long table set in the middle of the room, waiting.

"Hardly anyone is awake," she whispered as Kaeden carefully made his way toward her.

"There were a couple beds in the other room. Why were they not placed in there?"

"Nobody wanted to disturb your rest."

"They were also uncomfortable with me," Kaeden said.

Brighid shrugged. "Most have never seen that kind of power."

"I understand." At least Brighid had been there when he awoke. He wanted to ask what was next, but felt it was too early for that. Instead, he would enjoy the freedom he had now. "Would it be all right if we went outside? I would like to see the sunrise."

A few of the warriors began to stir.

Brighid glanced around and nodded. "Yes. Let's go out the side door. The main hall is also filled with Nordic warriors still sleeping."

The two crossed the room and exited through the door on the left. Colors of pink, orange, and yellow filled the sky with a scattering of clouds. The air smelled crisp and clean after a night of rain. Ahead stood the wall that encompassed the fortress. A set of stairs led to the top near where it met with the mountainside.

Brighid led the way between the fortress and wall to the stairs, then up until they were on the battlements. The sky continued to change, and a bird let out its first song of the morning. Kaeden followed Brighid along the pathway—wide enough for three men to walk abreast. To his right were thick stones that provided protection for those standing on top of the wall.

Her cloak fluttered behind her as she walked, and it took him a moment to realize it was his old grey cloak, the one he gave her the night he helped her escape. Her unbound hair flowed past the hood, and a few hairs caught in the wind. A soft smile spread across his face at the sight. He took a risk that night to free her, never knowing if she would rejoin the Nordic forces. Instead, she had found her way back to her people and shared the truth with them.

The sun was just peeking over the mountains and forests ahead in glorious light. Her words from last night rang in his mind as they rounded the corner.

I condemn you as a warrior of Nordica.

Brighid had stood up to Viessa before anyone else did. Including him. He'd thought he was ready to face her again, but the moment he heard her voice, everything froze inside him. Until Brighid spoke. Her courage and words broke through to his mind, giving him the strength to stand beside her and do the same.

"There is your sunrise." Brighid came to a stop just beyond the gates.

"Yes," Kaeden said, but he wasn't watching the sun. He was looking at Brighid. They had come through winter, through pain and snow. He had rescued her, and she had rescued him. Together, they had encountered the first Shadonae and won. But there was still much ahead. A war loomed before them. Two more Shadonae to confront. And an oath that would eventually destroy her people.

He would also need to tell her about their bonding and why she had seen the things she had. Maybe Selma was right and it was just a temporary connection. But . . .

Brighid glanced over at him, and the light of dawn lit upon her face, leaving a glow across her skin. Her eyes appeared bluer than the sky, and the half-sun tattoo around her left eye seemed to blaze like the sun behind her.

No, he didn't believe this was temporary. Whatever reason the Word chose to bind them, he would remain beside her if she allowed.

And together, maybe—just maybe—they would find a way to end this war.

ABOUT THE AUTHOR

Morgan L. Busse is a writer by day and a mother by night. She is the author of multiple series including The Ravenwood Saga and Skyworld series. She is a three-time Christy Award finalist and won the INSPY, Selah, and Carol Award for best in Christian speculative fiction. During her spare time she enjoys playing games, taking long walks, and dreaming about her next novel.

Visit her online at www.morganlbusse.com.

Read more by
Morgan L. Busse

The Nordic wars

The Follower of the Word trilogy

www.enclavepublishing.com